The Collected Shorter Supernatural & Weird Fiction of Algernon Blackwood Volume 5

ALGERNON BLACKWOOD

The Collected Shorter Supernatural & Weird Fiction of Algernon Blackwood Volume 5

Eleven Short Stories and Two Novelettes of the Strange and Unusual Including 'The Empty Sleeve', 'The Olive', 'The Pikestaffe Case', 'The Listener', 'The Doll' and 'Old Clothes'

Algernon Blackwood

LEONAUR

The Collected Shorter Supernatural & Weird Fiction of
Algernon Blackwood
Volume 5
Eleven Short Stories and Two Novelettes of the Strange and Unusual Including 'The
Empty Sleeve', 'The Olive', 'The Pikestaffe Case', 'The Listener', 'The Doll' and
'Old Clothes'
by Algernon Blackwood

Some of the stories in this volume were originally published as by
Algernon Blackwood in collaboration with an unknown contributor,
Wilfred Wilson. Oakpast Limited has undertaken reasonable research on the
subject, but also has been unable to fully identify this person.
Leonaur is an imprint of Oakpast Ltd

ISBN: 978-1-916535-30-5 (hardcover)
ISBN: 978-1-916535-31-2 (softcover)

http://www.leonaur.com

Publisher's Notes

The views expressed in this book are not necessarily
those of the publisher.

Contents

Old Clothes

1

Imaginative children with their odd questionings of life and their delicate nervous systems must be often a source of greater anxiety than delight to their parents, and Aileen, the child of my widowed cousin, impressed me from the beginning as being a strangely vivid specimen of her class. Moreover, the way she took to me from the first placed quasi-avuncular responsibilities upon my shoulders (in her mother's eyes), that I had no right, even as I had no inclination, to shirk. Indeed, I loved the queer, wayward, mysterious little being. Only it was not always easy to advise; and her somewhat marked peculiarities certainly called for advice of a skilled and special order.

It was not merely that her make-believe was unusually sincere and haunting, and that she would talk by the hour with invisible playmates (touching them, putting up her lips to be kissed, opening doors for them to pass in and out, and setting chairs, footstools and even flowers for them), for many children in my experience have done as much and done it with a vast sincerity; but that she also accepted what they told her with so steady a degree of conviction that their words influenced her life and, accordingly, her health.

They told her stories, apparently, in which she herself played a central part, stories, moreover, that were neither comforting nor wise. She would sit in a corner of the room, as both her mother and myself can vouch, face to face with some make-believe Occupant of the chair so carefully arranged; the footstool had been placed with precision, and sometimes she would move it a little this way or that; the table whereon rested the invisible elbows was beside her with a jar of flowers that changed according to the particular visitor.

And there she would wait motionless, perhaps an hour at a time, staring up into the viewless features of the person who was talking with her—who was telling her a story in which she played an exceedingly poignant part. Her face altered with the run of emotions, her eyes grew large and moist, and sometimes frightened; rarely she laughed, and rarely asked a whispered question, but more often sat there, tense and eager, uncannily absorbed in the inaudible tale falling from invisible lips—the tale of her own adventures.

But it was the terror inspired by these singular recitals that affected her delicate health as early as the age of eight, and when, owing to her mother's well-meant but ill-advised ridicule, she indulged them with more secrecy, the effect upon her nerves and character became so acute that I was summoned down upon a special advisory visit I scarcely appreciated.

"Now, George, what *do* you think I had better do? Dr. Hale insists upon more exercise and more companionship, sea air and all the rest of it, but none of these things seem to do any good."

"Have you taken her into your confidence, or rather has *she* taken you into hers?" I ventured mildly. The question seemed to give offence a little.

"Of course," was the emphatic answer. "The child has no secrets from her mother. She is perfectly devoted to me."

But you *have* tried to laugh her out of it, haven't you now?"

"Yes. But with such success that she holds these conversations far less than she used to—"

"Or more secretly?" was my comment, that was met with a superior shrug of the shoulders.

Then, after a further pause, in which my cousin's distress and my own affectionate interest in the whimsical imagination of my little niece combined to move me, I tried again—"Make-believe," I observed, "is always a bit puzzling to us older folk, because, though we indulge in it all our lives, we no longer believe in it; whereas children like Aileen—"

She interrupted me quickly—

"You know what I feel anxious about," she said, lowering her voice. "I think there may be cause for serious alarm." Then she added frankly, looking up with grave eyes into my face, "George, I want your help—your best help, please. You've always been a true friend."

I gave it her in calculated words.

"Theresa," I said with grave emphasis, "there is no trace of insanity on either side of the family, and my own opinion is that Aileen is perfectly well-balanced in spite of this too highly developed imagination. But, above all things, you must not drive it inwards by making fun of it. Lead it out. Educate it. Guide it by intelligent sympathy. Get her to tell you all about it, and so on. I think Aileen wants careful observing, perhaps—but nothing more."

For some minutes she watched my face in silence, her eyes intent, her features slightly twitching. I knew at once from her manner what she was driving at. She approached the subject with awkwardness and circumlocution, for it was something she dreaded, not feeling sure whether it was of heaven or of hell.

"You are very wonderful, George," she said at length, "and you have theories about almost everything—"

"Speculations," I admitted.

"And your hypnotic power is helpful, you know. Now—if—if you thought it safe, and that Providence would not be offended—"

"Theresa," I stopped her firmly before she had committed herself to the point where she would feel hurt by a refusal, "let me say at once that I do not consider a child a fit subject for hypnotic experiment, and I feel quite sure that an intelligent person like yourself will agree with me that it's unpermissible."

"I was only thinking of a little 'suggestion,'" she murmured.

"Which would come far better from the mother."

"If the mother had not already lost her power by using ridicule," she confessed meekly.

"Yes, you never should have laughed. Why did you, I wonder?"

An expression came into her eyes that I knew to be invariably with hysterical temperaments the precursor of tears. She looked round to make sure no one was listening.

"George," she whispered, and into the dusk of that September evening passed some shadow between us that left behind an atmosphere of sudden and inexplicable chill, "George, I wish—I wish it was *quite* clear to me that it really is all make-believe, I mean—"

"What do you mean?" I said, with a severity that was assumed to hide my own uneasiness. But the tears came the same instant in a flood that made any intelligent explanation out of the question.

The terror of the mother for her own blood burst forth.

"I'm frightened—horribly frightened," she said between the sobs.

"I'll go up and see the child myself," I said comfortingly at length when the storm had subsided. "I'll run up to the nursery. You mustn't be alarmed. Aileen's all right. I think I can help you in the matter a good deal."

2

In the nursery as usual Aileen was alone. I found her sitting by the open window, an empty chair opposite to her. She was staring at it—into it, but it is not easy to describe the certainty she managed to convey that there was some one sitting in that chair, talking with her. It was her manner that did it. She rose quickly, with a start as I came in, and made a half gesture in the direction of the empty chair as though to shake hands, then corrected herself quickly, and gave a friendly little nod of farewell or dismissal—then turned towards me. Incredible as it must sound, that chair looked at once slightly otherwise. It was empty.

"Aileen, what in the world are you up to?"

"*You* know, uncle," she replied, without hesitation.

"Oh, rather *I* know!" I said, trying to get into her mood so as later to get her out of it, "because I do the same thing with the people in my own stories. I talk to them too—"

She came up to my side, as though it were a matter of life and death.

"But do they *answer?*"

I realised the overwhelming sincerity, even the seriousness, of the question to her mind. The shadow evoked downstairs by my cousin had followed me up here. It touched me on the shoulder.

"Unless they answer," I told her, "they are not really alive, and the story hangs fire when people read it."

She watched me very closely a moment as we leaned out of the open window where the rich perfume of the Portuguese laurels came up from the lawns below. The proximity of the child brought a distinct atmosphere of its own, an atmosphere charged with suggestions, almost with faint pictures, as of things I had once known. I had often felt this before, and did not altogether welcome it, for the pictures seemed framed in some emotional setting that invariably escaped my analysis. I understood in a vague way what it was about the child that made her mother afraid. There flashed across me a fugitive sensation, utterly elusive yet painfully real, that she knew moments of suffering by rights she ought not to have known. Bizarre and unreasonable as the conception was, it was convincing. And it touched a profound sympathy in me.

Aileen undoubtedly was aware of this sympathy.

"It's Philip that talks to me *most* of the time," she volunteered, "and he's always, always explaining—but never quite finishes."

"Explaining what, dear little Child of the Moon?" I urged gently, giving her a name she used to love when she was smaller.

"Why he couldn't come in time to save me, of course," she said. "You see, they cut off both his hands."

I shall never forget the sensation these words of a child's mental adventure caused me, nor the kind of bitter reality they forced into me that they were true, and not merely a detail of some attempted rescue of a "Princess in a Tower." A vivid rush of thought seemed to focus my consciousness upon my own two wrists, as though I felt the pain of the operation she mentioned, and with a swift instinct that slipped into action before I could control it, I had hidden both hands from her sight in my coat pockets.

"And what else does 'Philip' tell you?" I asked gently.

Her face flushed. Tears came into her eyes, then fled away again lest they should fall from their softly-coloured nests.

"That he loved me so *awfully*," she replied; "and that he loved me to the very end, and that all his life after I was gone, and after they cut his hands off, he did nothing but pray for me—from the end of the world where he went to hide—"

I shook myself free with an effort from the enveloping atmosphere of tragedy, realizing that her imagination must be driven along brighter channels and that my duty must precede my interest.

"But you must get Philip to tell you all his funny and jolly adventures, too," I said, "the ones he had, you know, when his hands grew again—"

The expression that came into her face literally froze my blood.

"That's only making-up stories," she said icily. "They never did grow again. There *were* no happy or funny adventures."

I cast about in my mind for an inspiration how to help her mind into more wholesome ways of invention. I realised more than ever before the profundity of my affection for this strange, fatherless child, and how I would give my whole soul if I could help her and teach her joy. It was a real love that swept me, rooted in things deeper than I realised.

But, before the right word was given me to speak, I felt her nestle up against my side, and heard her utter the very phrase that for some time I had been dreading in the secret places of my soul she *would* utter. The sentence seemed to shake me within. I knew a hurried, passing moment of unspeakable pain that is utterly beyond me to reason about.

"*You* know," was what she said, "because it's *you* who are Philip!"

11

And the way she said it—so quietly, the words touched somehow with a gentle though compassionate scorn, yet made golden by a burning love that filled her little person to the brim—robbed me momentarily of all power of speech. I could only bend down and put my arm about her and kiss her head that came up barely to the level of my chin. I swear I loved that child as I never loved any other human being.

"Then Philip is going to teach you all sorts of jolly adventures with his new hands," I remember saying, with blundering good intention, "because he's no longer sad, and is full of fun, and loves you twice as much as ever!"

And I caught her up and carried her down the long stairs of the house out into the garden, where we joined the dogs and romped together until the face of the motherly Kempster at an upper window shouted down something stupid about bedtime, supper, or the rest of it, and Aileen, flushed yet with brighter eyes, ran into the house and, turning at the door, showed me her odd little face wreathed in smiles and laughter.

★★★★★★★★★★

For a long time, I paced to and fro with a cigar between the box hedges of the old-time garden, thinking of the child and her queer imaginings, and of the profoundly moving and disquieting sensations she stirred in me at the same time. Her face flitted by my side through the shadows. She was not pretty, properly speaking, but her appearance possessed an original charm that appealed to me strongly. Her head was big and, in some way, old-fashioned; her eyes, dark but not large, were placed close together, and she had a wide mouth that was certainly not beautiful. But the look of distressed and yearning passion that sometimes swept over these features, not otherwise prepossessing, changed her look into sudden beauty, a beauty of the soul, a soul that knew suffering and was acquainted with grief.

This, at least, is the way my own mind saw the child, and therefore the only way I can hope to make others see her. Were I a painter I might put her upon canvas in some imaginary portrait and call it, perhaps, "Reincarnation"—for I have never seen anything in child-life that impressed me so vividly with that odd idea of an old soul come back to the world in a new young body—a new Suit of Clothes.

But when I talked with my cousin after dinner, and consoled her with the assurance that Aileen was gifted with an unusually vivid imagination which time and ourselves must train to some more practical end—while I said all this, and more besides, two sentences the child had made use of kept ringing in my head. One—when she told me with merciless perception that I was only "making-up" stories; and the other, when she had informed me with that quiet rush of certainty and conviction that "Philip" was—myself.

3

A big-game expedition of some months put an end temporarily to my avuncular responsibilities; at least so far as action was concerned, for there were certain memories that held curiously vivid among all the absorbing turmoil of our camp life. Often, lying awake in my tent at night, or even following the tracks of our prey through the jungle, these pictures would jump out upon me and claim attention. Aileen's little face of suffering would come between me and the sight of my rifle; or her assurance that I was the "Philip" of her imagination would attack me with an accent of reality that seemed queer enough until I analysed it away.

And more than once I found myself thinking of her dark and serious countenance when she told how "Philip" had loved her to the end, and would have saved her if they had not cut off his hands. My own imagination, it seemed, was weaving the details of her child's invention into a story, for I never could think of this latter detail without positively experiencing a sensation of smarting pain in my wrists ...!

When I returned to England in the spring they had moved, I found, into a house by the sea, a tumbled-down old rookery of a building my cousin's father had rarely occupied during his lifetime, nor she been able to let since it had passed into her possession. An urgent letter summoned me thither, and I travelled down the very day after my arrival to the bleak Norfolk coast with a sense of foreboding in my heart that increased almost to a presentiment when the cab entered the long drive and I recognised the grey and gloomy walls of the old mansion. The sea air swept the gardens with its salt wash, and the moan of the surf was audible even up to the windows.

"I wonder what possessed her to come here?" was the first thought in my mind. "Surely the last place in the world to bring a morbid or too-sensitive child to!" My further dread that something had happened to the little child I loved so tenderly was partly dispelled, however, when my cousin met me at the door with open arms and smiling face, though the welcome I soon found, was chiefly due to the relief she gained from my presence. Something had happened to little Aileen, though not the final disaster that I dreaded.

She had suffered from nervous attacks of so serious a character during my absence that the doctor had insisted upon sea air, and my cousin, not with the best judgment, had seized upon the idea of making the old house serve the purpose. She had made a wing habitable for a few weeks; she hoped the entire change of scene would fill the little girl's mind with new and happier ideas. Instead—the result had been exactly the reverse. The child had wept copiously and hysterically the moment she set eyes on the old walls and smelt the odour of the sea.

But before we had been talking ten minutes there was a cry and a sound of rushing footsteps, and a scampering figure, with dark, flying hair, had dived headlong into my arms, and Aileen was sobbing—

"Oh, you've come, you've come at last! I am so awfully glad. I thought it would be the same as before, and you'd get caught." She ran from me next and kissed her mother, laughing with pleasure through her tears, and was gone from the room as quickly as she had come.

I caught my cousin's glance of frightened amazement.

"Now isn't that odd?" she exclaimed in a hushed voice. "Isn't that odd? Those are the tears of happiness,—the first time I've seen her smile since we came here last week."

But it rather nettled me, I think. "Why odd?" I asked. "Aileen loves me, it's delightful to—"

"Not that, not that!" she said quickly. "It's odd, I meant, she should have found you out So soon. She didn't even know you were back in England, and I'd sent her off to play on the sands with Kempster and the dogs so as to be sure of an opportunity of telling you everything before you saw her."

Our eyes met squarely, yet not with complete sympathy or comprehension.

"You see, she knew perfectly well you were here—the instant you came."

"But there's nothing in that," I asserted. "Children know things just as animals do. She scented her favourite uncle from the shore like a dog!"

And I laughed in her face.

That laugh perhaps was a mistake on my part. Its well-meant cheerfulness was possibly overdone. Even to myself it did not ring quite true.

"I do believe you are in league with her—against me," was the remark that greeted it, accompanied by an increase of that expression of

14

fear in the eyes I had divined the moment we met upon the doorstep. Finding nothing genuine to say in reply, I kissed the top of her head.

In due course, after the tea things had been removed, I learned the exact state of affairs, and even making due allowance for my cousin's excited exaggerations, there were things that seemed to me inexplicable enough on any ground of normal explanation. Slight as the details may seem when set down seriatim, their cumulative effect upon my own mind touched an impressive and disagreeable climax that I did my best to conceal from outward betrayal. As I sat in the great shadowy room, listening to my cousin's jerky description of "childish" things, it was borne in upon me that they might well have the profoundest possible significance.

I watched her eager, frightened face, lit only by the flickering flames the sharp spring evening made necessary, and thought of the subject of our conversation flitting about the dreary halls and corridors of the huge old building, a little figure of tragedy, laughing, crying and dreaming in a world entirely her own—and there stirred in me an unwelcome recognition of those mutinous and dishevelled forces that lie but thinly screened behind the common-place details of life and that now seemed ready to burst forth and play their mysterious *rôle* before our very eyes.

"Tell me *exactly* what has happened," I urged, with decision but sympathy.

"There's so little, when it's put into words, George; but—well, the thing that first upset me was that she—knew the whole place, though she's never been here before. She knew every passage and staircase, many of them that I did not know myself; she showed us an underground passage to the sea, that father himself didn't know; and she actually drew a scrawl of the house as it used to be three hundred years ago when the other wing was standing where the copper beeches grow now. It's accurate, too."

It seemed impossible to explain to a person of my cousin's temperament the theories of pre-natal memory and the like, or the possibility of her own knowledge being communicated telepathically to the brain of her own daughter. I said therefore very little, but listened with an uneasiness that grew horribly.

"She found her way about the gardens instantly, as if she had played in them all her life; and she keeps drawing figures of people—men and women—in old costumes, the sort of thing our ancestors wore, you know—"

"Well, well, well!" I interrupted impatiently; "what can be more natural? She is old enough to have seen pictures she can remember enough to copy—?"

"Of course," she resumed calmly, but with a calmness due to the terror that ate her very soul and swallowed up all minor emotions; "of course, but one of the faces she gets is—a *portrait*."

She rose suddenly and came closer to me across the big stone hearth, lowering her voice to a whisper, "George," she whispered, "it's the very image of that awful—de Lorne!"

The announcement, I admit, gave me a thrill, for that particular ancestor on my father's side had largely influenced my boyish imagination by the accounts of his cruelty and wickedness in days gone by. But I think now the shiver that ran down my back was due to the thought of my little Aileen practising her memory and pencil upon so vile an object. That, and my cousin's pale visage of alarm, combined to shake me. I said, however, what seemed wise and reasonable at the moment.

"You'll be claiming next, Theresa, that the house is haunted," I suggested.

She shrugged her shoulders with an indifference that was very eloquent of the strength of this other more substantial terror.

"That would be so easy to deal with," she said, without even looking up. "A ghost stays in one place. Aileen could hardly take it about with her."

I think we both enjoyed the pause that followed. It gave me time to collect my forces for what I knew was coming. It gave her time to get her further facts into some pretence of coherence.

"I told you about the belt?" she asked at length, weakly, and as though unutterable things she longed to disown forced the question to her unwilling lips.

The sentence shot into me like the thrust of a naked sword. . . . I shook my head.

"Well, even a year or two ago she had that strange dislike of wearing a belt with her frocks. We thought it was a whim, and did not humour her. Belts are necessary, you know, George," she tried to smile feebly. "But now it has come to such a point that I've had to give in."

"She dislikes a belt round her waist, you mean?" I asked, fighting a sudden inexplicable spasm in my heart.

"It makes her scream. The moment anything encloses her waist she sets up such a hubbub, and struggles so, and hides away, and I've been obliged to yield."

"But really, Theresa—"

"She declares it fastens her in, and she will never get free again, and all kinds of other things. Oh, her fear is dreadful, poor child. Her face gets that sort of awful grey, don't you know? Even Kempster, who if anything is too firm, had to give in."

"And what else, pray?" I disliked hearing these details intensely. It made me ache with a kind of anger that I could not at once relieve the child's pain.

"The way she spoke to me after Dr. Hale had left —you know how awfully kind and gentle he is, and how Aileen likes him and even plays with him and sits on his knee? Well, he was talking about her diet, regulating it and so forth, teasing her that she mustn't eat this and that, and the rest of it, when she turned that horrid grey again and jumped off his knee with her scream—that thin wailing scream she has that goes through me like a knife, George—and flew to the nursery and locked herself in with—what do you think?—with all the bread, apples, cold meat and other eatables she could find!"

Eatables!" I exclaimed, aware of another spasm of vivid pain.

"When I coaxed her out, hours later, she was trembling like a leaf and fell into my arms utterly exhausted, and all I could get her to tell me was this—which she repeated again and again with a sort of beseeching, appealing tone that made my heart bleed—"

She hesitated an instant.

"Tell me at once."

"'I shall starve again, I shall starve again,' were the words she used. She kept repeating it over and over between her sobs. "I shall be without anything to eat. I shall starve!' And, would you believe it, while she hid in that nursery cupboard, she had crammed so much cake and stuff into her little self that she was violently sick for a couple of days. Moreover, she now hates the sight of Dr. Hale so much, poor man, that it's useless for him to see her. It does more harm than good."

I had risen and begun to walk up and down the hall while she told me this. I said very little. In my mind strange thoughts tore and raced, standing erect before me out of unbelievably immense depths of shadow. There was nothing very pregnant I found to say, however, for theories and speculations are of small avail as practical help—unless two minds see eye to eye in them.

"And the rest?" I asked gently, coming behind the chair and resting both hands upon her shoulders. She got up at once and faced me.

I was afraid to show too much sympathy lest the tears should come.

"Oh, George," she exclaimed, "I *am* relieved you have come. You are really strong and comforting. To feel your great hands on my shoulders gives me courage. But, you know, truly and honestly I am frightened out of my very wits by the child—"

"You won't stay here, of course?"

"We leave at the end of this week," she replied. "You will not desert me till then, I know. And Aileen will be all right as long as you are here, for you have the most extraordinary effect on her for good."

"Bless her little suffering imagination," I said. "You can count on me. I'll send to town tonight for my things."

And then she told me about the room. It was simple enough, but it conveyed a more horrible certainty of something true than all the other details put together. For there was a room on the ground floor, intended to be used on wet days when the nursery was too far for muddy boots—and into this room Aileen could not go. Why? No one could tell.

The facts were that the first moment the child ran in, her mother close behind, she stopped, swayed, and nearly fell. Then, with shrieks that were even heard outside by the gardeners sweeping the gravel path, she flung herself headlong against the wall, against a particular corner of it that is to say, and beat it with her little fists until the skin broke and left stains upon the paper.

It all happened in less than a minute. The words she cried so frantically her mother was too shocked and flabbergasted to remember, or even to hear properly. Aileen nearly upset her in her bewildered efforts next to find the door and escape. And the first thing she did when escape was accomplished, was to drop in a dead faint upon the stone floor of the passage outside.

"Now, is *that* all make-believe?" whispered Theresa, unable to keep the shudder from her lips. "Is that all merely part of a story she has make up and plays a part in?"

We looked one another straight in the eyes for a space of some seconds. The dread in the mother's heart leaped out to swell a terror in my own—a terror of another kind, but greater.

"It is too late tonight," I said at length, "for it would only excite her unnecessarily; but tomorrow I will talk with Aileen. And—if it seems wise—I might—I might be able to help in other ways too," I added.

So, I did talk to her—next day.

I always had her confidence, this little dark-eyed maid, and there was an intimacy between us that made play and talk very delightful. Yet as a rule, without giving myself a satisfactory reason, I preferred talking with her in the sunlight. She was not eerie, bless her little heart of queerness and mystery, but she had a way of suggesting other ways of life and existence shouldering about us that made me look round in the dark and wonder what the shadows concealed or what waited round the next corner.

We were on the lawn, where the bushy yews drop thick shade, the soft air making tea possible out of doors, my cousin out driving to distant calls; and Aileen had invited herself and was messing about with my manuscripts in a way that vexed me, for I had been reading my fairy tales to her and she kept asking me questions that shamed my limited powers. I remember, too, that I was glad the collie ran to and fro past us, scampering and barking after the swallows on the lawn.

"Only *some* of your stories are true, aren't they?" she asked abruptly.

"How do you know that, young critic?" I had been waiting for an opening supplied by herself. Anything forced on my part she would have suspected.

"Oh, I can tell."

Then she came up and whispered without any hint of invitation on my part, "Uncle, it is true, isn't it, that I've been in other places with you? And isn't it only the things we did there that make the true stories?"

The opening was delivered all perfect and complete into my hands. I cannot conceive how it was I availed myself of it so queerly—I mean, how it was that the words and the name slipped out of their own accord as though I was saying something in a dream.

"Of course, my little Lady Aileen, because in imagination, you see, we—"

But before I had time to finish the sentence with which I hoped to coax out the true inwardness of her own distress, she was upon me in a heap. "

Oh," she cried, with a sudden passionate outburst, "then you *do* know my name? You know all the story—*our* story!"

She was very excited, face flushed, eyes dancing, all the emotions of a life charged to the brim with experience playing through her little person.

"Of course, Miss Inventor, I know your name," I said quickly, puzzled, and with a sudden dismay that was hideous, clutching at my throat.

"And all that we did in this place?" she went on, pointing with increased excitement to the thick, ivygrown walls of the old house.

My own emotion grew extraordinarily, a swift, rushing uneasiness upsetting all my calculations. For it suddenly came back to me that in calling her "Lady Aileen" I had not pronounced the name quite as usual. My tongue had played a trick with the consonants and vowels, though at the moment of utterance I had somehow failed to notice the change. "Aileen" and "Helen" are almost interchangeable sounds. . . . . . And it was "Lady Helen" that I had actually said.

The discovery took my breath away for an instant —and the way she had leaped upon the name to claim it.

"No one else, you see, knows me as 'Lady Helen,'" she continued whispering, "because that's only in our story, isn't it? And now I'm just Aileen Langton. But as long as you know, it's all right. Oh, I am so awf'ly glad you knew, most awf'ly, awfly glad."

I was momentarily at a loss for words. Keenly desirous to guide the child's "pain-stories" into wiser channels, and thus help her to relief, I hesitated a moment for the right clue. I murmured something soothing about "our story," while in my mind I searched vigorously for the best way of leading her on to explain all her terror of the belt, the fear of starvation, the room that made her scream, and all the rest. All that I was most anxious to get out of her little tortured mind and then replace it by some brighter dream.

But the insidious experience had shaken my confidence a little, and these explicable emotions destroyed my elder wisdom. The little Inventor had caught me away into the reality of her own "story" with a sense of conviction that was even beyond witchery. And the next sentence she almost instantly let loose upon me completed my discomfiture—

"With you," she said, still half whispering, "with you I could even go into the room. I never could—alone—!"

The spring wind whispering in the yews behind us brought in that moment something upon me from vanished childhood days that made me tremble. Some wave of lost passion—lost because I guessed not its origin or nature—surged through the depths of me, sending faint messages to the surface of my consciousness. Aileen, little mischief-maker, changed before my very eyes as she stood there close— changed into a tall sad figure that beckoned to me across seas of time and distance, with the haze of ages in her eyes and gestures, . . . I was obliged to focus my gaze upon her with a deliberate effort to see her again as the tumble-haired girl I was accustomed to. . . .

Then, sitting in the creaky garden chair, I drew her down upon my knee, determined to win the whole story from her mind. My back was to the house; she was perched at an angle, however, that enabled her to command the doors and windows. I mention this because, scarcely had I begun my attack, when I saw that her attention wandered, and that she seemed curiously uneasy. Once or twice, as she shifted her position to get a view of something that was going on over my shoulder, I was aware that a slight shiver passed from her small person down to my knees. She seemed to be expecting something—with dread.

"We'll make a special expedition, armed to the teeth," I said, with a laugh, referring to her singular words about the room. "We'll send Pat in first to bark at the cobwebs, and we'll take lots of provisions and—and water in case of a siege—and a file—"

I cannot pretend to understand why I chose those precise words— or why it was as though other thoughts than those I had intended rose up, clamouring for expression. It seemed all I could manage not to say a lot of other things about the room that could only have frightened instead of relieving her.

"Will you talk *into the wall* too?" she asked, turning her eyes down suddenly upon me with a little rush and flame of passion. And though I had not the faintest conception what she meant, the question sent an agony of yearning pain through me. "Talking into the wall," I instantly grasped, referred to the core of her trouble, the very central idea that frightened her and provided the suffering and terror of all her imaginings.

But I had no time to follow up the clue thus mysteriously offered to me, for almost at the same moment her eyes fixed themselves upon something behind me with an expression of tense horror, as though she saw the approach of a danger that might—kill.

"Oh, oh!" she cried under her breath, "he's coming! He's coming to take me! Uncle George—Philip—!"

The same impulse operated upon us simultaneously, it seems, for I sprang up with my fists clenched at the very instant she shot off my knee and stood with all her muscles rigid as though to resist attack. She was shaking dreadfully. Her face went the colour of linen.

"*Who's* coming——?" I began sharply, then stopped as I saw the figure of a man moving towards us from the house. It was the butler—the new butler who had arrived only that very afternoon. It is impossible to say what there was in his swift and silent approach that was abominable. The man was upon us, it seemed, almost as soon as I caught sight of him, and the same moment Aileen, with a bursting cry, looking wildly about her for a place to hide in, plunged headlong into my arms and buried her face in my coat.

Horribly perplexed, yet mortified that the servant should see my little friend in such a state, I did my best to pretend that it was all part of some mad game or other, and catching her up in my arms, I ran, calling the collie to follow with, "Come on, Pat! She's our prisoner!" —and only set her down when we were under the limes at the far end of the lawn. She was all white and ghostly from her terror, still looking frantically about her, trembling in such a way that I thought any minute she must collapse in a dead faint. She clung to me with very tight fingers. How I hated that man. Judging by the sudden violence of my loathing he might have been some monster who wanted to torture her....

"Let's go away, oh, much farther, ever so far away!" she whispered, and I took her by the hand, comforting her as best I could with words, while realising that the thing she wanted was my big arm about her to protect. My heart ached, oh, so fiercely, for her, but the odd thing about it was that I could not find anything of real comfort to say that I felt would be *true*. If I "made up" soothing rubbish, it would not deceive either of us and would only shake her confidence in me, so that I should lose any power I had to help. Had a tiger come upon her out of the wood I might as well have assured her it would not bite!

I did stammer something, however—

"It's only the new butler. He startled me, too; he came so softly, didn't he?" Oh! how eagerly I searched for a word that might make the thing seem as ordinary as possible—yet how vainly.

"But you know who he is—*really!*" she said in a crying whisper, running down the path and dragging me after her; "and if he gets me again ... oh! Oh!" and she shrieked aloud in the anguish of her fear.

That fear chased both of us down the winding path between the bushes.

"Aileen, darling," I cried, surrounding her with both arms and holding her very tight, "you need not be afraid. I'll always save you. I'll always be with you, dear child."

"Keep me in your big arms, always, always, won't you, Uncle—Philip?" She mixed both names. The choking stress of her voice wrung

22

me dreadfully. "Always, always, like in our story," she pleaded, hiding her little face again in my coat.

I really was at a complete loss to know what best to do; I hardly dared to bring her back to the house; the sight of the man, I felt, might be fatal to her already too delicately balanced reason, for I dreaded a fit or seizure if she chanced to run across him when I was not with her. My mind was easily made up on one point, however.

"I'll send him away at once, Aileen," I told her. "When you wake up tomorrow he'll be gone. Of course mother won't keep him."

This assurance seemed to bring her some measure of comfort, and at last, without having dared to win the whole story from her as I had first hoped, I got her back to the house by covert ways, and saw her myself upstairs to her own quarters. Also I took it upon myself to give the necessary orders. She must set no eye upon the man. Only, why was it that in my heart of hearts I longed for him to do something outrageous that should make it possible for me to break his very life at its source and kill him . . . ?

But my cousin, alarmed to the point of taking even frantic measures, finally had a sound suggestion to offer, namely that I should take the afflicted little child away with me the very next day, run down to Harwich and carry her off for a week of absolute change across the North Sea. And I, meanwhile, had reached the point where I had persuaded myself that the experiment I had hitherto felt unable to consent to had now become a permissible, even a necessary one. Hypnotism should win the story from that haunted mind without her being aware of it, and provided I could drive her deep enough into the trance state, I could then further wipe the memory from her outer consciousness so completely that she might know at last some happiness of childhood.

5

It was after ten o'clock, and I was still sitting in the big hall before the fire of logs, talking with lowered voice. My cousin sat opposite to me in a deep armchair. We had discussed the matter pretty fully, and the deep uneasiness we felt clothed not alone our minds but the very building with gloom. The fact that, instinctively, neither of us referred to the possible assistance of doctors is eloquent, I think, of the emotion that troubled us both so profoundly, the emotion, I mean, that sprang from the vivid sense of the reality of it all. No child's make-believe merely could have thus caught us away, or spread a net that entangled our minds to such a point of confusion and dismay. It was perfectly comprehensible to me now that my cousin should have cried in very helplessness before the convincing effects of the little girl's calamitous distress. Aileen was living through a Reality, not an Invention. This was the fact that haunted the shadowy halls and corridors behind us. Already I hated the very building. It seemed charged to the roof with the memories of melancholy and ancient pain that swept my heart with shivering, cold winds.

Purposely, however, I affected some degree of cheerfulness, and concealed from my cousin any mention of the attacks that certain emotions and alarms had made upon myself: I said nothing of my replacing "Lady Aileen" with "Lady Helen," nothing of my passing for "Philip," or of my sudden dashes of quasimemory arising from the child's inclusion of myself in her "story," and my own singular acceptance of the role. I did not consider it wise to mention *all* that the sight of the new servant with his sinister dark face and his method of stealthy approach had awakened in my thoughts.

None the less these things started constantly to the surface of my mind and doubtless betrayed themselves somewhere in my "atmosphere," sufficiently at least for a woman's intuition to divine them. I spoke passingly of the "room," and of Aileen's singular aversion for it, and of her remark about "talking to the wall." Yet strange thoughts pricked their way horribly into both our minds. In the hall the stuffed heads of deer and fox and badger stared upon us like masks of things still alive beneath their fur and dead skin.

"But what disturbs me more than all the rest of her delusions put together," said my cousin, peering at me with eyes that made no pretence of hiding dark things, "is her extraordinary knowledge of this place. I assure you, George, it was the most uncanny thing I've ever known when she showed me over and asked questions as if she had actually lived here." Her voice sank to a whisper, and she looked up startled. It seemed to me for a moment that someone was coming near to listen, moving stealthily upon us along the dark approaches to the hall.

"I can understand you found it strange," I began quickly. But she interrupted me at once. Clearly it gave her a certain relief to say the things and get them out of her mind where they hid, breeding new growths of abhorrence.

"George," she cried aloud, "there's a limit to imagination. Aileen knows. That's the awful thing—"

Something sprang into my throat. My eyes moistened.

"The horror of the belt—" she whispered, loathing her own words.

"Leave that thought alone," I said with decision. The detail pained me inexpressibly—beyond belief.

"I wish I could," she answered, "but if you had seen the look on her face when she struggled—and the—the frenzy she got into about the food and starving—I mean when Dr. Hale spoke—oh, if you had seen all that, you would understand that I—"

She broke off with a start. Someone had entered the hall behind us and was standing in the doorway at the far end. The listener had moved upon us from the dark. Theresa, though her back was turned, had felt the presence and was instantly upon her feet.

"You need not sit up, Porter," she said, in a tone that only thinly veiled the fever of apprehension behind, "we will put the lights out," and the man withdrew like a shadow. She exchanged a quick glance with me. A sensation of darkness that seemed to have come with the servant's presence was gone. It is wholly beyond me to explain why neither myself nor my cousin found anything to say for some minutes. But it was still more a mystery, I think, why the muscles of my two hands should have contracted involuntarily with a force that drove the nails into my palms, and why the violent impulse should have leaped into my blood to fling myself upon the man and strangle the life out of his neck before he could take another breath. I have never before or since experienced this apparently causeless desire to throttle anybody. I hope I never may again.

"He hangs about rather," was all my cousin said presently. "He's always watching us—" But my own thoughts were horribly busy, and I was marvelling how it was this ugly and sinister creature had ever come to be accepted in the story that Aileen lived, and that I was slowly coming to *believe* in.

It was a relief to me when, towards midnight, Theresa rose to go to bed. We had skirted through the horrors of the child's possessing misery without ever quite facing it, and as we stood there lighting the candles, our voices whispering, our minds charged with the strain of thoughts neither of us had felt it wise to utter, my cousin started back against the wall and stared up into the darkness above where the staircase climbed the well of the house. She uttered a cry. At first I thought she was going to collapse. I was only just in time to catch the candle.

All the emotions of fearfulness she had repressed during our long talk came out in that brief cry, and when I looked up to discover the cause I saw a small white figure come slowly down the wide stair-case and just about to step into the hall. It was Aileen, with bare feet, her dark hair tumbling down over her nightgown, her eyes wide open, an expression in them of anguished expectancy that her tender years could never possibly have known. She was walking steadily, yet somehow not quite as a child walks.

"Stop!" I whispered peremptorily to my cousin, putting my hand quickly over her mouth, and holding her back from the first movement of rescue, "don't wake her. She's walking in her sleep."

Aileen passed us like a white shadow, scarcely audible, and went straight across the hall. She was utterly unaware of our presence. Avoiding all obstructions of chairs and tables, moving with decision and purpose, the little figure dipped into the shadows at the far end and disappeared from view in the mouth of the corridor that had once—three hundred years ago–led into the wing where now the copper beeches grew upon open lawns. It was clearly a way familiar to her. And the instant I recovered from my surprise and moved after her to act, Theresa found her voice and cried aloud—a voice that broke the midnight silence with shrill discordance—

"George, oh, George. She's going to that awful room . . . . ."

"Bring the candle and come after me," I replied from halfway down the hall, "but do not interrupt unless I call for you," and was after the child at a pace to which the most singular medley of emotions I have ever known urged me imperiously. A sense of tragic disaster gripped my very vitals. All that I did seemed to rise out of some subconscious region of the mind where the haunting passions of a deeply buried past stirred in their sleep and woke.

"Helen!" I cried, "Lady Helen—" I was close upon the gliding figure. Aileen turned and for the first time saw me with eyes that seemed to waver between sleep and waking. They gazed straight at me over the flickering candle flame, then hesitated. In similar fashion the gesture of her little hands towards me was arrested before it had completed itself. She saw me, knew my presence, yet was uncertain who I was. It was astonishing the way I actually surprised this momentary indecision between the two personalities in her—caught the two phases of her consciousness at grips—discerned the Aileen of Today in the act of waking to know me as her "Uncle George," and that other Aileen of her great dark story, the "Helen" of some far Yesterday, that drew her in this condition of somnambulism to the scene in the past where our two lives were linked in her imagination. For it was quite clear to me that the child was dreaming in her sleep the action of the story she lived through in the vivid moments of her waking terror.

But the choice was swift. I just had time to signal Theresa to set the candle upon a shelf and wait, when she came up, stretched her hands out in completion of the original gesture, and fell into my arms with a smothered cry of love and anguish that, coming from those childish lips, I think is the most thrilling human sound I have ever known. She knew and saw me, but not as "Uncle" George of this present life.

"Oh, Philip!" she cried, "then you have come after all—"

"Of course, dear heart," I whispered. "Of course I have come. Did I not give my promise that I would?"

Her eyes searched my face, and then settled upon my hands that held her little cold wrists so tightly.

"But—but," she stammered in comment, "they are not cut! They have made you whole again. You will save me and get me out, and we—we—"

The expressions of her face ran together into a queer confusion of perplexity, and she seemed to totter on her feet. In another instant she would probably have wakened; again she felt the touch of uncertainty and doubt as to my identity. Her hands resisted the pressure of my own; she drew back half a step; into her eyes rose the shallower consciousness of the present. Once awake it would drive out the profoundly strange passion and mystery that haunted the corridors of thought and memory and plunged so obscurely into the inmost recesses of her being. For, once awake, I realised that I should lose her, lose the opportunity of getting the complete story. The chance was unique. I heard my cousin's footsteps approaching behind us down the passage on tiptoe—and I came to an immediate decision.

In the state of deep sleep, of course, the trance condition is very close, and many experiments had taught me that the human spirit can be subjected to the influence of hypnotism far more speedily when asleep than when awake; for if hypnotism means chiefly—as I then held it to mean—the merging of the little ineffectual surface-consciousness with the deep sea of the greater subliminal consciousness below, then the process has already been partially begun in normal slumber and its completion need be no very long or difficult matter. It was Aileen's very active subconsciousness that "invented" or "remembered" the dark story which haunted her life, her subconscious region too readily within tap. . . . By deepening her sleep state I could learn the whole story.

Stopping her mother's approach with a sign that I intended she should clearly understand, and which accordingly she did understand, I took immediate steps to plunge the spirit of this little sleep-walking child down again into the subconscious region that had driven her thus far, and wherein lay the potentialities of all her powers, of memory, knowledge and belief. Only the simplest passes were necessary, for she yielded quickly and easily; that first look came back into her eyes; she no longer wavered or hesitated, but drew close against me, with the name of "Philip" upon her lips, and together we moved down the long passage till we reached the door of her horrid room of terror.

And there, whether it was that Theresa's following with the candle disturbed the child—for the subconscious tie with the mother is of such unalterable power —or whether anxiety weakened my authority over her fluctuating mental state, I noticed that she again wavered and hesitated, looking up with eyes that saw partly "Uncle George," partly the "Philip" she remembered.

"We'll go in," I said firmly, "and you shall see that there is nothing to be afraid of." I opened the door, and the candle from behind threw a triangle of light into the darkness. It fell upon a bare floor, pictureless walls, and just tipped the high white ceiling overhead. I pushed the door still wider open and we went in hand in hand, Aileen shaking like a leaf in the wind.

How the scene lives in my mind, even as I write it today so many years after it took place: the little child in her nightgown facing me in that empty room of the ancient building, all the passionate emotions of a tragic history in the small young eyes, her mother like a ghost in the passage, afraid to come in, the tossing shadows thrown by the candle and the soft moan of the night wind against the outside walls.

I made further passes over the small flushed face and pressed my thumbs gently along the temples. "Sleep!" I commanded; "sleep—and remember!" My will poured over her being to control and protect. She passed still deeper into the trance condition in which the somnambulistic lucidity manifests itself and the deeper self gives up its dead. Her eyes grew wider, rounder, charged with memories as they fastened themselves upon my own. The present, which a few minutes before had threatened to claim her consciousness by waking her, faded. She saw me no longer as her familiar Uncle George, but as the faithful friend and lover of her great story, Philip, the man who had come to save her. There she stood in the atmosphere of bygone days, in the very room where she had known great suffering—this room that three centuries ago had led by a corridor into the wing of the house where now the beeches grew upon the lawns.

She came up close and put her thin bare arms about my neck and stared with peering, searching eyes into mine.

"Remember what happened here," I said resolutely. "Remember, and tell me."

Her brows contracted slightly as with the effort, and she whispered, glancing over her shoulder towards the farther end where the corridor once began, "It hurts a little, but I—I'm in your arms, Philip dear, and you will get me out, I know—"

"I hold you safe and you are in no danger, little one," I answered. "You can remember and speak without it hurting you. Tell me."

The suggestion, of course, operated instantly, for her face cleared, and she dropped a great sigh of relief. From time to time I continued the passes that held the trance condition firm.

Then she spoke in a low, silvery little tone that cut into me like a sword and searched my inmost parts. I seemed to bleed internally. I could have sworn that she spoke of things I knew as though I had lived through them.

"This was when I last saw you," she said, "this was the room where you were to fetch me and carry me away into happiness and safety from—him," and it was the voice and words of no mere child that said it; "and this was where you did come on that night of snow and wind. Through that window you entered;" she pointed to the deep, embrasured window behind us. "Can't you hear the storm? How it howls and screams! And the boom of the surf on the beach below. . . .You left the horses outside, the swift horses that were to carry us to the sea and away from all his cruelties, and then—"

She hesitated and searched for words or memories; her face darkened with pain and loathing.

"Tell me the rest," I ordered, "but forget all your own pain." And she smiled up at me with an expression of unbelievable tenderness and confidence while I drew the frail form closer.

"*You* remember, Philip," she went on, "you know just what it was, and how he and his men seized you the moment you stepped inside, and how you struggled and called for me, and heard me answer—"

"Far away—outside—" I interrupted quickly, helping her out of some flashing memory in my own deep heart that seemed to burn and leave a scar. "You answered from the lawn—"

"You thought it was the lawn, but really, you see, it was there—in there," and she pointed to the side of the room on my right. She shook dreadfully, and her voice dwindled most oddly in volume, as though coming from a distance—almost muffled."

"In there?" I asked it with a shudder that put ice and fire mingled in my blood.

"In the wall," she whispered. "You see, someone had betrayed us, and he knew you were coming. He walled me up alive in there, and only left two little holes for my eyes so that I could see. You heard my voice calling through those holes, but you never knew where I was. And then—"

Her knees gave way, and I had to hold her. She looked suddenly with torture in her eyes down the length of the room—towards the old wing of the house.

"You won't let him come," she pleaded beseechingly, and in her voice was the agony of death. "I thought I heard him. Isn't that his footsteps in the corridor?" She listened fearfully, her eyes trying to pierce the wall and see out on to the lawn.

"No one is coming, dear heart," I said, with conviction and authority. "Tell it all. Tell me everything."

"I saw the whole of it because I could not close my eyes," she continued. "There was an iron band round my waist fastening me in—an iron belt I never could escape from. The dust got into my mouth—I bit the bricks. My tongue was scraped and bleeding, but before they put in the last stones to smother me I saw them—cut both your hands off so that you could never save me—never let me out."

She dashed without warning from my side and flew up to the wall, beating it with her hands and crying aloud—

"Oh, you poor, poor thing. I know how awful it was. I remember—when I was in you and you wore and carried me, poor, poor body! That thunder of the last brick as they drove it in against the mouth, and the iron clamp that cut into the waist, and the suffocation and hunger and thirst!"

"What are you talking to in there?" I asked sternly, crushing down the tears.

The body I was in—the one he walled up—my body—my own body."

She flew back to my side. But even before my cousin had uttered that "mother-cry" that broke in upon the child's deeper consciousness, disturbing the memories, I had given the command with all the force of my being to "forget" the pain. And only those few who are familiar with the instantaneous changes of emotion that can be produced by suggestion under hypnosis will understand that Aileen came back to me from that moment of "talking to the wall" with laughter on her lips and in her eyes.

The small white figure with the cascade of dark hair tumbling over the nightgown ran up and jumped into my arms.

"But I saved you," I cried, "you were never properly walled-up; I got you out and took you away from him over the sea, and we were happy ever afterwards, like the people in the fairy tales." I drove the words into her with my utmost force, and inevitably she accepted them as the truth, for she clung to me with love and laughter all over her child's face of mystery, the horror fading out, the pain swept clean away. With kaleidoscopic suddenness the change came.

"So they never really cut your poor dead hands off at all," she said hesitatingly.

"Look How could they? There they are! And I first showed them to her and then pressed them against her little cheeks, drawing her mouth up to be kissed. "They're big enough still and strong enough to carry; you off to bed and stroke you into so deep a sleep that when you wake in the morning you will have forgotten everything about your dark story, about Philip, Lady Helen, the iron belt, the starvation, your cruel old husband, and all the rest of it. You'll wake up happy and jolly just like any other child—"

"If you say so, of course I shall," she answered, smiling into my eyes.

And it was just then there came in that touch of abomination that so nearly made my experiment a failure, for it came with a black force that threatened at first to discount all my "suggestion" and make it of no account. My new command that she should forget had apparently not yet fully registered itself in her being; the tract of deeper consciousness that constructed the "Story" had not sunk quite below the threshold. Thus she was still open to any detail of her former suffering that might obtrude itself with sufficient force. And such a detail *did* obtrude itself. This touch of abomination was calculated with a really superhuman ingenuity.

"Hark!" she cried—and it was that *scream in a whisper* that only utter terror can produce—"Hark! I hear his steps He's coming! Oh, I told you he was coming! He's in *that* passage!" pointing down the room. And she first sprang from my arms as though something burned her, and then almost instantly again flew back to my protection. In that interval of a few seconds she tore into the middle of the room, put her hand to her ear to listen, and then shaded her eyes in the act of peering down through the wall at the far end. She stared at the very place where in olden days the corridor had led into the vanished wing. The window my great-uncle had built into the wall now occupied the exact spot where the opening had been.

Theresa then for the first time came forward with a rush into the room, dropping the candle-grease over the floor. She clutched me by the arm. The three of us stood there—listening—listening apparently to nought but the sighing of the sea-wind about the walls, Aileen with her eyes buried in my coat. I was standing erect trying in vain to catch the new sound. I remember my cousin's face of chalk with the fluttering eyes and the candle held aslant.

Then suddenly she raised her hand and pointed over my shoulder. I thought her jaw would drop from her face. And she and the child both spoke in the same breath the two sharp phrases that brought the climax of the vile adventure upon us in that silent room of night.

They were like two pistol-shots.

"My God! There's a face watching us . . . . ." I heard her voice, all choked and dry.

And at the same second, Aileen— "Oh, oh He's seen us! . . . He's here! Look. . . . He'll get me . . . hide your hands, hide your poor hands!
. . . ."

And, turning to the place my cousin stared at, I saw sure enough that a face—apparently a living human face—was pressed against the window-pane, framed between two hands as it tried to peer upon us into the semi-obscurity of the room. I saw the swift momentary rolling of the two eyes as the candle glare fell upon them, and caught a glimpse even of the hunched-up shoulders behind, as their owner, standing outside upon the lawn, stooped down a little to see better. And though the apparition instantly withdrew, I recognised it beyond question as the dark and evil countenance of the butler. His breath still stained the window.

Yet the strange thing was that Aileen, struggling violently to bury herself amid the scanty folds of my coat, could not possibly have seen what we saw, for her face was turned from the window the entire time, and from the way I held her she could never for a single instant have been in a position to know. It all took place behind her back. . . . A moment later, with her eyes still hidden against me, I was carrying her swiftly in my arms across the hall and up the main staircase to the night nursery.

My difficulty with her was, of course, while she hovered between the two states of sleep and waking, for once I got her into bed and plunged her deeply again into the trance condition, I was easily able to control her slightest thought or emotion. Within ten minutes she was sleeping peacefully, her little face smoothed of all anxiety or terror, and my imperious command ringing from end to end of her consciousness that when she woke next morning all should be forgotten. She was finally to forget .. utterly and completely.

And, meanwhile, of course, the man, when I went with loathing and anger in my heart to his room in the servants' quarters, had a perfectly plausible explanation. He was in the act of getting ready for bed, he declared, when the noise had aroused his suspicions, and, as in duty bound, he had made a tour of the house outside, thinking to discover burglars. . . .

With a month's wages in his pocket, and a considerable degree of wonder in his soul, probably—for the man was guilty of nothing worse than innocently terrifying a child's imagination!—he went back to London the following day; and a few hours later I myself was travelling with Aileen and old Kempster over the blue waves of the North Sea, carrying her off, curiously enough, to freedom and happiness in the very way her "imagination" had pictured her escape in the "story" of long ago, when she was Lady Helen, held in bondage by a cruel husband, and I was Philip, her devoted lover.

Only this time her happiness was lasting and complete. Hypnotic suggestion had wiped from her mind the last vestige of her dreadful memories; her face was wreathed in jolly smiles; her enjoyment of the journey and our week in Antwerp was absolutely unclouded; she played and laughed with all the radiance of an unhaunted childhood, and her imagination was purged and healed.

And when we got back her mother had again moved her household gods to the original family mansion where she had first lived. Thither it was I took the restored child, and there it was my cousin and I looked up the old family records and verified certain details of the history of De Lorne, that wicked and semifabulous ancestor whose portrait hung in the dark corner of the stairs. That his life was evil to the brim I had always understood, but neither myself nor Theresa had known—at least had not consciously remembered—that he had married twice, and that his first wife, Lady Helen, had mysteriously disappeared, and Sir Philip Lansing, a neighbouring knight, supposed to be her lover, had soon afterwards emigrated to France and left his lands and property to go to ruin.

But another discovery I made, and kept to myself, had to do with that "room of terror" in the old Norfolk house where, on the plea of necessary renovation, I had the stones removed, and in the very spot where Aileen used to beat her hands against the bricks and "talk to the wall," the workmen under my own eyes laid bare the skeleton of a woman, fastened to the granite by means of a narrow iron band that encircled the waist—the skeleton of some unfortunate who had been walled-up alive and had come to her dreadful death by the pangs of hunger, thirst and suffocation centuries ago.

The Doll

Some nights are merely dark, others are dark in a suggestive way as though something ominous, mysterious, is going to happen. In certain remote outlying suburbs, at any rate, this seems true, where great spaces between the lamps go dead at night, where little happens, where a ring at the door is a summons almost, and people cry "Let's go to town!" In the villa gardens the mangy cedars sigh in the wind, but the hedges stiffen, there is a muffling of spontaneous activity.

On this particular November night, a moist breeze barely stirred the silver pine in the narrow drive leading to the "Laurels" where Colonel Masters lived. Colonel Hymber Masters, late of an Indian regiment, with many distinguished letters after his name. The housemaid in the limited staff being out, it was the cook who answered the bell when it rang with a sudden, sharp clang soon after ten o'clock—and gave an audible gasp half of surprise, half of fear. The bell's sudden clangour was an unpleasant and unwelcome sound. Monica, the colonel's adored yet rather neglected child, was asleep upstairs, but the cook was not frightened lest Monica be disturbed, nor because it seemed a bit late for the bell to ring so violently; she was frightened because when she opened the door to let the fine rain drive in, she saw a black man standing on the steps. There, in the wind and the rain, stood a tall, slim black man holding a parcel.

Dark-skinned, at any rate, he was, she reflected afterwards, whether negro, Hindu or Arab. Wearing a stained yellow mackintosh and dirty slouch hat, and "looking like a devil, so help me, God," he shoved the little parcel at her out of the gloom, the light from the hall flaring red into his gleaming eyes. "For Colonel Masters," he whispered rapidly, "and very special into his own personal touch and no one else." And he melted away into the night with his "strange foreign accent, his eyes of fire, and his nasty hissing voice."

He was gone, swallowed up in the wind and rain.

"But I saw his eyes," swore the cook the next morning to the housemaid, "his fiery eyes, and his nasty look, and his black hands and long thin fingers, and his nails all shiny pink, and he looked to me—if you know wot I mean—he looked like—death. . . ."

Thus the cook, so far as she was intelligently articulate next day, but standing now against the closed door with the small brown paper parcel in her hands, impressed by the orders that it was to be given into his personal touch, she was relieved by the fact that Colonel Masters never returned till after midnight and that she need not act at once. The reflection brought a certain comfort that restored her equanimity a little, though she still stood there, holding the parcel gingerly in her grimy hands, reluctant, hesitating, uneasy.

A parcel, even brought by a mysterious dark stranger, was not in itself frightening, yet frightened she certainly felt. Instinct and superstition worked perhaps; the wind, the rain, the fact of being alone in the house, the unexpected black man, these also contributed to her discomfort. A vague sense of horror touched her, her Irish blood stirred ancient dreams, so that she began to shake a little, as though the parcel contained something alive, explosive, poisonous, unholy almost as though it moved, and, her fingers loosening their hold, the parcel—dropped. It fell on the tiled floor with a queer, sharp clack, but it lay motionless.

She eyed it closely, cautiously, but, thank God, it did not move, an inert, brown-paper parcel. Brought by an errand boy in daylight, it might have been groceries, tobacco, even a mended shirt. She peeped and tinkered, that sharp clack puzzled her. Then, after a few minutes, remembering her duty, she picked it up gingerly even while she shivered. It was to be handed into the colonel's "personal touch." She compromised, deciding to place it on his desk and to tell him about it in the morning; only Colonel Masters, with those mysterious years in the East behind him, his temper and his tyrannical orders, was not easy of direct approach at the best of times, in the morning least of all.

The cook left it at that—that is, she left it on the desk in his study, but left out all explanations about its arrival. She had decided to be vague about such unimportant details, for Mrs. O'Reilly was afraid of Colonel Masters, and only his professed love of Monica made her believe that he was quite human. He paid her well, oh yes, and sometimes he smiled, and he was a handsome man, if a bit too dark for her fancy, yet he also paid her an occasional compliment about her curry, and that soothed her for the moment. They suited one another, at any rate, and she stayed, robbing him comfortably, if cautiously.

"It ain't no good," she assured the housemaid next day, "wot with that 'personal touch into his hands, and no one else,' and that black man's eyes and that crack when it came away in my hands and fell on the floor. It ain't no good, not to us nor anybody. No man as black as he was means lucky stars to anybody. A parcel indeed—with those devil's eyes—"

"What did you do with it?" enquired the housemaid.

The cook looked her up and down "Put it in the fire o' course," she replied. "On the stove if you want to know exact."

It was the housemaid's turn to look the cook up and down.

"I don't think," she remarked.

The cook reflected, probably because she found no immediate answer.

"Well," she puffed out presently, "D'you know wot I think? You don't. So, I'll tell you. It was something the master's afraid of, that's wot it was. He's afraid of something—ever since I been here, I've known that. And that's wot it was. He done somebody wrong in India long ago and that lanky black man brought wot's coming to him, and that's why I says I put it on the stove—see?" She dropped her voice. "It was a bloody idol," she whispered, "that's wot it was, that parcel, and he—why, he's a bloody secret worshipper." And she crossed herself "That's why I said I put it on the stove—see?"

The housemaid stared and gasped.

"And you mark my words, young Jane!" added the cook, turning to her dough.

And there the matter rested for a period, for the cook, being Irish, had more laughter in her than tears, and beyond admitting to the scared housemaid that she had not really burnt the parcel but had left it on the study table, she almost forgot the incident. It was not her job, in any case, to answer the front door. She had "delivered" the parcel. Her conscience was quite clear.

Thus, nobody "marked her words" apparently, for nothing untoward happened, as the way is in remote Suburbia, and Monica in her lonely play was happy, and Colonel Masters as tyrannical and grim as ever. The moist wintry wind blew through the silver pine, the rain beat against the bow window, and no one called. For a week this lasted, a longish time in uneventful Suburbia.

★★★★★★★★★★

But suddenly one morning Colonel Masters rang his study bell

37

and, the housemaid being upstairs, it was the cook who answered. He held a brown paper parcel in his hands, half opened, the string dangling.

"I found this on my desk. I haven't been in my room for a week. Who brought it? And when did it come?" His face, yellow as usual, held a fiery tinge.

Mrs. O'Reilly replied, post-dating the arrival vaguely.

"I asked *who* brought it?" he insisted sharply.

"A stranger," she fumbled. "Not anyone," she added nervously, "from hereabouts. No one I ever seen before. It was a man."

"What did he look like?" The question came like a bullet.

Mrs. O'Reilly was rather taken by surprise. "D-darkish," she stumbled. "Very darkish," she added, "if I saw him right. Only he came and went so quick I didn't get his face proper like, and . . ."

"Any message?" the colonel cut her short.

She hesitated. "There was no answer," she began, remembering former occasions.

"Any *message*, I asked you?" he thundered.

"No message, sir, none at all. And he was gone before I could get his name and address, sir, but I think it was a sort of black man, or it may have been the darkness of the night—I couldn't reely say, sir . . ."

In another minute she would have burst into tears or dropped to the floor in a faint, such was her terror of her employer especially when she was lying blind. The colonel, however, saved her both disasters by abruptly holding out the half-opened parcel towards her. He neither cross-examined nor cursed her as she had expected. He spoke with the curtness that betrayed anger and anxiety, almost it occurred to her, distress.

"Take it away and burn it," he ordered in his army voice, passing it into her outstretched hands. "Burn it," he repeated it, "or chuck the damned thing away." He almost flung it at her as though he did not want to touch it. "If the man comes back," he ordered in a voice of steel, "tell him it's been destroyed—and say it *didn't reach me*," laying tremendous emphasis on the final words. "You understand?" He almost chucked it at her.

"Yes, sir. Exactly, sir," and she turned and stumbled out, holding the parcel gingerly in her arms rather than in her hands and fingers, as though it contained something that might bite or sting.

Yet her fear had somehow lessened, for if he. Colonel Masters, could treat the parcel so contemptuously, why should she feel afraid of it. And, once alone in her kitchen among her household gods, she opened it. Turning back the thick paper wrappings, she started, and to her rather disappointed amazement, she found herself staring at nothing but a fair, waxen faced doll that could be bought in any toy-shop for one shilling and sixpence.

A commonplace little cheap doll! Its face was pallid, white, expressionless, its flaxen hair was dirty, its tiny ill-shaped hands and fingers lay motionless by its side, its mouth was closed, though somehow grinning, no teeth visible, its eyelashes ridiculously like a worn tooth brush, its entire presentment in its flimsy skirt, contemptible, harmless, even ugly. A doll! She giggled to herself, all fear evaporated.

"Gawd!" she thought. "The master must have a conscience like the floor of a parrot's cage! And worse than that!" She was too afraid of him to despise him, her feeling was probably more like pity. "At any rate," she reflected, "he had the wind up pretty bad. It was something else he expected—not a two-penny halfpenny doll!" Her warm heart felt almost sorry for him.

Instead of "chucking the damned thing away or burning it," however—for it was quite a nice-looking doll, she presented it to Monica, and Monica, having few new toys, instantly adored it, promising faithfully, as gravely warned by Mrs. O'Reilly, that she would never, never, let her father know she had it.

Her father. Colonel Hymber Masters, was, it seems, what's called a "disappointed" man, a man whose fate forced him to live in surroundings he detested, disappointed in his career probably, possibly in love as well, Monica a love-child doubtless, and limited by his pension to face daily conditions that he loathed.

He was a silent, bitter sort of fellow, no more than that, and not so much disliked in the neighbourhood, as misunderstood. A sombre man they reckoned him, with his dark, furrowed face and silent ways. Yet "dark" in the suburbs meant mysterious, and "silent" invited female fantasy to fill the vacuum. It's the frank, corn-haired man who invites sympathy and generous comment. He enjoyed his Bridge, however, and was accepted as a first-class player. Thus, he went out nightly, and rarely came back before midnight. He was welcome among the gamblers evidently, while the fact that he had an adored child at home softened the picture of this "mysterious" man. Monica, though rarely seen, appealed to the women of the neighbourhood, and "whatever her origin" said the gossips, "he loves her."

To Monica, meanwhile, in her rather play-less, toy-less life, the doll, her new treasure, was a spot of gold. The fact that it was a "secret" present from her father, added to its value. Many other presents had come to her like that; she thought nothing of it; only, he had never given her a doll before, and it spelt rapture. Never, never, would she betray her pleasure and delight; it should remain her secret and his; and that made her love it all the more.

She loved her father too, his taciturn silence was something she vaguely respected and adored. That's just like father," she always said, when a strange new present came, and she knew instinctively that she must never say *Thank you* for it, for that was part of the lovely game between them. But this doll was exceptionally marvellous.

"It's much more real and alive than my teddy bears," she told the cook, after examining it critically. "What ever made him think of it? Why, it even talks to me!" and she cuddled and fondled the half mis-shapen toy. "It's my baby," she cried taking it against her cheek.

For no teddy-bear could really be a child; cuddly bears were not offspring, whereas a doll was a potential baby. It brought sweetness, as both cook and governess realised, into a rather grim house, hope and tenderness, a maternal flavour almost, something anyhow that no young bear could possibly bring. A child, a human baby!

And yet both cook and governess—for both were present at the actual delivery—recalled later that Monica opened the parcel and recognised the doll with a yell of wild delight that seemed almost a scream of pain. There was this too high note of delirious exultation as though some instinctive horror of revulsion were instantly smothered and obliterated in a whirl of overmastering joy. It was Madame Jodzka who recalled—long afterwards—this singular contradiction.

"I did think she shrieked at it a bit, now you ask me," admitted Mrs. O'Reilly later, though at the actual moment all she said was "Oh, lovely, darling, ain't it a pet!" While all Madame Jodzka said was a cautionary "If you squash its mouth like that, Monica, it won't be able to breathe!"

While Monica, paying no attention to either of them, fell to cuddling the doll with ecstasy.

A cheap little flaxen-haired, waxen-faced doll.

That so strange a case should come to us at second hand is, admittedly, a pity; that so much of the information should reach us largely through a cook and housemaid and through a foreigner of question-able validity, is equally unfortunate. Where precisely the reported facts creep across the feathery frontier into the incredible and thence into the fantastic would need the spider's thread of the big telescopes to define. With the eye to the telescope, the thread of that New Zealand spider seems thick as a rope; but with the eye examining second-hand reports the thread becomes elusive gossamer.

★★★★★★★★★★

The Polish governess, Madame Jodzka, left the house rather abruptly. Though adored by Monica and accepted by Colonel Masters, she left not long after the arrival of the doll. She was a comely, youngish widow of birth and breeding, tactful, discreet, understanding. She adored Monica, and Monica was happy with her; she feared her employer, yet perhaps secretly admired him as the strong, silent, dominating Englishman. He gave her great freedom, she never took liberties, everything went smoothly. The pay was good and she needed it. Then, suddenly, she left.

In the suddenness of her departure, as in the odd reason she gave for leaving, lie doubtless the first hints of this remarkable affair, creeping across that "feathery frontier" into the incredible and fantastic. An understandable reason she gave for leaving was that she was too frightened to stay in the house another night. She left at twenty-four hours' notice. Her reason was absurd, even if understandable, because any woman might find herself so frightened in a certain building that it has become intolerable to her nerves. Foolish or otherwise, this is understandable. An *idée fixe*, an obsession, once lodged in the mind of a superstitious, therefore hysterically-favoured woman, cannot be dislodged by argument. It may be absurd, yet it is "understandable."

The story behind the reason for Madame Jodzka's sudden terror is another matter, and it is best given quite simply. It relates to the doll. She swears by all her gods that she saw the doll "walking by itself." It was walking in a disjointed, hoppity, hideous fashion across the bed in which Monica lay sleeping.

In the gleam of the night-light, Madame Jodzka swears she saw this happen. She was half inside the opened door, peeping in, as her habit, and duty decreed, to see if all was well with the child before going up to bed herself. The light, if faint, was clear. A jerky movement on the counterpane first caught her attention, for a smallish object seemed blundering awkwardly across its slippery silken surface. Something rolling, possibly, some object Monica had left outside on falling asleep rolling mechanically as the child shifted or turned over.

After staring for some seconds, she then saw that it was not merely an "object," since it had a living outline, nor was it rolling mechani-

41

cally, or sliding, as she had first imagined. It was horribly taking steps, small but quite deliberate steps as though alive. It had a tiny, dreadful face, it had an expressionless tiny face, and the face had eyes—small, brightly shining eyes, and the eyes looked straight at Madame Jodzka.

She watched for a few seconds thunderstruck, and then suddenly realised with a shock of utter horror that this small, purposive monster was the doll, Monica's doll! And this doll was moving towards her across the tumbled surface of the counterpane. It was coming in her direction—straight at her.

Madame Jodzka gripped herself, physically and mentally, making a great effort, it seems, to deny the abnormal, the incredible. She denied the ice in her veins and down her spine. She prayed. She thought frantically of her priest in Warsaw. Making no audible sound, she screamed in her mind. But the doll, quickening its pace, came hobbling straight towards her, its glassy eyes fixed hard upon her own

Then Madame Jodzka fainted.

★★★★★★★★★★

That she was, in some ways, a remarkable woman, with a sense of values, is clear from the fact that she realised this story "wouldn't wash," for she confided it only to the cook in cautious whispers, while giving her employer some more "washable" tale about a family death that obliged her to hurry home to Warsaw. Nor was there the slightest attempt at embroidery, for on recovering consciousness she had recovered her courage, too—and done a remarkable thing; she had compelled herself to investigate. Aided and fortified by her religion, she compelled herself to make an examination.

She had tiptoed further into the room, had made sure that Monica was sleeping peacefully, and that the doll lay—motionless—halfway down the counterpane. She gave it a long, concentrated look. Its lidless eyes, fringed by hideously ridiculous black lashes were fixed on space. Its expression was not so much innocent, as blankly stupid, idiotic, a mask of death that aped cheaply a pretence of life, where life could never be. Not ugly merely, it was revolting.

Madame Jodzka however, did more than study this visage with concentration, for with admirable pluck she forced herself to touch the little horror. She actually picked it up. Her faith, her deep religious conviction denied the former evidence of her senses. She had not seen movement. It was incredible, impossible. The fault lay somewhere in herself. This persuasion, at any rate, lasted long enough to enable her to touch the repulsive little toy, to pick it up, to lift it. She placed it steadily on the table near the bed between the bowl of flowers and the night-light, where it lay on its back helpless, innocent, yet horrible, and only then on shaking legs did she leave the room and go up to her own bed. That her fingers remained ice-cold until eventually she fell asleep can be explained, of course, too easily and naturally to claim examination.

★★★★★★★★★★

Whether imagined or actual, it must have been, none the less, a horrifying spectacle—a mechanical outline from a commercial factory walking like a living thing with a purpose. It holds the nightmare touch. To Madame Jodzka, protected since youth within cast-iron tenets, it came as a shock. And a shock dislocates. The sight smashed everything she knew as possible and real. The flow of her blood was interrupted, it froze, there came icy terror into her heart, her normal mechanism failed for a moment she fainted. And fainting seemed a natural result. Yet it was the shock of the incredible masquerade that gave her the courage to act. She loved Monica, apart from any consideration of paid duty. The sight of this tiny monstrosity strutting across the counterpane not far from the child's sleeping face and folded hands—it was this that enabled her to pick it up with naked fingers and set it out of reach. . . .

For hours, before falling asleep, she reviewed the incredible thing, alternately denying the facts, then accepting them, yet taking into sleep finally the assured conviction that her senses had not deceived her. There seems little, indeed, that in a court of law could have been advanced against her character for reliability, for sincerity, for the logic of her detailed account.

"I'm sorry," said Colonel Masters quietly, referring to her bereavement. He looked searchingly at her. "And Monica will miss you," he added with one of his rare smiles. "She needs you." Then just as she turned away, he suddenly extended his hand. "If perhaps later you can come back—do let me know. Your influence is—so helpful—and good."

She mumbled some phrase with a promise in it, yet she left with a queer, deep impression that it was not merely, not chiefly perhaps, Monica who needed her. She wished he had not used quite those words. A sense of shame lay in her, almost as though she were running away from duty, or at least from a chance to help God had put in her way. "Your influence is—so good."

★★★★★★★★★★

Already in the train and on the boat, conscience attacked her, biting, scratching, gnawing. She had deserted a child she loved, a child who needed her, because she was scared out of her wits. No, that was a one-sided statement. She had left a house because the Devil had come into it. No, that was only partially true. When a hysterical temperament, engrained since early childhood in fixed dogmas, begins to sift facts and analyse reactions, logic and common sense themselves become confused. Thought led one way, emotion another, and no honest conclusion dawned on her mind.

She hurried on to Warsaw, to a stepfather, a retired general whose gay life had no place for her and who would not welcome her return It was a derogatory prospect for this youngish widow who had taken a job in order to escape from his vulgar activities to return now empty-handed. Yet it was easier, perhaps, to face a stepfather's selfish anger than to go and tell Colonel Masters her real reason for leaving his service. Her conscience, too, troubled her on another score as thoughts and memories travelled backwards and half-forgotten details emerged.

Those spots of blood, for instance, mentioned by Mrs. O'Reilly, the superstitious Irish cook. She had made it a rule to ignore Mrs. O'Reilly's silly fairy tales, yet now she recalled suddenly those ridiculous discussions about the laundry list and the foolish remarks that the cook and housemaid had let fall.

"But there ain't no paint in a doll, I tell you. It's all sawdust and wax and muck," from the housemaid. "I know red paint when I sees it, and that ain't paint, it's blood."

And from Mrs. O'Reilly later: "Mother o' God! Another red blob! She's biting her fingernails—and that's not *my* job. . . !"

The red stains on sheets and pillow cases were puzzling certainly, but Madame Jodzka, hearing these remarks by chance as it were, had paid no particular attention to them at the moment. The laundry lists were hardly her affair. These ridiculous servants anyhow. . .! And yet, now in the train, those spots of red, be they paint or blood, crept back to trouble her.

Another thing, oddly enough, also troubled her—the ill-defined feeling that she was deserting a man who needed help, help that she could give. It was too vague to put into words. Was it based on his remark that her influence was "good" perhaps? She could not say. It was an intuition, and few intuitions bear analysis. Supporting it, however, was a conviction she had felt since first she entered the service of Colonel Masters, the conviction, namely, that he had a Past that frightened him. There was something he had done, something he regretted and was probably ashamed of, something at any rate, for which he feared retribution. A retribution, moreover, he expected; a punishment that would come like a thief in the night and seize him by the throat.

It was against this dreaded vengeance that her influence was "good," a protective influence possibly that her religion supplied, something on the side of the angels, in any case, that her personality provided.

Her mind worked thus, it seems; and whether a concealed admiration for this sombre and mysterious man, an admiration and protective instinct never admitted even to her inmost self, existed below the surface, hidden yet urgent, remains the secret of her own heart.

It was naturally and according to human nature, at any rate, that after a few weeks of her stepfather's outrageous behaviour in the house, his cruelty too, she decided to return. She prayed to her gods incessantly, also she found oppressive her sense of neglected duty and failure of self-respect. She returned to the soulless suburban villa. It was understandable; the welcome from Monica was also understandable, the relief and pleasure of Colonel Masters still more so. It was expressed, this latter, in a courteous message only, tactfully worded, as though she had merely left for brief necessity, for it was some days before she actually saw him to speak to. From cook and housemaid the welcome was voluble and—disquieting. There were no more inexplicable "spots of red," but there were other unaccountable happenings even more distressing.

"She's missed you something terrible," said Mrs. O'Reilly, "though she's found something else to keep her quiet—if you like to put it that way." And she made the sign of the cross.

"The doll?" asked Madame Jodzka with a start of shocked horror, forcing herself to come straight to the point and forcing herself also to speak lightly, casually.

"That's it, *Madame*. The bleeding doll."

The governess had heard the strange adjective many times already, but did not know whether to take it figuratively or not. She chose the latter.

"Blood?" she asked in a lowered voice.

The cook's body gave an odd jerk. "Well," she explained. "I meant more the way it goes on. Like a thing of flesh and blood, if you get me. And the way she treats it and plays with it," and her voice, while loud, had a hush of fear in it somewhere. She held her arms before her in a protective, shielding way, as though to ward off aggression.

"Scratches ain't proof of nothing," interjected the housemaid scornfully.

"You mean," asked Madame Jodzka gravely, "there's a question of—of injury—to someone?" She suppressed an involuntary gasp, but paid no attention to the maid's interruption otherwise.

Mrs. O'Reilly seemed to mis-manage her breath for a moment.

"It ain't Miss Monica it's after," she announced in a defiant whisper as soon as she recovered herself, "it's someone else. That's what I mean. And no man as black as he was," she let herself go, " ever brought no good into a house, not since I was born."

"Someone else—?" repeated Madame Jodzka almost to herself, seizing the vital words.

"You and yer black man!" interjected the housemaid. "Get along with yer! Thank God I ain't a Christian or anything like that! But I did 'ear them sort of jerky shuffling footsteps one night, I admit, and the doll did look bigger—swollen like—when I peeked in and looked—"

" Stop it!" cried Mrs. O'Reilly, " for you ain't saying what's true or what you reely know."

She turned to the governess.

"There's more talk what means nothing about this doll," she said by way of apology, " than all the fairy tales I was brought up with as a child in Mayo, and I—I wouldn't be believing anything of it."

Turning her back contemptuously on the chattering housemaid, she came close to Madame Jodzka.

"There's no harm coming to Miss Monica, *Madame*," she whispered vehemently, "you can be quite sure about her. Any trouble there may be is for someone else." And again she crossed herself.

Madame Jodzka, in the privacy of her room, reflected between her prayers. She felt a deep, a dreadful uneasiness.

A doll! A cheap, tawdry little toy made in factories by the hundred, by the thousand, a manufactured article of commerce for children to play with. . . But . . .

"The way. she treats it and plays with it . . ." rang on in her disturbed mind.

A doll! But for the maternal suggestion, a doll was a pathetic, even horrible plaything, yet to watch a child busy with it involved deep reflections, since here the future mother prophesied. The child fondles and caresses her doll with passionate love, cares for it, seeks its welfare, yet stuffs it down into the perambulator, its head and neck twisted, its limbs broken and contorted, leaving it atrociously upside down so that blood and breathing cannot possibly function, while she runs to the window to see if the rain has stopped or the sun has come out.

A blind and hideous automatism dictated by the race, provided nothing of more immediate interest interferes, yet a herd-instinct that overcomes all obstacles, its vitality insuperable. The maternity instinct defies, even denies death. The doll, whether left upside down on the floor with broken teeth and ruined eyes, or lovingly arranged to be overlaid in the night, squashed, tortured, mutilated, survives all cruelties and disasters, and asserts finally its immortal qualities. It is unkillable. It is beyond death.

A child with her doll, reflected Madame Jodzka, is an epitome of nature's remorseless and unconquerable passion, of her dominant purpose—the survival of the race. . . .

Such thoughts, influenced perhaps by her bitter subconscious grievance against nature for depriving her of a child of her own, were unable to hold that level for long; they soon dropped back to the concrete case that perplexed and frightened her—Monica and her flaxen haired, sightless, idiotic doll. In the middle of her prayers, falling asleep incontinently, she did not even dream of it, and she woke refreshed and vigorous, facing the fact that sooner or later, sooner probably, she would have to speak to her employer.

She watched and listened. She watched Monica; she watched the doll. All seemed as normal as in a thousand other homes. Her mind reviewed the position, and where mind and superstition clashed, the former held its own easily. During her evening off she enjoyed the local cinema, leaving the heated building with the conviction that coloured fantasy, benumbed the faculties, and that ordinary life was in itself prosaic. Yet before she had covered the half-mile to the house, her deep, unaccountable uneasiness returned with overmastering power.

Mrs, O'Reilly had seen Monica to bed for her, and it was Mrs. O'Reilly who let her in. Her face was like the dead.

"It's been talking," whispered the cook, even before she closed the door. She was white about the gills.

"Talking! Who's been talking? What do you mean?"

Mrs. O'Reilly closed the door softly. "Both," she stated with dramatic emphasis, then sat down and wiped her face. She looked distraught with fear.

Madame took command, if only a command based on dreadful insecurity.

"Both?" she repeated, in a voice deliberately loud so as to counteract the other's whisper. "What are you talking about?"

"They've both been talking—talking together," stated the cook.

The governess kept silent for a moment, fighting to deny a shrinking heart.

"You've heard them talking together, you mean?" she asked presently in a shaking voice that tried to be ordinary.

Mrs. O'Reilly nodded looking over her shoulder as she did so. Her nerves were, obviously, in rags. "I thought you'd never come back," she whimpered. "I could hardly stay in the house."

Madame looked intently into her frightened eyes.

"You heard . . .?" she asked quietly.

"I listened at the door. There were two voices. Different voices."

Madame Jodzka did not insist or cross-examine, as though acute fear helped her to a greater wisdom.

"You mean, Mrs. O'Reilly," she said in flat, quiet tones, "that you heard Miss Monica talking to her doll as she always does, and herself inventing the doll's answers in a changed voice? Isn't that what you mean you heard?"

But Mrs. O'Reilly was not to be shaken. By way of answer she crossed herself and shook her head.

She spoke in a low whisper. "Come up now and listen with me, *Madame*, and judge for yourself."

Thus, soon after midnight, and Monica long since asleep, these two, the cook and governess in a suburban villa, took up their places in the dark corridor outside a child's bedroom door. It was a quiet windless night; Colonel Masters, whom they both feared, doubtless long since gone to his room in another corner of the ungainly villa. It must have been a long dreary wait before sounds in the child's bedroom first became audible—the low quiet sound of voices talking audibly—two voices. A hushed, secretive, unpleasant sound in the room where Monica slept peacefully with her beloved doll beside her. Yet two voices assuredly, it was.

Both women sat erect, both crossed themselves involuntarily, exchanging glances. Both were bewildered, terrified. Both sat aghast.

What lay in Mrs. O'Reilly's superstitious mind, only the gods of "ould Oirela'nd" can tell, but what the Polish woman's contained was clear as a bell; it was not two voices talking, it was only one. Her ear was pressed against the crack in the door. She listened intently; shaking to the bone, she listened. Voices in sleep-talking, she remembered, changed oddly.

48

"The child's talking to herself in sleep," she whispered firmly, "and that's all it is, Mrs. O'Reilly. She's just talking in her sleep," she repeated with emphasis to the woman crowding against her shoulder as though in need of support. "Can't you hear it," she added loudly, half angrily, "isn't it the same voice always? Listen carefully and you'll see I'm right."

She listened herself more closely than before.

"Listen! Hark . . .!" she repeated in a breathless whisper, concentrating her mind upon the curious sound, "isn't that the same voice—answering itself?"

Yet, as she listened, another sound disturbed her concentration, and this time it seemed a sound behind her—a faint, rustling, shuffling sound rather like footsteps hurrying away on tiptoe. She turned her head sharply and found that she had been whispering to no one. There was no one beside her. She was alone in the darkened corridor. Mrs. O'Reilly was gone. From the well of the house below a voice came up in a smothered cry beneath the darkened stairs: "Mother o' God and all the Saints. . ." and more besides.

A gasp of surprise and alarm escaped her doubtless at finding herself deserted and alone but in the same instant, exactly as in the story books, came another sound that caught her breath still more aghast—the rattle of a key in the front door below. Colonel Masters, after all, had not yet come in and gone to bed as expected: he was coming in now. Would Mrs. O'Reilly have time to slip across the hall before he caught her? More—and worse—would he come up and peep into Monica's bedroom on his way up to bed, as he rarely did? Madame Jodzka listened, her nerves in rags. She heard him fling down his coat. He was a man quick in such actions. The stick or umbrella was banged down noisily, hastily. The same instant his step sounded on the stairs. He was coming up. Another minute and he would start into the passage where she crouched against Monica's door.

He was mounting rapidly, two stairs at a time.

She, too, was quick in action and decision. She thought in a flash. To be caught crouching outside the door was ludicrous, but to be caught inside the door would be natural and explicable. She acted at once.

With a palpitating heart, she opened the bedroom door and stepped inside. A second later she heard Colonel Masters' tread, as he stumped along the corridor up to bed. He passed the door. He went on. She heard this with intense relief.

Now, inside the room, the door closed behind her, she saw the picture clearly.

Monica, sound asleep, was playing with her beloved doll, but in her sleep. She was indubitably in deep slumber. Her fingers, however, were roughing the doll this way and that, as though some dream perplexed her. The child was mumbling in her sleep, though no words were distinguishable. Muffled sighs and groans issued from her lips. Yet another sound there certainly was, though it could not have issued from the child's mouth. Whence, then, did it come?

Madame Jodzka paused, holding her breath, her heart panting. She watched and listened intently. She heard squeaks and grunts, but a moment's examination convinced her whence these noises came. They did not come from Monica's lips. They issued indubitably from the doll she clutched and twisted in her dream. The joints, as Monica twisted them emitted these odd sounds, as though the sawdust in knees and elbows wheezed and squeaked against the unnatural rubbing. Monica obviously was wholly unconscious of these noises. As the doll's neck screwed round, the material—wax, thread, sawdust—produced this curious grating sound that was almost like syllables of a word or words.

Madame Jodzka stared and listened. She felt icy cold. Seeking for a natural explanation she found none. Prayer and terror raced in her helter-skelter. Her skin began to sweat.

Then, suddenly Monica, her expression peaceful and composed, turned over in her sleep, and the dreadful doll, released from the dream-clutch, fell to one side on the bed and lay apparently lifeless and inert. In which moment, to Madame Jodzka's unbelieving yet horrified ears, it continued to squeak and utter. It went on mouthing itself. Worse than that, the next instant it stood abruptly upright, rising on its twisted legs. It started moving. It began to move, walking crookedly, across the counterpane. Its glassy, sightless eyes, seemed to look straight at her.

It presented an inhuman and appalling picture, a picture of the utterly incredible. With a queer, hoppity motion of its broken legs and joints, it came fumbling and tumbling across the rough unevenness of the slippery counterpane towards her. Its appearance was deliberate and aggressive. The sounds, as of syllables, came with it—strange, meaningless syllables that yet managed to convey anger. It stumbled towards her like a living thing. Its whole presentment conveyed attack.

Once again, this effect of a mere child's toy, aping the life of some

50

awful monstrosity with purpose and passion in its hideous tiny outline, brought collapse to the plucky Polish governess. The rush of blood without control drained her heart, and a moment of unconsciousness supervened so that everything, as it were, turned black.

This time, however, the moment of dark unconsciousness passed instantly: it came and went, almost like a moment of forgetfulness in passion. Passionate it certainly was, for the reaction came upon her like a storm. With recovered consciousness a sudden rage rushed into her woman heart—perhaps a coward's rage, an exaggerated fury against her own weakness? It rushed, in any case, to help her. She staggered, caught her breath, clutched violently at the cupboard next her, and—recovered her self-control. A fury of resentment blazed through her, fury against this utterly incredible exhibition of a wax doll walking and squawking as though it were something intelligently alive that could utter syllables. Syllables, she felt convinced, in a language she did not know.

If the monstrous can paralyse, it also can affront. The sight and sound of this cheap factory toy behaving with a will and heart of its own stung her into an act of violence that became imperative. For it was more than she could stand. Irresistibly, she rushed forward. She hurled herself against it, her only available weapon the high-heeled shoe her foot kicked loose on the instant, determined to smash down the frightful apparition into fragments and annihilate it. Hysterical, no doubt, she was at the moment, and yet logical: the godless horror must be blotted out of visible existence. This one thing obsessed her—to destroy beyond a possibility of survival. It must be smashed into fragments, in dust.

They stood close, face to face, the glassy eyes staring into her own, her hand held high for the destruction she craved—but the hand did not fall. A stinging pain, sharp as a serpent's bite, darted suddenly through her fingers, wrist and arm, her grip was broken the shoe spun sideways across the room, and in the flickering light of the candle, it seemed to her, the whole room quivered. Paralysed and helpless, she stood utterly aghast. What gods or saints could come to aid her? None. Her own will alone could help her. Some effort, at any rate, she made, trembling, on the edge collapse: My God!" she heard her half whispering, strangled voice cry out. "It is not true! You are a lie! My God denies you! I call upon my God. . .!"

Whereupon, to her added horror, the dreadful little doll, waved a broken arm, squawked back at her, as though in definite answer the strange disjointed syllables she could not understand, syllables as though in another tongue. The same instant it collapsed abruptly on the counterpane like a toy balloon that had be pricked. It shrank down in a mutilated mess before her eyes, when Monica—added touch of horror—stirred uneasily in her sleep turning over and stretching out her hands as though feeling blindly for something that she missed. And this sight of the innocent sleeping child fumbling instinctively towards an incomprehensible evil and dangerous something that attracted her proved again too strong for the Polish woman to control.

The blackness intervened a second time.

It was undoubtedly a blur in memory that followed, emotion and superstition proving too much for common-sense to deal with. She just remembers violent, unreasoned action on her part before she came back to clearer consciousness in her own room, praying volubly on her knees against her own bed. The interval of transit down the corridor and upstairs remained a blank. Yet her shoe was with her, clutched tightly in her hand. And she remembered also having clutched an inert, waxen doll with frantic fingers, clutched and crushed and crumpled its awful little frame till the sawdust came spurting from its broken joints and its tiny body was mutilated beyond recognition, if not annihilated . . . then stuffing it down ruthlessly on a table far out of Monica's reach, Monica lying peacefully in deepest sleep.

She remembered that. She also saw the clear picture of the small monster lying upside down, grossly untidy, an obscene attitude in the disorder of its flimsy dress and exposed limbs, lying motionless, its eyes crookedly aglint, motionless, yet alive still, alive moreover with intense and malignant purpose.

No duration or intensity of prayer could obliterate the picture.

She knew now that a plain, face to face talk with her employer was essential; her conscience, her peace of mind, her sanity, her sense of duty all demanded this. Deliberately, and she was sure, rightly, she had never once risked a word with the child herself. Danger lay that way, the danger of emphasising something in the child's mind that was best left ignored. But with Colonel Masters, who paid her for her services, believed in her integrity, trusted her, with him there must be an immediate explanation.

An interview was absurdly difficult; in the first place because he loathed and avoided such occasions; secondly because he was so exceedingly impervious to approach, being so rarely even visible at all. At night he came home late, in the mornings no one dared go near him.

He expected the little household, once its routine established, to run itself. The only inmate who dared beard him was Mrs. O'Reilly, who periodically, once every six months, walked straight into his study, gave notice, received an addition to her wages, and then left him alone for another six months.

Madame Jodzka, knowing his habits, waylaid him in the hall next morning while Monica was lying down before lunch, as usual. He was on his way out and she had been watching from the upper landing. She had hardly set eyes on him since her return from Warsaw. His lean, upright figure, his dark, emotionless face, she thought magnificent. He was the perfect expression of the soldier. Her heart fluttered as she raced downstairs. Her carefully prepared sentences, however, evaporated when he stopped and looked at her, a jumble of wild words pouring from her in confused English instead. He cut her rigmarole short, though he listened politely enough at first.

"I'm so glad you were able to come back to us, as I told you. Monica missed you very much—"

"She has something now she plays with—"

"The very thing," he interrupted. "No doubt the kind of toy she needs. . .Your excellent judgment. . . Please tell me if there's anything else you think . . ." and he half turned as though to move away.

"But I didn't get it. It's a horrible—*horrible*—"

Colonel Masters uttered one of his rare laughs. "Of course, all children's toys are horrible, but if she's pleased with it. . . I haven't seen it. I'm no judge . . . If you can buy something better—" and he shrugged his shoulders.

"I didn't buy it," she cried desperately. "It was brought. It makes sounds by itself—syllables. I've seen it move—move by itself. It's a doll."

He turned from the front door which he had just reached as though he had been shot; the skin held a sudden pallor beneath the flush and something contradicted the blazing eyes, something that seemed to shrink.

"A doll," he repeated in a very quiet voice. "You said—a doll?"

But his eyes and face disconcerted her, so that she merely gave a fumbling account of a parcel that had been brought. His question about a parcel he had ordered strictly to be destroyed added to her confusion.

" Wasn't it?" he asked in a rasping whisper, as though a disobeyed order seemed incredible.

"It was thrown away, I believe," she prevaricated, unable to meet his eyes, anxious to protect the cook as well. "I think Monica—perhaps found it." She despised her lack of courage, but his intensity scattered her wits; she was conscious, moreover, of a strange desire not to give him pain, as though his safety and happiness, not Monica's, were at stake. "It—talks!—as well as moves," she cried desperately, forcing herself at last to look at him.

Colonel Masters seemed to stiffen; his breath caught oddly.

"You say Monica has it? Plays with it? You've seen movement and heard sounds like syllables?" He asked the questions in a low voice, almost as though talking to himself. "You've—listened?" he whispered.

Unable to find convincing words, she bowed her head, while some terror in him came across to her like a blast of icy wind. The man was afraid in his heart. Instead, however, of some explosive reply by way of blame or criticism, he spoke quietly, even calmly: "You did right to come and tell me this—quite right," adding then in so low a tone that she barely caught the ominous words, "for I have been expecting something of the sort. . . sooner or later. . . it was bound to come. . ." the voice dying away into the handkerchief he put to his face.

And abruptly then, as though aware of an appeal for sympathy, an emotional reaction swept her fear away. Stepping closer, she looked her employer straght in the eyes.

"See the child for yourself," she said with sudden firmness. "Come and listen with me. Come into the bedroom."

She saw him stagger. For a moment he said nothing.

"Who," he then asked, the low voice unsteady, "who brought that parcel?"

" A man, I believe."

There was a pause that seemed like minutes before his next question.

"White," he asked, " or—black?"

"Dark," she told him, " very dark."

He was shaking like a leaf, the skin of his face blanched; he leaned against the door, wilted, limp; unless she somehow took command there threatened a collapse she did not wish to witness.

"You shall come with me tonight," she said firmly, "and we shall listen together. Wait till I return now. I go for brandy," and a minute later as she came back breathless and watched him gulp down half a tumbler full, she knew that she had done right in telling him. His obedience proved it, though it seemed strange that cowardice should borrow from its like to produce courage.

"Tonight," she repeated, "tonight after your Bridge. We meet in the corridor outside the bedroom. I shall be there. At half-past twelve."

He pulled himself into an upright position, staring at her fixedly, making a movement of his head, half bow, half nod.

" Twelve thirty," he muttered, "in the passage outside the bedroom door," and using his stick heavily rather, he opened the door and passed out into the drive. She watched him go, aware that her fear had changed to pity, aware also that she watched the stumbling gait of a man too conscience-stricken to know a moment's peace, too frightened even to think of God.

Madame Jodzka kept the appointment; she had eaten no supper, but had stayed in her room—praying. She had first put Monica to bed.

"My doll," the child pleaded, good as gold, after being tucked up. "I must have my doll or else I'll never get to sleep," and Madame Jodzka had brought it with reluctant fingers, placing it on the night-table beside the bed,

"She'll sleep quite comfortably here, Monica, darling. Why not leave her outside the sheets?" It had been carefully mended, she noticed, patched together with pins and stitches.

The child grabbed at it. "I want her in bed beside me, close against me," she said with a happy smile. "We tell each other stories. If she's too far away I can't hear what she says." And she seized it with a cuddling pleasure that made the woman's heart turn cold.

"Of course, darling—if it helps you to fall asleep quickly, you shall have it," and Monica did not see the trembling fingers, not notice the horror in the face and voice. Indeed, hardly was the doll against her cheek on the pillow, her fingers half stroking the flaxen hair and pink wax cheeks, than her eyes closed, a sigh of deep content breathed out, and Monica was asleep.

Madame Jodzka, fearful of looking behind her, tiptoed to the door, and left the room. In the passage she wiped a cold sweat from her forehead. "God bless her and protect her," her heart murmured, "and may God forgive me if I've sinned."

She kept the appointment; she knew Colonel Masters would keep it, too.

It had been a long wait from eight o'clock till after midnight. With great determination she had kept away from the bedroom door, fearful lest she might hear a sound that would necessitate action on her part: she went to her room and stayed there. But praying exhausted itself, for it both excited and betrayed her. If her God could help, a brief request alone was needed. To go on praying for help hour by hour was not only an insult to her deity, but it also wore her out physically. She stopped, therefore, and read some pages of a Polish saint which she did not understand. Later she fell into a state of horrified nervous drowse. In due course, she slept. . .

A noise awoke her—steps going softly past her door. A glance at her watch showed eleven o'clock. The steps, though stealthy, were familiar. Mrs. O'Reilly was waddling up to bed. The sounds died away. Madame Jodzka, a trifle ashamed, though she hardly knew why, returned to her Polish saint, yet determined to keep her ears open. Then slept again. . .

What woke her a second time she could not tell. She was startled. She listened. The night was unpleasantly still, tlip house quiet as the grave. No casual traffic passed No wind stirred the gloomy evergreens in the drive. The world outside was silent. And then, as she saw by her watch that it was some minutes after midnight, a sharp click became audible that acted like a pistol shot to her keyed-up nerves. It was the front door closing softly. Steps followed across the hall below, then up the stairs, unsteadily a little. Colonel Masters had come in. He was coming up slowly, unwillingly she felt, to keep the appointment. Madame Jodzka started from her chair, looked in the glass, mumbled a quick confused prayer, and opened her door into the dark passage.

She stiffened, physically and mentally. "Now, he'll hear and perhaps see—for himself," she thought. "And God help him!"

She marched along the passage and reached the door of Monica's bedroom, listening with such intentness that she seemed to hear only the confused running murmur of her own blood. Having reached the appointed spot, she stood stock still and waited while his steps approached. A moment later his bulk blocked the passage,, shown up as a dark shadow by the light in the hall below. This bulk came nearer, came right up to her. She believed she said "Good evening," and that he mumbled something about "I said I'd come. . . damned nonsense. . ." or words to that effect, whereupon the couple stood side by side in the darkened silence of the corridor, remote from the rest of the house, and waited without further words. They stood shoulder to shoulder outside the door of Monica's bedroom. Her heart was knocking against her side.

She heard his breathing, there came a whiff of spirits, of stale tobacco smoke, his outline seemed to shift against the wall unsteadily, he moved his feet; and a sudden, extraordinary wave of emotion swept over her, half of protective maternal yearning, half almost of sexual desire, so that for a passing instant she burned to take him in her arms and kiss him savagely, and at the same time shield him from some appalling danger his blunt ignorance laid him open to.

With revulsion, pity, and a sense of sin and passion, she acknowledged this odd sudden weakness in herself, but the face of the Warsaw priest flashed across her fuddled mind the next instant. There was evil in the air. This meant the Devil. She felt herself trembling dreadfully, shaking in her shoes, losing her balance, her whole body leaning over, but leaning in his direction. A moment more and she must have fallen towards him, dropped into his arms.

A sound broke the silence, and she drew up just in time. It came from beyond the door, from inside the bedroom.

"Hark!" she whispered, her hand upon his arm, and while he made no movement, spoke no word, she saw his head and shoulders bend down toward the panel of the closed door. There was a noise, upon the other side, there were noises, Monica's voice distinctly recognisable, another slighter, shriller sound accompanying it, breaking in upon it, answering it. Two voices.

"Listen," she repeated in a whisper scarcely audible, and felt his warm hand grip her own so fiercely that it hurt her.

No words were distinguishable at first, just these odd broken sounds of two separate voices in that dark corridor of the silent house—the voice of a child, and the other a strange faint, hardly a human sound, while yet a voice.

"*Que le bon Dieu*—" she began, then faltered, breath failing her, for she saw Colonel Masters stoop down suddenly and do the last thing that would have occurred to her as likely: he put his eye to the keyhole and kept it there steadily, for the best part of a minute, his hand still gripping her own firmly. He knelt on one knee to keep his balance.

The sounds had ceased, no movement now stirred inside the room. The night-light, she knew, would show him clearly the pillows of the bed, Monica's head, the doll in her arms. Colonel Masters must see clearly anything there was to see, and he yet gave no sign that he saw anything. She experienced a queer sensation for a few seconds— almost as though she had perhaps imagined everything and proved herself a consummate, idiotic, hysterical fool. For a few seconds this ghastly thought flashed over her, the odd silence emphasising it. Had she been after all, just a crazy lunatic? Had her senses all deceived her?

Why should he see nothing, make no sign? Why had the voice, the voices, ceased? Not a murmur of any sort was audible in the room.

Then Colonel Masters, suddenly releasing his grip of her hand, shuffled on to both feet and stood up straight, while in the same instant she herself stiffened, trying to prepare for the angry scorn, the contemptuous abuse he was about to pour upon her. Protecting herself against this attack, expecting it, she was the more amazed at what she did hear:

"I saw it," came in a strangled whisper. "I saw it walk!"

She stood paralysed.

"It's watching me," he added, scarcely audible. "*Me!*"

The revulsion of feeling at first left her speechless; it was the sheer terror in his strangled whisper that restored a measure of self possession to her. Yet it was he who found words first, awful whispered words, words spoken to himself, it seemed, more than to her.

"It's what I've always feared—I knew it must come some day—yet not like this. Not this way."

Then immediately the voice in the room became audible, and it was a sweet and gentle voice, sincere and natural, with feeling in it—Monica's childish voice, pleading:

"Don't go, don't leave me! Come back into bed—please."

An incomprehensible sound followed, as though by way of answer. There were syllables in that faint, creaky tone Madame Jodzka recognised, but syllables she could not comprehend. They seemed to enter her like point of ice. She froze. And facing her stood the motionless, inanimate bulk of him, his outline, then leaned leaned over towards her, his lips so close to her own face that, as he spoke, she felt the breath upon her cheek.

"*Buth laga* . . ." she heard him repeat the syllables to himself again and again. " *Revenge*. . . in Hindustani. . . !" He drew a long, anguished breath. The sounds sank into her like drops of poison, the syllables she had heard several times already but had not understood. At last she understood their meaning. Revenge!

"I must go in, go in," he was mumbling to himself. "I must go in and face it." Her intuition was justified: the danger was not for Monica but for himself. Her sudden protective maternal instinct found its explanation too. The lethal power concentrated in that hideous puppet was aimed at him. He began to edge impetuously past her.

"No!" she cried. "I'll go? Let me go in!" pushing him aside with all her strength. But his hand was already on the knob and the next instant the door was open and he was inside the room. On the threshold they stood still a second side by side, though she was slightly behind, struggling to shove past him and stand protectively in front.

She stared across his shoulder, her eyes so wide open that the intense strain to note everything at once threatened to defeat jts own end. Sight, none the less, worked normally; she saw all there was to see, and that was—nothing; nothing unusual, that is, nothing abnormal, nothing terrifying, so that this second time the threat of anti-climax rose to her mind. Had she worked herself up to this peak of horror merely to behold Monica lying sound asleep in a safe and quiet room? The flickering night-light revealed no more than a child in natural slumber without a toy of any sort against her pillow.

There stood the glass of water beside the flowers in their saucer, the picture-book on the sill of the window within reach, the window opened a little at the bottom, and there also lay the calm face of Monica with eyes tight shut upon the pillow. Her breathing was deep and regular, no sign of disquiet anywhere, no hint of disturbance that might have accompanied that pleading sentence of two minutes ago, except that the bedclothes were perhaps somewhat tumbled. The counterpane humped itself in folds towards the foot of the bed, she noticed, as though Monica, finding it too warm, had tossed it away in sleep. No more than that.

In that first moment Colonel Masters and the governess took in this whole pretty picture complete. The room was so still that the child's breathing was distinctly audible. Their eyes roved all over. Nothing was anywhere in movement. Yet the same instant Madame Jodzka became aware that there *was* movement. Something stirred. The report came, perhaps, through her skin, for no sense announced it. It was undeniable; in that still, silent room there was movement somewhere, and with that unreported movement there was danger.

Certain, rightly or wrongly, that she herself was safe, also that the quietly sleeping child was safe, she was equally certain that Colonel Masters was the one in danger. She knew that in her very bones.

"Wait here by the door," she said almost peremptorily, as she felt him pushing past her further into the quiet room. "You saw it watching you. It's somewhere—Take care!"

She clutched at him, but he was already beyond her.

"Damned nonsense," he muttered and strode forward.

Never before in her whole life had she admired a man more than in this instant when she saw him moving towards what she knew to

59

be physical and spiritual danger—never before, and never again, was such a hideous and dreadful sight to be repeatable in a woman's life. Pity and horror drowned her in a sea of passionate, futile longing. A man going to meet his fate, it flashed over her, Was something none, without power to help, should witness. No human power can stay the course of the stars.

Her eye rested, as it were by chance, on the crumpled ridges and hollows of the discarded counterpane. These lay by the foot of the bed in shadow, confused a little in their contours and their masses. Had Monica not moved, they must have lain thus till morning. But Monica did move. At this particular moment she turned over in her sleep. She stretched her little legs before settling down in the new position, and this stretching squeezed and twisted the contours of the heavy counterpane at the foot of the bed.

The tiny landscape altered thus a fraction, its immediate detail shifted. And an outline—a very small outline—emerged. Hitherto, it had lain concealed among the shadows. It emerged now with disconcerting rapidity, as though a spring released it. Out of its nest of darkness it seemed almost to leap forward. Fast it came, supernaturally fast, its velocity actually shocking, for a shock came with it. It was exceedingly small, it was exceedingly dreadful, its head erect and venomous and the movement of its legs and arms, as of its bitter, glittering eyes, aping humanity. Malignant evil, personified and aggressive, shaped itself in this otherwise ridiculous outline.

It was the doll.

Racing with incredible security across the slippery surface of the crumpled silk counterpane, it dived and climbed and shot forward with an appearance of complete control and deliberate purpose. That it had a definite aim was overwhelmingly obvious. Its fixed, glassy eyes were concentrated upon a point beyond and behind the terrified governess, the point precisely where Colonel Masters, her employer, stood against her shoulder.

A frantic, half protective movement on her part, seemed lost in the air. . . .

She turned instinctively, putting an arm about his shoulders, which he instantly flung off.

"Let the bloody thing come," he cried. "I'll deal with it. . . !" He thrust her violently aside.

The doll came at him. The hinges of its diminutive broken arms and its jointed legs emitted a thin, creaking sound as it came darting—the syllables Madame Jodzka had already heard more than once. Syllables she had heard without understanding—"*buth laga*"—but syllables now packed with awful meaning: *Revenge.*

The sounds hissed and squeaked, yet clear as a bell as the beast advanced at this miraculous speed.

Before Colonel Masters could move an inch backwards or forwards in self protection, before he could command himself to any sort of action, or contrive the smallest measure of self defence, it was off the bed and at him. It settled. Savagely, its little jaws of tiny make-believe were bitten deep into Colonel Masters' throat, fastened tightly.

In a flash this happened, in a flash it was over. In Madame Jodzka's memory it remained like the impression of a lightning flash, simultaneously etched in black and white. It had happened in the present as though it had no past. It came and was gone again. Her faculties, as after a vivid lightning flash, were momentarily paralysed, without past or present. She had witnessed these awful things, but had not realized them. It was this lack of realisation that struck her motionless and dumb.

Colonel Masters, on the other hand, stood beside her quietly as though nothing unusual had happened, wholly master of himself, calm, collected. At the moment of attack no sound had left his lips, there had been no gesture even of defence. Whatever had come, he had apparently accepted. The words that now fell from his lips were, thus, all the more dreadful in their appalling common-placeness.

"Hadn't you better put that counterpane, straight a bit. . . Perhaps?"

Common sense, as always, enables the gas of hysteria to escape. Madame Jodzka gasped, but she obeyed. Automatically she moved across to do his bidding, yet aware, even as she thus moved, that he flicked something from his neck, as though a wasp, a mosquito, or some poisonous insect, had tried to sting him. She remembered no more than that, for he, in his calmness, had contributed nothing else.

Fumbling with the folds of slippery counterpane she tried to straighten out, she was startled to find that Monica was sitting up in bed, awake.

"Oh, Doska—you here!" the child exclaimed innocently, straight out of sleep and using the affectionate nickname. "And Daddy, too! Oh, my goodness. . . !"

"Sm-moothing your bed, darling," she stammered, hardly aware of what she said. "You ought to be asleep. I just looked into see. . ." She mumbled a few other automatic words.

"And Daddy with you!" repeated the child excitedly, sleep still about her, wondering what it all meant. "Ooh! Ooh!" holding out her arms.

This brief exchange of spoken words, though it takes a minute to describe, occurred simultaneously with the action—perhaps ten seconds all told, for while the governess fumbled with the counterpane, Colonel Masters was in the act of brushing something from his neck. Nothing else was audible, nothing but his quick gasp and sudden intake of breath: but something else—she swears it on her Warsaw priest—was visible. Madame Jodzka maintains by all her gods she saw this other thing.

In moments of paralysing stress it is not the senses that act less speedily nor with less precision; their action, on the contrary, is intensified and speeded up: what takes longer is the registration of their reports. The numbed brain causes the apparent delay; realization is slowed down.

Madame Jodzka thus only realised a fraction of a second later what her eyes had indubitably witnessed; a dark-skinned arm slanting in through the open window by the bed and snatching at a small object that lay on the floor after dropping from Colonel Masters' throat, then withdrawing again at lightning speed into the darkness of the night outside.

No one but herself, apparently, had seen this—it was almost supernaturally swift.

"And now you'll be asleep again in two minutes, lucky Monica," Colonel Masters was whispering over by the bed. "I just peeped in to see that you were all right. . ." His voice was thin, dreadfully soundless.

Madame Jodzka, against the door, frozen, terrified, looked on and listened.

"Are you quite well, Daddy? Sure? I had a dream, but it's gone now."

"Splendid. Never better in my life. But better still if I saw you sound asleep. Come now. I'll blow out this silly night-light, for that's what woke you up. I'll be bound."

He blew it out, he and the child blew it out together, the latter with sleepy laughter that then hushed. And Colonel Masters tiptoed to join Madame Jodzka at the door. "A lot of damned fuss about nothing," she heard him muttering in that same thin dreadful voice, and then, as they closed the door and stood a moment in the darkened passage, he did suddenly an unexpected thing. He took the Polish woman in his arms, held her fiercely to him for a second, kissed her vehemently, and flung her away.

"Bless you and thank you," he said in a low, angry voice. "You did your best. You made a great fight. But I got what I deserved. I've been waiting years for it." And he was off down the stairs to his own quarters. Half way down he stopped and looked up to where she stood against the rails. "Tell the doctor," he whispered hoarsely, "that I took a sleeping draught—an overdose." And he was gone.

And this was, roughly, what she did tell the doctor next morning when a hurried telephone summons brought him to the bed whereon a dead man lay with a swollen, blackened tongue. She told the same tale at the inquest too and an emptied bottle of a powerful sleeping-draught supported her. . .

And Monica, too young to realise grief beyond its trumpery meaning of a selfishly felt loss, never once—oddly enough—referred to the absence of her lovely doll that had comforted so many hours, proved such an intimate companion day and night in a life that held no other playmates. It seemed forgotten, expunged utterly, from her memory, as though it had ever existed at all. She stared blankly, stupidly, when a doll was mentioned: she preferred her worn-out teddy bears. The slate of memory in this particular, was wiped clean.

"They're so warm and comfy," she described her bears, "and they cuddle without tickling. Besides," she added innocently, "they don't squeak and try to slip away. . ."

Thus in the suburbs, where great spaces between the lamps go dead at night, where the moist wind comes whispering through the mournful branches of the silver-pines, where nothing happens and people cry "Let's go to town!" there are occasional stirrings among the dead dry bones that hide behind respectable villa walls. . . .

The Decoy

It belonged to the category of unlovely houses about which an ugly superstition clings, one reason being, perhaps, its inability to inspire interest in itself without assistance. It seemed too ordinary to possess individuality, much less to exert an influence. Solid and ungainly, its huge bulk dwarfing the park timber, its best claim to notice was a negative one—it was unpretentious.

From the little hill its expressionless windows stared across the Kentish Weald, indifferent to weather, dreary in winter, bleak in spring, unblessed in summer. Some colossal hand had tossed it down, then let it starve to death, a country mansion that might well strain the adjectives of advertisers and find inheritors with difficulty. Its soul had fled, said some; it had committed suicide, thought others; and it was an inheritor, before he killed himself in the library, who thought this latter, yielding, apparently, to an hereditary taint in the family. For two other inheritors followed suit, with an interval of twenty years between them, and there was no clear reason to explain the three disasters. Only the first owner, indeed, lived permanently in the house, the others using it in the summer months and then deserting it with relief. Hence, when John Burley, present inheritor, assumed possession, he entered a house about which clung an ugly superstition, based, nevertheless, upon a series of undeniably ugly facts.

This century deals harshly with superstitious folk, deeming them fools or charlatans; but John Burley, robust, contemptuous of half lights, did not deal harshly with them, because he did not deal with them at all. He was hardly aware of their existence. He ignored them as he ignored, say, the Esquimaux, poets, and other human aspects that did not touch his scheme of life. A successful business man, he concentrated on what was real; he dealt with business people. His philanthropy, on a big scale, was also real; yet, though he would have denied it vehemently, he had his superstition as well. No man exists without some taint of superstition in his blood; the racial heritage is too rich to be escaped entirely. Burley's took this form—that unless he gave his tithe to the poor he would not prosper. This ugly mansion, he decided, would make an ideal Convalescent Home.

"Only cowards or lunatics kill themselves," he declared flatly, when his use of the house was criticised. "I'm neither one nor t'other." He let out his gusty, boisterous laugh. In his invigorating atmosphere such weakness seemed contemptible, just as superstition in his presence seemed feeblest ignorance. Even its picturesqueness faded. "I can't conceive," he boomed, "can't even imagine to myself," he added emphatically, "the state of mind in which a man can *think* of suicide, much less do it." He threw his chest out with a challenging air. "I tell you, Nancy, it's either cowardice or mania. And I've no use for either."

Yet he was easy-going and good-humoured in his denunciation. He admitted his limitations with a hearty laugh his wife called noisy. Thus, he made allowances for the fairy fears of sailorfolk, and had even been known to mention haunted ships his companies owned. But he did so in the terms of tonnage and £ s. d. His scope was big; details were made for clerks.

His consent to pass a night in the mansion was the consent of a practical business man and philanthropist who dealt condescendingly with foolish human nature. It was based on the common-sense of tonnage and £ s. d. The local newspapers had revived the silly story of the suicides, calling attention to the effect of the superstition upon the fortunes of the house, and so, possibly, upon the fortunes of its present owner. But the mansion, otherwise a white elephant, was precisely ideal for his purpose, and so trivial a matter as spending a night in it should not stand in the way. "We must take people as we find them, Nancy."

His young wife had her motive, of course, in making the proposal, and, if she was amused by what she called "spook-hunting," he saw no reason to refuse her the indulgence. He loved her, and took her as he found her—late in life. To allay the superstitions of prospective staff and patients and supporters, all, in fact, whose goodwill was necessary to success, he faced this boredom of a night in the building before its opening was announced. "You see, John, if you, the owner, do this, it will nip damaging talk in the bud. If anything went wrong later it would only be put down to this suicide idea, this haunting influence. The Home will have a bad name from the start. There'll be endless trouble. It will be a failure."

"You think my spending a night there will stop the nonsense?" he inquired.

"According to the old legend it breaks the spell," she replied. "That's the condition, anyhow."

"But somebody's sure to die there sooner or later," he objected. "We can't prevent that."

"We can prevent people whispering that they died unnaturally." She explained the working of the public mind.

"I see," he replied, his lip curling, yet quick to gauge the truth of what she told him about collective instinct.

"Unless *you* take poison in the hall," she added laughingly, "or elect to hang yourself with your braces from the hat peg."

"I'll do it," he agreed, after a moment's thought. "I'll sit up with you. It will be like a honeymoon over again, you and I on the spree— eh?" He was even interested now; the boyish side of him was touched perhaps; but his enthusiasm was less when she explained that three was a better number than two on such an expedition.

"I've often done it before, John. We were always three."

"Who?" he asked bluntly. He looked wonderingly at her, but she answered that if anything went wrong a party of three provided a better margin for help. It was sufficiently obvious. He listened and agreed. "I'll get young Mortimer," he suggested. "Will he do?"

She hesitated. "Well—he's cheery; he'll be interested, too. Yes, he's as good as another." She seemed indifferent.

"And he'll make the time pass with his stories," added her husband.

So, Captain Mortimer, late officer on a T.B.D., a "cheery lad," afraid of nothing, cousin of Mrs. Burley, and now filling a good post in the company's London offices, was engaged as third hand in the expedition. But Captain Mortimer was young and ardent, and Mrs. Burley was young and pretty and ill-mated, and John Burley was a neglectful, and self-satisfied husband.

Fate laid the trap with cunning, and John Burley, blind-eyed, careless of detail, floundered into it. He also floundered out again, though in a fashion none could have expected of him.

The night agreed upon eventually was as near to the shortest in the year as John Burley could contrive—June 18th—when the sun set at 8:18 and rose about a quarter to four. There would be barely three hours of true darkness. "You're the expert," he admitted, as she explained that sitting through the actual darkness only was required, not necessarily from sunset to sunrise. "We'll do the thing properly.

Mortimer's not very keen, he had a dance or something," he added, noticing the look of annoyance that flashed swiftly in her eyes; "but he got out of it. He's coming." The pouting expression of the spoilt woman amused him. "Oh, no, he didn't need much persuading really," he assured her. "Some girl or other, of course. He's young, remember." To which no comment was forthcoming, though the implied comparison made her flush.

They motored from South Audley Street after an early tea, in due course passing Sevenoaks and entering the Kentish Weald; and, in order that the necessary advertisement should be given, the chauffeur, warned strictly to keep their purpose quiet, was to put up at the country inn and fetch them an hour after sunrise; they would breakfast in London. "He'll tell everybody," said his practical and cynical master; "the local newspaper will have it all next day. A few hours' discomfort is worthwhile if it ends the nonsense. We'll read and smoke, and Mortimer shall tell us yarns about the sea." He went with the driver into the house to superintend the arrangement of the room, the lights, the hampers of food, and so forth, leaving the pair upon the lawn.

"Four hours isn't much, but it's something," whispered Mortimer, alone with her for the first time since they started. "It's simply ripping of you to have got me in. You look divine tonight. You're the most wonderful woman in the world." His blue eyes shone with the hungry desire he mistook for love. He looked as if he had blown in from the sea, for his skin was tanned and his light hair bleached a little by the sun. He took her hand, drawing her out of the slanting sunlight towards the rhododendrons.

"I didn't, you silly boy. It was John suggested your coming." She released her hand with an affected effort. "Besides, you overdid it—pretending you had a dance."

"You could have objected," he said eagerly, "and didn't. Oh, you're too lovely, you're delicious!" He kissed her suddenly with passion. There was a tiny struggle, in which she yielded too easily, he thought.

"Harry, you're an idiot!" she cried breathlessly, when he let her go. "I really don't know how you dare! And John's your friend. Besides, you know"—she glanced round quickly—"it isn't safe here." Her eyes shone happily, her cheeks were flaming. She looked what she was, a pretty, young, lustful animal, false to ideals, true to selfish passion only. "Luckily," she added, "he trusts me too fully to think anything."

The young man, worship in his eyes, laughed gaily. "There's no harm in a kiss," he said. "You're a child to him, he never thinks of you as a woman. Anyhow, his head's full of ships and kings and sealing-wax," he comforted her, while respecting her sudden instinct which warned him not to touch her again, "and he never sees anything. Why, even at ten yards——"

From twenty yards away a big voice interrupted him, as John Burley came round a corner of the house and across the lawn towards them. The chauffeur, he announced, had left the hampers in the room on the first floor and gone back to the inn. "Let's take a walk round," he added, joining them, "and see the garden. Five minutes before sunset we'll go in and feed." He laughed. "We must do the thing faithfully, you know, mustn't we, Nancy? Dark to dark, remember. Come on, Mortimer"—he took the young man's arm—"a last look round before we go in and hang ourselves from adjoining hooks in the matron's room!" He reached out his free hand towards his wife.

"Oh, hush, John!" she said quickly. "I don't like—especially now the dusk is coming." She shivered, as though it were a genuine little shiver, pursing her lips deliciously as she did so; whereupon he drew her forcibly to him, saying he was sorry, and kissed her exactly where she had been kissed two minutes before, while young Mortimer looked on. "We'll take care of you between us," he said. Behind a broad back the pair exchanged a swift but meaning glance, for there was that in his tone which enjoined wariness, and perhaps after all he was not so blind as he appeared. They had their code, these two. "All's well," was signalled; "but another time be more careful!"

There still remained some minutes' sunlight before the huge red ball of fire would sink behind the wooded hills, and the trio, talking idly, a flutter of excitement in two hearts certainly, walked among the roses. It was a perfect evening, windless, perfumed, warm. Headless shadows preceded them gigantically across the lawn as they moved, and one side of the great building lay already dark; bats were flitting, moths darted to and fro above the azalea and rhododendron clumps. The talk turned chiefly on the uses of the mansion as a Convalescent Home, its probable running cost, suitable staff, and so forth.

"Come along," John Burley said presently, breaking off and turning abruptly, "we must be inside, actually inside, before the sun's gone. We must fulfil the conditions faithfully," he repeated, as though fond of the phrase. He was in earnest over everything in life, big or little, once he set his hand to it.

They entered, this incongruous trio of ghost-hunters, no one of them really intent upon the business in hand, and went slowly upstairs to the great room where the hampers lay. Already in the hall it was dark enough for three electric torches to flash usefully and help their steps as they moved with caution, lighting one corner after another. The air inside was chill and damp. "Like an unused museum," said Mortimer. "I can smell the specimens." They looked about them, sniffing.

"That's humanity," declared his host, employer, friend, "with cement and whitewash to flavour it"; and all three laughed as Mrs. Burley said she wished they had picked some roses and brought them in. Her husband was again in front on the broad staircase, Mortimer just behind him, when she called out.

"I don't like being last," she exclaimed. It's so black behind me in the hall. I'll come between you two," and the sailor took her outstretched hand, squeezing it, as he passed her up. "There's a figure, remember," she said hurriedly, turning to gain her husband's attention, as when she touched wood at home. "A figure is seen; that's part of the story. The figure of a man." She gave a tiny shiver of pleasurable, half-imagined alarm as she took his arm.

"I hope we shall see it," he mentioned prosaically.

"I hope we shan't," she replied with emphasis. "It's only seen before—something happens." Her husband said nothing, while Mortimer remarked facetiously that it would be a pity if they had their trouble for nothing. "Something can hardly happen to all three of us," he said lightly, as they entered a large room where the paper-hangers had conveniently left a rough table of bare planks. Mrs. Burley, busy with her own thoughts, began to unpack the sandwiches and wine. Her husband strolled over to the window. He seemed restless.

"So this," his deep voice startled her, "is where one of us"—he looked round him—"is to——"

"John!" She stopped him sharply, with impatience. "Several times already I've begged you." Her voice rang rather shrill and querulous in the empty room, a new note in it. She was beginning to feel the atmosphere of the place, perhaps. On the sunny lawn it had not touched her, but now, with the fall of night, she was aware of it, as shadow called to shadow and the kingdom of darkness gathered power. Like a great whispering gallery, the whole house listened.

"Upon my word, Nancy," he said with contrition, as he came and sat down beside her, "I quite forgot again. Only I cannot take it seriously. It's so utterly unthinkable to me that a man——"

"But why evoke the idea at all?" she insisted in a lowered voice, that snapped despite its faintness. "Men, after all, don't do such things for nothing."

"We don't know everything in the universe, do we?" Mortimer put in, trying clumsily to support her. "All I know just now is that I'm famished and this veal and ham pie is delicious." He was very busy with his knife and fork. His foot rested lightly on her own beneath the table; he could not keep his eyes off her face; he was continually passing new edibles to her.

"No," agreed John Burley, "not everything. You're right there."

She kicked the younger man gently, flashing a warning with her eyes as well, while her husband, emptying his glass, his head thrown back, looked straight at them over the rim, apparently seeing nothing. They smoked their cigarettes round the table, Burley lighting a big cigar. "Tell us about the figure, Nancy?" he inquired. "At least there's no harm in that. It's new to me. I hadn't heard about a figure." And she did so willingly, turning her chair sideways from the dangerous, reckless feet. Mortimer could now no longer touch her.

"I know very little," she confessed; "only what the paper said. It's a man. . . . And he changes."

"How changes?" asked her husband. "Clothes, you mean, or what?"

Mrs. Burley laughed, as though she was glad to laugh. Then she answered: "According to the story, he shows himself each time to the man——"

"The man who——?"

"Yes, yes, of course. He appears to the man who dies—as himself."

"H'm," grunted her husband, naturally puzzled. He stared at her.

"Each time the chap saw his own double"—Mortimer came this time usefully to the rescue—"before he did it."

Considerable explanation followed, involving much psychic jargon from Mrs. Burley, which fascinated and impressed the sailor, who thought her as wonderful as she was lovely, showing it in his eyes for all to see. John Burley's attention wandered. He moved over to the window, leaving them to finish the discussion between them; he took no part in it, made no comment even, merely listening idly and watching them with an air of absent-mindedness through the cloud of cigar smoke round his head.

He moved from window to window, ensconcing himself in turn in each deep embrasure, examining the fastenings, measuring the thickness of the stonework with his handkerchief. He seemed restless, bored, obviously out of place in this ridiculous expedition. On his big massive face lay a quiet, resigned expression his wife had never seen before. She noticed it now as, the discussion ended, the pair tidied away the *débris* of dinner, lit the spirit lamp for coffee and laid out a supper which would be very welcome with the dawn. A draught passed through the room, making the papers flutter on the table. Mortimer turned down the smoking lamps with care.

"Wind's getting up a bit—from the south," observed Burley from his niche, closing one-half of the casement window as he said it. To do this, he turned his back a moment, fumbling for several seconds with the latch, while Mortimer, noting it, seized his sudden opportunity with the foolish abandon of his age and temperament. Neither he nor his victim perceived that, against the outside darkness, the interior of the room was plainly reflected in the window-pane. One reckless, the other terrified, they snatched the fearful joy, which might, after all, have been lengthened by another full half-minute, for the head they feared, followed by the shoulders, pushed through the side of the casement still open, and remained outside, taking in the night.

"A grand air," said his deep voice, as the head drew in again, "I'd like to be at sea a night like this." He left the casement open and came across the room towards them. "Now," he said cheerfully, arranging a seat for himself, "let's get comfortable for the night. Mortimer, we expect stories from you without ceasing, until dawn or the ghost arrives. Horrible stories of chains and headless men, remember. Make it a night we shan't forget in a hurry." He produced his gust of laughter.

They arranged their chairs, with other chairs to put their feet on, and Mortimer contrived a footstool by means of a hamper for the smallest feet; the air grew thick with tobacco smoke; eyes flashed and answered, watched perhaps as well; ears listened and perhaps grew wise; occasionally, as a window shook, they started and looked round; there were sounds about the house from time to time, when the entering wind, using broken or open windows, set loose objects rattling.

But Mrs. Burley vetoed horrible stories with decision. A big, empty mansion, lonely in the country, and even with the comfort of John Burley and a lover in it, has its atmosphere. Furnished rooms are far less ghostly. This atmosphere now came creeping everywhere, through spacious halls and sighing corridors, silent, invisible, but all-pervading, John Burley alone impervious to it, unaware of its soft attack upon the nerves. It entered possibly with the summer night wind, but possibly it was always there. . . . And Mrs. Burley looked often at her husband, sitting near her at an angle; the light fell on his fine strong face; she felt that, though apparently so calm and quiet, he was really very rest-less; something about him was a little different; she could not define it; his mouth seemed set as with an effort; he looked, she thought curi-ously to herself, patient and very dignified; he was rather a dear after all. Why did she think the face inscrutable? Her thoughts wandered vaguely, unease, discomfort among them somewhere, while the heated blood—she had taken her share of wine—seethed in her.

Burley turned to the sailor for more stories. "Sea and wind in them," he asked. "No horrors, remember!" and Mortimer told a tale about the shortage of rooms at a Welsh seaside place where spare rooms fetched fabulous prices, and one man alone refused to let—a retired captain of a South Seas trader, very poor, a bit crazy appar-ently. He had two furnished rooms in his house worth twenty guineas a week. The rooms faced south; he kept them full of flowers; but he would not let. An explanation of his unworldly obstinacy was not forthcoming until Mortimer—they fished together—gained his con-fidence. "The South Wind lives in them," the old fellow told him. "I keep them free for her."

"For *her?*"

"It was on the South Wind my love came to me," said the other softly; "and it was on the South Wind that she left——"

It was an odd tale to tell in such company, but he told it well.

"Beautiful," thought Mrs. Burley. Aloud she said a quiet, "Thank you. By 'left,' I suppose he meant she died or ran away?"

John Burley looked up with a certain surprise. "We ask for a story," he said, "and you give us a poem." He laughed. "You're in love, Mor-timer," he informed him, "and with my wife probably."

"Of course, I am, sir," replied the young man gallantly. "A sailor's heart, you know," while the face of the woman turned pink, then white. She knew her husband more intimately than Mortimer did, and there was something in his tone, his eyes, his words, she did not like. Harry was an idiot to choose such a tale. An irritated annoyance stirred in her, close upon dislike. "Anyhow, it's better than horrors," she said hurriedly.

"Well," put in her husband, letting forth a minor gust of laugh-ter, "it's possible, at any rate. Though one's as crazy as the other." His meaning was not wholly clear. "If a man really loved," he added in his blunt fashion, "and was tricked by her, I could almost conceive his——"

"Oh, don't preach, John, for Heaven's sake. You're so dull in the pulpit." But the interruption only served to emphasize the sentence which, otherwise, might have been passed over.

"Could conceive his finding life so worthless," persisted the other, "that——" He hesitated. "But there, now, I promised I wouldn't," he went on, laughing good-humouredly. Then, suddenly, as though in spite of himself, driven it seemed: "Still, under such conditions, he might show his contempt for human nature and for life by——"

It was a tiny stifled scream that stopped him this time.

"John, I hate, I loathe you, when you talk like that. And you've broken your word again." She was more than petulant; a nervous anger sounded in her voice. It was the way he had said it, looking from them towards the window, that made her quiver. She felt him suddenly as a man; she felt afraid of him.

Her husband made no reply; he rose and looked at his watch, leaning sideways towards the lamp, so that the expression of his face was shaded. "Two o'clock," he remarked. "I think I'll take a turn through the house. I may find a workman asleep or something. Anyhow, the light will soon come now." He laughed; the expression of his face, his tone of voice, relieved her momentarily. He went out. They heard his heavy tread echoing down the carpetless long corridor.

Mortimer began at once. "Did he mean anything?" he asked breathlessly. "He doesn't love you the least little bit, anyhow. He never did. I do. You're wasted on him. You belong to me." The words poured out. He covered her face with kisses. "Oh, I didn't mean *that*," he caught between the kisses.

The sailor released her, staring. "What then?" he whispered. "Do you think he saw us on the lawn?" He paused a moment, as she made no reply. The steps were audible in the distance still. "I know!" he exclaimed suddenly. "It's the blessed house he feels. That's what it is. He doesn't like it."

A wind sighed through the room, making the papers flutter; something rattled; and Mrs. Burley started. A loose end of rope swinging from the paperhanger's ladder caught her eye. She shivered slightly.

"He's different," she replied in a low voice, nestling very close again, "and so restless. Didn't you notice what he said just now—that under certain conditions he could understand a man"—she hesitated—"doing it," she concluded, a sudden drop in her voice. "Harry," she looked full into his eyes, "that's not like him. He didn't say that for nothing."

"Nonsense! He's bored to tears, that's all. And the house is getting

74

on your nerves, too." He kissed her tenderly. Then, as she responded, he drew her nearer still and held her passionately, mumbling incoherent words, among which "nothing to be afraid of" was distinguishable. Meanwhile, the steps were coming nearer.

She pushed him away. "You must behave yourself. I insist. You shall, Harry," then buried herself in his arms, her face hidden against his neck—only to disentangle herself the next instant and stand clear of him. "I hate you, Harry," she exclaimed sharply, a look of angry annoyance flashing across her face. "And I *hate* myself. Why do you treat me——?" She broke off as the steps came closer, patted her hair straight, and stalked over to the open window.

"I believe after all you're only playing with me," he said viciously. He stared in surprised disappointment, watching her. "It's him you really love," he added jealously. He looked and spoke like a petulant spoilt boy.

She did not turn her head. "He's always been fair to me, kind and generous. He never blames me for anything. Give me a cigarette and don't play the stage hero. My nerves are on edge, to tell you the truth." Her voice jarred harshly, and as he lit her cigarette, he noticed that her lips were trembling; his own hand trembled too.

He was still holding the match, standing beside her at the window-sill, when the steps crossed the threshold and John Burley came into the room. He went straight up to the table and turned the lamp down. "It was smoking," he remarked. "Didn't you see?"

"I'm sorry, sir," and Mortimer sprang forward, too late to help him. "It was the draught as you pushed the door open."

The big man said, "Ah!" and drew a chair over, facing them. "It's just *the* very house," he told them. "I've been through every room on this floor. It will make a splendid Home, with very little alteration, too." He turned round in his creaking wicker chair and looked up at his wife, who sat swinging her legs and smoking in the window embrasure. "Lives will be saved inside these old walls. It's a good investment," he went on, talking rather to himself it seemed. "People will die here, too——"

"Hark!" Mrs. Burley interrupted him. "That noise—what is it?" A faint thudding sound in the corridor or in the adjoining room was audible, making all three look round quickly, listening for a repetition, which did not come. The papers fluttered on the table, the lamps smoked an instant.

"Wind," observed Burley calmly, "our little friend, the South Wind.

75

Something blown over again, that's all." But, curiously, the three of them stood up. "I'll go and see," he continued. "Doors and windows are all open to let the paint dry." Yet he did not move; he stood there watching a white moth that dashed round and round the lamp, flopping heavily now and again upon the bare deal table.

"Let me go, sir," put in Mortimer eagerly. He was glad of the chance; for the first time he, too, felt uncomfortable. But there was another who, apparently, suffered a discomfort greater than his own and was accordingly even more glad to get away.

"I'll go," Mrs. Burley announced, with decision. "I'd like to. I haven't been out of this room since we came. I'm not an atom afraid."

It was strange that for a moment she did not make a move either; it seemed as if she waited for something. For perhaps fifteen seconds no one stirred or spoke. She knew by the look in her lover's eyes that he had now become aware of the slight, indefinite change in her husband's manner, and was alarmed by it. The fear in him woke her contempt; she suddenly despised the youth, and was conscious of a new, strange yearning towards her husband; against her worked nameless pressures, troubling her being. There was an alteration in the room, she thought; something had come in.

The trio stood listening to the gentle wind outside, waiting for the sound to be repeated; two careless, passionate young lovers and a man stood waiting, listening, watching in that room; yet it seemed there were five persons altogether and not three, for two guilty consciences stood apart and separate from their owners. John Burley broke the silence.

"Yes, you go, Nancy. Nothing to be afraid of—there. It's only wind." He spoke as though he meant it.

Mortimer bit his lips. "I'll come with you," he said instantly. He was confused. "Let's all three go. I don't think we ought to be separated."

But Mrs. Burley was already at the door. "I insist," she said, with a forced laugh. "I'll call if I'm frightened," while her husband, saying nothing, watched her from the table.

"Take this," said the sailor, flashing his electric torch as he went over to her. "Two are better than one." He saw her figure exquisitely silhouetted against the black corridor beyond; it was clear she wanted to go; any nervousness in her was mastered by a stronger emotion still; she was glad to be out of their presence for a bit. He had hoped to snatch a word of explanation in the corridor, but her manner stopped him. Something else stopped him, too.

"First door on the left," he called out, his voice echoing down the empty length. "That's the room where the noise came from. Shout if you want us."

He watched her moving away, the light held steadily in front of her, but she made no answer, and he turned back to see John Burley lighting his cigar at the lamp chimney, his face thrust forward as he did so. He stood a second, watching him, as the lips sucked hard at the cigar to make it draw; the strength of the features was emphasised to sternness. He had meant to stand by the door and listen for the least sound from the adjoining room, but now found his whole attention focused on the face above the lamp.

In that minute he realised that Burley had wished—had meant— his wife to go. In that minute also he forgot his love, his shameless, selfish little mistress, his worthless, caddish little self. For John Burley looked up. He straightened slowly, puffing hard and quickly to make sure his cigar was lit, and faced him. Mortimer moved forward into the room, self-conscious, embarrassed, cold.

"Of course, it was only wind," he said lightly, his one desire being to fill the interval while they were alone with commonplaces. He did not wish the other to speak, "Dawn wind, probably." He glanced at his wristwatch. "It's half-past two already, and the sun gets up at a quarter to four. It's light by now, I expect. The shortest night is never quite dark." He rambled on confusedly, for the other's steady, silent stare embarrassed him. A faint sound of Mrs. Burley moving in the next room made him stop a moment. He turned instinctively to the door, eager for an excuse to go.

"That's nothing," said Burley, speaking at last and in a firm quiet voice. "Only my wife, glad to be alone—my young and pretty wife. She's all right. I know her better than you do. Come in and shut the door."

Mortimer obeyed. He closed the door and came close to the table, facing the other, who at once continued.

"If I thought," he said, in that quiet deep voice, "that you two were serious"—he uttered his words very slowly, with emphasis, with intense severity—"do you know what I should do? I will tell you, Mortimer. I should like one of us two—you or myself—to remain in this house, dead."

His teeth gripped his cigar tightly; his hands were clenched; he went on through a half-closed mouth. His eyes blazed steadily.

"I trust her so absolutely—understand me?—that my belief in

women, in human beings, would go. And with it the desire to live. Understand me?"

Each word to the young careless fool was a blow in the face, yet it was the softest blow, the flash of a big deep heart, that hurt the most. A dozen answers—denial, explanation, confession, taking all guilt upon himself—crowded his mind, only to be dismissed. He stood motionless and silent, staring hard into the other's eyes. No word passed his lips; there was no time in any case.

It was in this position that Mrs. Burley, entering at that moment, found them. She saw her husband's face; the other man stood with his back to her. She came in with a little nervous laugh. "A bell-rope swinging in the wind and hitting a sheet of metal before the fireplace," she informed them. And all three laughed together then, though each laugh had a different sound. "But I hate this house," she added. "I wish we had never come."

"The moment there's light in the sky," remarked her husband quietly, "we can leave. That's the contract; let's see it through. Another half-hour will do it. Sit down, Nancy, and have a bite of something." He got up and placed a chair for her. "I think I'll take another look round." He moved slowly to the door. "I may go out on to the lawn a bit and see what the sky is doing."

It did not take half a minute to say the words, yet to Mortimer it seemed as though the voice would never end. His mind was confused and troubled. He loathed himself, he loathed the woman through whom he had got into this awkward mess.

The situation had suddenly become extremely painful; he had never imagined such a thing; the man he had thought blind had after all seen everything—known it all along, watched them, waited. And the woman, he was now certain, loved her husband; she had fooled him, Mortimer, all along, amusing herself.

"I'll come with you, sir. Do let me," he said suddenly. Mrs. Burley stood pale and uncertain between them. She looked scared. What has happened, she was clearly wondering.

"No, no, Harry"—he called him "Harry" for the first time—"I'll be back in five minutes at most. My wife mustn't be alone either." And he went out.

The young man waited till the footsteps sounded some distance down the corridor, then turned, but he did not move forward; for the first time he let pass unused what he called "an opportunity." His passion had left him; his love, as he once thought it, was gone. He looked at the pretty woman near him, wondering blankly what he had ever seen there to attract him so wildly. He wished to Heaven he was out of it all. He wished he were dead. John Burley's words suddenly appalled him.

One thing he saw plainly—she was frightened. This opened his lips.

"What's the matter?" he asked, and his hushed voice shirked the familiar Christian name. "Did you see anything?" He nodded his head in the direction of the adjoining room. It was the sound of his own voice addressing her coldly that made him abruptly see himself as he really was, but it was her reply, honestly given, in a faint even voice, that told him she saw her own self too with similar clarity. God, he thought, how revealing a tone, a single word can be!

"I saw—nothing. Only I feel uneasy—dear." That "dear" was a call for help.

"Look here," he cried, so loud that she held up a warning finger, "I'm—I've been a damned fool, a cad! I'm most frightfully ashamed. I'll do anything—*anything* to get it right." He felt cold, naked, his worthlessness laid bare; she felt, he knew, the same. Each revolted suddenly from the other. Yet he knew not quite how or wherefore this great change had thus abruptly come about, especially on her side. He felt that a bigger, deeper emotion than he could understand was working on them, making mere physical relationships seem empty, trivial, cheap and vulgar. His cold increased in face of this utter ignorance.

"Uneasy?" he repeated, perhaps hardly knowing exactly why he said it. "Good Lord, but he can take care of himself——"

"Oh, *he* is a man," she interrupted; "yes."

Steps were heard, firm, heavy steps, coming back along the corridor. It seemed to Mortimer that he had listened to this sound of steps all night, and would listen to them till he died. He crossed to the lamp and lit a cigarette, carefully this time, turning the wick down afterwards. Mrs. Burley also rose, moving over towards the door, away from him. They listened a moment to these firm and heavy steps, the tread of a man, John Burley. A man ... and a philanderer, flashed across Mortimer's brain like fire, contrasting the two with fierce contempt for himself. The tread became less audible. There was distance in it. It had turned in somewhere.

"There!" she exclaimed in a hushed tone. "He's gone in."

"Nonsense! It passed us. He's going out on to the lawn."

The pair listened breathlessly for a moment, when the sound of steps came distinctly from the adjoining room, walking across the boards, apparently towards the window.

"There!" she repeated. "He did go in." Silence of perhaps a minute followed, in which they heard each other's breathing. "I don't like his being alone—in there," Mrs. Burley said in a thin faltering voice, and moved as though to go out. Her hand was already on the knob of the door, when Mortimer stopped her with a violent gesture.

"Don't! For God's sake, don't!" he cried, before she could turn it. He darted forward. As he laid a hand upon her arm a thud was audible through the wall. It was a heavy sound, and this time there was no wind to cause it.

"It's only that loose swinging thing," he whispered thickly, a dreadful confusion blotting out clear thought and speech.

"There was no loose swaying thing at all," she said in a failing voice, then reeled and swayed against him. "I invented that. There was nothing." As he caught her, staring helplessly, it seemed to him that a face with lifted lids rushed up at him. He saw two terrified eyes in a patch of ghastly white. Her whisper followed, as she sank into his arms. "It's John. He's——"

At which instant, with terror at its climax, the sound of steps suddenly became audible once more—the firm and heavy tread of John Burley coming out again into the corridor. Such was their amazement and relief that they neither moved nor spoke. The steps drew nearer. The pair seemed petrified; Mortimer did not remove his arms, nor did Mrs. Burley attempt to release herself. They stared at the door and waited. It was pushed wider the next second, and John Burley stood beside them. He was so close he almost touched them—there in each other's arms.

"Jack, dear!" cried his wife, with a searching tenderness that made her voice seem strange.

He gazed a second at each in turn. "I'm going out on to the lawn for a moment," he said quietly. There was no expression on his face; he did not smile, he did not frown; he showed no feeling, no emotion—just looked into their eyes, and then withdrew round the edge of the door before either could utter a word in answer. The door swung to behind him. He was gone.

"He's going to the lawn. He said so." It was Mortimer speaking, but his voice shook and stammered. Mrs. Burley had released herself. She stood now by the table, silent, gazing with fixed eyes at nothing, her lips parted, her expression vacant. Again she was aware of an alteration in the room; something had gone out. . . . He watched her a second, uncertain what to say or do. It was the face of a drowned person, occurred to him. Something intangible, yet almost visible stood between them in that narrow space. Something had ended, there before his eyes, definitely ended. The barrier between them rose higher, denser. Through this barrier her words came to him with an odd whispering remoteness.

"Harry. . . . You saw? You noticed?"

"What d'you mean?" he said gruffly. He tried to feel angry, contemptuous, but his breath caught absurdly.

"Harry—he was different. The eyes, the hair, the"—her face grew like death—"the twist in his face——"

"What on earth are you saying? Pull yourself together." He saw that she was trembling down the whole length of her body, as she leaned against the table for support. His own legs shook. He stared hard at her.

"Altered, Harry . . . altered." Her horrified whisper came at him like a knife. For it was true. He, too, had noticed something about the husband's appearance that was not quite normal. Yet, even while they talked, they heard him going down the carpetless stairs; the sounds ceased as he crossed the hall; then came the noise of the front door banging, the reverberation even shaking the room a little where they stood.

Mortimer went over to her side. He walked unevenly.

"My dear! For God's sake—this is sheer nonsense. Don't let yourself go like this. I'll put it straight with him—it's all my fault." He saw by her face that she did not understand his words; he was saying the wrong thing altogether; her mind was utterly elsewhere. "He's all right," he went on hurriedly. "He's out on the lawn now——"

He broke off at the sight of her. The horror that fastened on her brain plastered her face with deathly whiteness.

"That was not John at all!" she cried, a wail of misery and terror in her voice. She rushed to the window and he followed. To his immense relief a figure moving below was plainly visible. It was John Burley. They saw him in the faint grey of the dawn, as he crossed the lawn, going away from the house. He disappeared.

"There you are! See?" whispered Mortimer reassuringly. "He'll be back in——" when a sound in the adjoining room, heavier, louder than before, cut appallingly across his words, and Mrs. Burley, with that wailing scream, fell back into his arms. He caught her only just in time, for she stiffened into ice, daft with the uncomprehended terror of it all, and helpless as a child.

"Darling, my darling—oh, God!" He bent, kissing her face wildly. He was utterly distraught.

"Harry! Jack—oh, oh!" she wailed in her anguish. "It took on his likeness. It deceived us . . . to give him time. He's done it."

She sat up suddenly. "Go," she said, pointing to the room beyond, then sank fainting, a dead weight in his arms.

He carried her unconscious body to a chair, then entering the adjoining room he flashed his torch upon the body of her husband hanging from a bracket in the wall. He cut it down five minutes too late.

Running Wolf

The man who enjoys an adventure outside the general experience of the race, and imparts it to others, must not be surprised if he is taken for either a liar or a fool, as Malcolm Hyde, hotel clerk on a holiday, discovered in due course. Nor is "enjoy" the right word to use in describing his emotions; the word he chose was probably "survive."

When he first set eyes on Medicine Lake he was struck by its still, sparkling beauty, lying there in the vast Canadian backwoods; next, by its extreme loneliness; and, lastly—a good deal later, this—by its combination of beauty, loneliness, and singular atmosphere, due to the fact that it was the scene of his adventure.

"It's fairly stiff with big fish," said Morton of the Montreal Sporting Club. "Spend your holiday there—up Mattawa way, some fifteen miles west of Stony Creek. You'll have it all to yourself except for an old Indian who's got a shack there. Camp on the east side—if you'll take a tip from me." He then talked for half an hour about the wonderful sport; yet he was not otherwise very communicative, and did not suffer questions gladly, Hyde noticed. Nor had he stayed there very long himself. If it was such a paradise as Morton, its discoverer and the most experienced rod in the province, claimed, why had he himself spent only three days there?

"Ran short of grub," was the explanation offered; but to another friend he had mentioned briefly, "flies," and to a third, so Hyde learned later, he gave the excuse that his half-breed "took sick," necessitating a quick return to civilization.

Hyde, however, cared little for the explanations; his interest in these came later. "Stiff with fish" was the phrase he liked. He took the Canadian Pacific train to Mattawa, laid in his outfit at Stony Creek, and set off thence for the fifteen-mile canoe-trip without a care in the world.

Travelling light, the portages did not trouble him; the water was swift and easy, the rapids negotiable; everything came his way, as the saying is. Occasionally he saw big fish making for the deeper pools, and was sorely tempted to stop; but he resisted. He pushed on between the immense world of forests that stretched for hundreds of miles, known to deer, bear, moose, and wolf, but strange to any echo of human tread, a deserted and primeval wilderness. The autumn day was calm, the water sang and sparkled, the blue sky hung cloudless over all, ablaze with light. Toward evening he passed an old beaver-dam, rounded a little point, and had his first sight of Medicine Lake. He lifted his dripping paddle; the canoe shot with silent glide into calm water. He gave an exclamation of delight, for the loveliness caught his breath away.

Though primarily a sportsman, he was not insensible to beauty. The lake formed a crescent, perhaps four miles long, its width between a mile and half a mile. The slanting gold of sunset flooded it. No wind stirred its crystal surface. Here it had lain since the redskin's god first made it; here it would lie until he dried it up again. Towering spruce and hemlock trooped to its very edge, majestic cedars leaned down as if to drink, crimson *sumachs* shone in fiery patches, and maples gleamed orange and red beyond belief. The air was like wine, with the silence of a dream.

It was here the red men formerly "made medicine," with all the wild ritual and tribal ceremony of an ancient day. But it was of Morton, rather than of Indians, that Hyde thought. If this lonely, hidden paradise was really stiff with big fish, he owed a lot to Morton for the information. Peace invaded him, but the excitement of the hunter lay below.

He looked about him with quick, practised eye for a camping-place before the sun sank below the forests and the half-lights came. The Indian's shack, lying in full sunshine on the eastern shore, he found at once; but the trees lay too thick about it for comfort, nor did he wish to be so close to its inhabitant. Upon the opposite side, however, an ideal clearing offered. This lay already in shadow, the huge forest darkening it toward evening; but the open space attracted. He paddled over quickly and examined it. The ground was hard and dry, he found, and a little brook ran tinkling down one side of it into the lake. This outfall, too, would be a good fishing spot. Also, it was sheltered. A few low willows marked the mouth.

An experienced camper soon makes up his mind. It was a perfect site, and some charred logs, with traces of former fires, proved that he was not the first to think so. Hyde was delighted. Then, suddenly, disappointment came to tinge his pleasure. His kit was landed, and preparations for putting up the tent were begun, when he recalled a detail that excitement had so far kept in the background of his mind—Morton's advice. But not Morton's only, for the storekeeper at Stony Creek had reinforced it. The big fellow with straggling moustache and stooping shoulders, dressed in shirt and trousers, had handed him out a final sentence with the bacon, flour, condensed milk, and sugar. He had repeated Morton's half-forgotten words:

"Put yer tent on the east shore. I should," he had said at parting.

He remembered Morton, too, apparently. "A shortish fellow, brown as an Indian and fairly smelling of the woods. Travelling with Jake, the half-breed." That assuredly was Morton. "Didn't stay long, now, did he?" he added in a reflective tone.

"Going Windy Lake way, are yer? Or Ten Mile Water, maybe?" he had first inquired of Hyde.

"Medicine Lake."

"Is that so?" the man said, as though he doubted it for some obscure reason. He pulled at his ragged moustache a moment. "Is that so, now?" he repeated. And the final words followed him downstream after a considerable pause—the advice about the best shore on which to put his tent.

All this now suddenly flashed back upon Hyde's mind with a tinge of disappointment and annoyance, for when two experienced men agreed, their opinion was not to be lightly disregarded. He wished he had asked the storekeeper for more details. He looked about him, he reflected, he hesitated. His ideal camping-ground lay certainly on the forbidden shore. What in the world, he pondered, could be the objection to it?

But the light was fading; he must decide quickly one way or the other. After staring at his unpacked dunnage and the tent, already half erected, he made up his mind with a muttered expression that consigned both Morton and the storekeeper to less pleasant places. "They must have *some* reason," he growled to himself; "fellows like that usually know what they're talking about. I guess I'd better shift over to the other side—for tonight, at any rate."

He glanced across the water before actually reloading. No smoke rose from the Indian's shack. He had seen no sign of a canoe. The man, he decided, was away. Reluctantly, then, he left the good camping-ground and paddled across the lake, and half an hour later his tent was up, firewood collected, and two small trout were already caught for supper. But the bigger fish, he knew, lay waiting for him on the other side by the little outfall, and he fell asleep at length on his bed of balsam boughs, annoyed and disappointed, yet wondering how a mere sentence could have persuaded him so easily against his own better judgment. He slept like the dead; the sun was well up before he stirred.

But his morning mood was a very different one. The brilliant light, the peace, the intoxicating air, all this was too exhilarating for the mind to harbour foolish fancies, and he marvelled that he could have been so weak the night before. No hesitation lay in him anywhere. He struck camp immediately after breakfast, paddled back across the strip of shining water, and quickly settled in upon the forbidden shore, as he now called it, with a contemptuous grin. And the more he saw of the spot, the better he liked it. There was plenty of wood, running water to drink, an open space about the tent, and there were no flies. The fishing, moreover, was magnificent. Morton's description was fully justified, and "stiff with big fish" for once was not an exaggeration.

The useless hours of the early afternoon he passed dozing in the sun, or wandering through the underbrush beyond the camp. He found no sign of anything unusual. He bathed in a cool, deep pool; he revelled in the lonely little paradise. Lonely it certainly was, but the loneliness was part of its charm; the stillness, the peace, the isolation of this beautiful backwoods' lake delighted him. The silence was divine. He was entirely satisfied.

After a brew of tea, he strolled toward evening along the shore, looking for the first sign of a rising fish. A faint ripple on the water, with the lengthening shadows, made good conditions. *Plop* followed *plop*, as the big fellows rose, snatched at their food, and vanished into the depths. He hurried back. Ten minutes later he had taken his rods and was gliding cautiously in the canoe through the quiet water.

So good was the sport, indeed, and so quickly did the big trout pile up in the bottom of the canoe that, despite the growing lateness, he found it hard to tear himself away. "One more," he said, "and then I really will go." He landed that "one more," and was in act of taking it off the hook, when the deep silence of the evening was curiously disturbed. He became abruptly aware that someone watched him. A pair of eyes, it seemed, were fixed upon him from some point in the surrounding shadows.

Thus, at least, he interpreted the odd disturbance in his happy mood; for thus he felt it. The feeling stole over him without the slightest warning. He was not alone. The slippery big trout dropped from his fingers. He sat motionless, and stared about him.

Nothing stirred; the ripple on the lake had died away; there was no wind; the forest lay a single purple mass of shadow; the yellow sky, fast fading, threw reflections that troubled the eye and made distances uncertain. But there was no sound, no movement; he saw no figure anywhere. Yet he knew that someone watched him, and a wave of quite unreasoning terror gripped him. The nose of the canoe was against the bank. In a moment, and instinctively, he shoved it off and paddled into deeper water. The watcher, it came to him also instinctively, was quite close to him upon that bank. But where? And who? Was it the Indian?

Here, in deeper water, and some twenty yards from the shore, he paused and strained both sight and hearing to find some possible clue. He felt half ashamed, now that the first strange feeling passed a little. But the certainty remained. Absurd as it was, he felt positive that someone watched him with concentrated and intent regard. Every fibre in his being told him so; and though he could discover no figure, no new outline on the shore, he could even have sworn in which clump of willow bushes the hidden person crouched and stared. His attention seemed drawn to that particular clump.

The water dripped slowly from his paddle, now lying across the thwarts. There was no other sound. The canvas of his tent gleamed dimly. A star or two were out. He waited. Nothing happened.

Then, as suddenly as it had come, the feeling passed, and he knew that the person who had been watching him intently had gone. It was as if a current had been turned off; the normal world flowed back; the landscape emptied as if someone had left a room. The disagreeable feeling left him at the same time, so that he instantly turned the canoe in to the shore again, landed, and, paddle in hand, went over to examine the clump of willows he had singled out as the place of concealment. There was no one there, of course, nor any trace of recent human occupancy. No leaves, no branches stirred, nor was a single twig displaced; his keen and practised sight detected no sign of tracks upon the ground.

Yet, for all that, he felt positive that a little time ago someone had crouched among these very leaves and watched him. He remained absolutely convinced of it. The watcher, whether Indian, hunter, stray lumberman, or wandering half-breed, had now withdrawn, a search was useless, and dusk was falling. He returned to his little camp, more disturbed perhaps than he cared to acknowledge. He cooked his supper, hung up his catch on a string, so that no prowling animal could get at it during the night, and prepared to make himself comfortable until bedtime. Unconsciously, he built a bigger fire than usual, and found himself peering over his pipe into the deep shadows beyond the firelight, straining his ears to catch the slightest sound. He remained generally on the alert in a way that was new to him.

A man under such conditions and in such a place need not know discomfort until the sense of loneliness strikes him as too vivid a reality. Loneliness in a backwoods camp brings charm, pleasure, and a happy sense of calm until, and unless, it comes too near. It should remain an ingredient only among other conditions; it should not be directly, vividly noticed. Once it has crept within short range, however, it may easily cross the narrow line between comfort and discomfort, and darkness is an undesirable time for the transition. A curious dread may easily follow—the dread lest the loneliness suddenly be disturbed, and the solitary human feel himself open to attack.

For Hyde, now, this transition had been already accomplished; the too intimate sense of his loneliness had shifted abruptly into the worse condition of no longer being quite alone. It was an awkward moment, and the hotel clerk realised his position exactly. He did not quite like it. He sat there, with his back to the blazing logs, a very visible object in the light, while all about him the darkness of the forest lay like an impenetrable wall. He could not see a foot beyond the small circle of his camp-fire; the silence about him was like the silence of the dead. No leaf rustled, no wave lapped; he himself sat motionless as a log.

Then again, he became suddenly aware that the person who watched him had returned, and that same intent and concentrated gaze as before was fixed upon him where he lay. There was no warning; he heard no stealthy tread or snapping of dry twigs, yet the owner of those steady eyes was very close to him, probably not a dozen feet away. This sense of proximity was overwhelming.

It is unquestionable that a shiver ran down his spine. This time, moreover, he felt positive that the man crouched just beyond the firelight, the distance he himself could see being nicely calculated, and straight in front of him. For some minutes he sat without stirring a single muscle, yet with each muscle ready and alert, straining his eyes in vain to pierce the darkness, but only succeeding in dazzling his sight with the reflected light. Then, as he shifted his position slowly, cautiously, to obtain another angle of vision, his heart gave two big thumps against his ribs and the hair seemed to rise on his scalp with the sense of cold that shot horribly up his spine. In the darkness facing him he saw two small and greenish circles that were certainly a pair of eyes, yet not the eyes of Indian, hunter, or of any human being. It was a pair of animal eyes that stared so fixedly at him out of the night. And this certainly had an immediate and natural effect upon him.

For, at the menace of those eyes, the fears of millions of long dead hunters since the dawn of time woke in him. Hotel clerk though he was, heredity surged through him in an automatic wave of instinct. His hand groped for a weapon. His fingers fell on the iron head of his small camp axe, and at once he was himself again. Confidence returned; the vague, superstitious dread was gone. This was a bear or wolf that smelt his catch and came to steal it. With beings of that sort, he knew instinctively how to deal, yet admitting, by this very instinct, that his original dread had been of quite another kind.

"I'll damned quick find out what it is," he exclaimed aloud, and snatching a burning brand from the fire, he hurled it with good aim straight at the eyes of the beast before him.

The bit of pitch-pine fell in a shower of sparks that lit the dry grass this side of the animal, flared up a moment, then died quickly down again. But in that instant of bright illumination, he saw clearly what his unwelcome visitor was. A big timber wolf sat on its hindquarters, staring steadily at him through the firelight. He saw its legs and shoulders, he saw its hair, he saw also the big hemlock trunks lit up behind it, and the willow scrub on each side. It formed a vivid, clear-cut picture shown in clear detail by the momentary blaze. To his amazement, however, the wolf did not turn and bolt away from the burning log, but withdrew a few yards only, and sat there again on its haunches, staring, staring as before. Heavens, how it stared! He "shoo-ed" it, but without effect; it did not budge. He did not waste another good log on it, for his fear was dissipated now; a timber wolf was a timber wolf, and it might sit there as long as it pleased, provided it did not try to steal his catch. No alarm was in him anymore. He knew that wolves were harmless in the summer and autumn, and even when "packed" in the winter, they would attack a man only when suffering desperate hunger. So, he lay and watched the beast, threw bits of stick in its direction, even talked to it, wondering only that it never moved. "You can stay there for ever, if you like," he remarked to it aloud, "for you cannot get at my fish, and the rest of the grub I shall take into the tent with me!"

The creature blinked its bright green eyes, but made no move.

Why, then, if his fear was gone, did he think of certain things as he rolled himself in the Hudson Bay blankets before going to sleep? The immobility of the animal was strange, its refusal to turn and bolt was still stranger. Never before had he known a wild creature that was not afraid of fire. Why did it sit and watch him, as with purpose in its dreadful eyes? How had he felt its presence earlier and instantly? A timber wolf, especially a solitary timber wolf, was a timid thing, yet this one feared neither man nor fire. Now, as he lay there wrapped in his blankets inside the cosy tent, it sat outside beneath the stars, beside the fading embers, the wind chilly in its fur, the ground cooling beneath its planted paws, watching him, steadily watching him, perhaps until the dawn.

It was unusual, it was strange. Having neither imagination nor tradition, he called upon no store of racial visions. Matter of fact, a hotel clerk on a fishing holiday, he lay there in his blankets, merely wondering and puzzled. A timber wolf was a timber wolf and nothing more. Yet this timber wolf—the idea haunted him—was different. In a word, the deeper part of his original uneasiness remained. He tossed about, he shivered sometimes in his broken sleep; he did not go out to see, but he woke early and unrefreshed.

Again, with the sunshine and the morning wind, however, the incident of the night before was forgotten, almost unreal. His hunting zeal was uppermost. The tea and fish were delicious, his pipe had never tasted so good, the glory of this lonely lake amid primeval forests went to his head a little; he was a hunter before the Lord, and nothing else. He tried the edge of the lake, and in the excitement of playing a big fish, knew suddenly that it, the wolf, was there. He paused with the rod, exactly as if struck. He looked about him, he looked in a definite direction.

The brilliant sunshine made every smallest detail clear and sharp—boulders of granite, burned stems, crimson *sumach*, pebbles along the shore in neat, separate detail—without revealing where the watcher hid. Then, his sight wandering farther inshore among the tangled undergrowth, he suddenly picked up the familiar, half-expected outline. The wolf was lying behind a granite boulder, so that only the head, the muzzle, and the eyes were visible. It merged in its background. Had he not known it was a wolf, he could never have separated it from the landscape. The eyes shone in the sunlight.

There it lay. He looked straight at it. Their eyes, in fact, actually met full and square. "Great Scott!" he exclaimed aloud, "why, it's like looking at a human being!" From that moment, unwittingly, he established a singular personal relation with the beast. And what followed confirmed this undesirable impression, for the animal rose instantly and came down in leisurely fashion to the shore, where it stood looking back at him. It stood and stared into his eyes like some great wild dog, so that he was aware of a new and almost incredible sensation—that it courted recognition.

"Well! well!" he exclaimed again, relieving his feelings by addressing it aloud, "if this doesn't beat everything I ever saw! What d'you want, anyway?"

He examined it now more carefully. He had never seen a wolf so big before; it was a tremendous beast, a nasty customer to tackle, he reflected, if it ever came to that. It stood there absolutely fearless and full of confidence. In the clear sunlight he took in every detail of it—a huge, shaggy, lean-flanked timber wolf, its wicked eyes staring straight into his own, almost with a kind of purpose in them. He saw its great jaws, its teeth, and its tongue, hung out, dropping saliva a little. And yet the idea of its savagery, its fierceness, was very little in him.

He was amazed and puzzled beyond belief. He wished the Indian would come back. He did not understand this strange behaviour in an animal. Its eyes, the odd expression in them, gave him a queer, unusual, difficult feeling. Had his nerves gone wrong, he almost wondered.

The beast stood on the shore and looked at him. He wished for the first time that he had brought a rifle. With a resounding smack he brought his paddle down flat upon the water, using all his strength, till the echoes rang as from a pistol-shot that was audible from one end of the lake to the other. The wolf never stirred. He shouted, but the beast remained unmoved. He blinked his eyes, speaking as to a dog, a domestic animal, a creature accustomed to human ways. It blinked its eyes in return.

At length, increasing his distance from the shore, he continued fishing, and the excitement of the marvellous sport held his attention—his surface attention, at any rate. At times he almost forgot the attendant beast; yet whenever he looked up, he saw it there. And worse; when he slowly paddled home again, he observed it trotting along the shore as though to keep him company. Crossing a little bay, he spurted, hoping to reach the other point before his undesired and undesirable attendant. Instantly the brute broke into that rapid, tireless lope that, except on ice, can run down anything on four legs in the woods. When he reached the distant point, the wolf was waiting for him.

He raised his paddle from the water, pausing a moment for reflection; for this very close attention—there were dusk and night yet to come—he certainly did not relish. His camp was near; he had to land; he felt uncomfortable even in the sunshine of broad day, when, to his keen relief, about half a mile from the tent, he saw the creature suddenly stop and sit down in the open. He waited a moment, then paddled on. It did not follow. There was no attempt to move; it merely sat and watched him. After a few hundred yards, he looked back. It was still sitting where he left it. And the absurd, yet significant, feeling came to him that the beast divined his thought, his anxiety, his dread, and was now showing him, as well as it could, that it entertained no hostile feeling and did not meditate attack.

He turned the canoe toward the shore; he landed; he cooked his supper in the dusk; the animal made no sign. Not far away it certainly lay and watched, but it did not advance. And to Hyde, observant now in a new way, came one sharp, vivid reminder of the strange atmosphere into which his commonplace personality had strayed: he suddenly recalled that his relations with the beast, already established, had progressed distinctly a stage further. This startled him, yet without the accompanying alarm he must certainly have felt twenty-four hours before. He had an understanding with the wolf. He was aware of friendly thoughts toward it. He even went so far as to set out a few big fish on the spot where he had first seen it sitting the previous night.

"If he comes," he thought, "he is welcome to them. I've got plenty, anyway." He thought of it now as "he."

Yet the wolf made no appearance until he was in the act of entering his tent a good deal later. It was close on ten o'clock, whereas nine was his hour, and late at that, for turning in. He had, therefore, unconsciously been waiting for him. Then, as he was closing the flap, he saw the eyes close to where he had placed the fish. He waited, hiding himself, and expecting to hear sounds of munching jaws; but all was silence. Only the eyes glowed steadily out of the background of pitch darkness. He closed the flap. He had no slightest fear. In ten minutes, he was sound asleep.

He could not have slept very long, for when he woke up, he could see the shine of a faint red light through the canvas, and the fire had not died down completely. He rose and cautiously peeped out. The air was very cold; he saw his breath. But he also saw the wolf, for it had come in, and was sitting by the dying embers, not two yards away from where he crouched behind the flap. And this time, at these very close quarters, there was something in the attitude of the big wild thing that caught his attention with a vivid thrill of startled surprise and a sudden shock of cold that held him spellbound. He stared, unable to believe his eyes; for the wolf's attitude conveyed to him something familiar that at first, he was unable to explain. Its pose reached him in the terms of another thing with which he was entirely at home. What was it? Did his senses betray him? Was he still asleep and dreaming?

Then, suddenly, with a start of uncanny recognition, he knew. Its attitude was that of a dog. Having found the clue, his mind then made an awful leap. For it was, after all, no dog its appearance aped, but something nearer to himself, and more familiar still. Good heavens! It sat there with the pose, the attitude, the gesture in repose of something almost human. And then, with a second shock of biting wonder, it came to him like a revelation. The wolf sat beside that camp-fire as a man might sit.

Before he could weigh his extraordinary discovery, before he could examine it in detail or with care, the animal, sitting in this ghastly fashion, seemed to feel his eyes fixed on it. It slowly turned and looked him in the face, and for the first time Hyde felt a full-blooded, super-stitious fear flood through his entire being. He seemed transfixed with that nameless terror that is said to attack human beings who suddenly face the dead, finding themselves bereft of speech and movement. This moment of paralysis certainly occurred. Its passing, however, was as singular as its advent. For almost at once he was aware of something beyond and above this mockery of human attitude and pose, some-thing that ran along unaccustomed nerves and reached his feeling, even perhaps his heart.

The revulsion was extraordinary, its result still more extraordinary and unexpected. Yet the fact remains. He was aware of another thing that had the effect of stilling his terror as soon as it was born. He was aware of appeal, silent, half expressed, yet vastly pathetic. He saw in the savage eyes a beseeching, even a yearning, expression that changed his mood as by magic from dread to natural sympathy. The great grey brute, symbol of cruel ferocity, sat there beside his dying fire and ap-pealed for help.

This gulf betwixt animal and human seemed in that instant bridged. It was, of course, incredible. Hyde, sleep still possibly clinging to his inner being with the shades and half shapes of dream yet about his soul, acknowledged, how he knew not, the amazing fact. He found himself nodding to the brute in half consent, and instantly, without more ado, the lean grey shape rose like a wraith and trotted off swiftly, but with stealthy tread, into the background of the night.

When Hyde woke in the morning his first impression was that he must have dreamed the entire incident. His practical nature asserted itself. There was a bite in the fresh autumn air; the bright sun allowed no half lights anywhere; he felt brisk in mind and body. Reviewing what had happened, he came to the conclusion that it was utterly vain to speculate; no possible explanation of the animal's behaviour occurred to him; he was dealing with something entirely outside his experience. His fear, however, had completely left him. The odd sense of friendliness remained. The beast had a definite purpose, and he himself was included in that purpose. His sympathy held good.

But with the sympathy there was also an intense curiosity. "If it shows itself again," he told himself, "I'll go up close and find out what it wants." The fish laid out the night before had not been touched.

It must have been a full hour after breakfast when he next saw the brute; it was standing on the edge of the clearing, looking at him in the way now become familiar. Hyde immediately picked up his axe and advanced toward it boldly, keeping his eyes fixed straight upon its own. There was nervousness in him, but kept well under; nothing betrayed it; step by step he drew nearer until some ten yards separated them. The wolf had not stirred a muscle as yet. Its jaws hung open, its eyes observed him intently; it allowed him to approach without a sign of what its mood might be. Then, with these ten yards between them, it turned abruptly and moved slowly off, looking back first over one shoulder and then over the other, exactly as a dog might do, to see if he was following.

A singular journey it was they then made together, animal and man. The trees surrounded them at once, for they left the lake behind them, entering the tangled bush beyond. The beast, Hyde noticed, obviously picked the easiest track for him to follow; for obstacles that meant nothing to the four-legged expert, yet were difficult for a man, were carefully avoided with an almost uncanny skill, while yet the general direction was accurately kept. Occasionally there were windfalls to be surmounted; but though the wolf bounded over these with ease, it was always waiting for the man on the other side after he had laboriously climbed over. Deeper and deeper into the heart of the lonely forest they penetrated in this singular fashion, cutting across the arc of the lake's crescent, it seemed to Hyde; for after two miles or so, he recognised the big rocky bluff that overhung the water at its northern end.

This outstanding bluff he had seen from his camp, one side of it falling sheer into the water; it was probably the spot, he imagined, where the Indians held their medicine-making ceremonies, for it stood out in isolated fashion, and its top formed a private plateau not easy of access. And it was here, close to a big spruce at the foot of the bluff upon the forest side, that the wolf stopped suddenly and for the first time since its appearance gave audible expression to its feelings. It sat down on its haunches, lifted its muzzle with open jaws, and gave vent to a subdued and long-drawn howl that was more like the wail of a dog than the fierce barking cry associated with a wolf.

By this time Hyde had lost not only fear, but caution too; nor, oddly enough, did this warning howl revive a sign of unwelcome emotion in him. In that curious sound he detected the same message that the eyes conveyed—appeal for help. He paused, nevertheless, a little startled, and while the wolf sat waiting for him, he looked about him quickly. There was young timber here; it had once been a small clearing, evidently. Axe and fire had done their work, but there was evidence to an experienced eye that it was Indians and not white men who had once been busy here. Some part of the medicine ritual, doubtless, took place in the little clearing, thought the man, as he advanced again towards his patient leader. The end of their queer journey, he felt, was close at hand.

He had not taken two steps before the animal got up and moved very slowly in the direction of some low bushes that formed a clump just beyond. It entered these, first looking back to make sure that its companion watched. The bushes hid it; a moment later it emerged again. Twice it performed this pantomime, each time, as it reappeared, standing still and staring at the man with as distinct an expression of appeal in the eyes as an animal may compass, probably. Its excitement, meanwhile, certainly increased, and this excitement was, with equal certainty, communicated to the man. Hyde made up his mind quickly. Gripping his axe tightly, and ready to use it at the first hint of malice, he moved slowly nearer to the bushes, wondering with something of a tremor what would happen.

If he expected to be startled, his expectation was at once fulfilled; but it was the behaviour of the beast that made him jump. It positively frisked about him like a happy dog. It frisked for joy. Its excitement was intense, yet from its open mouth no sound was audible. With a sudden leap, then, it bounded past him into the clump of bushes, against whose very edge he stood, and began scraping vigorously at the ground. Hyde stood and stared, amazement and interest now banishing all his nervousness, even when the beast, in its violent scraping, actually touched his body with its own.

He had, perhaps, the feeling that he was in a dream, one of those fantastic dreams in which things may happen without involving an adequate surprise; for otherwise the manner of scraping and scratching at the ground must have seemed an impossible phenomenon. No wolf, no dog certainly, used its paws in the way those paws were working. Hyde had the odd, distressing sensation that it was hands, not paws, he watched. And yet, somehow, the natural, adequate surprise he should have felt was absent. The strange action seemed not entirely unnatural. In his heart some deep hidden spring of sympathy and pity stirred instead. He was aware of pathos.

The wolf stopped in its task and looked up into his face. Hyde acted without hesitation then. Afterwards he was wholly at a loss to explain his own conduct. It seemed he knew what to do, divined what was asked, expected of him. Between his mind and the dumb desire yearning through the savage animal there was intelligent and intelligible communication. He cut a stake and sharpened it, for the stones would blunt his axe-edge. He entered the clump of bushes to complete the digging his four-legged companion had begun. And while he worked, though he did not forget the close proximity of the wolf, he paid no attention to it; often his back was turned as he stooped over the laborious clearing away of the hard earth; no uneasiness or sense of danger was in him anymore.

The wolf sat outside the clump and watched the operations. Its concentrated attention, its patience, its intense eagerness, the gentleness and docility of the grey, fierce, and probably hungry brute, its obvious pleasure and satisfaction, too, at having won the human to its mysterious purpose—these were colours in the strange picture that Hyde thought of later when dealing with the human herd in his hotel again. At the moment he was aware chiefly of pathos and affection. The whole business was, of course, not to be believed, but that discovery came later, too, when telling it to others.

The digging continued for fully half an hour before his labour was rewarded by the discovery of a small whitish object. He picked it up and examined it—the finger-bone of a man. Other discoveries then followed quickly and in quantity. The *cache* was laid bare. He collected nearly the complete skeleton. The skull, however, he found last, and might not have found at all but for the guidance of his strangely alert companion. It lay some few yards away from the central hole now dug, and the wolf stood nuzzling the ground with its nose before Hyde understood that he was meant to dig exactly in that spot for it.

Between the beast's very paws his stake struck hard upon it. He scraped the earth from the bone and examined it carefully. It was perfect, save for the fact that some wild animal had gnawed it, the teeth-marks being still plainly visible. Close beside it lay the rusty iron head of a tomahawk. This and the smallness of the bones confirmed him in his judgment that it was the skeleton not of a white man, but of an Indian.

During the excitement of the discovery of the bones one by one, and finally of the skull, but, more especially, during the period of intense interest while Hyde was examining them, he had paid little, if any, attention to the wolf. He was aware that it sat and watched him, never moving its keen eyes for a single moment from the actual operations, but of sign or movement it made none at all. He knew that it was pleased and satisfied, he knew also that he had now fulfilled its purpose in a great measure. The further intuition that now came to him, derived, he felt positive, from his companion's dumb desire, was perhaps the cream of the entire experience to him. Gathering the bones together in his coat, he carried them, together with the tomahawk, to the foot of the big spruce where the animal had first stopped. His leg actually touched the creature's muzzle as he passed.

It turned its head to watch, but did not follow, nor did it move a muscle while he prepared the platform of boughs upon which he then laid the poor worn bones of an Indian who had been killed, doubtless, in sudden attack or ambush, and to whose remains had been denied the last grace of proper tribal burial. He wrapped the bones in bark; he laid the tomahawk beside the skull; he lit the circular fire round the pyre, and the blue smoke rose upward into the clear bright sunshine of the Canadian autumn morning till it was lost among the mighty trees far overhead.

In the moment before actually lighting the little fire he had turned to note what his companion did. It sat five yards away, he saw, gazing intently, and one of its front paws was raised a little from the ground. It made no sign of any kind. He finished the work, becoming so absorbed in it that he had eyes for nothing but the tending and guarding of his careful ceremonial fire. It was only when the platform of boughs collapsed, laying their charred burden gently on the fragrant earth among the soft wood ashes, that he turned again, as though to show the wolf what he had done, and seek, perhaps, some look of satisfaction in its curiously expressive eyes. But the place he searched was empty. The wolf had gone.

He did not see it again; it gave no sign of its presence anywhere; he was not watched. He fished as before, wandered through the bush about his camp, sat smoking round his fire after dark, and slept peacefully in his cosy little tent. He was not disturbed. No howl was ever audible in the distant forest, no twig snapped beneath a stealthy tread, he saw no eyes. The wolf that behaved like a man had gone for ever.

It was the day before he left that Hyde, noticing smoke rising from the shack across the lake, paddled over to exchange a word or two with the Indian, who had evidently now returned. The Indian came down to meet him as he landed, but it was soon plain that he spoke very little English. He emitted the familiar grunts at first; then bit by bit Hyde stirred his limited vocabulary into action. The net result, however, was slight enough, though it was certainly direct:

"You camp there?" the man asked, pointing to the other side.

"Yes."

"Wolf come?"

"Yes."

"You see wolf?"

"Yes."

The Indian stared at him fixedly a moment, a keen, wondering look upon his coppery, creased face.

"You 'fraid wolf?" he asked after a moment's pause.

"No," replied Hyde, truthfully. He knew it was useless to ask questions of his own, though he was eager for information. The other would have told him nothing. It was sheer luck that the man had touched on the subject at all, and Hyde realized that his own best *rôle* was merely to answer, but to ask no questions. Then, suddenly, the Indian became comparatively voluble. There was awe in his voice and manner.

"Him no wolf. Him big medicine wolf. Him spirit wolf."

Whereupon he drank the tea the other had brewed for him, closed his lips tightly, and said no more. His outline was discernible on the shore, rigid and motionless, an hour later, when Hyde's canoe turned the corner of the lake three miles away, and landed to make the portages up the first rapid of his homeward stream.

It was Morton who, after some persuasion, supplied further details of what he called the legend. Some hundred years before, the tribe that lived in the territory beyond the lake began their annual medicine-making ceremonies on the big rocky bluff at the northern end; but no medicine could be made. The spirits, declared the chief medicine man, would not answer. They were offended. An investigation followed. It was discovered that a young brave had recently killed a wolf, a thing strictly forbidden, since the wolf was the totem animal of the tribe. To make matters worse, the name of the guilty man was Running Wolf. The offence being unpardonable, the man was cursed and driven from the tribe:

"Go out. Wander alone among the woods, and if we see you, we slay you. Your bones shall be scattered in the forest, and your spirit shall not enter the Happy Hunting Grounds till one of another race shall find and bury them."

"Which meant," explained Morton laconically, his only comment on the story, "probably forever."

The Glamour of the Snow

1

Hibbert, always conscious of two worlds, was in this mountain village conscious of three. It lay on the slopes of the Valais Alps, and he had taken a room in the little post office, where he could be at peace to write his book, yet at the same time enjoy the winter sports and find companionship in the hotels when he wanted it.

The three worlds that met and mingled here seemed to his imaginative temperament very obvious, though it is doubtful if another mind less intuitively equipped would have seen them so well-defined. There was the world of tourist English, civilised, quasi-educated, to which he belonged by birth, at any rate; there was the world of peasants to which he felt himself drawn by sympathy—for he loved and admired their toiling, simple life; and there was this other—which he could only call the world of Nature. To this last, however, in virtue of a vehement poetic imagination, and a tumultuous pagan instinct fed by his very blood, he felt that most of him belonged. The others borrowed from it, as it were, for visits. Here, with the soul of Nature, hid his central life.

Between all three was conflict—potential conflict. On the skating-rink each Sunday the tourists regarded the natives as intruders; in the church the peasants plainly questioned: "Why do you come? We are here to worship; you to stare and whisper!" For neither of these two worlds accepted the other.

And neither did Nature accept the tourists, for it took advantage of their least mistakes, and indeed, even of the peasant-world "accepted" only those who were strong and bold enough to invade her savage domain with sufficient skill to protect themselves from several forms of—death.

Now Hibbert was keenly aware of this potential conflict and want of harmony; he felt outside, yet caught by it—torn in the three direc-

101

tions because he was partly of each world, but wholly in only one. There grew in him a constant, subtle effort—or, at least, desire—to unify them and decide positively to which he should belong and live in. The attempt, of course, was largely subconscious. It was the natural instinct of a richly imaginative nature seeking the point of equilibrium, so that the mind could feel at peace and his brain be free to do good work.

Among the guests no one especially claimed his interest. The men were nice but undistinguished—athletic schoolmasters, doctors snatching a holiday, good fellows all; the women, equally various—the clever, the would-be-fast, the dare-to-be-dull, the women "who understood," and the usual pack of jolly dancing girls and "flappers." And Hibbert, with his forty odd years of thick experience behind him, got on well with the lot; he understood them all; they belonged to definite, pre-digested types that are the same the world over, and that he had met the world over long ago.

But to none of them did he belong. His nature was too "multiple" to subscribe to the set of shibboleths of any one class. And, since all liked him, and felt that somehow, he seemed outside of them—spectator, looker-on—all sought to claim him.

In a sense, therefore, the three worlds fought for him: natives, tourists, Nature. . . .

It was thus began the singular conflict for the soul of Hibbert. *In his own soul*, however, it took place. Neither the peasants nor the tourists were conscious that they fought for anything. And Nature, they say, is merely blind and automatic.

The assault upon him of the peasants may be left out of account, for it is obvious that they stood no chance of success. The tourist world, however, made a gallant effort to subdue him to themselves. But the evenings in the hotel, when dancing was not in order, were—English. The provincial imagination was set upon a throne and worshipped heavily through incense of the stupidest conventions possible. Hibbert used to go back early to his room in the post office to work.

"It is a mistake on my part to have *realised* that there is any conflict at all," he thought, as he crunched home over the snow at midnight after one of the dances.

"It would have been better to have kept outside it all and done my work. Better," he added, looking back down the silent village street to the church tower, "and—safer."

The adjective slipped from his mind before he was aware of it. He turned with an involuntary start and looked about him. He knew perfectly well what it meant—this thought that had thrust its head up from the instinctive region. He understood, without being able to express it fully, the meaning that betrayed itself in the choice of the adjective. For if he had ignored the existence of this conflict he would at the same time, have remained outside the arena. Whereas now he had entered the lists. Now this battle for his soul must have issue. And he knew that the spell of Nature was greater for him than all other spells in the world combined—greater than love, revelry, pleasure, greater even than study. He had always been afraid to let himself go. His pagan soul dreaded her terrific powers of witchery even while he worshipped.

The little village already slept. The world lay smothered in snow. The chalet roofs shone white beneath the moon, and pitch-black shadows gathered against the walls of the church. His eye rested a moment on the square stone tower with its frosted cross that pointed to the sky: then travelled with a leap of many thousand feet to the enormous mountains that brushed the brilliant stars. Like a forest rose the huge peaks above the slumbering village, measuring the night and heavens.

They beckoned him. And something born of the snowy desolation, born of the midnight and the silent grandeur, born of the great listening hollows of the night, something that lay 'twixt terror and wonder, dropped from the vast wintry spaces down into his heart—and called him. Very softly, unrecorded in any word or thought his brain could compass, it laid its spell upon him. Fingers of snow brushed the surface of his heart. The power and quiet majesty of the winter's night appalled him. . . .

Fumbling a moment with the big unwieldy key, he let himself in and went upstairs to bed. Two thoughts went with him—apparently quite ordinary and sensible ones:

"What fools these peasants are to sleep through such a night!" And the other:

"Those dances tire me. I'll never go again. My work only suffers in the morning." The claims of peasants and tourists upon him seemed thus in a single instant weakened.

The clash of battle troubled half his dreams. Nature had sent her Beauty of the Night and won the first assault. The others, routed and dismayed, fled far away.

2

"Don't go back to your dreary old post office. We're going to have supper in my room—something hot. Come and join us. Hurry up!"

There had been an ice carnival, and the last party, tailing up the snow-slope to the hotel, called him. The Chinese lanterns smoked and sputtered on the wires; the band had long since gone. The cold was bitter and the moon came only momentarily between high, driving clouds. From the shed where the people changed from skates to snow-boots he shouted something to the effect that he was "following"; but no answer came; the moving shadows of those who had called were already merged high up against the village darkness. The voices died away. Doors slammed. Hibbert found himself alone on the deserted rink.

And it was then, quite suddenly, the impulse came to—stay and skate alone. The thought of the stuffy hotel room, and of those noisy people with their obvious jokes and laughter, oppressed him. He felt a longing to be alone with the night; to taste her wonder all by himself there beneath the stars, gliding over the ice. It was not yet midnight, and he could skate for half an hour. That supper party, if they noticed his absence at all, would merely think he had changed his mind and gone to bed.

It was an impulse, yes, and not an unnatural one; yet even at the time it struck him that something more than impulse lay concealed behind it. More than invitation, yet certainly less than command, there was a vague queer feeling that he stayed because he had to, almost as though there was something he had forgotten, overlooked, left undone. Imaginative temperaments are often thus; and impulse is ever weakness. For with such ill-considered opening of the doors to hasty action may come an invasion of other forces at the same time—forces merely waiting their opportunity perhaps!

He caught the fugitive warning even while he dismissed it as absurd, and the next minute he was whirling over the smooth ice in delightful curves and loops beneath the moon. There was no fear of collision. He could take his own speed and space as he willed. The shadows of the towering mountains fell across the rink, and a wind of ice came from the forests, where the snow lay ten feet deep. The hotel lights winked and went out. The village slept. The high wire netting could not keep out the wonder of the winter night that grew about him like a presence. He skated on and on, keen exhilarating pleasure in his tingling blood, and weariness all forgotten.

And then, midway in the delight of rushing movement, he saw a figure gliding behind the wire netting, watching him. With a start that almost made him lose his balance—for the abruptness of the new arrival was so unlooked for—he paused and stared. Although the light was dim, he made out that it was the figure of a woman and that she was feeling her way along the netting, trying to get in. Against the white background of the snow-field he watched her rather stealthy efforts as she passed with a silent step over the banked-up snow. She was tall and slim and graceful; he could see that even in the dark. And then, of course, he understood.

It was another adventurous skater like himself, stolen down unawares from hotel or chalet, and searching for the opening. At once, making a sign and pointing with one hand, he turned swiftly and skated over to the little entrance on the other side.

But even before he got there, there was a sound on the ice behind him and, with an exclamation of amazement he could not suppress, he turned to see her swerving up to his side across the width of the rink. She had somehow found another way in.

Hibbert, as a rule, was punctilious, and in these free-and-easy places, perhaps, especially so. If only for his own protection he did not seek to make advances unless some kind of introduction paved the way. But for these two to skate together in the semi-darkness without speech, often of necessity brushing shoulders almost, was too absurd to think of. Accordingly, he raised his cap and spoke. His actual words he seems unable to recall, nor what the girl said in reply, except that she answered him in accented English with some commonplace about doing figures at midnight on an empty rink. Quite natural it was, and right. She wore grey clothes of some kind, though not the customary long gloves or sweater, for indeed her hands were bare, and presently when he skated with her, he wondered with something like astonishment at their dry and icy coldness.

And she was delicious to skate with—supple, sure, and light, fast as a man yet with the freedom of a child, sinuous and steady at the same time. Her flexibility made him wonder, and when he asked where she had learned she murmured—he caught the breath against his ear and recalled later that it was singularly cold—that she could hardly tell, for she had been accustomed to the ice ever since she could remember.

But her face he never properly saw. A muffler of white fur buried her neck to the ears, and her cap came over the eyes. He only saw that she was young. Nor could he gather her hotel or chalet, for she pointed vaguely, when he asked her, up the slopes. "Just over there—" she said, quickly taking his hand again. He did not press her; no doubt she wished to hide her escapade. And the touch of her hand thrilled him more than anything he could remember; even through his thick glove he felt the softness of that cold and delicate softness.

The clouds thickened over the mountains. It grew darker. They talked very little, and did not always skate together. Often, they separated, curving about in corners by themselves, but always coming together again in the centre of the rink; and when she left him thus Hibbert was conscious of—yes, of missing her. He found a peculiar satisfaction, almost a fascination, in skating by her side. It was quite an adventure—these two strangers with the ice and snow and night!

Midnight had long since sounded from the old church tower before they parted. She gave the sign, and he skated quickly to the shed, meaning to find a seat and help her take her skates off. Yet when he turned—she had already gone. He saw her slim figure gliding away across the snow ... and hurrying for the last time round the rink alone he searched in vain for the opening she had twice used in this curious way.

"How very queer!" he thought, referring to the wire netting. "She must have lifted it and wriggled under ...!"

Wondering how in the world she managed it, what in the world had possessed him to be so free with her, and who in the world she was, he went up the steep slope to the post office and so to bed, her promise to come again another night still ringing delightfully in his ears. And curious were the thoughts and sensations that accompanied him. Most of all, perhaps, was the half suggestion of some dim memory that he had known this girl before, had met her somewhere, more—that she knew him. For in her voice—a low, soft, windy little voice it was, tender and soothing for all its quiet coldness—there lay some faint reminder of two others he had known, both long since gone: the voice of the woman he had loved, and—the voice of his mother.

But this time through his dreams there ran no clash of battle. He was conscious, rather, of something cold and clinging that made him think of sifting snowflakes climbing slowly with entangling touch and thickness round his feet. The snow, coming without noise, each flake so light and tiny none can mark the spot whereon it settles, yet the mass of it able to smother whole villages, wove through the very texture of his mind—cold, bewildering, deadening effort with its clinging network of ten million feathery touches.

3

In the morning Hibbert realised he had done, perhaps, a foolish thing. The brilliant sunshine that drenched the valley made him see this, and the sight of his work-table with its typewriter, books, papers, and the rest, brought additional conviction. To have skated with a girl alone at midnight, no matter how innocently the thing had come about, was unwise—unfair, especially to her. Gossip in these little winter resorts was worse than in a provincial town. He hoped no one had seen them. Luckily the night had been dark. Most likely none had heard the ring of skates.

Deciding that in future he would be more careful, he plunged into work, and sought to dismiss the matter from his mind.

But in his times of leisure the memory returned persistently to haunt him. When he "skied," "luged," or danced in the evenings, and especially when he skated on the little rink, he was aware that the eyes of his mind forever sought this strange companion of the night. A hundred times he fancied that he saw her, but always sight deceived him. Her face he might not know, but he could hardly fail to recognise her figure. Yet nowhere among the others did he catch a glimpse of that slim young creature he had skated with alone beneath the clouded stars. He searched in vain.

Even his inquiries as to the occupants of the private chalets brought no results. He had lost her. But the queer thing was that he felt as though she were somewhere close; he *knew* she had not really gone. While people came and left with every day, it never once occurred to him that she had left. On the contrary, he felt assured that they would meet again.

This thought he never quite acknowledged. Perhaps it was the wish that fathered it only. And, even when he did meet her, it was a question how he would speak and claim acquaintance, or whether *she* would recognise himself. It might be awkward. He almost came to dread a meeting, though "dread," of course, was far too strong a word to describe an emotion that was half delight, half wondering anticipation.

Meanwhile the season was in full swing. Hibbert felt in perfect health, worked hard, skied, skated, luged, and at night danced fairly often—in spite of his decision. This dancing was, however, an act of subconscious surrender; it really meant he hoped to find her among the whirling couples. He was searching for her without quite acknowledging it to himself; and the hotel-world, meanwhile, thinking it had won him over, teased and chaffed him. He made excuses in a similar vein; but all the time he watched and searched and—waited.

For several days the sky held clear and bright and frosty, bitterly cold, everything crisp and sparkling in the sun; but there was no sign of fresh snow, and the skiers began to grumble. On the mountains was an icy crust that made "running" dangerous; they wanted the frozen, dry, and powdery snow that makes for speed, renders steering easier and falling less severe. But the keen east wind showed no signs of changing for a whole ten days. Then, suddenly, there came a touch of softer air and the weather-wise began to prophesy.

Hibbert, who was delicately sensitive to the least change in earth or sky, was perhaps the first to feel it. Only he did not prophesy. He knew through every nerve in his body that moisture had crept into the air, was accumulating, and that presently a fall would come. For he responded to the moods of Nature like a fine barometer.

And the knowledge, this time, brought into his heart a strange little wayward emotion that was hard to account for—a feeling of unexplained uneasiness and disquieting joy. For behind it, woven through it rather, ran a faint exhilaration that connected remotely somewhere with that touch of delicious alarm, that tiny anticipating "dread," that so puzzled him when he thought of his next meeting with his skating companion of the night. It lay beyond all words, all telling, this queer relationship between the two; but somehow the girl and snow ran in a pair across his mind.

Perhaps for imaginative writing-men, more than for other workers, the smallest change of mood betrays itself at once. His work at any rate revealed this slight shifting of emotional values in his soul. Not that his writing suffered, but that it altered, subtly as those changes of sky or sea or landscape that come with the passing of afternoon into evening—imperceptibly. A subconscious excitement sought to push outwards and express itself . . . and, knowing the uneven effect such moods produced in his work, he laid his pen aside and took instead to reading that he had to do.

Meanwhile the brilliance passed from the sunshine, the sky grew slowly overcast; by dusk the mountain tops came singularly close and sharp; the distant valley rose into absurdly near perspective. The moisture increased, rapidly approaching saturation point, when it must fall in snow. Hibbert watched and waited.

And in the morning the world lay smothered beneath its fresh white carpet. It snowed heavily till noon, thickly, incessantly, chokingly, a foot or more; then the sky cleared, the sun came out in splendour, the wind shifted back to the east, and frost came down upon the mountains with its keenest and most biting tooth. The drop in the temperature was tremendous, but the skiers were jubilant. Next day the "running" would be fast and perfect. Already the mass was settling, and the surface freezing into those moss-like, powdery crystals that make the ski run almost of their own accord with the faint "sishing" as of a bird's wings through the air.

4

That night there was excitement in the little hotel-world, first because there was a *bal* costume, but chiefly because the new snow had come. And Hibbert went—felt drawn to go; he did not go in costume, but he wanted to talk about the slopes and skiing with the other men, and at the same time....

Ah, there was the truth, the deeper necessity that called. For the singular connection between the stranger and the snow again betrayed itself, utterly beyond explanation as before, but vital and insistent. Some hidden instinct in his pagan soul—heaven knows how he phrased it even to himself, if he phrased it at all—whispered that with the snow the girl would be somewhere about, would emerge from her hiding place, would even look for him.

Absolutely unwarranted it was. He laughed while he stood before the little glass and trimmed his moustache, tried to make his black tie sit straight, and shook down his dinner jacket so that it should lie upon the shoulders without a crease. His brown eyes were very bright. "I look younger than I usually do," he thought. It was unusual, even significant, in a man who had no vanity about his appearance and certainly never questioned his age or tried to look younger than he was. Affairs of the heart, with one tumultuous exception that left no fuel for lesser subsequent fires, had never troubled him.

The forces of his soul and mind not called upon for "work" and obvious duties, all went to Nature. The desolate, wild places of the earth were what he loved; night, and the beauty of the stars and snow. And this evening he felt their claims upon him mightily stirring. A rising wildness caught his blood, quickened his pulse, woke longing and passion too. But chiefly snow. The snow whirred softly through his thoughts like white, seductive dreams. . . . For the snow had come;

109

and She, it seemed, had somehow come with it—into his mind.

And yet he stood before that twisted mirror and pulled his tie and coat askew a dozen times, as though it mattered. "What in the world is up with me?" he thought. Then, laughing a little, he turned before leaving the room to put his private papers in order. The green morocco desk that held them he took down from the shelf and laid upon the table. Tied to the lid was the visiting card with his brother's London address "in case of accident." On the way down to the hotel he wondered why he had done this, for though imaginative, he was not the kind of man who dealt in presentiments. Moods with him were strong, but ever held in leash.

"It's almost like a warning," he thought, smiling. He drew his thick coat tightly round the throat as the freezing air bit at him. "Those warnings one reads of in stories sometimes . . .!"

A delicious happiness was in his blood. Over the edge of the hills across the valley rose the moon. He saw her silver sheet the world of snow. Snow covered all. It smothered sound and distance. It smothered houses, streets, and human beings. It smothered—life.

5

In the hall there was light and bustle; people were already arriving from the other hotels and chalets, their costumes hidden beneath many wraps. Groups of men in evening dress stood about smoking, talking "snow" and "skiing." The band was tuning up. The claims of the hotel-world clashed about him faintly as of old. At the big glass windows of the verandah, peasants stopped a moment on their way home from the *café* to peer. Hibbert thought laughingly of that conflict he used to imagine. He laughed because it suddenly seemed so unreal. He belonged so utterly to Nature and the mountains, and especially to those desolate slopes where now the snow lay thick and fresh and sweet, that there was no question of a conflict at all.

The power of the newly fallen snow had caught him, proving it without effort. Out there, upon those lonely reaches of the moonlit ridges, the snow lay ready—masses and masses of it—cool, soft, inviting. He longed for it. It awaited him. He thought of the intoxicating delight of skiing in the moonlight....

Thus, somehow, in vivid flashing vision, he thought of it while he stood there smoking with the other men and talking all the "shop" of skiing.

And, ever mysteriously blended with this power of the snow,

poured also through his inner being the power of the girl. He could not disabuse his mind of the insinuating presence of the two together. He remembered that queer skating-impulse of ten days ago, the impulse that had let her in. That any mind, even an imaginative one, could pass beneath the sway of such a fancy was strange enough; and Hibbert, while fully aware of the disorder, yet found a curious joy in yielding to it. This insubordinate centre that drew him towards old pagan beliefs had assumed command. With a kind of sensuous pleasure, he let himself be conquered.

And snow that night seemed in everybody's thoughts. The dancing couples talked of it; the hotel proprietors congratulated one another; it meant good sport and satisfied their guests; everyone was planning trips and expeditions, talking of slopes and telemarks, of flying speed and distance, of drifts and crust and frost. Vitality and enthusiasm pulsed in the very air; all were alert and active, positive, radiating currents of creative life even into the stuffy atmosphere of that crowded ball-room. And the snow had caused it, the snow had brought it; all this discharge of eager sparkling energy was due primarily to the—Snow.

But in the mind of Hibbert, by some swift alchemy of his pagan yearnings, this energy became transmuted. It rarefied itself, gleaming in white and crystal currents of passionate anticipation, which he transferred, as by a species of electrical imagination, into the personality of the girl—the Girl of the Snow. She somewhere was waiting for him, expecting him, calling to him softly from those leagues of moonlit mountain. He remembered the touch of that cool, dry hand; the soft and icy breath against his cheek; the hush and softness of her presence in the way she came and the way she had gone again—like a flurry of snow the wind sent gliding up the slopes.

She, like himself, belonged out there. He fancied that he heard her little windy voice come sifting to him through the snowy branches of the trees, calling his name . . . that haunting little voice that dived straight to the centre of his life as once, long years ago, two other voices used to do. . . .

But nowhere among the costumed dancers did he see her slender figure. He danced with one and all, distrait and absent, a stupid partner as each girl discovered, his eyes ever turning towards the door and windows, hoping to catch the luring face, the vision that did not come . . . and at length, hoping even against hope. For the ball-room thinned; groups left one by one, going home to their hotels and chalets; the band tired obviously; people sat drinking lemon-squashes at the little tables, the men mopping their foreheads, everybody ready for bed.

It was close on midnight. As Hibbert passed through the hall to get his overcoat and snow-boots, he saw men in the passage by the "sport-room," greasing their ski against an early start. Knapsack luncheons were being ordered by the kitchen swing doors. He sighed. Lighting a cigarette, a friend offered him, he returned a confused reply to some question as to whether he could join their party in the morning. It seemed he did not hear it properly. He passed through the outer vestibule between the double glass doors, and went into the night.

The man who asked the question watched him go, an expression of anxiety momentarily in his eyes.

"Don't think he heard you," said another, laughing. "You've got to shout to Hibbert, his mind's so full of his work."

"He works too hard," suggested the first, "full of queer ideas and dreams."

But Hibbert's silence was not rudeness. He had not caught the invitation, that was all. The call of the hotel-world had faded. He no longer heard it. Another wilder call was sounding in his ears.

For up the street he had seen a little figure moving. Close against the shadows of the baker's shop it glided—white, slim, enticing.

6

And at once into his mind passed the hush and softness of the snow—yet with it a searching, crying wildness for the heights. He knew by some incalculable, swift instinct she would not meet him in the village street. It was not there, amid crowding houses, she would speak to him. Indeed, already she had disappeared, melted from view up the white vista of the moonlit road. Yonder, he divined, she waited where the highway narrowed abruptly into the mountain path beyond the chalets.

It did not even occur to him to hesitate; mad though it seemed, and was—this sudden craving for the heights with her, at least for open spaces where the snow lay thick and fresh—it was too imperious to be denied. He does not remember going up to his room, putting the sweater over his evening clothes, and getting into the fur gauntlet gloves and the helmet cap of wool. Most certainly he has no recollection of fastening on his ski; he must have done it automatically. Some faculty of normal observation was in abeyance, as it were. His mind was out beyond the village—out with the snowy mountains and the moon.

Henri Défago, putting up the shutters over his *café* windows, saw him pass, and wondered mildly: "*Un monsieur qui fait du ski à cette heure! Il est Anglais, donc . . .!*" He shrugged his shoulders, as though a man had the right to choose his own way of death. And Marthe Perotti, the hunchback wife of the shoemaker, looking by chance from her window, caught his figure moving swiftly up the road. She had other thoughts, for she knew and believed the old traditions of the witches and snow-beings that steal the souls of men. She had even heard, 'twas said, the dreaded "synagogue" pass roaring down the street at night, and now, as then, she hid her eyes. "They've called to him ... and he must go," she murmured, making the sign of the cross.

But no one sought to stop him. Hibbert recalls only a single incident until he found himself beyond the houses, searching for her along the fringe of forest where the moonlight met the snow in a bewildering frieze of fantastic shadows. And the incident was simply this—that he remembered passing the church. Catching the outline of its tower against the stars, he was aware of a faint sense of hesitation. A vague uneasiness came and went—jarred unpleasantly across the flow of his excited feelings, chilling exhilaration. He caught the instant's discord, dismissed it, and—passed on. The seduction of the snow smothered the hint before he realised that it had brushed the skirts of warning.

And then he saw her. She stood there waiting in a little clear space of shining snow, dressed all in white, part of the moonlight and the glistening background, her slender figure just discernible.

"I waited, for I knew you would come," the silvery little voice of windy beauty floated down to him. "You *had* to come."

"I'm ready," he answered, "I knew it too."

The world of Nature caught him to its heart in those few words—the wonder and the glory of the night and snow. Life leaped within him. The passion of his pagan soul exulted, rose in joy, flowed out to her. He neither reflected nor considered, but let himself go like the veriest schoolboy in the wildness of first love.

"Give me your hand," he cried, "I'm coming . . .!"

"A little farther on, a little higher," came her delicious answer. "Here it is too near the village—and the church."

And the words seemed wholly right and natural; he did not dream of questioning them; he understood that, with this little touch of civilisation in sight, the familiarity he suggested was impossible. Once out upon the open mountains, 'mid the freedom of huge slopes and towering peaks, the stars and moon to witness and the wilderness of snow to watch, they could taste an innocence of happy intercourse free from the dead conventions that imprison literal minds.

He urged his pace, yet did not quite overtake her. The girl kept always just a little bit ahead of his best efforts. . . . And soon they left the trees behind and passed on to the enormous slopes of the sea of snow that rolled in mountainous terror and beauty to the stars. The wonder of the white world caught him away. Under the steady moonlight it was more than haunting. It was a living, white, bewildering power that deliciously confused the senses and laid a spell of wild perplexity upon the heart. It was a personality that cloaked, and yet revealed, itself through all this sheeted whiteness of snow. It rose, went with him, fled before, and followed after. Slowly it dropped lithe, gleaming arms about his neck, gathering him in. . . .

Certainly, some soft persuasion coaxed his very soul, urging him ever forwards, upwards, on towards the higher icy slopes. Judgment and reason left their throne, it seemed, completely, as in the madness of intoxication. The girl, slim and seductive, kept always just ahead, so that he never quite came up with her. He saw the white enchantment of her face and figure, something that streamed about her neck flying like a wreath of snow in the wind, and heard the alluring accents of her whispering voice that called from time to time: "A little farther on, a little higher. . . . Then we'll run home together!"

Sometimes he saw her hand stretched out to find his own, but each time, just as he came up with her, he saw her still in front, the hand and arm withdrawn. They took a gentle angle of ascent. The toil seemed nothing. In this crystal, wine-like air fatigue vanished. The sishing of the ski through the powdery surface of the snow was the only sound that broke the stillness; this, with his breathing and the rustle of her skirts, was all he heard. Cold moonshine, snow, and silence held the world. The sky was black, and the peaks beyond cut into it like frosted wedges of iron and steel. Far below the valley slept, the village long since hidden out of sight. He felt that he could never tire. . . . The sound of the church clock rose from time to time faintly through the air—more and more distant.

"Give me your hand. It's time now to turn back."

"Just one more slope," she laughed. "That ridge above us. Then we'll make for home." And her low voice mingled pleasantly with the purring of their ski. His own seemed harsh and ugly by comparison.

"But I have never come so high before. It's glorious! This world of silent snow and moonlight—and *you*. You're a child of the snow, I swear. Let me come up—closer—to see your face—and touch your little hand."

Her laughter answered him.

"Come on! A little higher. Here we're quite alone together."

"It's magnificent," he cried. "But why did you hide away so long? I've looked and searched for you in vain ever since we skated—" he was going to say "ten days ago," but the accurate memory of time had gone from him; he was not sure whether it was days or years or minutes. His thoughts of earth were scattered and confused.

"You looked for me in the wrong places," he heard her murmur just above him. "You looked in places where I never go. Hotels and houses kill me. I avoid them." She laughed—a fine, shrill, windy little laugh.

"I loathe them too—"

He stopped. The girl had suddenly come quite close. A breath of ice passed through his very soul. She had touched him.

"But this awful cold!" he cried out, sharply, "this freezing cold that takes me. The wind is rising; it's a wind of ice. Come, let us turn . . .!"

But when he plunged forward to hold her, or at least to look, the girl was gone again. And something in the way she stood there a few feet beyond, and stared down into his eyes so steadfastly in silence, made him shiver. The moonlight was behind her, but in some odd way he could not focus sight upon her face, although so close. The gleam of eyes he caught, but all the rest seemed white and snowy as though he looked beyond her—out into space. . . .

The sound of the church bell came up faintly from the valley far below, and he counted the strokes—five. A sudden, curious weakness seized him as he listened. Deep within it was, deadly yet somehow sweet, and hard to resist. He felt like sinking down upon the snow and lying there. . . . They had been climbing for five hours. . . . It was, of course, the warning of complete exhaustion.

With a great effort he fought and overcame it. It passed away as suddenly as it came.

"We'll turn," he said with a decision he hardly felt. "It will be dawn before we reach the village again. Come at once. It's time for home."

The sense of exhilaration had utterly left him. An emotion that was akin to fear swept coldly through him. But her whispering answer turned it instantly to terror—a terror that gripped him horribly and turned him weak and unresisting.

"Our home is—*here!*" A burst of wild, high laughter, loud and shrill, accompanied the words. It was like a whistling wind. The wind *had* risen, and clouds obscured the moon. "A little higher—where we cannot hear the wicked bells," she cried, and for the first time seized him deliberately by the hand. She moved, was suddenly close against his face. Again, she touched him.

And Hibbert tried to turn away in escape, and so trying, found for the first time that the power of the snow—that other power which does not exhilarate but deadens effort—was upon him. The suffocating weakness that it brings to exhausted men, luring them to the sleep of death in her clinging soft embrace, lulling the will and conquering all desire for life—this was awfully upon him. His feet were heavy and entangled. He could not turn or move.

The girl stood in front of him, very near; he felt her chilly breath upon his cheeks; her hair passed blindingly across his eyes; and that icy wind came with her. He saw her whiteness close; again, it seemed, his sight passed through her into space as though she had no face. Her arms were round his neck. She drew him softly downwards to his knees. He sank; he yielded utterly; he obeyed. Her weight was upon him, smothering, delicious. The snow was to his waist.... She kissed him softly on the lips, the eyes, all over his face. And then she spoke his name in that voice of love and wonder, the voice that held the accent of two others—both taken over long ago by Death—the voice of his mother, and of the woman he had loved.

He made one more feeble effort to resist. Then, realising even while he struggled that this soft weight about his heart was sweeter than anything life could ever bring, he let his muscles relax, and sank back into the soft oblivion of the covering snow. Her wintry kisses bore him into sleep.

7

They say that men who know the sleep of exhaustion in the snow find no awakening on the hither side of death.... The hours passed and the moon sank down below the white world's rim. Then, suddenly, there came a little crash upon his breast and neck, and Hibbert—woke.

He slowly turned bewildered, heavy eyes upon the desolate mountains, stared dizzily about him, tried to rise. At first his muscles would not act; a numbing, aching pain possessed him. He uttered a long, thin cry for help, and heard its faintness swallowed by the wind. And then he understood vaguely why he was only warm—not dead. For this very wind that took his cry had built up a sheltering mound of driven snow against his body while he slept. Like a curving wave it ran beside him. It was the breaking of its over-toppling edge that caused the crash, and the coldness of the mass against his neck that woke him.

Dawn kissed the eastern sky; pale gleams of gold shot every peak with splendour; but ice was in the air, and the dry and frozen snow blew like powder from the surface of the slopes. He saw the points of his ski projecting just below him. Then he—remembered. It seems he had just strength enough to realise that, could he but rise and stand, he might fly with terrific impetus towards the woods and village far beneath. The ski would carry him. But if he failed and fell . . .!

How he contrived it Hibbert never knew; this fear of death somehow called out his whole available reserve force. He rose slowly, balanced a moment, then, taking the angle of an immense zigzag, started down the awful slopes like an arrow from a bow. And automatically the splendid muscles of the practised skier and athlete saved and guided him, for he was hardly conscious of controlling either speed or direction. The snow stung face and eyes like fine steel shot; ridge after ridge flew past; the summits raced across the sky; the valley leaped up with bounds to meet him. He scarcely felt the ground beneath his feet as the huge slopes and distance melted before the lightning speed of that descent from death to life.

He took it in four mile-long zigzags, and it was the turning at each corner that nearly finished him, for then the strain of balancing taxed to the verge of collapse the remnants of his strength.

Slopes that have taken hours to climb can be descended in a short half-hour on ski, but Hibbert had lost all count of time. Quite other thoughts and feelings mastered him in that wild, swift dropping through the air that was like the flight of a bird. For ever close upon his heels came following forms and voices with the whirling snow-dust. He heard that little silvery voice of death and laughter at his back. Shrill and wild, with the whistling of the wind past his ears, he caught its pursuing tones; but in anger now, no longer soft and coaxing. And it was accompanied; she did not follow alone. It seemed a host of these flying figures of the snow chased madly just behind him. He felt them furiously smite his neck and cheeks, snatch at his hands and try to entangle his feet and ski in drifts. His eyes they blinded, and they caught his breath away.

The terror of the heights and snow and winter desolation urged him forward in the maddest race with death a human being ever knew; and so terrific was the speed that before the gold and crimson had left the summits to touch the ice-lips of the lower glaciers, he saw the friendly forest far beneath swing up and welcome him.

And it was then, moving slowly along the edge of the woods, he saw a light. A man was carrying it. A procession of human figures was passing in a dark line laboriously through the snow. And—he heard the sound of chanting.

Instinctively, without a second's hesitation, he changed his course. No longer flying at an angle as before, he pointed his ski straight down the mountain-side. The dreadful steepness did not frighten him. He knew full well it meant a crashing tumble at the bottom, but he also knew it meant a doubling of his speed—with safety at the end. For, though no definite thought passed through his mind, he understood that it was the village *curé* who carried that little gleaming lantern in the dawn, and that he was taking the Host to a chalet on the lower slopes—to some peasant *in extremis*. He remembered her terror of the church and bells. She feared the holy symbols.

There was one last wild cry in his ears as he started, a shriek of the wind before his face, and a rush of stinging snow against closed eyelids—and then he dropped through empty space. Speed took sight from him. It seemed he flew off the surface of the world.

★★★★★★★★★★

Indistinctly he recalls the murmur of men's voices, the touch of strong arms that lifted him, and the shooting pains as the ski were unfastened from the twisted ankle . . . for when he opened his eyes again to normal life, he found himself lying in his bed at the post office with the doctor at his side. But for years to come the story of "mad Hibbert's" skiing at night is recounted in that mountain village. He went, it seems, up slopes, and to a height that no man in his senses ever tried before. The tourists were agog about it for the rest of the season, and the very same day two of the bolder men went over the actual ground and photographed the slopes. Later Hibbert saw these photographs. He noticed one curious thing about them—though he did not mention it to any one:

There was only a single track.

The Empty Sleeve

1

The Gilmer brothers were a couple of fussy and pernickety old bachelors of a rather retiring, not to say timid, disposition. There was grey in the pointed beard of John, the elder, and if any hair had remained to William it would also certainly have been of the same shade. They had private means. Their main interest in life was the collection of violins, for which they had the instinctive *flair* of true connoisseurs. Neither John nor William, however, could play a single note. They could only pluck the open strings. The production of tone, so necessary before purchase, was done vicariously for them by another.

The only objection they had to the big building in which they occupied the roomy top floor was that Morgan, liftman and caretaker, insisted on wearing a billycock with his uniform after six o'clock in the evening, with a result disastrous to the beauty of the universe. For "Mr. Morgan," as they called him between themselves, had a round and pasty face on the top of a round and conical body. In view, however, of the man's other rare qualities—including his devotion to themselves—this objection was not serious.

He had another peculiarity that amused them. On being found fault with, he explained nothing, but merely repeated the words of the complaint.

"Water in the bath wasn't really hot this morning, Morgan!"

"Water in the bath not reely 'ot, wasn't it, sir?"

Or, from William, who was something of a faddist:

"My jar of sour milk came up late yesterday, Morgan."

"Your jar sour milk come up late, sir, yesterday?"

Since, however, the statement of a complaint invariably resulted in its remedy, the brothers had learned to look for no further explanation. Next morning the bath *was* hot, the sour milk *was* "brortup" punctually. The uniform and billycock hat, though, remained an eyesore and source of oppression.

On this particular night John Gilmer, the elder, returning from a Masonic rehearsal, stepped into the lift and found Mr. Morgan with his hand ready on the iron rope.

"Fog's very thick outside," said Mr. John pleasantly; and the lift was a third of the way up before Morgan had completed his customary repetition: "Fog very thick outside, yes, sir." And Gilmer then asked casually if his brother were alone, and received the reply that Mr. Hyman had called and had not yet gone away.

Now this Mr. Hyman was a Hebrew, and, like themselves, a connoisseur in violins, but, unlike themselves, who only kept their specimens to look at, he was a skilful and exquisite player. He was the only person they ever permitted to handle their pedigree instruments, to take them from the glass cases where they reposed in silent splendour, and to draw the sound out of their wondrous painted hearts of golden varnish. The brothers loathed to see his fingers touch them, yet loved to hear their singing voices in the room, for the latter confirmed their sound judgment as collectors, and made them certain their money had been well spent. Hyman, however, made no attempt to conceal his contempt and hatred for the mere collector. The atmosphere of the room fairly pulsed with these opposing forces of silent emotion when Hyman played and the Gilmers, alternately writhing and admiring, listened. The occasions, however, were not frequent. The Hebrew only came by invitation, and both brothers made a point of being in. It was a very formal proceeding—something of a sacred rite almost.

John Gilmer, therefore, was considerably surprised by the information Morgan had supplied. For one thing, Hyman, he had understood, was away on the Continent.

"Still in there, you say?" he repeated, after a moment's reflection.

"Still in there, Mr. John, sir." Then, concealing his surprise from the liftman, he fell back upon his usual mild habit of complaining about the billycock hat and the uniform.

"You really should try and remember, Morgan," he said, though kindly. "That hat does *not* go well with that uniform!"

Morgan's pasty countenance betrayed no vestige of expression. "'At don't go well with the yewniform, sir," he repeated, hanging up the disreputable bowler and replacing it with a gold-braided cap from the peg. "No, sir, it don't, do it?" he added cryptically, smiling at the transformation thus effected.

And the lift then halted with an abrupt jerk at the top floor. By somebody's carelessness the landing was in darkness, and, to make things worse, Morgan, clumsily pulling the iron rope, happened to knock the billycock from its peg so that his sleeve, as he stooped to catch it, struck the switch and plunged the scene in a moment's complete obscurity.

And it was then, in the act of stepping out before the light was turned on again, that John Gilmer stumbled against something that shot along the landing past the open door. First, he thought it must be a child, then a man, then—an animal. Its movement was rapid yet stealthy. Starting backwards instinctively to allow it room to pass, Gilmer collided in the darkness with Morgan, and Morgan incontinently screamed. There was a moment of stupid confusion. The heavy framework of the lift shook a little, as though something had stepped into it and then as quickly jumped out again. A rushing sound followed that resembled footsteps, yet at the same time was more like gliding—someone in soft slippers or stockinged feet, greatly hurrying. Then came silence again. Morgan sprang to the landing and turned up the electric light. Mr. Gilmer, at the same moment, did likewise to the switch in the lift. Light flooded the scene. Nothing was visible.

"Dog or cat, or something, I suppose, wasn't it?" exclaimed Gilmer, following the man out and looking round with bewildered amazement upon a deserted landing. He knew quite well, even while he spoke, that the words were foolish.

"Dog or cat, yes, sir, or—something," echoed Morgan, his eyes narrowed to pin-points, then growing large, but his face stolid.

"The light should have been on." Mr. Gilmer spoke with a touch of severity. The little occurrence had curiously disturbed his equanimity. He felt annoyed, upset, uneasy.

For a perceptible pause the liftman made no reply, and his employer, looking up, saw that, besides being flustered, he was white about the jaws. His voice, when he spoke, was without its normal assurance. This time he did not merely repeat. He explained.

"The light *was* on, sir, when last *I* come up!" he said, with emphasis, obviously speaking the truth. "Only a moment ago," he added.

Mr. Gilmer, for some reason, felt disinclined to press for explanations. He decided to ignore the matter.

Then the lift plunged down again into the depths like a diving-bell into water; and John Gilmer, pausing a moment first to reflect, let himself in softly with his latch-key, and, after hanging up hat and coat in the hall, entered the big sitting-room he and his brother shared in common.

The December fog that covered London like a dirty blanket had penetrated, he saw, into the room. The objects in it were half shrouded in the familiar yellowish haze.

2

In dressing-gown and slippers, William Gilmer, almost invisible in his armchair by the gas-stove across the room, spoke at once. Through the thick atmosphere his face gleamed, showing an extinguished pipe hanging from his lips. His tone of voice conveyed emotion, an emotion he sought to suppress, of a quality, however, not easy to define.

"Hyman's been here," he announced abruptly. "You must have met him. He's this very instant gone out."

It was quite easy to see that something had happened, for "scenes" leave disturbance behind them in the atmosphere. But John made no immediate reference to this. He replied that he had seen no one—which was strictly true—and his brother thereupon, sitting bolt upright in the chair, turned quickly and faced him. His skin, in the foggy air, seemed paler than before.

"That's odd," he said nervously.

"What's odd?" asked John.

"That you didn't see—anything. You ought to have run into one another on the doorstep." His eyes went peering about the room. He was distinctly ill at ease. "You're positive you saw no one? Did Morgan take him down before you came? Did Morgan see him?" He asked several questions at once.

"On the contrary, Morgan told me he was still here with you. Hyman probably walked down, and didn't take the lift at all," he replied. "That accounts for neither of us seeing him." He decided to say nothing about the occurrence in the lift, for his brother's nerves, he saw plainly, were on edge.

William then stood up out of his chair, and the skin of his face changed its hue, for whereas a moment ago it was merely pale, it had now altered to a tint that lay somewhere between white and a livid grey. The man was fighting internal terror. For a moment these two brothers of middle age looked each other straight in the eye. Then John spoke:

"What's wrong, Billy?" he asked quietly. "Something's upset you. What brought Hyman in this way—unexpectedly? I thought he was still in Germany."

The brothers, affectionate and sympathetic, understood one another perfectly. They had no secrets. Yet for several minutes the younger one made no reply. It seemed difficult to choose his words apparently.

"Hyman played, I suppose—on the fiddles?" John helped him, wondering uneasily what was coming. He did not care much for the individual in question, though his talent was of such great use to them.

The other nodded in the affirmative, then plunged into rapid speech, talking under his breath as though he feared someone might overhear. Glancing over his shoulder down the foggy room, he drew his brother close.

"Hyman came," he began, "unexpectedly. He hadn't written, and I hadn't asked him. You hadn't either, I suppose?"

John shook his head.

"When I came in from the dining-room I found him in the passage. The servant was taking away the dishes, and he had let himself in while the front door was ajar. Pretty cool, wasn't it?"

"He's an original," said John, shrugging his shoulders. "And you welcomed him?" he asked.

"I asked him in, of course. He explained he had something glorious for me to hear. Silenski had played it in the afternoon, and he had bought the music since. But Silenski's 'Strad' hadn't the power—it's thin on the upper strings, you remember, unequal, patchy—and he said no instrument in the world could do it justice but our 'Joseph'—the small Guarnerius, you know, which he swears is the most perfect in the world."

"And what was it? Did he play it?" asked John, growing more uneasy as he grew more interested. With relief he glanced round and saw the matchless little instrument lying there safe and sound in its glass case near the door.

"He played it—divinely: a Zigeuner Lullaby, a fine, passionate, rushing bit of inspiration, oddly misnamed 'lullaby.' And, fancy, the fellow had memorised it already! He walked about the room on tiptoe while he played it, complaining of the light——"

"Complaining of the light?"

"Said the thing was crepuscular, and needed dusk for its full effect. I turned the lights out one by one, till finally there was only the glow of the gas logs. He insisted. You know that way he has with him? And then he got over me in another matter: insisted on using some special strings he had brought with him, and put them on, too, himself—thicker than the A and E *we* use."

For though neither Gilmer could produce a note, it was their pride that they kept their precious instruments in perfect condition for playing, choosing the exact thickness and quality of strings that suited the temperament of each violin; and the little Guarnerius in question always "sang" best, they held, with thin strings.

"Infernal insolence," exclaimed the listening brother, wondering what was coming next. "Played it well, though, didn't he, this Lullaby thing?" he added, seeing that William hesitated. As he spoke, he went nearer, sitting down close beside him in a leather chair.

"Magnificent! Pure fire of genius!" was the reply with enthusiasm, the voice at the same time dropping lower. "Staccato like a silver hammer; harmonics like flutes, clear, soft, ringing; and the tone—well, the G string was a baritone, and the upper registers creamy and mellow as a boy's voice. John," he added, "that Guarnerius is the very pick of the period and"—again he hesitated—"Hyman loves it. He'd give his soul to have it."

The more John heard, the more uncomfortable it made him. He had always disliked this gifted Hebrew, for in his secret heart he knew that he had always feared and distrusted him. Sometimes he had felt half afraid of him; the man's very forcible personality was too insistent to be pleasant. His type was of the dark and sinister kind, and he possessed a violent will that rarely failed of accomplishing its desire.

"Wish I'd heard the fellow play," he said at length, ignoring his brother's last remark, and going on to speak of the most matter-of-fact details he could think of. "Did he use the Dodd bow, or the Tourte? That Dodd I picked up last month, you know, is the most perfectly balanced I have ever——"

He stopped abruptly, for William had suddenly got upon his feet and was standing there, searching the room with his eyes. A chill ran down John's spine as he watched him.

"What is it, Billy?" he asked sharply. "Hear anything?"

William continued to peer about him through the thick air.

"Oh, nothing, probably," he said, an odd catch in his voice; "only—— I keep feeling as if there was somebody listening. Do you think, perhaps"—he glanced over his shoulder—"there is someone at the door? I wish—I wish you'd have a look, John."

John obeyed, though without great eagerness. Crossing the room slowly, he opened the door, then switched on the light. The passage leading past the bathroom towards the bedrooms beyond was empty. The coats hung motionless from their pegs.

"No one, of course," he said, as he closed the door and came back to the stove. He left the light burning in the passage. It was curious the way both brothers had this impression that they were not alone, though only one of them spoke of it.

"Used the Dodd or the Tourte, Billy—which?" continued John in the most natural voice he could assume.

But at that very same instant the water started to his eyes. His brother, he saw, was close upon the thing he really had to tell. But he had stuck fast.

3

By a great effort John Gilmer composed himself and remained in his chair. With detailed elaboration he lit a cigarette, staring hard at his brother over the flaring match while he did so. There he sat in his dressing-gown and slippers by the fireplace, eyes downcast, fingers playing idly with the red tassel. The electric light cast heavy shadows across the face. In a flash then, since emotion may sometimes express itself in attitude even better than in speech, the elder brother understood that Billy was about to tell him an unutterable thing.

By instinct he moved over to his side so that the same view of the room confronted him.

"Out with it, old man," he said, with an effort to be natural. "Tell me what you saw."

Billy shuffled slowly round and the two sat side by side, facing the fog-draped chamber.

"It was like this," he began softly, "only I was standing instead of sitting, looking over to that door as you and I do now. Hyman moved to and fro in the faint glow of the gas logs against the far wall, playing that 'crepuscular' thing in his most inspired sort of way, so that the music seemed to issue from himself rather than from the shining bit of wood under his chin, when—I noticed something coming over me that was"—he hesitated, searching for words—"that wasn't *all* due to the music," he finished abruptly.

"His personality put a bit of hypnotism on you, eh?"

William shrugged his shoulders.

"The air was thickish with fog and the light was dim, cast upwards upon him from the stove," he continued. "I admit all that. But there wasn't light enough to throw shadows, you see, and——"

"Hyman looked queer?" the other helped him quickly.

Billy nodded his head without turning.

"Changed there before my very eyes"—he whispered it—"turned animal——"

"Animal?" John felt his hair rising.

"That's the only way I can put it. His face and hands and body turned otherwise than usual. I lost the sound of his feet. When the bow-hand or the fingers on the strings passed into the light, they were"—he uttered a soft, shuddering little laugh—"furry, oddly divided, the fingers massed together. And he paced stealthily. I thought every instant the fiddle would drop with a crash and he would spring at me across the room."

"My dear chap——"

"He moved with those big, lithe, striding steps one sees"—John held his breath in the little pause, listening keenly—"one sees those big brutes make in the cages when their desire is aflame for food or escape, or—or fierce, passionate desire for anything they want with their whole nature——"

"The big felines!" John whistled softly.

"And every minute getting nearer and nearer to the door, as though he meant to make a sudden rush for it and get out."

"With the violin! Of course, you stopped him?"

"In the end. But for a long time, I swear to you, I found it difficult to know what to do, even to move. I couldn't get my voice for words of any kind; it was like a spell."

"It *was* a spell," suggested John firmly.

"Then, as he moved, still playing," continued the other, "he seemed to grow smaller; to shrink down below the line of the gas. I thought I should lose sight of him altogether. I turned the light up suddenly. There he was over by the door—crouching."

"Playing on his knees, you mean?"

William closed his eyes in an effort to visualize it again.

"Crouching," he repeated, at length, "close to the floor. At least, I think so. It all happened so quickly, and I felt so bewildered, it was hard to see straight. But at first, I could have sworn he was half his natural size. I called to him, I think I swore at him—I forget exactly, but I know he straightened up at once and stood before me down there in the light"—he pointed across the room to the door—"eyes gleaming, face white as chalk, perspiring like midsummer, and gradually filling out, straightening up, whatever you like to call it, to his natural size and appearance again. It was the most horrid thing I've ever seen."

"As an—animal, you saw him still?"

126

"No; human again. Only much smaller."

"What did he say?"

Billy reflected a moment.

"Nothing that I can remember," he replied. "You see, it was all over in a few seconds. In the full light, I felt so foolish, and nonplussed at first. To see him normal again baffled me. And, before I could collect myself, he had let himself out into the passage, and I heard the front door slam. A minute later—the same second almost, it seemed—you came in. I only remember grabbing the violin and getting it back safely under the glass case. The strings were still vibrating."

The account was over. John asked no further questions. Nor did he say a single word about the lift, Morgan, or the extinguished light on the landing. There fell a longish silence between the two men; and then, while they helped themselves to a generous supply of whisky-and-soda before going to bed, John looked up and spoke:

"If you agree, Billy," he said quietly, "I think I might write and suggest to Hyman that we shall no longer have need for his services."

And Billy, acquiescing, added a sentence that expressed something of the singular dread lying but half concealed in the atmosphere of the room, if not in their minds as well:

"Putting it, however, in a way that need not offend him."

"Of course. There's no need to be rude, is there?"

Accordingly, next morning the letter was written; and John, saying nothing to his brother, took it round himself by hand to the Hebrew's rooms near Euston. The answer he dreaded was forthcoming:

"Mr. Hyman's still away abroad," he was told. "But we're forwarding letters; yes. Or I can give you 'is address if you'll prefer it." The letter went, therefore, to the number in Königstrasse, Munich, thus obtained.

Then, on his way back from the insurance company where he went to increase the sum that protected the small Guarnerius from loss by fire, accident, or theft, John Gilmer called at the offices of certain musical agents and ascertained that Silenski, the violinist, was performing at the time in Munich. It was only some days later, though, by diligent inquiry, he made certain that at a concert on a certain date the famous *virtuoso* had played a Zigeuner Lullaby of his own composition—the very date, it turned out, on which he himself had been to the Masonic rehearsal at Mark Masons' Hall.

John, however, said nothing of these discoveries to his brother William.

4

It was about a week later when a reply to the letter came from
Munich—a letter couched in somewhat offensive terms, though it
contained neither words nor phrases that could actually be found fault
with. Isidore Hyman was hurt and angry. On his return to London a
month or so later, he proposed to call and talk the matter over. The
offensive part of the letter lay, perhaps, in his definite assumption that
he could persuade the brothers to resume the old relations. John, however, wrote a brief reply to the effect that they had decided to buy no
new fiddles; their collection being complete, there would be no occasion for them to invite his services as a performer. This was final. No
answer came, and the matter seemed to drop. Never for one moment,
though, did it leave the consciousness of John Gilmer. Hyman had said
that he would come, and come assuredly he would. He secretly gave
Morgan instructions that he and his brother for the future were always
"out" when the Hebrew presented himself.

"He must have gone back to Germany, you see, almost at once after his visit here that night," observed William—John, however, making no reply.

One night towards the middle of January the two brothers came
home together from a concert in Queen's Hall, and sat up later than
usual in their sitting-room discussing over their whisky and tobacco
the merits of the pieces and performers. It must have been past one
o'clock when they turned out the lights in the passage and retired
to bed. The air was still and frosty; moonlight over the roofs—one
of those sharp and dry winter nights that now seem to visit London
rarely.

"Like the old-fashioned days when we were boys," remarked William, pausing a moment by the passage window and looking out across
the miles of silvery, sparkling roofs.

"Yes," added John; "the ponds freezing hard in the fields, rime on
the nursery windows, and the sound of a horse's hoofs coming down
the road in the distance, eh?" They smiled at the memory, then said
good night, and separated. Their rooms were at opposite ends of the
corridor; in between were the bathroom, dining-room, and sitting-
room. It was a long, straggling flat. Half an hour later both brothers
were sound asleep, the flat silent, only a dull murmur rising from the
great city outside, and the moon sinking slowly to the level of the
chimneys.

Perhaps two hours passed, perhaps three, when John Gilmer, sitting up in bed with a start, wide-awake and frightened, knew that some-one was moving about in one of the three rooms that lay between him and his brother. He had absolutely no idea why he should have been frightened, for there was no dream or nightmare-memory that he brought over from unconsciousness, and yet he realized plainly that the fear he felt was by no means a foolish and unreasoning fear. It had a cause and a reason. Also—which made it worse—it was fully war-ranted. Something in his sleep, forgotten in the instant of waking, had happened that set every nerve in his body on the watch. He was posi-tive only of two things—first, that it was the entrance of this person, moving so quietly there in the flat, that sent the chills down his spine; and, secondly, that this person was *not* his brother William.

John Gilmer was a timid man. The sight of a burglar, his eyes black-masked, suddenly confronting him in the passage, would most likely have deprived him of all power of decision—until the burglar had either shot him or escaped. But on this occasion some instinct told him that it was no burglar, and that the acute distress he experienced was not due to any message of ordinary physical fear. The thing that had gained access to his flat while he slept had first come—he felt sure of it—into his room, and had passed very close to his own bed, before going on. It had then doubtless gone to his brother's room, visiting them both stealthily to make sure they slept. And its mere passage through his room had been enough to wake him and set these drops of cold perspiration upon his skin. For it was—he felt it in every fibre of his body—something hostile.

The thought that it might at that very moment be in the room of his brother, however, brought him to his feet on the cold floor, and set him moving with all the determination he could summon towards the door. He looked cautiously down an utterly dark passage; then crept on tiptoe along it. On the wall were old-fashioned weapons that had belonged to his father; and feeling a curved, sheathless sword that had come from some Turkish campaign of years gone by, his fingers closed tightly round it, and lifted it silently from the three hooks whereon it lay. He passed the doors of the bathroom and dining-room, making instinctively for the big sitting-room where the violins were kept in their glass cases. The cold nipped him. His eyes smarted with the effort to see in the darkness. Outside the closed door he hesitated.

Putting his ear to the crack, he listened. From within came a faint sound of someone moving. The same instant there rose the sharp, deli-cate "ping" of a violin-string being plucked; and John Gilmer, with nerves that shook like the vibrations of that very string, opened the door wide with a fling and turned on the light at the same moment. The plucked string still echoed faintly in the air.

The sensation that met him on the threshold was the well-known one that things had been going on in the room which his unexpected arrival had that instant put a stop to. A second earlier and he would have discovered it all in the act. The atmosphere still held the feeling of rushing, silent movement with which the things had raced back to their normal, motionless positions. The immobility of the furniture was a mere attitude hurriedly assumed, and the moment his back was turned the whole business, whatever it might be, would begin again. With this presentment of the room, however—a purely imaginative one—came another, swiftly on its heels.

For one of the objects, less swift than the rest, had not quite regained its "attitude" of repose. It still moved. Below the window curtains on the right, not far from the shelf that bore the violins in their glass cases, he made it out, slowly gliding along the floor. Then, even as his eye caught it, it came to rest.

And, while the cold perspiration broke out all over him afresh, he knew that this still moving item was the cause both of his waking and of his terror. This was the disturbance whose presence he had divined in the flat without actual hearing, and whose passage through his room, while he yet slept, had touched every nerve in his body as with ice. Clutching his Turkish sword tightly, he drew back with the utmost caution against the wall and watched, for the singular impression came to him that the movement was not that of a human being crouching, but rather of something that pertained to the animal world. He remembered, flash-like, the movements of reptiles, the stealth of the larger felines, the undulating glide of great snakes. For the moment, however, it did not move, and they faced one another.

The other side of the room was but dimly lighted, and the noise he made clicking up another electric lamp brought the thing flying forward again—towards himself. At such a moment it seemed absurd to think of so small a detail, but he remembered his bare feet, and, genuinely frightened, he leaped upon a chair and swished with his sword through the air about him. From this better point of view, with the increased light to aid him, he then saw two things—first, that the glass case usually covering the Guarnerius violin had been shifted; and, secondly, that the moving object was slowly elongating itself into an upright position. Semi-erect, yet most oddly, too, like a creature on its hind legs, it was coming swiftly towards him. It was making for the door—and escape.

The confusion of ghostly fear was somehow upon him so that he was too bewildered to see clearly, but he had sufficient self-control, it seemed, to recover a certain power of action; for the moment the advancing figure was near enough for him to strike, that curved scimitar flashed and whirred about him, with such misdirected violence, however, that he not only failed to strike it even once, but at the same time lost his balance and fell forward from the chair whereon he perched—straight into it.

And then came the most curious thing of all, for as he dropped, the figure also dropped, stooped low down, crouched, dwindled amazingly in size, and rushed past him close to the ground like an animal on all fours. John Gilmer screamed, for he could no longer contain himself. Stumbling over the chair as he turned to follow, cutting and slashing wildly with his sword, he saw halfway down the darkened corridor beyond the scuttling outline of, apparently, an enormous—cat!

The door into the outer landing was somehow ajar, and the next second the beast was out, but not before the steel had fallen with a crashing blow upon the front disappearing leg, almost severing it from the body.

It was dreadful. Turning up the lights as he went, he ran after it to the outer landing. But the thing he followed was already well away, and he heard, on the floor below him, the same oddly gliding, slithering, stealthy sound, yet hurrying, that he had heard weeks before when something had passed him in the lift and Morgan, in his terror, had likewise cried aloud.

For a time, he stood there on that dark landing, listening, thinking, trembling; then turned into the flat and shut the door. In the sitting-room he carefully replaced the glass case over the treasured violin, puzzled to the point of foolishness, and strangely routed in his mind. For the violin itself, he saw, had been dragged several inches from its cushioned bed of plush.

Next morning, however, he made no allusion to the occurrence of the night. His brother apparently had not been disturbed.

5

The only thing that called for explanation—an explanation not fully forthcoming—was the curious aspect of Mr. Morgan's countenance. The fact that this individual gave notice to the owners of the building, and at the end of the month left for a new post, was, of course, known to both brothers; whereas the story he told in explanation of his face was known only to the one who questioned him about it—John. And John, for reasons best known to himself, did not pass it on to the other. Also, for reasons best known to himself, he did not cross-question the liftman about those singular marks, or report the matter to the police.

Mr. Morgan's pasty visage was badly scratched, and there were red lines running from the cheek into the neck that had the appearance of having been produced by sharp points viciously applied—claws. He had been disturbed by a noise in the hall, he said, about three in the morning, a scuffle had ensued in the darkness, but the intruder had got clear away....

"A cat or something of the kind, no doubt," suggested John Gilmer at the end of the brief recital. And Morgan replied in his usual way: "A cat, or something of the kind, Mr. John, no doubt."

All the same, he had not cared to risk a second encounter, but had departed to wear his billycock and uniform in a building less haunted.

Hyman, meanwhile, made no attempt to call and talk over his dismissal. The reason for this was only apparent, however, several months later when, quite by chance, coming along Piccadilly in an omnibus, the brothers found themselves seated opposite to a man with a thick black beard and blue glasses. William Gilmer hastily rang the bell and got out, saying something half intelligible about feeling faint. John followed him.

"Did you see who it was?" he whispered to his brother the moment they were safely on the pavement.

John nodded.

"Hyman, in spectacles. He's grown a beard, too."

"Yes, but did you also notice——"

"What?"

"He had an empty sleeve."

"An empty sleeve?"

"Yes," said William; "he's lost an arm."

There was a long pause before John spoke. At the door of their club the elder brother added:

"Poor devil! He'll never again play on"—then, suddenly changing the preposition—"*with* a pedigree violin!"

And that night in the flat, after William had gone to bed, he looked up a curious old volume he had once picked up on a second-hand bookstall, and read therein quaint descriptions of how the "desire-body of a violent man" may assume animal shape, operate on concrete matter even at a distance; and, further, how a wound inflicted thereon can reproduce itself upon its physical counterpart by means of the mysterious so-called phenomenon of "repercussion."

The Olive

He laughed involuntarily as the olive rolled towards his chair across the shiny parquet floor of the hotel dining-room.

His table in the cavernous *salle manger* was apart: he sat alone, a solitary guest; the table from which the olive fell and rolled towards him was some distance away. The angle, however, made him an unlikely objective. Yet the lob-sided, juicy thing, after hesitating once or twice *en route* as it plopped along, came to rest finally against his feet.

It settled with an inviting, almost an aggressive air. And he stooped and picked it up, putting it rather self-consciously, because of the girl from whose table it had come, on the white tablecloth beside his plate.

Then, looking up, he caught her eye, and saw that she too was laughing, though not a bit self-consciously. As she helped herself to the *hors d'oeuvres* a false move had sent it flying. She watched him pick the olive up and set it beside his plate. Her eyes then suddenly looked away again—at her mother—questioningly.

The incident was closed. But the little oblong, succulent olive lay beside his plate, so that his fingers played with it. He fingered it automatically from time to time until his lonely meal was finished.

When no one was looking he slipped it into his pocket, as though, having taken the trouble to pick it up, this was the very least he could do with it. Heaven alone knows why, but he then took it upstairs with him, setting it on the marble mantelpiece among his field glasses, tobacco tins, ink-bottles, pipes and candlestick. At any rate, he kept it—the moist, shiny, lob-sided, juicy little oblong olive. The hotel lounge wearied him; he came to his room after dinner to smoke at his ease, his coat off and his feet on a chair; to read another chapter of Freud, to write a letter or two he didn't in the least want to write, and then go to bed at ten o'clock.

But this evening the olive kept rolling between him and the thing he read; it rolled between the paragraphs, between the lines; the ol-

135

ive was more vital than the interest of these eternal "complexes" and "suppressed desires."

The truth was that he kept seeing the eyes of the laughing girl beyond the bouncing olive. She had smiled at him in such a natural, spontaneous, friendly way before her mother's glance had checked her—a smile, he felt, that might lead to acquaintance on the morrow.

He wondered! A thrill of possible adventure ran through him.

She was a merry-looking sort of girl, with a happy, half-roguish face that seemed on the lookout for somebody to play with. Her mother, like most of the people in the big hotel, was an invalid; the girl, a dutiful and patient daughter. They had arrived that very day apparently. A laugh is a revealing thing, he thought as he fell asleep to dream of a lob-sided olive rolling consciously towards him, and of a girl's eyes that watched its awkward movements, then looked up into his own and laughed. In his dream the olive had been deliberately and cleverly dispatched upon its uncertain journey. It was a message.

He did not know, of course, that the mother, chiding her daughter's awkwardness, had muttered:

"There you are again, child! True to your name, you never see an olive without doing something queer and odd with it!"

A youngish man, whose knowledge of chemistry, including invisible inks and such-like mysteries, had proved so valuable to the Censor's Department that for five years he had overworked without a holiday, the Italian Riviera had attracted him, and he had come out for a two months' rest. It was his first visit. Sun, mimosa, blue seas and brilliant skies had tempted him; exchange made a pound worth forty, fifty, sixty and seventy shillings. He found the place lovely, but somewhat untenanted.

Having chosen at random, he had come to a spot where the companionship he hoped to find did not exist. The place languished after the war, slow to recover; the colony of resident English was scattered still; travellers preferred the coast of France with Mentone and Monte Carlo to enliven them. The country, moreover, was distracted by strikes. The electric light failed one week, letters the next, and as soon as the electricians and postal-workers resumed, the railways stopped running. Few visitors came, and the few who came soon left.

He stayed on, however, caught by the sunshine and the good exchange, also without the physical energy to discover a better, livelier place. He went for walks among the olive groves, he sat beside the sea and palms, he visited shops and bought things he did not want because the exchange made them seem cheap, he paid immense "extras" in his weekly bill, then chuckled as he reduced them to shillings and found that a few pence covered them; he lay with a book for hours among the olive groves.

The olive groves! His daily life could not escape the olive groves; to olive groves, sooner or later, his walks, his expeditions, his meanderings by the sea, his shopping—all led him to these ubiquitous olive groves.

If he bought a picture postcard to send home, there was sure to be an olive grove in one corner of it. The whole place was smothered with olive groves, the people owed their incomes and existence to these irrepressible trees. The villages among the hills swam roof-deep in them. They swarmed even in the hotel gardens.

The guide books praised them as persistently as the residents brought them, sooner or later, into every conversation. They grew lyrical over them:

"And how do you like our olive trees? Ah, you think them pretty. At first, most people are disappointed. They grow on one."

"They do," he agreed.

"I'm glad you appreciate them. I find them the embodiment of grace. And when the wind lifts the under-leaves across a whole mountain slope—why, it's wonderful, isn't it? One realises the meaning of 'olive-green'."

"One does," he sighed. "But all the same I should like to get one to eat—an olive, I mean."

"Ah, to eat, yes. That's not so easy. You see, the crop is—"

"Exactly," he interrupted impatiently, weary of the habitual and evasive explanations. "But I should like to taste the fruit. I should like to enjoy one."

For, after a stay of six weeks, he had never once seen an olive on the table, in the shops, nor even on the street barrows at the market place. He had never tasted one. No one sold olives, though olive trees were a drug in the place; no one bought them, no one asked for them; it seemed that no one wanted them. The trees, when he looked closely, were thick with a dark little berry that seemed more like a sour sloe than the succulent, delicious spicy fruit associated with its name.

Men climbed the trunks, everywhere shaking the laden branches and hitting them with long bamboo poles to knock the fruit off, while women and children, squatting on their haunches, spent laborious hours filling baskets underneath, then loading mules and donkeys with their daily "catch." But an olive to eat was unobtainable. He had never cared for olives, but now he craved with all his soul to feel his teeth in one.

"*Ach!* But it is the Spanish olive that you *eat*," explained the head waiter, a German "from Basel." "These are for oil only." After which he disliked the olive more than ever—until that night when he saw the first eatable specimen rolling across the shiny parquet floor, propelled towards him by the careless hand of a pretty girl, who then looked up into his eyes and smiled.

He was convinced that Eve, similarly, had rolled the apple towards Adam across the emerald sward of the first garden in the world.

He slept usually like the dead. It must have been something very real that made him open his eyes and sit up in bed alertly. There was a noise against his door. He listened. The room was still quite dark. It was early morning. The noise was not repeated.

"Who's there?" he asked in a sleepy whisper. "What is it?"

The noise came again. Someone was scratching on the door. No, it was somebody tapping.

"What do you want?" he demanded in a louder voice. "Come in," he added, wondering sleepily whether he was presentable. Either the hotel was on fire or the porter was waking the wrong person for some sunrise expedition.

Nothing happened. Wide awake now, he turned the switch on, but no light flooded the room. The electricians, he remembered with a curse, were out on strike. He fumbled for the matches, and as he did so a voice in the corridor became distinctly audible. It was just outside his door.

"Aren't you ready?" he heard. "You sleep for ever."

And the voice, although never having heard it before, he could not have recognised it, belonged, he knew suddenly, to the girl who had let the olive fall. In an instant he was out of bed. He lit a candle.

"I'm coming," he called softly, as he slipped rapidly into some clothes. "I'm sorry I've kept you. I shan't be a minute."

"Be quick then!" he heard, while the candle flame slowly grew, and he found his garments. Less than three minutes later he opened the door and, candle in hand, peered into the dark passage.

"Blow it out!" came a peremptory whisper. He obeyed, but not quick enough. A pair of red lips emerged from the shadows. There was a puff, and the candle was extinguished. "I've got my reputation to consider. We mustn't be seen, of course!"

The face vanished in the darkness, but he had recognised it—the shining skin, the bright glancing eyes. The sweet breath touched his cheek. The candlestick was taken from him by a swift, deft movement. He heard it knock the wainscoting as it was set down. He went out into a pitch-black corridor, where a soft hand seized his own and led him—by a back door, it seemed—out into the open air of the hill-side immediately behind the hotel.

He saw the stars. The morning was cool and fragrant, the sharp air waked him, and the last vestiges of sleep went flying. He had been drowsy and confused, had obeyed the summons without thinking. He now realised suddenly that he was engaged in an act of madness.

The girl, dressed in some flimsy material thrown loosely about her head and body, stood a few feet away, looking, he thought, like some figure called out of dreams and slumber of a forgotten world, out of legend almost. He saw her evening shoes peep out; he divined an evening dress beneath the gauzy covering. The light wind blew it close against her figure. He thought of a nymph.

"I say—but haven't you been to bed?" he asked stupidly. He had meant to expostulate, to apologise for his foolish rashness, to scold and say they must go back at once. Instead, this sentence came. He guessed she had been sitting up all night. He stood still a second, staring in mute admiration, his eyes full of bewildered question.

"Watching the stars," she met his thought with a happy laugh. "Orion has touched the horizon. I came for you at once. We've got just four hours!" The voice, the smile, the eyes, the reference to Orion, swept him off his feet. Something in him broke loose, and flew wildly, recklessly to the stars.

"Let us be off!" he cried, "before the Bear tilts down. Already Alcyone begins to fade. I'm ready. Come!"

She laughed. The wind blew the gauze aside to show two ivory white limbs. She caught his hand again, and they scampered together up the steep hillside towards the woods. Soon the big hotel, the villas, the white houses of the little town where natives and visitors still lay soundly sleeping, were out of sight. The farther sky came down to meet them. The stars were paling, but no sign of actual dawn was yet visible. The freshness stung their cheeks.

Slowly, the heavens grew lighter, the east turned rose, the outline of the trees defined themselves, there was a stirring of the silvery green leaves. They were among olive groves—but the spirits of the trees were dancing. Far below them, a pool of deep colour, they saw the ancient sea. They saw the tiny specks of distant fishing-boats. The sailors were singing to the dawn, and birds among the mimosa of the hanging gardens answered them.

Pausing a moment at length beneath a gaunt old tree, whose struggle to leave the clinging earth had tortured its great writhing arms and trunk, they took their breath, gazing at one another with eyes full of happy dreams.

"You understood so quickly," said the girl, "my little message. I knew by your eyes and ears you would." And she first tweaked his ears with two slender fingers mischievously, then laid her soft palm with a momentary light pressure on both eyes.

"You're half-and-half, at any rate," she added, looking him up and down for a swift instant of appraisement, "if you're not altogether." The laughter showed her white, even little teeth.

"You know how to play, and that's something," she added. Then, as if to herself, "You'll be altogether before I've done with you."

"Shall I?" he stammered, afraid to look at her.

Puzzled, some spirit of compromise still lingering in him, he knew not what she meant; he knew only that the current of life flowed increasingly through his veins, but that her eyes confused him.

"I'm longing for it," he added. "How wonderfully you did it! They roll so awkwardly——"

"Oh, that!" She peered at him through a wisp of hair. "You've kept it, I hope."

"Rather. It's on my mantelpiece——"

"You're sure you haven't eaten it?" and she made a delicious mimicry with her red lips, so that he saw the tip of a small pointed tongue.

"I shall keep it," he swore, "as long as these arms have life in them," and he seized her just as she was crouching to escape, and covered her with kisses.

"I knew you longed to play," she panted, when he released her. "Still, it was sweet of you to pick it up before another got it."

"Another!" he exclaimed.

"The gods decide. It's a lob-sided thing, remember. It can't roll straight." She looked oddly mischievous, elusive.

He stared at her.

"If it had rolled elsewhere—and another had picked it up——?" he began.

"I should be with that other now!" And this time she was off and away before he could prevent her, and the sound of her silvery laughter mocked him among the olive trees beyond. He was up and after her in a second, following her slim whiteness in and out of the old-world grove, as she flitted lightly, her hair flying in the wind, her figure flashing like a ray of sunlight or the race of foaming water—till at last he caught her and drew her down upon his knees, and kissed her wildly, forgetting who and where and what he was.

"Hark!" she whispered breathlessly, one arm close about his neck. "I hear their footsteps. Listen! It is the pipe!"

"The pipe——!" he repeated, conscious of a tiny but delicious shudder.

For a sudden chill ran through him as she said it. He gazed at her. The hair fell loose about her cheeks, flushed and rosy with his hot kisses. Her eyes were bright and wild for all their softness. Her face, turned sideways to him as she listened, wore an extraordinary look that for an instant made his blood run cold. He saw the parted lips, the small white teeth, the slim neck of ivory, the young bosom panting from his tempestuous embrace. Of an unearthly loveliness and bright-ness she seemed to him, yet with this strange, remote expression that touched his soul with sudden terror.

Her face turned slowly.

"Who *are* you?" he whispered. He sprang to his feet without wait-ing for her answer.

He was young and agile; strong, too, with that quick response of muscle they have who keep their bodies well; but he was no match for her. Her speed and agility outclassed his own with ease. She leapt. Before he had moved one leg forward towards escape, she was cling-ing with soft, supple arms and limbs about him, so that he could not free himself, and as her weight bore him downwards to the ground, her lips found his own and kissed them into silence. She lay buried again in his embrace, her hair across his eyes, her heart against his heart, and he forgot his question, forgot his little fear, forgot the very world he knew. . . .

"They come, they come," she cried gaily. "The Dawn is here. Are you ready?"

"I've been ready for five thousand years," he answered, leaping to his feet beside her.

"Altogether!" came upon a sparkling laugh that was like wind among the olive leaves.

Shaking her last gauzy covering from her, she snatched his hand, and they ran forward together to join the dancing throng now crowding up the slope beneath the trees. Their happy singing filled the sky. Decked with vine and ivy, and trailing silvery green branches, they poured in a flood of radiant life along the mountain side. Slowly they melted away into the blue distance of the breaking dawn, and, as the last figure disappeared, the sun came up slowly out of a purple sea.

They came to the place he knew—the deserted earthquake village—and a faint memory stirred in him. He did not actually recall that he had visited it already, had eaten his sandwiches with "hotel friends" beneath its crumbling walls; but there was a dim troubling sense of familiarity—nothing more. The houses still stood, but pigeons lived in them, and weasels, stoats and snakes had their uncertain homes in ancient bedrooms. Not twenty years ago the peasants thronged its narrow streets, through which the dawn now peered and cool wind breathed among dew-laden brambles.

"I know the house," she cried, "the house where we would live!" and raced, a flying form of air and sunlight, into a tumbled cottage that had no roof, no floor or windows. Wild bees had hung a nest against the broken wall.

He followed her. There was sunlight in the room, and there were flowers. Upon a rude, simple table lay a bowl of cream, with eggs and honey and butter close against a home-made loaf. They sank into each other's arms upon a couch of fragrant grass and boughs against the window where wild roses bloomed . . . and the bees flew in and out.

It was Bussana, the so-called earthquake village, because a sudden earthquake had fallen on it one summer morning when all the inhabitants were at church. The crashing roof killed sixty, the tumbling walls another hundred, and the rest had left it where it stood.

"The Church," he said, vaguely remembering the story. "They were at prayer——"

The girl laughed carelessly in his ear, setting his blood in a rush and quiver of delicious joy. He felt himself untamed, wild as the wind and animals. "The true God claimed His own," she whispered. "He came back. Ah, they were not ready—the old priests had seen to that. But he came. They heard his music. Then his tread shook the olive groves, the old ground danced, the hills leapt for joy——"

"And the houses crumbled," he laughed as he pressed her closer to his heart—

"And now we've come back!" she cried merrily. "We've come back to worship and be glad!" She nestled into him, while the sun rose higher.

"I hear them—hark!" she cried, and again leapt, dancing from his side. Again he followed her like wind. Through the broken window they saw the naked fauns and nymphs and satyrs rolling, dancing, shaking their soft hoofs amid the ferns and brambles. Towards the appalling, ruptured church they sped with feet of light and air. A roar of happy song and laughter rose.

"Come!" he cried. "We must go too."

Hand in hand they raced to join the tumbling, dancing throng. She was in his arms and on his back and flung across his shoulders, as he ran. They reached the broken building, its whole roof gone sliding years ago, its walls a-tremble still, its shattered shrines alive with nesting birds.

"Hush!" she whispered in a tone of awe, yet pleasure. "He is there!" She pointed, her bare arm outstretched above the bending heads.

There, in the empty space, where once stood sacred Host and Cup, he sat, filling the niche sublimely and with awful power. His shaggy form, benign yet terrible, rose through the broken stone. The great eyes shone and smiled. The feet were lost in brambles.

"God!" cried a wild, frightened voice yet with deep worship in it—and the old familiar panic came with portentous swiftness. The great Figure rose.

The birds flew screaming, the animals sought holes, the worshippers, laughing and glad a moment ago, rushed tumbling over one another for the doors.

"He goes again! Who called? Who called like that? His feet shake the ground!"

"It is the earthquake!" screamed a woman's shrill accents in ghastly terror.

"Kiss me—one kiss before we forget again. . . !" sighed a laughing, passionate voice against his ear. "Once more your arms, your heart beating on my lips. . . ! You recognised his power. You are now altogether! We shall remember!"

But he woke, with the heavy bedclothes stuffed against his mouth and the wind of early morning sighing mournfully about the hotel walls.

★★★★★★★★★★★★★★★★

"Have they left again—those ladies?" he inquired casually of the head waiter, pointing to the table. "They were here last night at dinner."

"Who do you mean?" replied the man, stupidly, gazing at the spot

143

indicated with a face quite blank. "Last night—at dinner?" He tried to think.

"An English lady, elderly, with—her daughter———" at which moment precisely the girl came in alone. Lunch was over, the room empty. There was a second's difficult pause. It seemed ridiculous not to speak. Their eyes met. The girl blushed furiously.

He was very quick for an Englishman. "I was allowing myself to ask after your mother," he began. "I was afraid"—he glanced at the table laid for one—"she was not well, perhaps?"

"Oh, but that's very kind of you, I'm sure." She smiled. He saw the small white even teeth. . . .

And before three days had passed, he was so deeply in love that he simply couldn't help himself.

"I believe," he said lamely, "this is yours. You dropped it, you know. Er—may I keep it? It's only an olive."

They were, of course, in an olive grove when he asked it, and the sun was setting.

She looked at him, looked him up and down, looked at his ears, his eyes. He felt that in another second her little fingers would slip up and tweak the first, or close the second with a soft pressure———

"Tell me," he begged: "did you dream anything—that first night I saw you?"

She took a quick step backwards. "No," she said, as he followed her more quickly still, "I don't think I did. But," she went on breathlessly as he caught her up, "I knew—from the way you picked it up———"

"Knew what?" he demanded, holding her tightly so that she could not get away again.

"That you were already half and half, but would soon be altogether."

And, as he kissed her, he felt her soft little fingers tweak his ears.

The Call

The incident—story it never was, perhaps—began tamely, almost meanly; it ended upon a note of strange, unearthly wonder that has haunted him ever since. In Headley's memory, at any rate, it stands out as the loveliest, the most amazing thing he ever witnessed. Other emotions, too, contributed to the vividness of the picture. That he had felt jealousy towards his old pal, Arthur Deane, shocked him in the first place; it seemed impossible until it actually happened. But that the jealousy was proved afterwards to have been without a cause shocked him still more. He felt ashamed and miserable.

For him, the actual incident began when he received a note from Mrs. Blondin asking him to the Priory for a weekend, or for longer, if he could manage it.

Captain Arthur Deane, she mentioned, was staying with her at the moment, and a warm welcome awaited him. Iris she did not mention—Iris Manning, the interesting and beautiful girl for whom it was well known he had a considerable weakness. He found a good-sized house party; there was fishing in the little Sussex river, tennis, golf not far away, while two motor cars brought the remoter country across the downs into easy reach. Also, there was a bit of duck shooting for those who cared to wake at 3 a.m. and paddle upstream to the marshes where the birds were feeding.

"Have you brought your gun?" was the first thing Arthur said to him when he arrived. "Like a fool, I left mine in town."

"I hope you haven't," put in Miss Manning; "because if you have I must get up one fine morning at three o'clock." She laughed merrily, and there was an undernote of excitement in the laugh.

Captain Headley showed his surprise. "That you were a Diana had escaped my notice, I'm ashamed to say," he replied lightly. "Yet I've known you some years, haven't I?" He looked straight at her, and the soft yet searching eye, turning from his friend, met his own securely.

She was appraising him, for the hundreth time, and he, for the hundreth time, was thinking how pretty she was, and wondering how long the prettiness would last after marriage.

"I'm not," he heard her answer. "That's just it. But I've promised."

"Rather!" said Arthur gallantly. "And I shall hold you to it," he added still more gallantly—too gallantly, Headley thought. "I couldn't possibly get up at cockcrow without a very special inducement, could I, now? You know me, Dick!"

"Well, anyhow, I've brought my gun," Headley replied evasively, "so you've no excuse, either of you. You'll have to go." And while they were laughing and chattering about it, Mrs. Blondin clinched the matter for them. Provisions were hard to come by; the larder really needed a brace or two of birds; it was the least they could do in return for what she called amusingly her "Armistice hospitality."

"So, I expect you to get up at three," she chaffed them, "and return with your Victory birds."

It was from this preliminary skirmish over the tea-table on the law five minutes after his arrival that Dick Headley realised easily enough the little game in progress. As a man of experience, just on the wrong side of forty, it was not difficult to see the cards each held. He sighed. Had he guessed an intrigue was on foot he would not have come, yet he might have known that wherever his hostess was, there were the vultures gathered together. Matchmaker by choice and instinct, Mrs. Blondin could not help herself. True to her name, she was always balancing on matrimonial tightropes—for others.

Her cards, at any rate, were obvious enough; she had laid them on the table for him. He easily read her hand. The next twenty-four hours confirmed this reading. Having made up her mind that Iris and Arthur were destined for each other, she had grown impatient; they had been ten days together, yet Iris was still free. They were good friends only. With calculation, she, therefore, took a step that must bring things further. She invited Dick Headley, whose weakness for the girl was common knowledge. The card was indicated; she played it. Arthur must come to the point or see another man carry her off. This, at least, she planned, little dreaming that the dark King of Spades would interfere.

Miss Manning's hand also was fairly obvious, for both men were extremely eligible *partis*. She was getting on; one or other was to become her husband before the party broke up. This, in crude language, was certainly in her cards, though, being a nice and charming girl, she might camouflage it cleverly to herself and others. Her eyes, on each man in turn when the shooting expedition was being discussed, revealed her part in the little intrigue clearly enough. It was all, thus far, as commonplace as could be.

But there were two more hands Headley had to read—his own and his friend's; and these, he admitted honestly, were not so easy. To take his own first. It was true he was fond of the girl and had often tried to make up his mind to ask her. Without being conceited, he had good reason to believe his affection was returned and that she would accept him. There was no ecstatic love on either side, for he was no longer a boy of twenty, nor was she unscathed by tempestuous love affairs that had scorched the first bloom from her face and heart. But they understood one another; they were an honest couple; she was tired of flirting; both wanted to marry and settle down. Unless a better man turned up, she probably would say "Yes" without humbug or delay. It was this last reflection that brought him to the final hand he had to read.

Here he was puzzled. Arthur Deane's *rôle* in the teacup strategy, for the first time since they had known one another, seemed strange, uncertain. Why? Because, though paying no attention to the girl openly, he met her clandestinely, unknown to the rest of the house-party, and above all without telling his intimate pal—at three o'clock in the morning.

The house-party was in full swing, with a touch of that wild, reckless gaiety which followed the end of the war: "Let us be happy before a worse thing comes upon us," was in many hearts. After a crowded day they danced till early in the morning, while doubtful weather prevented the early shooting expedition after duck. The third night Headley contrived to disappear early to bed. He lay there thinking. He was puzzled over his friend's *rôle*, over the clandestine meeting in particular. It was the morning before, waking very early, he had been drawn to the window by an unusual sound—the cry of a bird. Was it a bird? In all his experience he had never heard such a curious, half-singing call before. He listened a moment, thinking it must have been a dream, yet with the odd cry still ringing in his ears. It was repeated close beneath his open window, a long, low-pitched cry with three distinct following notes in it.

He sat up in bed and listened hard. No bird that he knew could make such sounds. But it was not repeated a third time, and out of sheer curiosity he went to the window and looked out. Dawn was creeping over the distant downs; he saw their outline in the grey pearly light; he saw the lawn below, stretching down to the little river at the bottom, where a curtain of faint mist hung in the air. And on this lawn, he also saw Arthur Deane—with Iris Manning.

Of course, he reflected, they were going after the duck. He turned to look at his watch; it was three o'clock. The same glance, however, showed him his gun standing in the corner. So, they were going without a gun. A sharp pang of unexpected jealousy shot through him. He was just going to shout out something or other, wishing them good luck, or asking if they had found another gun, perhaps, when a cold touch crept down his spine. The same instant his heart contracted. Deane had followed the girl into the summer-house, which stood on the right. It was *not* the shooting expedition at all. Arthur was meeting her for another purpose. The blood flowed back, filling his head. He felt an eavesdropper, a sneak, a detective; but, for all that, he felt also jealous. And his jealousy seemed chiefly because Arthur had not told him.

Of this, then, he lay thinking in bed on the third night. The following day he had said nothing, but had crossed the corridor and put the gun in his friend's room. Arthur, for his part, had said nothing either. For the first time in their long, long friendship, there lay a secret between them. To Headley the unexpected revelation came with pain.

For something like a quarter of a century these two had been bosom friends; they had camped together, been in the army together, taken their pleasure together, each the full confidant of the other in all the things that go to make up men's lives. Above all, Headley had been the one and only recipient of Arthur's unhappy love story. He knew the girl, knew his friend's deep passion, and also knew his terrible pain when she was lost at sea. Arthur was burnt out, finished, out of the running, so far as marriage was concerned. He was not a man to love a second time. It was a great and poignant tragedy. Headley, as confidant, knew all. But more than that—Arthur, on his side, knew his friend's weakness for Iris Manning, knew that a marriage was still possible and likely between them. They were true as steel to one another, and each man, oddly enough, had once saved the other's life, thus adding to the strength of a great natural tie.

Yet now one of them, feigning innocence by day, even indifference, secretly met his friend's girl by night, and kept the matter to himself. It seemed incredible. With his own eyes Headley had seen him on the lawn, passing in the faint grey light through the mist into the summer-house, where the girl had just preceded him. He had not seen her face, but he had seen the skirt sweep round the corner of the wooden pillar. He had not waited to see them come out again.

So, he now lay wondering what *rôle* his old friend was playing in this little intrigue that their hostess, Mrs. Blondin, helped to stage. And, oddly enough, one minor detail stayed in his mind with a curious vividness. As naturalist, hunter, nature-lover, the cry of that strange bird, with its three mournful notes, perplexed him exceedingly.

A knock came at his door, and the door pushed open before he had time to answer. Deane himself came in.

"Wise man," he exclaimed in an easy tone, "got off to bed. Iris was asking where you were." He sat down on the edge of the mattress, where Headley was lying with a cigarette and an open book he had not read. The old sense of intimacy and comradeship rose in the latter's heart. Doubt and suspicion faded. He prized his great friendship. He met the familiar eyes. "Impossible," he said to himself, "absolutely impossible! He's not playing a game; he's not a rotter!" He pushed over his cigarette case, and Arthur lighted one.

"Done in," he remarked shortly, with the first puff. "Can't stand it anymore. I'm off to town tomorrow."

Headley stared in amazement. "Fed up already?" he asked. "Why, I rather like it. It's quite amusing. What's wrong, old man?"

"This match-making," said Deane bluntly. "Always throwing that girl at my head. If it's not the duck-shooting stunt at 3 a.m., it's something else. She doesn't care for me and I don't care for her. Besides——"

He stopped, and the expression of his face changed suddenly. A sad, quiet look of tender yearning came into his clear brown eyes.

"*You* know, Dick," he went on in a low, half-reverent tone. "I don't want to marry. I never can."

Dick's heart stirred within him. "Mary," he said, understandingly.

The other nodded, as though the memories were still too much for him. "I'm still miserably lonely for her," he said. "Can't help it simply. I feel utterly lost without her. Her memory to me is everything." He looked deep into his pal's eyes. "I'm married to that," he added very firmly.

They pulled their cigarettes a moment in silence. They belonged to the male type that conceals emotion behind schoolboy language.

"It's hard luck," said Headley gently, "rotten luck, old man, I understand." Arthur's head nodded several times in succession as he smoked.

He made no remark for some minutes. Then presently he said, as though it had no particular importance—for thus old friends show frankness to each other—"Besides, anyhow, it's you the girl's dying for, not me. She's blind as a bat, old Blondin. Even when I'm with her—thrust with her by that old matchmaker for my sins—it's you she talks about. All the talk leads up to you and yours. She's devilish fond of you." He paused a moment and looked searchingly into his friend's face. "I say, old man—are you—I mean, do you mean business there? Because—excuse me interfering—but you'd better be careful. She's a good sort, you know, after all."

"Yes, Arthur, I do like her a bit," Dick told him frankly. "But I can't make up my mind quite. You see, it's like this——"

And they talked the matter over as old friends will, until finally Arthur chucked his cigarette into the grate and got up to go. "Dead to the world," he said, with a yawn. "I'm off to bed. Give you a chance, too," he added with a laugh. It was after midnight.

The other turned, as though something had suddenly occurred to him.

"By the bye, Arthur," he said abruptly, "what bird makes this sound? I heard it the other morning. Most extraordinary cry. You know everything that flies. What is it?" And, to the best of his ability, he imitated the strange three-note cry he had heard in the dawn two mornings before.

To his amazement and keen distress, his friend, with a sound like a stifled groan, sat down upon the bed without a word. He seemed startled. His face was white. He stared. He passed a hand, as in pain, across his forehead.

"Do it again," he whispered, in a hushed, nervous voice. "Once again—for me."

And Headley, looking at him, repeated the queer notes, a sudden revulsion of feeling rising through him. "He's fooling me after all," ran in his heart, "my old, old pal——"

There was silence for a full minute. Then Arthur, stammering a bit, said lamely, a certain hush in his voice still: "Where in the world did you hear that—and *when?*"

Dick Headley sat up in bed. He was not going to lose this friendship, which, to him, was more than the love of woman. He must help. His pal was in distress and difficulty. There were circumstances, he realized, that might be too strong for the best man in the world—sometimes. No, by God, he would play the game and help him out!

"Arthur, old chap," he said affectionately, almost tenderly. "I heard it two mornings ago—on the lawn below my window here. It woke me up. I—I went to look. Three in the morning, about."

Arthur amazed him then. He first took another cigarette and lit it steadily. He looked round the room vaguely, avoiding, it seemed, the other's eyes. Then he turned, pain in his face, and gazed straight at him.

"You saw—nothing?" he asked in a louder voice, but a voice that had something very real and true in it. It reminded Headley of the voice he heard when he was fainting from exhaustion, and Arthur had said, "Take it, I tell you. I'm all right," and had passed over the flask, though his own throat and sight and heart were black with thirst. It was a voice that had command in it, a voice that did not lie because it could not—yet did lie and could lie—when occasion warranted.

Headley knew a second's awful struggle.

"Nothing," he answered quietly, after his little pause. "Why?"

For perhaps two minutes his friend hid his face. Then he looked up.

"Only," he whispered, "because that was our secret lover's cry. It seems so strange you heard it and not I. I've felt her so close of late—Mary!"

The white face held very steady, the firm lips did not tremble, but it was evident that the heart knew anguish that was deep and poignant. "We used it to call each other—in the old days. It was our private call. No one else in the world knew it but Mary and myself."

Dick Headley was flabbergasted. He had no time to think, however.

"It's odd you should hear it and not I," his friend repeated. He looked hurt, bewildered, wounded. Then suddenly his face brightened. "I know," he cried suddenly. "You and I are pretty good pals. There's a tie between us and all that. Why, it's tel—telepathy, or whatever they call it. That's what it is."

He got up abruptly. Dick could think of nothing to say but to repeat the other's words. "Of course, of course. That's it," he said, "telepathy." He stared—anywhere but at his pal.

"Night, night!" he heard from the door, and before he could do more than reply in similar vein Arthur was gone.

He lay for a long time, thinking, thinking. He found it all very strange. Arthur in this emotional state was new to him. He turned it over and over. Well, he had known good men behave queerly when wrought up. That recognition of the bird's cry was strange, of course, but—he knew the cry of a bird when he heard it, though he might not know the actual bird. That was no human whistle. Arthur was—inventing. No, that was not possible. He was worked up, then, over something, a bit hysterical perhaps.

It had happened before, though in a milder way, when his heart attacks came on. They affected his nerves and head a little, it seemed. He was a deep sort, Dick remembered. Thought turned and twisted in him, offering various solutions, some absurd, some likely. He was a nervous, high-strung fellow underneath, Arthur was. He remembered that. Also, he remembered, anxiously again, that his heart was not quite sound, though what that had to do with the present tangle he did not see.

Yet it was hardly likely that he would bring in Mary as an invention, an excuse—Mary, the most sacred memory in his life, the deepest, truest, best. He had sworn, anyhow, that Iris Manning meant nothing to him.

Through all his speculations, behind every thought, ran this horrid working jealousy. It poisoned him. It twisted truth. It moved like a wicked snake through mind and heart. Arthur, gripped by his new, absorbing love for Iris Manning, lied. He couldn't believe it, he didn't believe it, he wouldn't believe it—yet jealousy persisted in keeping the idea alive in him. It was a dreadful thought. He fell asleep on it.

But his sleep was uneasy with feverish, unpleasant dreams that rambled on in fragments without coming to conclusion. Then, suddenly, the cry of the strange bird came into his dream. He started, turned over, woke up. The cry still continued. It was not a dream. He jumped out of bed.

The room was grey with early morning, the air fresh and a little chill. The cry came floating over the lawn as before. He looked out, pain clutching at his heart. Two figures stood below, a man and a girl, and the man was Arthur Deane. Yet the light was so dim, the morning being overcast, that had he not expected to see his friend, he would scarcely have recognised the familiar form in that shadowy outline that stood close beside the girl. Nor could he, perhaps, have recognized Iris Manning. Their backs were to him. They moved away, disappearing again into the little summerhouse, and this time—he saw it beyond question—the two were hand in hand. Vague and uncertain as the figures were in the early twilight, he was sure of that.

The first disagreeable sensation of surprise, disgust, anger that sickened him turned quickly, however, into one of another kind altogether. A curious feeling of superstitious dread crept over him, and a shiver ran again along his nerves.

"Hallo, Arthur!" he called from the window. There was no answer. His voice was certainly audible in the summer-house. But no one came. He repeated the call a little louder, waited in vain for thirty seconds, then came, the same moment, to a decision that even surprised himself, for the truth we he could no longer bear the suspense of waiting. He must see his friend at once and have it out with him. He turned and went deliberately down the corridor to Deane's bedroom. He would wait there for his return and know the truth from his own lips. But also, another thought had come—the gun. He had quite forgotten it—the safety-catch was out of order. He had not warned him.

He found the door closed but not locked; opening it cautiously, he went in.

But the unexpectedness of what he saw gave him a genuine shock. He could hardly suppress a cry. Everything in the room was neat and orderly, no sign of disturbance anywhere, and it was not empty. There, in bed, before his very eyes, was Arthur. The clothes were turned back a little; he saw the pyjamas open at the throat; he lay sound asleep, deeply, peacefully asleep.

So surprised, indeed, was Headley that, after staring a moment, almost unable to believe his sight, he then put out a hand and touched him gently, cautiously on the forehead. But Arthur did not stir or wake; his breathing remained deep and regular. He lay sleeping like a baby.

Headley glanced round the room, noticed the gun in the corner where he himself had put it the day before, and then went out, closing the door behind him softly.

Arthur Deane, however, did not leave for London as he had intended, because he felt unwell and kept to his room upstairs. It was only a slight attack, apparently, but he must lie quiet. There was no need to send for a doctor; he knew just what to do; these passing attacks were common enough. He would be up and about again very shortly. Headley kept him company, saying no single word of what had happened. He read aloud to him, chatted and cheered him up. He had no other visitors. Within twenty-four hours he was himself once more. He and his friend had planned to leave the following day.

But Headley, that last night in the house, felt an odd uneasiness and could not sleep. All night long he sat up reading, looking out of the window, smoking in a chair where he could see the stars and hear the wind and watch the huge shadow of the downs. The house lay very still as the hours passed. He dozed once or twice. Why did he sit up in this unnecessary way? Why did he leave his door ajar so that the slightest sound of another door opening, or of steps passing along the corridor, must reach him? Was he anxious for his friend? Was he suspicious? What was his motive, what his secret purpose?

Headley did not know, and could not even explain it to himself. He felt uneasy, that was all he knew. Not for worlds would he have let himself go to sleep or lose full consciousness that night. It was very odd; he could not understand himself. He merely obeyed a strange, deep instinct that bade him wait and watch. His nerves were jumpy; in his heart lay some inexplicable anxiety that was pain.

The dawn came slowly; the stars faded one by one; the line of the downs showed their grand bare curves against the sky; cool and cloudless the September morning broke above the little Sussex pleasure house. He sat and watched the east grow bright. The early wind brought a scent of marshes and the sea into his room. Then suddenly it brought a sound as well—the haunting cry of the bird with its three following notes. And this time there came an answer.

Headley knew then why he had sat up. A wave of emotion swept him as he heard—an emotion he could not attempt to explain. Dread, wonder, longing seized him. For some seconds he could not leave his chair because he did not dare to. The low-pitched cries of call and answer rang in his ears like some unearthly music. With an effort he started up, went to the window and looked out.

This time the light was sharp and clear. No mist hung in the air. He saw the crimsoning sky reflected like a band of shining metal in the reach of river beyond the lawn. He saw dew on the grass, a sheet of pallid silver. He saw the summer-house, empty of any passing figures. For this time the two figures stood plainly in view before his eyes upon the lawn. They stood there, hand in hand, sharply defined, unmistakable in form and outline, their faces, moreover, turned upwards to the window where he stood, staring down in pain and amazement at them—at Arthur Deane and *Mary*.

They looked into his eyes. He tried to call, but no sound left his throat. They began to move across the dew-soaked lawn. They went, he saw, with a floating, undulating motion towards the river shining in the dawn. Their feet left no marks upon the grass. They reached the bank, but did not pause in their going. They rose a little, floating like silent birds across the river. Turning in midstream, they smiled towards him, waved their hands with a gesture of farewell, then, rising still higher into the opal dawn, their figures passed into the distance slowly, melting away against the sunlit marshes and the shadowing downs beyond. They disappeared.

Headley never quite remembers actually leaving the window, crossing the room, or going down the passage. Perhaps he went at once, perhaps he stood gazing into the air above the downs for a considerable time, unable to tear himself away. He was in some marvellous dream, it seemed. The next thing he remembers, at any rate, was that he was standing beside his friend's bed, trying, in his distraught anguish of heart, to call him from that sleep which, on earth, knows no awakening.

The Sacrifice

1

Limasson was a religious man, though of what depth and quality were unknown, since no trial of ultimate severity had yet tested him. An adherent of no particular creed, he yet had his gods; and his self-discipline was probably more rigorous than his friends conjectured. He was so reserved. Few guessed, perhaps, the desires conquered, the passions regulated, the inner tendencies trained and schooled—not by denying their expression, but by transmuting them alchemically into nobler channels. He had in him the makings of an enthusiastic devotee, and might have become such but for two limitations that prevented.

He loved his wealth, labouring to increase it to the neglect of other interests; and, secondly, instead of following up one steady line of search, he scattered himself upon many picturesque theories, like an actor who wants to play all parts rather than concentrate on one. And the more picturesque the part, the more he was attracted. Thus, though he did his duty unshrinkingly and with a touch of love, he accused himself sometimes of merely gratifying a sensuous taste in spiritual sensations. There was this unbalance in him that argued want of depth.

As for his gods—in the end he discovered their reality by first doubting, then denying their existence.

It was this denial and doubt that restored them to their thrones, converting his dilettante skirmishes into genuine, deep belief; and the proof came to him one summer in early June when he was making ready to leave town for his annual month among the mountains.

With Limasson mountains, in some inexplicable sense, were a passion almost, and climbing so deep a pleasure that the ordinary scrambler hardly understood it. Grave as a kind of worship it was to him; the preparations for an ascent, the ascent itself in particular, involved a concentration that seemed symbolical as of a ritual. He not only loved the heights, the massive grandeur, the splendour of vast proportions blocked in space, but loved them with a respect that held a touch of awe.

The emotion mountains stirred in him, one might say, was of that profound, incalculable kind that held kinship with his religious feelings, half realised though these were. His gods had their invisible thrones somewhere among the grim, forbidding heights. He prepared himself for this annual mountaineering with the same earnestness that a holy man might approach a solemn festival of his church.

And the impetus of his mind was running with big momentum in this direction, when there fell upon him, almost on the eve of starting, a swift series of disasters that shook his being to its last foundations, and left him stunned among the ruins. To describe these is unnecessary. People said, 'One thing after another like that! What appalling luck! Poor wretch!' then wondered, with the curiosity of children, how in the world he would take it. Due to no apparent fault of his own, these disasters were so sudden that life seemed in a moment shattered, and his interest in existence almost ceased. People shook their heads and thought of the emergency exit. But Limasson was too vital a man to dream of annihilation. Upon him it had a different effect—he turned and questioned what he called his gods. They did not answer or explain. For the first time in his life, he doubted. A hair's breadth beyond lay definite denial.

The ruin in which he sat, however, was not material; no man of his age, possessed of courage and a working scheme of life, would permit disaster of a material order to overwhelm him. It was collapse of a mental, spiritual kind, an assault upon the roots of character and temperament. Moral duties laid suddenly upon him threatened to crush. His *personal* existence was assailed, and apparently must end. He must spend the remainder of his life caring for others who were nothing to him.

No outlet showed, no way of escape, so diabolically complete was the combination of events that rushed his inner trenches. His faith was shaken. A man can but endure so much, and remain human. For him the saturation point seemed reached. He experienced the spiritual equivalent of that physical numbness which supervenes when pain has touched the limit of endurance. He laughed, grew callous, then mocked his silent gods.

It is said that upon this state of blank negation there follows sometimes a condition of lucidity which mirrors with crystal clearness the forces driving behind life at a given moment, a kind of clairvoyance that brings explanation and therefore peace. Limasson looked for this in vain.

There was the doubt that questioned, there was the sneer that mocked the silence into which his questions fell; but there was neither answer nor explanation, and certainly not peace. There was no relief. In this tumult of revolt, he did none of the things his friends suggested or expected; he merely followed the line of least resistance. He yielded to the impetus that was upon him when the catastrophe came. To their indignant amazement he went out to his mountains.

All marvelled that at such a time he could adopt so trivial a line of action, neglecting duties that seemed paramount; they disapproved. Yet in reality he was taking no definite action at all, but merely drifting with the momentum that had been acquired just before. He was bewildered with so much pain, confused with suffering, stunned with the crash that flung him helpless amid undeserved calamity. He turned to the mountains as a child to its mother, instinctively. Mountains had never failed to bring him consolation, comfort, peace. Their grandeur restored proportion whenever disorder threatened life. No calculation, properly speaking, was in his move at all; but a blind desire for a violent physical reaction such as climbing brings. And the instinct was more wholesome than he knew.

In the high upland valley among lonely peaks whither Limasson then went, he found in some measure the proportion he had lost. He studiously avoided thinking; he lived in his muscles recklessly. The region with its little Inn was familiar to him; peak after peak he attacked, sometimes with, but more often without a guide, until his reputation as a sane climber, a laurelled member of all the foreign Alpine Clubs, was seriously in danger. That he overdid it physically is beyond question, but that the mountains breathed into him some portion of their enormous calm and deep endurance is also true.

His gods, meanwhile, he neglected utterly for the first time in his life. If he thought of them at all, it was as tinsel figures imagination had created, figures upon a stage that merely decorated life for those whom pretty pictures pleased. Only—he had left the theatre and their make-believe no longer hypnotised his mind. He realised their impotence and disowned them. This attitude, however, was subconscious; he lent to it no substance, either of thought or speech. He ignored rather than challenged their existence.

And it was somewhat in this frame of mind—thinking little, feeling even less—that he came out into the hotel vestibule after dinner one evening, and took mechanically the bundle of letters the porter handed to him. They had no possible interest for him; in a corner where the big steam-heater mitigated the chilliness of the hall, he idly sorted them. The score or so of other guests, chiefly expert climbing men, were trailing out in twos and threes from the dining-room; but he felt as little interest in them as in his letters: no conversation could alter facts, no written phrases change his circumstances.

At random, then, he opened a business letter with a typewritten address—it would probably be impersonal, less of a mockery, therefore, than the others with their tiresome sham condolences. And, in a sense, it was impersonal; sympathy from a solicitor's office is mere formula, a few extra ticks upon the universal keyboard of a Remington. But as he read it, Limasson made a discovery that startled him into acute and bitter sensation. He had imagined the limit of bearable suffering and disaster already reached. Now, in a few dozen words, his error was proved convincingly. The fresh blow was dislocating.

This culminating news of additional catastrophe disclosed within him entirely new reaches of pain, of biting, resentful fury. Limasson experienced a momentary stopping of the heart as he took it in, a dizziness, a violent sensation of revolt whose impotence induced almost physical nausea. He felt like—death.

'Must I suffer all things?' flashed through his arrested intelligence in letters of fire.

There was a sullen rage in him, a dazed bewilderment, but no positive suffering as yet. His emotion was too sickening to include the smaller pains of disappointment; it was primitive, blind anger that he knew. He read the letter calmly, even to the neat paragraph of machine-made sympathy at the last, then placed it in his inner pocket. No outward sign of disturbance was upon him; his breath came slowly; he reached over to the table for a match, holding it at arm's length lest the sulphur fumes should sting his nostrils.

And in that moment, he made his second discovery. The fact that further suffering was still possible included also the fact that some touch of resignation had been left in him, and therefore some vestige of belief as well. Now, as he felt the crackling sheet of stiff paper in his pocket, watched the sulphur die, and saw the wood ignite, this remnant faded utterly away. Like the blackened end of the match, it shrivelled and dropped off. It vanished. Savagely, yet with an external calmness that enabled him to light his pipe with untrembling hand, he addressed his futile deities. And once more in fiery letters there flashed across the darkness of his passionate thought:

'Even this you demand of me—this cruel, ultimate sacrifice?'

And he rejected them, bag and baggage; for they were a mockery and a lie. With contempt he repudiated them for ever. The stage of doubt had passed. He denied his gods. Yet, with a smile upon his lips; for what were they after all but the puppets his religious fancy had imagined? They never had existed. Was it, then, merely the picturesque, sensational aspect of his devotional temperament that had created them? That side of his nature, in any case, was dead now, killed by a single devastating blow. The gods went with it.

Surveying what remained of his life, it seemed to him like a city that an earthquake has reduced to ruins. The inhabitants think no worse thing could happen. Then comes the fire.

★★★★★★★★★★★★★

Two lines of thought, it seems, then developed parallel in him and simultaneously, for while underneath he stormed against this culminating blow, his upper mind dealt calmly with the project of a great expedition he would make at dawn. He had engaged no guide. As an experienced mountaineer, he knew the district well; his name was tolerably familiar, and in half an hour he could have settled all details, and retired to bed with instructions to be called at two. But, instead, he sat there waiting, unable to stir, a human volcano that any moment might break forth into violence. He smoked his pipe as quietly as though nothing had happened, while through the blazing depths of him ran ever this one self-repeating statement: 'Even this you demand of me, this cruel, ultimate sacrifice!. . .' His self-control, dynamically estimated, just then must have been very great and, thus repressed, the store of potential energy accumulated enormously.

With thought concentrated largely upon this final blow, Limasson had not noticed the people who streamed out of the *salle à manger* and scattered themselves in groups about the hall. Some individual, now and again, approached his chair with the idea of conversation, then, seeing his absorption, turned away. Even when a climber whom he slightly knew reached across him with a word of apology for the matches, Limasson made no response, for he did not see him. He noticed nothing. In particular he did not notice two men who, from an opposite corner, had for some time been observing him. He now looked up—by chance?—and was vaguely aware that they were discussing him. He met their eyes across the hall, and started.

For at first, he thought he knew them. Possibly he had seen them about in the hotel—they seemed familiar—yet he certainly had never spoken with them. Aware of his mistake, he turned his glance elsewhere, though still vividly conscious of their attention. One was a clergyman or a priest; his face wore an air of gravity touched by sadness, a sternness about the lips counteracted by a kindling beauty in the eyes that betrayed enthusiasm nobly regulated. There was a suggestion of stateliness in the man that made the impression very sharp. His clothing emphasised it. He wore a dark tweed suit that was strict in its simplicity. There was austerity in him somewhere.

His companion, perhaps by contrast, seemed inconsiderable in his conventional evening dress. A good deal younger than his friend, his hair, always a tell-tale detail, was a trifle long; the thin fingers that flourished a cigarette wore rings; the face, though picturesque, was flippant, and his entire attitude conveyed a certain insignificance. Gesture, that faultless language which challenges counterfeit, betrayed unbalance somewhere. The impression he produced, however, was shadowy compared to the sharpness of the other. 'Theatrical' was the word in Limasson's mind, as he turned his glance elsewhere. But as he looked away, he fidgeted. The interior darkness caused by the dreadful letter rose about him. It engulfed him. Dizziness came with it....

Far away the blackness was fringed with light, and through this light, stepping with speed and carelessness as from gigantic distance, the two men, suddenly grown large, came at him. Limasson, in self-protection, turned to meet them. Conversation he did not desire. Somehow, he had expected this attack.

Yet the instant they began to speak—it was the priest who opened fire—it was all so natural and easy that he almost welcomed the diversion. A phrase by way of introduction—and he was speaking of the summits. Something in Limasson's mind turned over. The man was a serious climber, one of his own species. The sufferer felt a certain relief as he heard the invitation, and realised, though dully, the compliment involved.

'If you felt inclined to join us—if you would honour us with your company,' the man was saying quietly, adding something then about 'your great experience' and 'invaluable advice and judgment.'

Limasson looked up, trying hard to concentrate and understand.

'The Tour du Néant?' he repeated, mentioning the peak proposed. Rarely attempted, never conquered, and with an ominous record of disaster, it happened to be the very summit he had meant to attack himself next day.

'You have engaged guides?' He knew the question foolish.

'No guide will try it,' the priest answered, smiling, while his companion added with a flourish, 'but we—we need no guide—if *you* will come.'

'You are unattached, I believe? You are alone?' the priest enquired, moving a little in front of his friend, as though to keep him in the background.

'Yes,' replied Limasson. 'I am quite alone.'

He was listening attentively, but with only part of his mind. He realised the flattery of the invitation. Yet it was like flattery addressed to someone else. He felt himself so indifferent, so—dead. These men wanted his skilful body, his experienced mind; and it was his body and mind that talked with them, and finally agreed to go. Many a time, expeditions had been planned in just this way, but tonight he felt there was a difference. Mind and body signed the agreement, but his soul, listening elsewhere and looking on, was silent. With his rejected gods it had left him, though hovering close still. It did not interfere; it did not warn; it even approved; it sang to him from great distance that this expedition cloaked another. He was bewildered by the clashing of his higher and his lower mind.

'At one in the morning, then, if that will suit you . . .' the older man concluded.

'I'll see to the provisions,' exclaimed the younger enthusiastically, 'and I shall take my telephoto for the summit. The porters can come as far as the Great Tower. We're over six thousand feet here already, you see, so . . .' and his voice died away in the distance as his companion led him off.

Limasson saw him go with relief. But for the other man he would have declined the invitation. At heart he was indifferent enough. What decided him really was the coincidence that the Tour du Néant was the very peak he had intended to attack himself *alone*, and the curious feeling that this expedition cloaked another somehow—almost that these men had a hidden motive. But he dismissed the idea—it was not worth thinking about. A moment later he followed them to bed. So careless was he of the affairs of the world, so dead to mundane interests, that he tore up his other letters and tossed them into a corner of the room—unread.

2

Once in his chilly bedroom he realised that his upper mind had permitted him to do a foolish thing; he had drifted like a schoolboy into an unwise situation. He had pledged himself to an expedition with two strangers, an expedition for which normally he would have chosen his companions with the utmost caution. Moreover, he was guide; they looked to him for safety, while yet it was they who had arranged and planned it. But who were these men with whom he proposed to run grave bodily risks? He knew them as little as they knew him. Whence came, he wondered, the curious idea that this climb was really planned by another who was no one of them?

The thought slipped idly across his mind; going out by one door, it came back, however, quickly by another. He did not think about it more than to note its passage through the disorder that passed with him just then for thinking. Indeed, there was nothing in the whole world for which he cared a single brass farthing. As he undressed for bed, he said to himself: 'I shall be called at one ... but why am I going with these two on this wild plan?. . . And who made the plan?'...

It seemed to have settled itself. It came about so naturally and easily, so quickly. He probed no deeper. He didn't care. And for the first time he omitted the little ritual, half prayer, half adoration, it had always been his custom to offer to his deities upon retiring to rest. He no longer recognised them.

How utterly broken his life was! How blank and terrible and lonely! He felt cold, and piled his overcoats upon the bed, as though his mental isolation involved a physical effect as well. Switching off the light by the door, he was in the act of crossing the floor in the darkness when a sound beneath the window caught his ear. Outside there were voices talking. The roar of falling water made them indistinct, yet he was sure they were voices, and that one of them he knew. He stopped still to listen. He heard his own name uttered—'John Limasson.' They ceased. He stood a moment shivering on the boards, then crawled into bed beneath the heavy clothing. But in the act of settling down, they began again. He raised himself again hurriedly to listen. What little wind there was passed in that moment down the valley, carrying off the roar of falling water; and into the moment's space of silence dropped fragments of definite sentences:

'They are close, you say—close down upon the world?' It was the voice of the priest surely.

'For days they have been passing,' was the answer—a rough, deep tone that might have been a peasant's, and a kind of fear in it, 'for all my flocks are scattered.'

'The signs are sure? You know them?'

'Tumult,' was the answer in much lower tones. 'There has been tumult in the mountains. . . .'

There was a break then as though the voices sank too low to be heard. Two broken fragments came next, end of a question—beginning of an answer.

'. . . the opportunity of a lifetime?'

'. . . if he goes of his own free will, success is sure. For acceptance is . . .'

And the wind, returning, bore back the sound of the falling water, so that Limasson heard no more. . . .

An indefinable emotion stirred in him as he turned over to sleep. He stuffed his ears lest he should hear more. He was aware of a sinking of the heart that was inexplicable. What in the world were they talking about, these two? What was the meaning of these disjointed phrases? There lay behind them a grave significance almost solemn. That 'tumult in the mountains' was somehow ominous, its suggestion terrible and mighty. He felt disturbed, uncomfortable, the first emotion that had stirred in him for days. The numbness melted before its faint awakening. Conscience was in it—he felt vague prickings—but it was deeper far than conscience.

Somewhere out of sight, in a region life had as yet not plumbed, the words sank down and vibrated like pedal notes. They rumbled away into the night of undecipherable things. And, though explanation failed him, he felt they had reference somehow to the morrow's expedition: how, what, wherefore, he knew not; his name had been spoken—then these curious sentences; that was all. Yet tomorrow's expedition, what was it but an expedition of impersonal kind, not even planned by himself? Merely his own plan taken and altered by others—made over? His personal business, his personal life, were not really in it at all.

The thought startled him a moment. He had no personal life. . .!

Struggling with sleep, his brain played the endless game of disentanglement without winning a single point, while the under-mind in him looked on and smiled—because it *knew*. Then, suddenly, a great peace fell over him. Exhaustion brought it perhaps. He fell asleep; and next moment, it seemed, he was aware of a thundering at the door and an unwelcome growling voice, *''s ist bald ein Uhr, Herr! Aufstehen!'*

Rising at such an hour, unless the heart be in it, is a sordid and depressing business; Limasson dressed without enthusiasm, conscious that thought and feeling were exactly where he had left them on going to sleep. The same confusion and bewilderment were in him; also, the same deep solemn emotion stirred by the whispering voices. Only long habit enabled him to attend to detail, and ensured that nothing was forgotten. He felt heavy and oppressed, a kind of anxiety about him; the routine of preparation he followed gravely, utterly untouched by the customary joy; it was mechanical.

Yet through it ran the old familiar sense of ritual, due to the practice of so many years, that cleansing of mind and body for a big Ascent—like initiatory rites that once had been as important to him as those of some priest who approached the worship of his deity in the temples of ancient time. He performed the ceremony with the same care as though no ghost of vanished faith still watched him, beckoning from the air as formerly.... His knapsack carefully packed, he took his ice-axe from beside the bed, turned out the light, and went down the creaking wooden stairs in stockinged feet, lest his heavy boots should waken the other sleepers. And in his head still rang the phrase he had fallen asleep on—as though just uttered:

'The signs are sure; for days they have been passing—close down upon the world. The flocks are scattered. There has been tumult—tumult in the mountains.' The other fragments he had forgotten. But who were 'they'? And why did the word bring a chill of awe into his blood?

And as the words rolled through him Limasson felt tumult in his thoughts and feelings too. There had been tumult in his life, and all his joys were scattered—joys that hitherto had fed his days. The signs were sure. Something was close down upon his little world—passing—sweeping. He felt a touch of terror.

Outside in the fresh darkness of very early morning the strangers stood waiting for him. Rather, they seemed to arrive in the same instant as himself, equally punctual. The clock in the church tower sounded one. They exchanged low greetings, remarked that the weather promised to hold good, and started off in single file over soaking meadows towards the first belt of forest. The porter—mere peasant, unfamiliar of face and not connected with the hotel—led the way with a hurricane lantern. The air was marvellously sweet and fragrant. In the sky overhead the stars shone in their thousands. Only the noise of falling water from the heights, and the regular thud of their heavy boots broke the stillness. And, black against the sky, towered the enormous pyramid of the Tour du Néant they meant to conquer.

Perhaps the most delightful portion of a big ascent is the beginning in the scented darkness while the thrill of possible conquest lies still far off. The hours stretch themselves queerly; last night's sunset might be days ago; sunrise and the brilliance coming seem in another week, part of dim futurity like children's holidays. It is difficult to realise that this biting cold before the dawn, and the blazing heat to come, both belong to the same today.

There were no sounds as they toiled slowly up the zigzag path through the first fifteen hundred feet of pine-woods; no one spoke; the clink of nails and ice-axe points against the stones was all they heard. For the roar of water was felt rather than heard; it beat against the ears and the skin of the whole body at once. The deeper notes were below them now in the sleeping valley; the shriller ones sounded far above, where streams just born out of ponderous snow-beds tinkled sharply . . . .

The change came delicately. The stars turned a shade less brilliant, a softness in them as of human eyes that say farewell. Between the highest branches the sky grew visible. A sighing air smoothed all their crests one way; moss, earth, and open spaces brought keen perfumes; and the little human procession, leaving the forest, stepped out into the vastness of the world above the tree-line. They paused while the porter stooped to put his lantern out. In the eastern sky was colour. The peaks and crags rushed closer.

Was it the Dawn? Limasson turned his eyes from the height of sky where the summits pierced a path for the coming day, to the faces of his companions, pale and wan in the early twilight. How small, how insignificant they seemed amid this hungry emptiness of desolation. The stupendous cliffs fled past them, led by headstrong peaks crowned with eternal snows. Thin lines of cloud, trailing half way up precipice and ridge, seemed like the swish of movement—as though he caught the earth turning as she raced through space.

The four of them, timid riders on the gigantic saddle, clung for their lives against her titan ribs, while currents of some majestic life swept up at them from every side. He drew deep draughts of the rarefied air into his lungs. It was very cold. Avoiding the pallid, insignificant faces of his companions, he pretended interest in the porter's operations; he stared fixedly on the ground. It seemed twenty minutes before the flame was extinguished, and the lantern fastened to the pack behind. This Dawn was unlike any he had seen before.

For, in reality, all the while, Limasson was trying to bring order out of the extraordinary thoughts and feelings that had possessed him during the slow forest ascent, and the task was not crowned with much success. The Plan, made by others, had taken charge of him, he felt; and he had thrown the reins of personal will and interest loosely upon its steady gait. He had abandoned himself carelessly to what might come. Knowing that he was leader of the expedition, he yet had suffered the porter to go first, taking his own place as it was appointed to him, behind the younger man, but before the priest.

In this order, they had plodded, as only experienced climbers plod, for hours without a rest, until half way up a change had taken place. He had wished it, and instantly it was effected. The priest moved past him, while his companion dropped to the rear—the companion who forever stumbled in his speed, whereas the older man climbed surely, confidently.

And thereafter Limasson walked more easily—as though the relative positions of the three were of importance somehow. The steep ascent of smothering darkness through the woods became less arduous. He was glad to have the younger man behind him.

For the impression had strengthened as they climbed in silence that this ascent pertained to some significant Ceremony, and the idea had grown insistently, almost stealthily, upon him. The movements of himself and his companions, especially the positions each occupied relatively to the other, established some kind of intimacy that resembled speech, suggesting even question and answer. And the entire performance, while occupying hours by his watch, it seemed to him more than once, had been in reality briefer than the flash of a passing thought, so that he saw it within himself—pictorially. He thought of a picture worked in colours upon a strip of elastic. Someone pulled the strip, and the picture stretched. Or someone released it again, and the picture flew back, reduced to a mere stationary speck. All happened in a single speck of time.

And the little change of position, apparently so trivial, gave point to this singular notion working in his under-mind—that this ascent was a ritual and a ceremony as in older days, its significance approaching revelation, however, for the first time—now. Without language, this stole over him; no words could quite describe it. For it came to him that these three formed a unit, himself being in some fashion yet the acknowledged principal, the leader. The labouring porter had no place in it, for this first toiling through the darkness was a preparation, and when the actual climb began, he would disappear, while Limasson himself went first.

This idea that they took part together in a Ceremony established itself firmly in him, with the added wonder that, though so often done, he performed it now for the first time with full comprehension, knowledge, truth. Empty of personal desire, indifferent to an ascent that formerly would have thrilled his heart with ambition and delight, he understood that climbing had ever been a ritual for his soul and of his soul, and that power must result from its sincere accomplishment. It was a symbolical ascent.

In words this did not come to him. He felt it, never criticising. That is, he neither rejected nor accepted. It stole most sweetly, grandly, over him. It floated into him while he climbed, yet so convincingly that he had felt his relative position must be changed. The younger man held too prominent a post, or at least a wrong one—in advance. Then, after the change, effected mysteriously as though all recognised it, this line of certainty increased, and there came upon him the big, strange knowledge that all of life is a Ceremony on a giant scale, and that by performing the movements accurately, with sincere fidelity, there may come—knowledge. There was gravity in him from that moment.

This ran in his mind with certainty. Though his thought assumed no form of little phrases, his brain yet furnished detailed statements that clinched the marvellous thing with simile and incident which daily life might apprehend: That knowledge arises from action; that to do the thing invites the teaching and explains it.

Action, moreover, is symbolical; a group of men, a family, an entire nation, engaged in those daily movements which are the working out of their destiny, perform a Ceremony which is in direct relation somewhere to the pattern of greater happenings which are the teachings of the Gods. Let the body imitate, reproduce—in a bedroom, in a wood—anywhere—the movements of the stars, and the meaning of those stars shall sink down into the heart. The movements constitute a script, a language.

To mimic the gestures of a stranger is to understand his mood, his point of view—to establish a grave and solemn intimacy. Temples are everywhere, for the entire earth is a temple, and the body, House of Royalty, is the biggest temple of them all. To ascertain the pattern its movements trace in daily life, *could* be to determine the relation of that particular ceremony to the Cosmos, and so learn power. The entire system of Pythagoras, he realised, could be taught without a single word—by movements; and in everyday life even the commonest act and vulgarest movement are part of some big Ceremony—a message from the Gods. Ceremony, in a word, is three-dimensional language, and action, therefore, is the language of the Gods. The Gods he had denied were speaking to him . . . passing with tumult close across his broken life.... Their passage it was, indeed, that had caused the breaking!

In this cryptic, condensed fashion the great fact came over him—that he and these other two, here and now, took part in some great Ceremony of whose ultimate object as yet he was in ignorance. The impact with which it dropped upon his mind was tremendous. He realised it most fully when he stepped from the darkness of the forest and entered the expanse of glimmering, early light; up till this moment his mind was being prepared only, whereas now he knew. The innate desire to worship which all along had been his, the momentum his religious temperament had acquired during forty years, the yearning to have proof, in a word, that the Gods he once acknowledged were really true, swept back upon him with that violent reaction which denial had aroused.

He wavered where he stood. . . .

Looking about him, then, while the others rearranged burdens the returning porter now discarded, he perceived the astonishing beauty of the time and place, feeling it soak into him as by the very pores of his skin. From all sides this beauty rushed upon him. Some radiant, *wingéd* sense of wonder sped past him through the silent air. A thrill of ecstasy ran down every nerve. The hair of his head stood up. It was far from unfamiliar to him, this sight of the upper mountain world awakening from its sleep of the summer night, but never before had he stood shuddering thus at its exquisite cold glory, nor felt its significance as now, so mysteriously *within himself.*

Some transcendent power that held sublimity was passing across this huge desolate plateau, far more majestic than the mere sunrise among mountains he had so often witnessed. There was Movement. He understood why he had seen his companions insignificant. Again, he shivered and looked about him, touched by a solemnity that held deep awe.

Personal life, indeed, was wrecked, destroyed, but something greater was on the way. His fragile alliance with a spiritual world was strengthened. He realised his own past insolence. He became afraid.

3

The treeless plateau, littered with enormous boulders, stretched for miles to right and left, grey in the dusk of very early morning. Behind him dropped thick guardian pine-woods into the sleeping valley that still detained the darkness of the night. Here and there lay patches of deep snow, gleaming faintly through thin rising mist; singing streams of icy water spread everywhere among the stones, soaking the coarse rough grass that was the only sign of vegetation. No life was visible; nothing stirred; nor anywhere was movement, but of the quiet trailing mist and of his own breath that drifted past his face like smoke. Yet through the splendid stillness there *was* movement; that sense of absolute movement which results in stillness—it was owing to the stillness that he became aware of it—so vast, indeed, that only immobility could express it.

Thus, on the calmest day in summer, may the headlong rushing of the earth through space seem more real than when the tempest shakes the trees and water on its surface; or great machinery turn with such vertiginous velocity that it appears steady to the deceived function of the eye. For it was not through the eye that this solemn Movement made itself known, but rather through a massive sensation that owned his entire body as its organ. Within the league-long amphitheatre of enormous peaks and precipices that enclosed the plateau, piling themselves upon the horizon, Limasson felt the outline of a Ceremony extended. The pulses of its grandeur poured into him where he stood. Its vast design was knowable because they themselves had traced— were even then tracing—its earthly counterpart in little. And the awe in him increased.

'This light is false. We have an hour yet before the true dawn,' he heard the younger man say lightly. 'The summits still are ghostly. Let us enjoy the sensation, and see what we can make of it.'

And Limasson, looking up startled from his reverie, saw that the far-away heights and towers indeed were heavy with shadow, faint still with the light of stars. It seemed to him they bowed their awful heads and that their stupendous shoulders lowered. They drew together, shutting out the world.

'True,' said his companion, 'and the upper snows still wear the spectral shine of night. But let us now move faster, for we travel very light. The sensations you propose will but delay and weaken us.'

He handed a share of the burdens to his companion and to Limasson. Slowly they all moved forward, and the mountains shut them in.

And two things Limasson noted then, as he shouldered his heavier pack and led the way: first, that he suddenly knew their destination though its purpose still lay hidden; and, secondly, that the porter's leaving before the ascent proper began signified finally that ordinary climbing was not their real objective. Also—the dawn was a lifting of inner veils from off his mind, rather than a brightening of the visible earth due to the nearing sun. Thick darkness, indeed, draped this enormous, lonely amphitheatre where they moved.

'You lead us well,' said the priest a few feet behind him, as he picked his way unfalteringly among the boulders and the streams.

'Strange that I do so,' replied Limasson in a low tone, 'for the way is new to me, and the darkness grows instead of lessening.' The language seemed hardly of his choosing. He spoke and walked as in a dream.

Far in the rear the voice of the younger man called plaintively after them:

'You go so fast, I can't keep up with you,' and again he stumbled and dropped his ice-axe among the rocks. He seemed for ever stooping to drink the icy water, or clambering off the trail to test the patches of snow as to quality and depth. 'You're missing all the excitement,' he cried repeatedly. 'There are a hundred pleasures and sensations by the way.'

They paused a moment for him to overtake them; he came up panting and exhausted, making remarks about the fading stars, the wind upon the heights, new routes he longed to try up dangerous couloirs, about everything, it seemed, except the work in hand. There was eagerness in him, the kind of excitement that saps energy and wastes the nervous force, threatening a probable collapse before the arduous object is attained.

'Keep to the thing in hand,' replied the priest sternly. 'We are not really going fast; it is you who are scattering yourself to no purpose. It wears us all. We must husband our resources,' and he pointed significantly to the pyramid of the Tour du Néant that gleamed above them at an incredible altitude.

'We are here to amuse ourselves; life is a pleasure, a sensation, or it is nothing,' grumbled his companion; but there was a gravity in the tone of the older man that discouraged argument and made resistance difficult. The other arranged his pack for the tenth time, twisting his axe through an ingenious scheme of straps and string, and fell silently into line behind his leaders. Limasson moved on again ... and the darkness at length began to lift. Far overhead, at first, the snowy summits shone with a hue less spectral; a delicate pink spread softly from the east; there was a freshening of the chilly wind; then suddenly the highest peak that topped the others by a thousand feet of soaring rock, stepped sharply into sight, half golden and half rose.

At the same instant, the vast Movement of the entire scene slowed down; there came one or two terrific gusts of wind in quick succession; a roar like an avalanche of falling stones boomed distantly—and Limasson stopped dead and held his breath.

For something blocked the way before him, something he knew he could not pass. Gigantic and unformed, it seemed part of the architecture of the desolate waste about him, while yet it bulked there, enormous in the trembling dawn, as belonging neither to plain nor mountain. Suddenly it was there, where a moment before had been mere emptiness of air. Its massive outline shifted into visibility as though it had risen from the ground. He stood stock still. A cold that was not of this world turned him rigid in his tracks. A few yards behind him the priest had halted too. Farther in the rear they heard the stumbling tread of the younger man, and the faint calling of his voice—a feeble broken sound as of a man whom sudden fear distressed to helplessness.

'We're off the track, and I've lost my way,' the words came on the still air. 'My axe is gone ... let us put on the rope!. . . Hark! Do you hear that roar?' And then a sound as though he came slowly groping on his hands and knees.

'You have exhausted yourself too soon,' the priest answered sternly. 'Stay where you are and rest, for we go no farther. This is the place we sought.'

There was in his tone a kind of ultimate solemnity that for a moment turned Limasson's attention from the great obstacle that blocked his farther way. The darkness lifted veil by veil, not gradually, but by a series of leaps as when someone inexpertly turns a wick. He perceived then that not a single Grandeur loomed in front, but that others of similar kind, some huger than the first, stood all about him, forming an enclosing circle that hemmed him in.

Then, with a start, he recovered himself. Equilibrium and common sense returned. The trick that sight had played upon him, assisted by the rarefied atmosphere of the heights and by the witchery of dawn, was no uncommon one, after all. The long straining of the eyes to pick the way in an uncertain light so easily deceives perspective. Delusion ever follows abrupt change of focus. These shadowy encircling forms were but the rampart of still distant precipices whose giant walls framed the tremendous amphitheatre to the sky.

Their closeness was a mere gesture of the dusk and distance.

The shock of the discovery produced an instant's unsteadiness in him that brought bewilderment. He straightened up, raised his head, and looked about him. The cliffs, it seemed to him, shifted back instantly to their accustomed places; as though after all they *had* been close; there was a reeling among the topmost crags; they balanced fearfully, then stood still against a sky already faintly crimson. The roar he heard, that might well have seemed the tumult of their hurrying speed, was in reality but the wind of dawn that rushed against their ribs, beating the echoes out with angry wings. And the lines of trailing mist, streaking the air like proofs of rapid motion, merely coiled and floated in the empty spaces.

He turned to the priest, who had moved up beside him.

'How strange,' he said, 'is this beginning of new light. My sight went all astray for a passing moment. I thought the mountains stood right across my path. And when I looked up just now it seemed they all ran back.' His voice was small and lost in the great listening air.

The man looked fixedly at him. He had removed his slouch hat, hot with the long ascent, and as he answered, a long thin shadow flitted across his features. A breadth of darkness dropped about them. It was as though a mask were forming. The face that now was covered had been—naked. He was so long in answering that Limasson heard his mind sharpening the sentence like a pencil.

He spoke very slowly. '*They* move perhaps even as Their powers move, and Their minutes are our years. Their passage ever is in tumult. There is disorder then among the affairs of men; there is confusion in their minds. There may be ruin and disaster, but out of the wreckage shall issue strong, fresh growth. For like a sea, They pass.'

There was in his mien a grandeur that seemed borrowed marvellously from the mountains. His voice was grave and deep; he made no sign or gesture; and in his manner was a curious steadiness that breathed through the language a kind of sacred prophecy.

Long, thundering gusts of wind passed distantly across the precipices as he spoke. The same moment, expecting apparently no rejoinder to his strange utterance, he stooped and began to unpack his knapsack. The change from the sacerdotal language to this commonplace and practical detail was singularly bewildering.

'It is the time to rest,' he added, 'and the time to eat. Let us prepare.' And he drew out several small packets and laid them in a row upon the ground. Awe deepened over Limasson as he watched, and with it a great wonder too. For the words seemed ominous, as though this man, upon the floor of some vast Temple, said: 'Let us prepare a sacrifice...!' There flashed into him, out of depths that had hitherto concealed it, a lightning clue that hinted at explanation of the entire strange proceeding—of the abrupt meeting with the strangers, the impulsive acceptance of their project for the great ascent, their grave behaviour as though it were a Ceremonial of immense design, his change of position, the bewildering tricks of sight, and the solemn language, finally, of the older man that corroborated what he himself had deemed at first illusion. In a flying second of time this all swept through him— and with it the sharp desire to turn aside, retreat, to run away.

Noting the movement, or perhaps divining the emotion prompting it, the priest looked up quickly. In his tone was a coldness that seemed as though this scene of wintry desolation uttered words:

'You have come too far to think of turning back. It is not possible. You stand now at the gates of birth—and death. All that might hinder, you have so bravely cast aside. Be brave now to the end.'

And, as Limasson heard the words, there dropped suddenly into him a new and awful insight into humanity, a power that unerringly discovered the spiritual necessities of others, and therefore of himself. With a shock he realised that the younger man who had accompanied them with increasing difficulty as they climbed higher and higher— was but a shadow of reality. Like the porter, he was but an encumbrance who impeded progress. And he turned his eyes to search the desolate landscape.

'You will not find him,' said his companion, 'for he is gone. Never, unless you weakly call, shall you see him again, nor desire to hear his voice.' And Limasson realised that in his heart he had all the while disapproved of the man, disliked him for his theatrical fondness of sensation and effect, more, that he had even hated and despised him. Starvation might crawl upon him where he had fallen and eat his life away before he would stir a finger to save him. It was with the older man he now had dreadful business in hand.

'I am glad,' he answered, 'for in the end he must have proved my death—our death!'

And they drew closer round the little circle of food the priest had laid upon the rocky ground, an intimate understanding linking them together in a sympathy that completed Limasson's bewilderment. There was bread, he saw, and there was salt; there was also a little flask of deep red wine. In the centre of the circle was a miniature fire of sticks the priest had collected from the bushes of wild rhododendron. The smoke rose upwards in a thin blue line. It did not even quiver, so profound was the surrounding stillness of the mountain air, but far away among the precipices ran the boom of falling water, and behind it again, the muffled roar as of peaks and snow-fields that swept with a rolling thunder through the heavens.

'They are passing,' the priest said in a low voice, 'and They know that you are here. You have now the opportunity of a lifetime; for, if you yield acceptance of your own free will, success is sure. You stand before the gates of birth and death. They offer you life.'

'Yet . . . I denied Them!' He murmured it below his breath.

'Denial is evocation. You called to them, and They have come. The sacrifice of your little personal life is all They ask. Be brave—and yield it.'

He took the bread as he spoke, and, breaking it in three pieces, he placed one before Limasson, one before himself, and the third he laid upon the flame which first blackened and then consumed it.

'Eat it and understand,' he said, 'for it is the nourishment that shall revive your fading life.'

Next, with the salt, he did the same. Then, raising the flask of wine, he put it to his lips, offering it afterwards to his companion. When both had drunk there still remained the greater part of the contents. He lifted the vessel with both hands reverently towards the sky. He stood upright.

'The blood of your personal life I offer to Them in your name. By the renunciation which seems to you as death shall you pass through the gates of birth to the life of freedom beyond. For the ultimate sacrifice that They ask of you is—this.'

And bending low before the distant heights, he poured the wine upon the rocky ground.

For a period of time Limasson found no means of measuring, so terrible were the emotions in his heart, the priest remained in this attitude of worship and obeisance. The tumult in the mountains ceased. An absolute hush dropped down upon the world. There seemed a pause in the inner history of the universe itself. All waited—till he rose again. And, when he did so, the mask that had for hours now been spreading across his features, was accomplished. The eyes gazed sternly down into his own. Limasson looked—and recognised. He stood face to face with the man whom he knew best of all others in the world

. . . himself.

There had been death. There had also been that recovery of splendour which is birth and resurrection.

And the sun that moment, with the sudden surprise that mountains only know, rushed clear above the heights, bathing the landscape and the standing figure with a stainless glory. Into the vast Temple where he knelt, as into that greater inner Temple which is mankind's true House of Royalty, there poured the completing Presence which is—Light.

'For in this way, and in this way only, shall you pass from death to life,' sang a chanting voice he recognised also now for the first time as indubitably his own.

It was marvellous. But the birth of light is ever marvellous. It was anguish; but the pangs of resurrection since time began have been accomplished by the sweetness of fierce pain. For the majority still lie in the pre-natal stage, unborn, unconscious of a definite spiritual existence. In the womb they grope and stifle, depending ever upon another. Denial is ever the call to life, a protest against continued darkness for deliverance. Yet birth is the ruin of all that has hitherto been depended on. There comes then that standing alone which at first seems desolate isolation. The tumult of destruction precedes release.

Limasson rose to his feet, stood with difficulty upright, looked about him from the figure so close now at his side to the snowy summit of that Tour du Néant he would never climb. The roar and thunder of *Their* passage was resumed. It seemed the mountains reeled.

'They are passing,' sang the voice that was beside him and within him too, 'but They have known you, and your offering is accepted. When They come close upon the world there is ever wreckage and disaster in the affairs of men. They bring disorder and confusion into the mind, a confusion that seems final, a disorder that seems to threaten death. For there is tumult in Their Presence, and apparent chaos that seems the abandonment of order. Out of this vast ruin, then, there issues life in new design. The dislocation is its entrance, the dishevelment its strength. There has been birth. . . .'

The sunlight dazzled his eyes. That distant roar, like a wind, came close and swept his face. An icy air, as from a passing star, breathed over him.

'Are you prepared?' he heard.

He knelt again. Without a sign of hesitation or reluctance, he bared his chest to the sun and wind. The flash came swiftly, instantly, descending into his heart with unerring aim. He saw the gleam in the air, he felt the fiery impact of the blow, he even saw the stream gush forth and sink into the rocky ground, far redder than the wine....

★★★★★★★★★★★★★★

He gasped for breath a moment, staggered, reeled, collapsed ... and within the moment, so quickly did all happen, he was aware of hands that supported him and helped him to his feet. But he was too weak to stand. They carried him up to bed. The porter, and the man who had reached across him for the matches five minutes before, intending conversation, stood, one at his feet and the other at his head. As he passed through the vestibule of the hotel, he saw the people staring, and in his hand, he crumpled up the unopened letters he had received so short a time ago.

'I really think—I can manage alone,' he thanked them. 'If you will set me down, I can walk. I felt dizzy for a moment.'

'The heat in the hall——' the gentleman began in a quiet, sympathetic voice.

They left him standing on the stairs, watching a moment to see that he had quite recovered. Limasson walked up the two flights to his room without faltering. The momentary dizziness had passed. He felt quite himself again, strong, confident, able to stand alone, able to move forward, able to *climb*.

The Pikestaffe Case

1

The vitality of old governesses deserves an explanatory memo-randum by a good physiologist. It is remarkable. They tend to survive the grown-up married men and women they once taught as children. They hang on for ever, as a man might put it crudely, a man, that is, who, taught by one of them in his earliest schoolroom days, would answer enquiries fifty years later without enthusiasm: "Oh, we keep her going, yes. She doesn't want for anything!"

Miss Helena Speke had taught the children of a distinguished fam-ily, and these distinguished children, with expensive progeny of their own now, still kept her going. They had clubbed together, seeing that Miss Speke retained her wonderful health, and had established her in a nice little house where she could take respectable lodgers—men for preference—giving them the three B's—bed, bath, and breakfast. Be-ing a capable woman. Miss Speke more than made both ends meet. She wanted for nothing. She kept going.

Applicants for her rooms, especially for the first-floor suite, had to be recommended. She had a stern face for those who rang the bell without a letter in their pockets. She never advertised. Indeed, there was no need to do so. The two upper floors had been occupied by the same tenants for many years—a chief clerk in a branch bank and a re-tired clergyman respectively. It was only the best suite that sometimes "happened to be vacant at the moment." From two guineas inclusive before the war, her price for this had been raised, naturally, to four, the tenant paying his gas-stove, light, and bath extra. Breakfast—she prided herself legitimately on her good breakfasts—was included.

For a long time now this first-floor suite had been unoccupied. The cost of living worried Miss Speke, as it worried most other peo-ple. Her servant was cheap but incompetent, and once she could let the suite, she meant to engage a better one. The distinguished children were scattered out of reach about the world; the eldest had been killed in the war; a married one, a woman, lived in India; another married one was in the throes of divorce—an expensive business; and the fourth, the most generous and last, found himself in the Bankruptcy Court, and so was unable to help.

It was in these conditions that Miss Speke, her vitality impaired, decided to advertise. Although she inserted the words "references essential," she meant in her heart to use her own judgment, and if a likely gentleman presented himself and agreed to pay her price, she might accept him. The clergyman and the bank official upstairs were a protection, she felt. She invariably mentioned them to applicants:

"I have a clergyman of the Church of England on the top floor. He's been with me for eleven years. And a banker has the floor below. Mine is a very quiet house, you see."

These words formed part of the ritual she recited in the hall, facing her proposed tenants on the linoleum by the hat-rack; and it was these words she addressed to the tall, thin, pale-faced man with scanty hair and spotless linen, who informed her that he was a tutor, a teacher of higher mathematics to the sons of various families—he mentioned some first-class names where references could be obtained—a student besides and something of an author in his leisure hours. His pupils he taught, of course, in their respective houses, one being in Belgrave Square, another in The Albany; it was only after tea, or in the evenings, that he did his own work. All this he explained briefly, but with great courtesy of manner.

Mr. Thorley was well spoken, with a gentle voice, kind, far-seeing eyes, and an air of being lonely and uncared for that touched some forgotten, dried-up spring in Miss Speke's otherwise rather cautious heart. He looked every inch a scholar—"and a gentleman," as she explained afterwards to everybody who was interested in him, these being numerous, of unexpected kinds, and all very close, not to say unpleasantly close, questioners indeed.

But what chiefly influenced her in his favour was the fact, elicited in conversation, that years ago he had been a caller at the house in Portman Square where she was governess to the distinguished family. She did not exactly remember him, but he had certainly known Lady Araminta, the mother of her charges.

Thus, it was that Mr. Thorley—John Laking Thorley, M.A., of Jesus College, Cambridge—was accepted by Miss Speke as tenant of her best suite on the first floor at the price mentioned, breakfast included, winning her confidence so fully that she never went to the trouble even of taking up the references he gave her. She liked him, she felt safe with him, she pitied him. He had not bargained, nor tried to beat her down. He just reflected a moment, then agreed. He proved, indeed, an exemplary lodger, early to bed and not too early to rise, of regular habits, thoughtful of the expensive new servant, careful with towels, electric light, and ink-stains, prompt in his payments, and never once troubling her with complaints or requests, as other lodgers did, not excepting the banker and the clergyman.

Moreover, he was a tidy man, who never lost anything, because he invariably put everything in its proper place and thus knew exactly where to look for it. She noticed this tidiness at once.

Miss Speke, especially in the first days of his tenancy, studied him, as she studied all her lodgers. She studied his room when he was out "of a morning." At her leisure she did this, knowing he would never break in and disturb her unexpectedly. She was neither prying nor inquisitive, she assured herself, but she was curious. "I have a right to know something about the gentlemen who sleep under my roof with me," was the way she put it in her own mind. His clothes, she found, were ample, including evening dress, white gloves, and an opera hat. He had plenty of boots and shoes. His linen was good. His wardrobe, indeed, though a trifle uncared for, especially his socks, was a gentleman's wardrobe.

Only one thing puzzled her. The full-length mirror, standing on mahogany legs—a present from the generous "child," now in the Bankruptcy Court, and, a handsome thing, a special attraction in the best suite—this fine mirror Mr. Thorley evidently did not like. The second or third morning he was with her she went to his bedroom before the servant had done it up, and saw, to her surprise, that this full-length glass stood with its back to the room. It had been placed close against the wall in a corner, its unattractive back turned outward.

"It gave me quite a shock to see it," as she said afterwards. "And such a handsome piece, too!"

Her first thought, indeed, sent a cold chill down her energetic spine. "He's cracked it!" But it was not cracked. She paused in some amazement, wondering why her new lodger had done this thing; then she turned the mirror again into its proper position, and left the room. Next morning, she found it again with its face close against the wall. The following day it was the same—she turned it round, only to find it the next morning again with its back to the room.

She asked the servant, but the servant knew nothing about it.

"He likes it that way, I suppose, mum," was all Sarah said. "I never laid a 'and on it once."

Miss Speke, after much puzzled consideration, decided it must be something to do with the light. Mr. Thorley, she remembered, wore horn-rimmed spectacles for reading. She scented a mystery. It caused her a slight—oh, a very slight—feeling of discomfort. Well, if he did not like the handsome mirror, she could perhaps use it in her own room. To see it neglected hurt her a little. Not many furnished rooms could boast a full-length glass, she reflected. A few days later, meeting Mr. Thorley on the linoleum before the hat-rack, she enquired if he was quite comfortable, and if the breakfast was to his liking. He was polite and even cordial. Everything was perfect, he assured her. He had never been so well looked after. And the house was so quiet.

"And the bed, Mr. Thorley? You sleep well, I hope." She drew nearer to the subject of the mirror, but with caution. For some reason she found a difficulty in actually broaching it. It suddenly dawned upon her that there was something queer about his treatment of that full-length glass. She was by no means fanciful, Miss Speke, retired governess; only the faintest suspicion of something odd brushed her mind and vanished. But she did feel something. She found it impossible to mention the handsome thing outright.

"There's nothing you would like changed in the room, or altered?" she enquired with a smile, "or—in any way put different—perhaps?"

Mr. Thorley hesitated for a moment. A curious expression, half sad, half yearning, she thought, lit on his thoughtful face for one second and was gone. The idea of moving anything seemed distasteful to him.

"Nothing, Miss Speke, I thank you," he replied courteously, but without delay. "Everything is really as I like it." Then, with a little bow, he asked: "I trust my typewriter disturbs nobody. Please let me know if it does."

Miss Speke assured him that nobody minded the typewriter in the least, nor even heard it, and, with another charming little bow and a smile, Mr, Thorley went out to give his lessons in the higher mathematics.

"There!" she reflected, "and I never even asked him!" It had been impossible.

From the window she watched him going down the street, his head bent, evidently in deep thought, his books beneath his arm, looking, she thought, every inch the gentleman and the scholar that he undoubtedly was. His personality left a very strong impression on her mind. She found herself rather wondering about him. As he turned the corner Miss Speke owned to two things that rose simultaneously in her mind: first, the relief that the lodger was out for the day and could be counted upon not to return unexpectedly; secondly, that it would interest her to slip up and see what kind of books he read.

A minute later she was in his sitting-room. It was already swept and dusted, the breakfast cleared away, and the books, she saw, lay partly on the table where he had just left them and partly on the broad mantelpiece he used as a shelf. She was alone, the servant was downstairs in the kitchen. She examined Mr. Thorley's books.

The examination left her bewildered and uninspired. "I couldn't make them out at all," she put it. But they were evidently what she called costly volumes, and that she liked. "Something to do with his work, I suppose—mathematics, and all that," she decided, after turning over pages covered with some kind of hieroglyphics, symbols being a word she did not know in that connection. There was no printing, there were no sentences, there was nothing she could lay hold of, and the diagrams she thought perhaps were Euclid, or possibly astronomical.

Most of the names were odd and quite unknown to her. Gauss! Minowski! Lobatchewski! And it affronted her that some of these were German. A writer named Einstein was popular with her lodger' and that, she felt, was a pity, as well as a mistake in taste. It all alarmed her a little; or, rather she felt that touch of respect, almost of awe, pertaining to some world entirely beyond her ken. She was rather glad when the search—it was a duty—ended.

"There's nothing there," she reflected, meaning there was nothing that explained his dislike of the full-length mirror. And, disappointed, yet with a faint relief, she turned to his private papers. These, since he was a tidy man, were in a drawer. Mr. Thorley never left anything lying about. Now, a letter Miss Speke would not have thought of reading, but papers, especially learned papers, were another matter.

Conscience, nevertheless, did prick her faintly as she cautiously turned over sheaf after sheaf of large white foolscap, covered with designs, and curves, and diagrams in ink, the ink he never spilt, and assuredly in his recent handwriting. And it was among these foolscap sheets that she suddenly came upon one sheet in particular that caught her attention and even startled her. In the centre, surrounded by scriggly hierglyphics, numbers, curves and lines meaningless to her, she saw a drawing of the full-length mirror. Some of the curves ran into it and through it, emerging on the other side. She knew it was *the* mirror because its exact measurements were indicated in red ink.

This, as mentioned, startled her. What could it mean? she asked herself, staring intently at the curious sheet, as though it must somehow yield its secret to prolonged even if unintelligent enquiry. "It looks like an experiment or something," was the furthest her mind could probe into the mystery, though this, she admitted, was not very far. Holding the paper at various angles, even upside down, she examined it with puzzled curiosity, then slowly laid it down again in the exact place whence she had taken it. That faint breath of alarm had again suddenly brushed her soul, as though she approached a mystery, she had better leave unsolved.

"It's very strange——" she began, carefully closing the drawer, but unable to complete the sentence even in her mind. "I don't think I like it—quite," and she turned to go out. It was just then that something touched her face tickling one cheek, something fine as a cobweb, something in the air. She picked it away. It was a thread of silk, extremely fine, so fine, indeed, that it might almost have been a spider's web of gossamer such as one sees floating over the garden lawn on a sunny morning. Miss Speke brushed it away, giving it no further thought, and went about her usual daily duties.

2

But in her mind was established now a vague uneasiness, though so vague that at first she did not recognise it. Her thought would suddenly pause. "Now, what is it? "she would ask herself. "Something's on my mind. What is it I've forgotten? "The picture of her first-floor lodger appeared, and she knew at once. "Oh, yes, it's that mirror and the diagrams, of course." Some taut wire of alarm was quivering at the back of her mind. It was akin to those childhood alarms that pertain to the big unexplained mysteries no parent can elucidate because no parent knows. "Only God can tell that," says the parent, evading the insoluble problem. "I'd better not think about it," was the analogous conclusion reached by Miss Speke. Meanwhile the impression the new lodger's personality made upon her mind perceptibly deepened. He seemed to her full of power, above little things, a man of intense and mysterious mental life. He was constantly and somewhat possessingly in her thoughts. The mere thought of him, she found, stimulated her.

It was just before lunchen, as she returned from her morning marketing, that the servant drew her attention to certain marks upon the carpet of Mr. Thorley's sitting-room. She had discovered them as she handled the vacuum cleaner—faint, short lines drawn by dark chalk or crayons, in shape like the top or bottom right-angle of a square bracket, and sometimes with a tiny arrow shown as well. There were occasional other marks, too, that Miss Speke recognised as the hiero-glyphics she called squiggles.

Mistress and servant examined them together in a stooping posi-tion. They found others on the bedroom carpet, too, only these were not straight; they were small curved lines; and about the feet of the full-length mirror they clustered in a quantity, segments of circles, some large, some small. They looked as if someone had snipped off curly hair, or pared his finger-nails with sharp scissors, only consider-ably larger, and they were so faint that they were only visible when the sunlight fell upon them.

"I knew they was drawn on," said Sarah, puzzled, yet proud that she had found them, "because they didn't come up with the dust and fluff.

"I'll—speak to Mr. Thorley," Was the only comment Miss Speke made. "I'll tell him." Her voice was not quite steady, but the girl ap-parently noticed nothing.

"There's all this too, please, mum." She pointed to a number of fine silk threads she had collected upon a bit of newspaper, preparatory to the dustbin. "They was stuck on the cupboard door and the walls, stretched all across the room, but rather 'igh up. I only saw them by chance. One caught on my face."

Miss Speke stared, touched, examined for some seconds without speaking. She remembered the thread that had tickled her own cheek. She looked enquiringly round the room, and the servant, following her suggestion, indicated where the threads had been attached to walls and furniture. No marks, however, were left; there was no damage done.

"I'll mention it to Mr. Thorley," said her mistress briefly, unwilling to discuss the matter with the new servant, much less to admit that she was uncomfortably at sea. "Mr. Thorley," she added, as though there was nothing unusual, "is a high mathematician. He makes—measure-ments and—calculations of that sort." She had not sufficient control of her voice to be more explicit, and she went from the room aware that, unaccountably, she was trembling. She had first gathered up the threads, meaning to show them to her lodger when she demanded an explanation. But the explanation was delayed, for—to state it bluntly—she was afraid to ask him for it.

She put it off till the following morning, then till the day after, and, finally, she decided to say nothing about the matter at all. "I'd better leave it, perhaps, after all," she persuaded herself. "There's no damage done, anyhow. I'd better not enquire." All the same she did not like it. By the end of the week, however, she was able to pride herself upon her restraint and tact; the marks on the carpet, rubbed out by the girl, were not renewed, and the fine threads of silk were never again found stretching through the air from wall to furniture. Mr. Thorley had evidently noticed their removal and had discontinued what he had observed was an undesirable performance. He was a scholar and a gentleman. But he was more. He was frank and straight-dealing. One morning he asked to see his landlady and told her all about it himself.

"Oh," he said in his pleasantest, easiest manner when she came into the room, "I wanted to tell you, Miss Speke—indeed, I meant to do so long before this—about the marks I made on your carpets"—he smiled apologetically—"and the silk threads I stretched. I use them for measurements—for problems I set my pupils, and one morning I left them there by mistake. The marks easily rub out. But I will use scraps of paper instead another time. I can pin these on—if you will kindly tell your excellent servant not to touch them—er—they're rather important to me."

He smiled again charmingly, and his face wore the wistful, rather yearning expression that had already appealed to her. The eyes, it struck her, were very brilliant. "Any damage," he added—"though, I assure you, none is possible really—I would, of course, make good to you. Miss Speke."

"Thank you, Mr. Thorley," was all Miss Speke could find to say, so confused was her mind by troubling thoughts and questions she dared not express. "Of course—this is my best suite, you see."

It was all most amicable and pleasant between them.

"I wonder—have my books come?" he asked, as he went out. "Ah, there they are, I do believe!" he exclaimed, for through the open front door a van was seen discharging a very large packing-case.

"Your books, Mr. Thorley?" Miss Speke murmured, noting the size of the package with dismay. "But I'm afraid—you'll hardly find space to put them in," she stammered. "The rooms—er"—she did not wish to disparage them—"are so small, aren't they?"

Mr. Thorley smiled delightfully. "Oh, please do not trouble on that account," he said. "I shall find space all right, I assure you. It's merely a question of knowing where and how to put them," and he proceeded to give the men instructions.

A few days later a second case arrived.

"I'm expecting some instruments, too," he mentioned casually, "mathematical instruments," and he again assured her with his confident smile that she need have no anxiety on the score of space. Nor would he dent the walls or scrape the furniture the least little bit. There was always room, he reminded her gently again, provided one knew how to stow things away. Both books and instruments were necessary to his work. Miss Speke need feel no anxiety at all.

But Miss Speke felt more than anxiety, she felt uneasiness, she felt a singular growing dread. There lay in her a seed of distress that began to sprout rapidly. Everything arrived as Mr. Thorley has announced, case upon case was unpacked in his room by his own hands. The straw and wood she used for firing purposes, there was no mess, no litter, no untidiness, nor were walls and furniture injured in any way. What caused her dread to deepen into something bordering upon actual alarm was the fact that, on searching Mr. Thorley's rooms when he was out, she could discover no trace of any of the things that had arrived. There was no sign of either books or instruments.

Where had he stored them? Where could they lie concealed? She asked herself innumerable questions, but found no answer to them. These stores, enough to choke and block the room, had been brought in through the sitting-room door. They could not possibly have been taken out again. They had not been taken out. Yet no trace of them was anywhere to be seen. It was very strange, she thought; indeed, it was more than strange. She felt excited. She felt a touch of hysterical alarm.

Meanwhile, thin strips of white paper, straight, angled, curved, were pinned upon the carpet; threads of finest silk again stretched overhead connecting the top of the door lintel with the window, the high cupboard with the curtain rods—yet too high to be brushed away merely by the head of anyone moving in the room. And the full-length mirror still stood with its face close against the wall.

The mystery of these aerial entanglements increased Miss Speke's alarm considerably. What could their purpose be? "Thank God," she thought, "this isn't war time!" She knew enough to realise their meaning was not "wireless." That they bore some relation to the lines on the carpet and to the diagrams and curves upon the paper, she grasped vaguely. But what it all meant baffled her and made her feel quite stupid. Where all the books and instruments had disappeared added to her bewilderment. She felt more and more perturbed. A vague, uncertain fear was worse than something definite she could face and deal with. Her fear increased. Then, suddenly, yet with a reasonable enough excuse, Sarah gave notice.

For some reason Miss Speke did not argue with the girl. She preferred to let the real meaning of her leaving remain unexpressed. She just let her go. But the fact disturbed her extraordinarily.

Sarah had given every satisfaction, there had been no sign of a grievance, no complaint, the work was not hard, the pay was good. It was simply that the girl preferred to leave. Miss Speke attributed it to Mr. Thorley. She became more and more disturbed in mind. Also she found herself, more and more, avoiding her lodger, whose regular habits made such avoidance an easy matter. Knowing his hours of exit and entrance, she took care to be out of the way. At the mere sound of his step she flew to cover.

The new servant, a stupid, yet not inefficient country girl, betrayed no reaction of any sort, no unfavourable reaction at at any rate. Having received her instructions, Lizzie did her work without complaint from either side. She did not remove the paper and the thread, nor did she mention them. She seemed just the country clod she was. Miss Speke, however, began to have restless nights. She contracted an unpleasant habit: she lay awake—listening.

3

As the result of one of these sleepless nights she came to the abrupt conclusion that she would be happier without Mr. Thorley in the house—only she had not the courage to ask him to leave. The truth was she had not the courage to speak to him at all, much less to give him notice, however nicely.

After much cogitation she hit upon a plan that promised well: she sent him a carefully worded letter explaining that, owing to increased cost of living, she found herself compelled to raise his terms. The "raise" was more than considerable, it was unreasonable, but he paid what she demanded, sending down a cheque for three months in advance with his best compliments. The letter somehow made her tremble. It was at this stage she first became aware of the existence in her of other feelings than discomfort, uneasiness, and alarm. These other feelings, being in contradiction of her dread, were difficult to describe, but their result was plain—she did not really wish Mr. Thorley to go after all. His friendly "compliments", his refusal of her hint, caused her a secret pleasure. It was not the cheque at the increased rate that pleased her—it was simply the fact that her lodger meant to stay.

It might be supposed that some delayed sense of romance had been stirred in her, but this really was not the case at all. Her pleasure was due to another source, but to a source uncommonly obscure and very strange. She feared him, feared his presence, above all, feared going into his room, while yet there was something about the mere idea of Mr. Thorley that entranced her. Another thing may as well be told at once—she herself faced it boldly—she would enter his dreaded room, when he was out, and would deliberately linger there. There was an odd feeling in the room that gave her pleasure, and more than pleasure—happiness.

Surrounded by the enigmas of his personality, by the lines and curves of white paper pinned upon her carpet, by the tangle of silken threads above her head, by the mysterious books, the more than mysterious diagrams in his drawer—yet all these, even the dark perplexity of the rejected mirror and the vanished objects, were forgotten in the curious sense of happiness she derived from merely sitting in his room. Her fear contained this other remarkable ingredient—an uncommon sense of joy, of liberty, of freedom. She felt *exaltée,*

She could not explain it, she did not attempt to do so. She would go shaking and trembling into his room, and a few minutes later this sense of uncommon happiness—of release, almost of escape, she felt it—would steal over her as though in her dried-up frozen soul spring had burst upon midwinter, as though something that crawled had suddenly most gloriously found wings. An indescribable exhilaration caught her.

Under this influence the dingy street turned somehow radiant, and the front door of her poor lodging-house opened upon blue seas, yellow sands, and mountains carpeted with flowers. Her whole life, painfully repressed and crushed down in the dull service of convential nonentities, flashed into colour, movement, and adventure. Nothing confined her. She was no longer limited. She knew advance in all possible directions. She knew the stars. She knew escape!

An attempt has been made to describe for her what she never could have described herself.

Tbe reaction, upon coming out again, was painful. Her life in the past as a governess, little better than a servant; her life in the present as lodging-house keeper; her struggle with servants, with taxes, with daily expenses; her knowledge that no future but a mere "living" lay in front of her until the grave was reached—these overwhelmed her with an intense depression that the contrast rendered almost insupportable. Whereas in his room she had perfume, freedom, liberty, and wonder—the wonder of some entirely new existence.

Thus, briefly, while Miss Speke longed for Mr. Thorley to leave her house, she became obsessed with the fear that one day he really would go. Her mind, it is seen, became uncommonly disturbed; her lodger's presence being undoubtedly the cause. Her nights were now more than restless, they were sleepless. Whence came, she asked herself repeatedly in the dark watches, her fear? Whence came, too, her strange enchantment?

It was at this juncture, then, that a further item of perplexity was added to her mind. Miss Speke, as has been seen, was honourably disposed; she respected the rights of others, their property as well. Yet, included in the odd mood of elation the room and its atmosphere caused her, was also a vagrant, elusive feeling that the intimate, the personal—above all, the personal—had lost their original rigidity. Small individual privacies, secrecy, no longer held their familiar meaning quite. The idea that most things in life were to be shared slipped into her. A "secret," to this expansive mood, was a childish attitude.

At any rate, it was while lingering in her lodger's attractive room one day—a habit now—that she did something that caused her surprise, yet did not shock her. She saw an open letter lying on his table—and she read it.

Rather than an actual letter, however, it seemed a note, a memorandum. It began "To J. L. T."

In a boyish writing, the meaning of the language escaped her entirely. She understood the strange words as little as she understood the phases of the moon, while yet she derived from their perusal a feeling of mysterious beauty, similar to the emotions the changes of that lovely satellite stirred in her:

To J. L. T.
I followed your instructions, though with intense effort and difficulty. I woke at 4 o'clock. About ten minutes later, as you said might happen, I woke a *second time*. The change into the second state was as great as the change from sleeping to waking, in the ordinary meaning of these words. But I could not

remain 'awake'. I fell asleep again in about a minute—back into the usual waking state, I mean. Description in words is impossible, as you know. What I felt was too terrific to feel for long. The new energy must presently have *burned me up*. It frightened me—as you warned me it would. And this fear, no doubt, was the cause of my 'falling asleep' again so quickly.

Cannot we arrange a Call for Help for similar occasions in future?

G. P.

Against this note Mr. Thorley had written various strangest "squiggles"; higher mathematics, Miss Speke supposed. In the opposite margin, also in her lodger's writing, were these words:

We must agree on a word to use when frightened. *Help*, or *Help me*, seems the best. To be uttered with the whole being.

Mr. Thorley had added a few other notes. She read them without the faintest prick of conscience. Though she understood no single sentence, a thrill of deep delight ran through her:

It amounts, of course, to a new direction; a direction at right angles to all we know, a new direction in oneself, a new direction—in living. But it can, perhaps, be translated into mathematicd terms by the intellect. This, however, only a simile at best. Cannot be experienced that way. Actual experience possible only to *changed consciousness*. But good to become mathematically accustomed to it. The mathematical experiments are worth it. They induce the mind, at any rate, to dwell upon the new direction. This helps. . .

Miss Speke laid down the letter exactly where she had found it. No shame was in her. "G. P." she knew, meant Gerald Pikestaffe; he was one of her lodger's best pupils, the one in Belgrave Square. Her feeling of mysterious elation, as already mentioned, seemed above all such matters as small secrecies or petty personal privacies. She had read a "private" letter without remorse. One feeling only caused in her a certain commonplace emotion: the feeling that, while she read the letter, her lodger was present, watching her. He seemed close behind her, looking over her shoulder almost, observing her acts, her mood, her very thoughts—yet not objecting. He was aware, at any rate, of what she did. . . .

It was under these circumstances that she bethought herself of her old tenant, the retired clergyman on the top floor, and sought his aid. The consolation of talking to another would be something, yet when the interview began all she could manage to say was that her mind was troubled and her heart not quite as it should be, and that she "didn't know what to do about it all." For the life of her she could not find more definite words. To mention Mr. Thorley she found suddenly utterly impossible.

"Prayer," the old man interrupted her half-way, "prayer, my dear lady. Prayer, I find," he repeated smoothly, "is always the best course in all one's troubles and perplexities. Leave it to God. He knows. And in His good time He will answer." He advised her to read the Bible and Longfellow. She added Florence Barclay to the list and followed his advice. The books, however, comforted her very little.

After some hesitation she then tried her other tenant. But the "banker" stopped her even sooner than the clergyman had done. MacPherson was very prompt:

"I can give you another ten shillings or maybe half a guinea," he said briskly. "Times are deeficult, I know. But I can't do more. If that's suffeecient I shall be delighted to stay on—" and, with a nod and a quick smile that settled the matter then and there, he was through the door and down the steps on the way to his office.

It was evident that Miss Speke must face her troubles alone, a fact, for the rest, life had already taught her. The loyal, courageous spirit in her accepted the situation. The alternate moods of happiness and depression, meanwhile, began to wear her out. "If only Mr. Thorley would go! If only Mr. Thorley will not go!" For some weeks now she had successfully avoided him. He made no requests nor complaints. His habits were as regular as sunrise, his payments likewise. Not even the servant mentioned him. He became a shadow in the house.

Then, with the advent of summer-time, he came home, as it were, an hour earlier than usual. He invariably worked from 5.30 to 7.30, when he went out for his dinner. Tea he always had at a pupil's house. It was a light evening, caused by the advance of the clock, and Miss Speke, mending her underwear at the window, suddenly perceived his figure coming down the street.

She watched, fascinated. Of two instincts—to hide herself, or to wait there and catch his eye—she obeyed the latter. She had not seen him for several weeks, and a deep thrill of happiness ran through her. His walk was peculiar, she noticed at once; he did not walk in a straight line. His tall, thin outline flowed down the pavement in long, sweeping curves, yet quite steadily. He was not drunk. He came nearer; he was not twenty feet away; at ten feet she saw his face clearly, and received a shock. It was worn, and thin, and wasted, but a light of happiness, of something more than happiness indeed, shone in it. He reached the area railings.

He looked up. His face seemed ablaze. Their eyes met, his with no start of recognition, hers with a steady stare of wonder. She ran into the passage, and before Mr. Thorley had time to use his latch-key she had opened the door for him herself. Little she knew, as she stood there trembling, that she stood also upon the threshold of an amazing adventure.

Face to face with him her presence of mind deserted her. She could only look up into that worn and wasted face, into those happy, severe, and brilliant eyes, where yet burned a strange expression of wistful yearning, of uncommon wonder, of something that seemed not of this world quite. Such an expression she had never seen before upon any human countenance. Its light dazzled her. There was uncommon fire in the eyes. It enthralled her. The same instant, as she stood there gazing at him without a single word, either of welcome or enquiry, it flashed across her that he needed something from her. He needed help, her help. It was a far-fetched notion, she was well aware, but it came to her iiresistibly. The conviction was close to her, closer than her skin.

It was this knowledge, doubtless, that enabled her to hear without resentment the strange words he at once made use of:

"Ah, I thank you. Miss Speke, I thank you," the thin lips parting in a smile, the shining eyes lit with an emotion of more than ordinary welcome. "You cannot know what a relief it is to me to see you. You are so sound, so wholesome, so ordinary, so—forgive me, I beg—so commonplace."

He was gone past her and upstairs into his sitting-room. She heard the key turn softly. She was aware that she had not shut the front door. She did so, then went back, trembling, happy, frightened, into her own room. She had a curious, rushing feeling, both frightful and bewildering, that the room did not contain her. . . . She was still sitting there two hours later, when she heard Mr. Thorley's step come down the stairs and leave the house. She was still sitting there when she held him return, open the door with his key, and go up to his sitting-room. The interval might have been two minutes or two weeks, instead of two hours merely. And all this time she had the wondrous sensation that the room did not contain her. The walls and ceilings did not shut her in. She was out of the room. Escape had come very close to her. She was out of the house . . . out of herself as well. . . .

4

She went early to bed, taking this time the Bible with her. Her strange sensations had passed, they had left her gradually. She had made herself a cup of tea and had eaten a soft-boiled egg and some bread-and-butter. She felt more normal again, but her nerves were unusually sensitive. It was a comfort to know there were two men in the house with her, two worthy men, a clergyman and a banker. The Bible, the banker, the clergyman, with Mrs. Barclay and Longfellow not far from her bed, were certainly a source of comfort to her.

The traffic died away, the rumbling of the distant motor-buses ceased, and, with the passing of the hours, the night became intensely still.

It was April. Her window was opened at the top and she could smell the cool, damp air of coming spring. Soothed by the books she began to feel drowsy. She glanced at the clock—it was just on two—then blew out the candle and prepared to sleep. Her thoughts turned automatically to Mr. Thorley, lying asleep on the floor above, his threads and paper strips and mysterious diagrams all about him— when, suddenly, a voice broke through the silence with a cry for help. It was a man's voice, and it sounded a long way off. But she recognised it instantly, and she sprang out of bed without a trace of fear. It was Mr. Thorley calling, and in the voice was anguish,

"He's in trouble? In danger! He needs help? I knew it!" ran rapidly through her mind, as she lit the candle with fingers that did not tremble. The clock showed three. She had slept a full hour. She opened the door and peered into the passage, but saw no one there; the stairs, too, were empty. The call was not repeated.

"Mr. Thorley!" she cried aloud. "Mr. Thorley! Do you want anything?" And by the sound of her voice she realised how distant and muffled his own had been. "I'm coming!"

She stood there waiting, but no answer came. There was no sound. She realised the uncommon stillness of the night.

"Did you call me?" she tried again, but with less confidence. "Can I do anything for you?"

Again there was no answer; nothing stirred; the house was silent as the grave. The linoleum felt cold against her bare feet, and she stole back to get her slippers and a dressing-gown, while a hundred pos-

194

sibilities flashed through her mind at once. Oddly enough, she never once thought of burglars, nor of fire, nor, indeed, of any ordinary situation that required ordinary help. Why this was so she could not say. No ordinary fear, at any rate, assailed her in that moment, nor did she feel the smallest touch of nervousness about her own safety.

"Was it—I wonder—a dream?" she asked herself as she pulled the dressing-gown about her. "Did I dream that voice?" when the thrilling cry broke forth again, startling her so that she nearly dropped the candle:

"Help! Help! Help me!"

Very distinct, yet muffled as by distance, it was beyond all question the voice of Mr. Thorley. What she had taken for anguish in it she now recognised was terror. It sounded on the floor above, it was the closed door doubtless that caused the muffled effect of distance.

Miss Speke ran along the passage instantly, and with extraordinary speed for an elderly woman; she was half-way up the stairs in a moment, when, just as she reached the first little landing by the bathroom and turned to begin the second flight, the voice came again: "Help! Help!" but this time with a difference that, truth to tell, did set her nerves unpleasantly aquiver. For there were two voices instead of one, and they were not upstairs at all. Both were below her in the passage she had just that moment left. Close they were behind her. One, moreover, was not the voice of Mr. Thorley. It was a boy's clear soprano. Both called for help together, and both held a note of terror that made her heart shake.

Under these conditions it may be forgiven to Miss Speke that she lost her balance and reeled against the wall, clutching the banisters for a moment's support. Yet her courage did not fail her. She turned instantly and quickly went downstairs again—to find the passage empty of any living figure. There was no one visible. There was only silence, a motionless hat-rack, the door of her own room slightly ajar, and shadows.

"Mr. Thorley!" she called. "Mr. Thorley!" her voice not quite so loud and confident as before. It had a whisper in it. No answer came. She repeated the words, her tone with still less volume. Only a faint echoes that seemed to linger unduly came in response. Peering into her own room she found it exactly as she had left it. The dining-room, facing it, was likewise empty. Yet a moment before she had plainly heard two voices calling for help within a few yards of where she stood. Two voices! What could it mean? She noticed now for the first time a peculiar freshness in the air a sharpness, almost a perfume, as though all the windows were wide open, and the air of coming spring was in the house.

Terror, though close, had not yet actually gripped her. That she had gone crazy occurred to her, but only to be dismissed. She was quite sane and self-possessed. The changing direction of the sounds lay beyond all explanation, but an explanation, she was positive, there must be. The odd freshness in the air was heartening, and seemed to brace her. No, terror had not yet really gripped her. Ideas of summoning the servant, the clergyman, the banker, these she equally dismissed. It was no ordinary help that was needed, not theirs at any rate. She went boldly upstairs again and knocked at Mr. Thorley's bedroom door. She knocked again and again, loud enough to waken him, if he had perchance called out in sleep, but not loud enough to disturb her other tenants. No answer came. There was no sound within. No light shone through the cracks. With his sitting-room the same conditions held.

It was the strangeness of the second voice that now stole over her with a deadly fear. She found herself cold and shivering. As she, at length, went slowly downstairs again the cries were suddenly audible once more. She heard both voices; "Help! Help! Help me!" Then silence. They were fainter this time. Far away, they sounded, withdrawn curiously into some remote distance, yet ever with the same anguish, the same terror in them as before. The direction, however, this time she could not tell at all. In a sense they seemed both close and far, both above her and below; they seemed—it was the only way she could describe the astounding thing—in any direction, or in all directions.

Miss Speke was really terrified at last. The strange, full horror of it gripped her, turning her heart suddenly to ice. The two voices, the terror in them, the extraordinary impression that they had withdrawn further into some astounding distance—this overcame her. She became appalled. Staggering into her room, she reached the bed and fell upon it in a senseless heap. She had fainted.

5

She slept late, owing probably to exhausted nerves. Though usually up and about by 7.30, it was after nine when the servant woke her. She sprawled half in the bed, half out; the candle, which luckily had extinguished itself in falling, lay upon the carpet. The events of the night came slowly back to her as she watched the servant's face. The girl was white and shaking.

"Are you ill, mum?" Lizzie asked anxiously in a whisper; then, without waiting for an answer, blurted out what she had really come in to say: "Mr. Thorley, mum! I can't get into his room. There's no answer." The girl was very frightened.

Mr. Thorley invariably had breakfast at 8 o'clock, and was out of the house punctually at 8,45.

"Was he ill in the night—perhaps—do you think?" Miss Speke said. It was the nearest she could get to asking if the girl had heard the voices. She had admirable control of herself by this time. She got up, still in her dressing-gown and slippers.

"Not that I know of, mum," was the reply.

"Come," said her mistress firmly. "We'll go in." And they went upstairs together.

The bedroom door, as the girl had said, was closed, but the sitting-room was open. Miss Speke led the way. The freshness of the night before lay still in the air, she noticed, though the windows were all closed tightly. There was an exhilarating sharpness, a delightful tang as of open space. She particularly mentions this. On the carpet, as usual, lay the strips of white paper, fastened with small pins, and the silk threads, also as usual, stretched across from lintel to cupboard, from window to bracket. Miss Speke brushed several of them from her face.

The door into the bedroom she opened, and went boldly in, followed mofe cautiously by the girl. "There's nothing to be afraid of," said her mistress firmly. The bed, she saw, had not been slept in. Everything was neat and tidy. The long mirror stood close against the wall, showing its ugly back as usual, while about its four feet clustered the curved strips of paper Miss Speke had grown accustomed to.

"Pull the blinds up, Lizzie," she said in a quiet voice.

The light now enabled her to see everything quite clearly. There were silken threads, she noticed distinctly, stretching from bed to window, and though both windows were closed there was this strange sweetness in the air as of a flowering spring garden. She sniffed it with a curious feeling of pleasure, of freedom, of release, though Lizzie, apparently, noticed nothing of all this.

"There's his 'at and mackintosh," the girl whispered in a frightened voice, pointing to the hooks on the door. "And the umbrella in the corner. But I don't see 'is boots, mum. They weren't put out to be cleaned."

Miss Speke turned and looked at her, voice and manner under full command. "What do you mean?" she asked.

"Mr. Thorley ain't gone out, mum," was the reply in a tremulous tone.

At that very moment a faint, distant cry was audible in a man's voice: "Help! Help!" Immediately after it a soprano, fainter still, called from what seemed even greater distance: "Help me!" The direction was not ascertainable. It seemed both in the room, yet far away outside in space above the roofs. A glance at the girl convinced Miss Speke that she had heard nothing.

"Mr. Thorley is not here" whispered Miss Speke, one hand upon the brass bed-rail for support.

The room was undeniably empty.

"Leave everything exactly as it is," ordered her mistress as they went out. Tears stood in her eyes, she lingered a moment on the threshold, but the sounds were not repeated. "Exactly as it is,", she repeated, closing the bedroom and then the sitting-room door behind her. She locked the latter, putting the key in her pocket. Two days later, as Mr. Thorley had not returned, she informed the police. But Mr. Thorley never returned. He had disappeared completely. He left no trace. He was never heard of again, though—once—he was seen.

Yet, this is not entirely accurate perhaps, for he was seen twice, in the sense that he was seen by two persons, and though he was not "heard of," he was certainly heard. Miss Speke heard his voice from time to time. She heard it in the daytime and at night; calling for help and always with the same words she had first heard: "Help! Help! Help me!" It sounded very far away, withdrawn into immense distance, the distance ever increasing. Occasionally she heard the boy's voice with it; they called together sometimes; she never heard the soprano voice alone.

But the anguish and terror she had first noticed were no longer present. Alarm had gone out of them. It was more like an echo that she heard. Through all the hubbub, confusion and distressing annoyance of the police search and enquiry, the voice and voices came to her, though she never mentioned them to a single living soul, not even to her old tenants, the clergyman and the banker. They kept their rooms on—which was about all she could have asked of them. The best suite was never let again. It was kept locked and empty. The dust accumulated. The mirror remained untouched, its face against the wall.

The voices, meanwhile, grew more and more faint; the distance seemed to increase; soon the voice of the boy was no longer heard at all, only the cry of Mr. Thorley, her mysterious but perfect lodger, sang distantly from time to time, both in the sunshine and in the still darkness of the night hours. The direction whence it came, too, remained, as before, undeterminable. It came from anywhere and everywhere—from above, below, on all sides. It had become, too, a pleasant, even a happy sound; no dread belonged to it any more. The intervals grew longer then; days first, then weeks passed without a sound; and invariably, after these increasing intervals, the voice had become fainter, weaker, withdrawn into ever greater and greater distance. With the coming of the warm spring days it grew almost inaudible. Finally, with the great summer heats, it died away completely.

6

The disappearance of Mr. Thorley, however, had caused no public disturbance on its own account, nor until it was bracketed with another disappearance, that of one of his pupils, Sir Mark Pikestaffe's son. The Pikestaffe Case then became a daily mystery that filled the papers. Mr. Thorley was of no consequence, whereas Sir Mark was a figure in the public eye.

Mr. Thorley's life, as enquiry proved, held no mystery. He had left everything in order. He did not owe a penny. He owned, indeed, considerable property, both in land and securities, and teaching mathematics, especially to promising pupils, seemed to have been a hobby merely. A half-brother called eventually to take away his few possessions, but the books and instruments he had brought into the lodging-house were never traced. He was a scholar and a gentleman to the last, a man, too, it appeared, of immense attainments and uncommon ability, one of the greatest mathematical brains, if the modest obituaries were to be believed, the world has ever known.

His name now passed into oblivion. He left no record of his researches or achievements. Out of some mysterious sense of loyalty and protection Miss Speke never mentioned his peculiar personal habits. The strips of paper, as the silken threads, she had carefully removed and destroyed long before the police came to make their search of his rooms. . . .

But the disappearance of young Gerald Pikestaffe raised a tremendous hubbub. It was some days before the two disappearances were connected, both having occurred on the same night, it was then proved. The boy, a lad of great talent, promising a brilliant future, and the favourite pupil of the older man, his tutor, had not even left the house. His room was empty—and that was all. He left no clue, no trace. Terrible hints and suggejstions were, of course, spread far and wide, but there was not a scrap of evidence forthcoming to support them, Gerald Pikestaffe and Mr. Thorley, at the same moment of the same night, vanished from the face of the earth and were no more seen. The matter ended there. The one link between them appeared to have been an amazing, an exceptional gift for higher mathematico. The Pikestaffe Case merely added one more to the insoluble mysteries with which commonplace daily life is sprinkled.

It was some six weeks to a month after the event that Miss Speke received a letter from one of her former charges, the most generous one, now satisfactorily finished with the Bankruptcy Court. He had honourably discharged his obligations; he was doing well; he wrote and asked Miss Speke to put him up for a week or two. "And do please give me Mr. Thorley's room," he asked. "The case thrilled me, and I should like to sleep in that room. I always loved mysteries, you remember . . . There's something very mysterious about this thing. Besides, I knew the P. boy a little—an astounding genius, if ever there was one."

Though it cost her much effort and still more hesitation, she consented finally. She prepared the rooms herself. There was a new servant, Lizzie having given notice the day after the disappearance, and the older woman who now waited upon the clergy man and the banker was not quite to be trusted with the delicate job. Miss Speke, entering the empty rooms on tiptoe, a strange trepidation in her heart, but that same heart firm with courage, drew up the blinds, swept the floors, dusted the furniture, and made the bed. All she did with her own hands. Only the full-length mirror she did not touch.

What terror still was in her clung to that handsome piece. It was haunted by memories. For her it was still both wonderful and somehow awful. The ghost of her strange experience hid invisibly in its polished, if now unseen, depths. She dared not handle it, far less move it from the resting-place where it rested in peace. His hands had placed it there. To her it was sacred.

It had been given to her by Colonel Lyle, who would now occupy the room, stand on the wondrous carpet, move through the air where once the jnysterious silks had floated, sleep in the very bed itself. All this he could do, but the mirror he must not touch.

"I'll explain to him a little. I'll beg him not to move it. He's very understanding," she said to herself, as she went out to buy some flowers for the sitting-room. Colonel Lyle was expected that very afternoon. Lilac, she remembered, was what he always liked. It took her longer than she expected to find really fresh bunches, of the colour that he preferred, and when she got back it was time to be thinking about his tea. The sun's rays fell slanting down the dingy street, touching it with happy gold. This, with thoughts of the tea-kettle and what vase would suit the flowers best, filled her mind as she passed along the linoleum in the narrow hall—then noticed suddenly a new hat and coat hanging on the usually empty pegs. Colonel Lyle had arrived before his time.

"He's already come," she said to herself with a little gasp. A heavy dread settled instantly on her spirit. She stood a moment motionless in the passage, the lilac blossoms in her hand. She was listening.

"The gentleman's come, mum," she heard the servant say, and at the same moment saw her at the top of the kitchen stairs in the hall. "He went up to his room, mum."

Miss Speke held out the flowers. With an effort to make her voice sound ordinary she gave an order about them. "Put them in water, Mary, please. The double vase will do." She watched the woman take them slowly, oh, so slowly, from her. But her mind was elsewhere. It was still listening. And after the woman had gone down to the kitchen again slowly, oh, so slowly, she stood motionless for some minutes, listening, still intently listening. But no sound broke the quiet of the afternoon. She heard only the blundering noises made by the woman in the kitchen below. On the floor above was—silence.

Miss Speke then turned and went upstairs.

Now, Miss Speke admits frankly that she was "in a state," meaning thereby, doubtless, that her nerves were tightly strung. Her heart was thumping, her ears and eyes strained to their utmost capacity; her hands, she remembers, felt a little cold, and her legs moved uncertainly. She denies, however, that her "state," though it may be described as nervous, could have betrayed her into either invention or delusion. What she saw she saw, and nothing can shake her conviction. Colonel Lyle, besides, is there to support her in the main outline, and Colonel Lyle, when first he had entered the room, was certainly not "in a state," whatever excuses he may have offered later to comfort her.

Moreover, to counteract her trepidation, she says that, as she pushed the door wide open—it was already ajar—the original mood of elation met her in the face with its lift of wonder and release. This modified her dread. She declares that joy rushed upon her, and that

201

her "nerves "were on the instant entirely forgotten.

"What I saw, I saw," remains her emphatic and unshakable verdict. "I saw—everything."

The first thing she saw admitted certainly of no doubt. Colonel Lyle lay huddled up againt the further wall, half upon the carpet and half-leaning on the wainscoting. He was unconscious. One arm was stretched towards the mirror, the hand still clutching one of its mahogany feet. And the mirror had been moved. It turned now slightly more towards the room.

The picture, indeed, told its own story, a story Colonel Lyle himself repeated afterwards when he had recovered. He was surprised to find the mirror—his mirror—with its face to the wall; he went forward to put it in its proper position; in doing this he looked into it; he saw something, and—the next thing he knew—Miss Speke was bringing him round.

She explains, further, that her overmastering curiosity to look into the mirror, as Colonel Lyle had evidently looked himself, prevented her from immediately rendering first-aid to that gentleman, as she unquestionably should have done. Instead, she crossed the room, stepped over his huddled form, turned the mirror a little further round towards her, and looked straight into it.

The eye, apparently, takes in a great deal more than the mind is consciously aware of having "seen" at the moment. Miss Speke saw everything, she claims. But details certainly came back to her later, details she had not been aware of at the time. At the moment, however, her impressions, though extremely vivid, were limited to certain outstanding items. These items were—that her own reflection was not visible, no picture of herself being there; that Mr. Thorley and a boy—she recognised the Pikestafh; lad from the newspaper photographs she had seen—were plainly there, and that books and instruments in great quantity filled all the nearer space, blocking up the foreground.

Beyond, behind, stretching in all directions, she affirms, was empty space that produced upon her the effect of the infinite heavens as seen in a clear night sky. This space was prodigious, yet in some way not alarming. It did not terrify; rather it comforted, and, in a sense, uplifted. A diffused soft light pervaded the huge panorama. There were no shadows, there were no high lights.

Curiously enough, however, the absence of any reproduction of herself did not at first strike her as at all out of the way; she noticed the fact, no more than that; it was, perhaps, naturally, the deep shock of seeing Mr. Thorley and the boy that held her absolutely spell-bound, arresting her faculties as though they had been frozen.

Mr. Thorley was moving to and fro, his body bent, his hand thrown forward. He looked as natural as in life. He moved steadily, as with a purpose, now nearer, now further, but his figure always bent as though he were intent upon something in his hands. The boy moved, too, but with a more gentle, less vigorous, motion that suggested floating. He followed the larger figure, keeping close, his face raised from time to time as though his companion spoke to him. The expression that he wore was quiet, peaceful, happy, and intent. He was absorbed in what he was doing at the moment. Then, suddenly, Mr. Thorley straightened himself up. He turned. Miss Speke saw his face for the first time. He looked into her eyes. The face blazed with light. The gaze was straight, and full, and clear. It betrayed recognition. Mr. Thorley smiled at her.

In a very few seconds she was aware of all this, of its main outlines, at any rate. She saw the moving, living figures in the midst of this stupendous and amazing space. The overwhelming surprise it caused her prevented, apparently, the lesser emotion of personal alarm; fear she certainly did not feel at first. It was when Mr. Thorley looked at her with his brilliant eyes and blazing smile that her heart gave its violent jump, missed a beat or two, then began hammering against her ribs like released machinery that has gone beyond control. She was aware of the happy glory in the face, a face that was thin to emaciation, almost transparent, yet wearing an expression that was no longer earthly. Then, as he smiled, he came towards her; he beckoned; he stretched both hands out, while the boy looked up and watched.

Mr. Thorley's advance, however, had two distracting peculiarities— that as he drew nearer he moved not in a straight line, but in a curve. As a skater performing "edges," though on both feet instead of on one, he swept gracefully and with incredible speed in her direction. The other peculiarity was that with each step nearer his figure grew smaller. It lessened in height. He seemed, indeed, to be moving in two directions at once. He became diminutive.

The sight ought by rights to have paralysed her, yet it produced again, instead of terror, an effect of exhilaration she could not possibly account for. There came once again that fine elation to her mind. Not only did all desire to resist die away almost before it was born, but more, she felt its opposite—an overpowering wish to join him. The tiny hands were still stretched out to greet her, to draw her in, to welcome her; the smile upon the diminutive face, as it came nearer and nearer, was enchanting. She heard his voice then:

"Come, come to us! Here reality is nearer, and there is liberty....!"

The voice was very close and loud as in life, but it was not in front. It was behind her. Against her very ear it sounded in the air behind her back. She moved one foot forward; she raised her arms. She felt herself being sucked in—into that glorious space. There was an indescribable change in her whole being.

The cumulative effect of so many amazing happenings, all of them contrary to nature, should have been destructive to her reason. Their combined shock should have dislocated her system somewhere and have laid her low. But with every individual, it seems, the breaking-point is different. Her system, indeed, was dislocated, and a moment later and she was certainly laid low, yet it was not the effect of the figure, the voice, the gliding approach of Mr. Thorley that produced this. It was the flaw of little human egoism that brought her down.

For it was in this instant that she first realised the absence of her own reflection in the mirror. The fact, though noticed before, had not entered her consciousness as such. It now definitely did so. The arms she lifted in greeting had no reflected counterpart. Her figure, she realised with a shock of terror, was not there. She dropped, then, like a stricken animal, one outstretched hand clutching the frame of the mirror as she did so.

"Gracious God!" she heard herself scream as she collapsed. She heard, too, the crash of the falling mirror which she overturned and brought down with her.

Whether the noise brought Colonel Lyle round, or whether it was the combined weight of Miss Speke and the handsome piece upon his legs that roused him, is of no consequence. He stirred, opened his eyes, disentangled himself and proceeded, not without astonishment, to render first-aid to the unconscious lady.

The explanations that followed are, equally, of little consequence.

His own attack, he considered, was chiefly due to fatigue, to violent indigestion, and to the after-effects of his protracted bankruptcy proceedings. Thus, at any rate, he assured Miss Speke. He added, however, that he had received rather a shock from the handsome piece, for, surprised at finding it turned to the wall, he had replaced it and looked into it, but had not seen himself reflected. This had amazed him a good deal, yet what amazed him still more was that he had seen something moving in the depths of the glass.

"I saw a face," he said, and it was a face I knew. It was Gerald Pikestaffe. Behind him was another figure, the figure of a man, whose face I could not see." A mist rose before his eyes, his head swam a bit, and he evidently swayed for some unaccountable reason. It was a blow received in falling that stunned him momentarily.

He stood over her, while he fanned her face; her swoon was of brief duration; she recovered quickly; she listened to his story with a quiet mind. The after-effect of too great wonder leaves no room for pettier emotions, and traces of the exhilaration she had experienced were still about her heart and soul.

"Is it smashed?" was the first thing she asked, to which Colonel Lyle made no answer at first, merely pointing to the carpet where the frame of the long mirror lay in broken fragments.

"There was no glass, you see," he said presently. He, too, was quiet, his manner very earnest; his voice, though subdued as by a hint of awe, betrayed the glow of some intense inner excitement that lit fire in his eyes as well. "He had cut it out long ago, of course. He used the empty framework, merely."

"Eh?" said Miss Speke, looking down incredulously, but finding no sign of splinters on the floor.

Her companion smiled. "We shall find it about somewhere if we look," he said calmly, which, indeed, proved later true—lying flat beneath the carpet under the bed. "His measurements and calculations led—probably by chance—towards the mirror"—he seemed speaking to himself more than to his bewildered listener—"perhaps by chance, perhaps by knowledge," he continued, "up to the mirror—and then through it." He looked down at Miss Speke and laughed a little. "So, like Alice, he went through it, too, taking his books and instruments, the boy as well, all with him. The boy, that is, had the knowledge too."

"I only know one thing," said Miss Speke, unable to follow him or find meaning in his words, "I shall never let these rooms again. I shall lock them up."

Her companion collected the broken pieces and made a little heap of them.

"And I shall pray for him," added Miss Speke, as he led her presently downstairs to her own quarters. "I shall never cease to pray for him as long as I live."

"He hardly needs that," murmured Colonel Lyle, but to himself. "The first terror has long since left him. He's found the new direction—and moved along it."

The Listener

Sept 4.—I have hunted all over London for rooms sotted to my income—£120 a year—and have at last found them. Two rooms, without modern conveniences, it is true, and in an old, ramshackle building, but within a stone's throw of P—— Place and in an eminently respectable street. The rent is only £25 a year. I had begun to despair when at last I found them by chance. The chance was a mere chance, and unworthy of record. I had to sign a lease for a year, and I did so willingly. The furniture from our old place in H——shire, which has been stored so long, will just suit them.

Oct. 1.—Here I am in my two rooms, in the centre of London, and not far from the offices of the periodicals where occasionally I dispose of an article or two. The building is at the end of a *cul-de-sac*. The alley is well paved and clean, and lined chiefly with the backs of sedate and institutional-looking buildings. There is a stable in it. My own house is dignified with the title of "Chambers." I feel as if one day the honour must prove too much for it, and it will swell with pride—and fall asunder. It is very old. The floor of my sitting-room has valleys and low hills on it, and the top of the door slants away from the ceiling with a glorious disregard of what is usual. They must have quarrelled—fifty years ago—and, have been going apart ever since.

Oct 2.—My landlady is old and thin, with a faded, dusty face. She is uncommunicative. The few words she utters seem to cost her pain. Probably her lungs are half choked with dust. She keeps my rooms as free from this commodity as possible, and has the assistance of a strong girl who brings up the breakfast and lights the fire. As I have said already, she is not communicative. In reply to pleasant efforts on my part she informed me briefly that I was the only occupant of the house at present. My rooms had not been occupied for some years. There had been other gentlemen upstairs, but they had left.

She never looks straight at me when she speaks, but fixes her dim eyes on my middle waistcoat button, till I get nervous and begin to think it isn't on straight, or is the wrong sort of button altogether.

Oct. 8.—My week's book is nicely kept, and so far is reasonable. Milk and sugar 7d., bread 6d., butter 8d., marmalade 6d., eggs 1s. 8d., laundress 2s. 9d., oil 6d., attendance 5s.; total 12s. 2d.

The landlady has a son who, she told me, is "somethink on a homnibus." He comes occasionally to see her. I think he drinks, for he talks very loud, regardless of the hour of the day or night, and tumbles about over the furniture downstairs.

All the morning I sit indoors writing—articles; verses for the comic papers; a novel I've been "at" for three years, and concerning which I have dreams; a children's book, in which the imagination has free rein; and another book which is to last as long as myself, since it is an honest record of my soul's advance or retreat in the struggle of life. Besides these, I keep a book of poems which I use as a safety valve, and concerning which I have no dreams whatsoever. Between the lot I am always occupied. In the afternoons I generally try to take a walk for my health's sake, through Regent's Park, into Kensington Gardens, or farther afield to Hampstead Heath.

Oct. 10.—Everything went wrong today. I have two eggs for breakfast. This morning one of them was bad. I rang the bell for Emily. When she came in, I was reading the paper, and, without looking up, I said, "Egg's bad."

"Oh, is it, sir?" she said; "I'll get another one," and went out, taking the egg with her. I waited my breakfast for her return, which was in five minutes. She put the new egg on the table and went away. But, when I looked down, I saw that she had taken away the good egg and left the bad one—all green and yellow—in the slop basin. I rang again.

"You've taken the wrong egg," I said.

"Oh!" she exclaimed; "I thought the one I took down didn't smell so *very* bad." In due time she returned with the good egg, and I resumed my breakfast with two eggs, but less appetite. It was all very trivial, to be sure, but so stupid that I felt annoyed. The character of that egg influenced everything I did. I wrote a bad article, and tore it up. I got a bad headache. I used bad words—to myself. Everything was bad, so I "chucked" work and went for a long walk.

I dined at a cheap chop-house on my way back, and reached home about nine o'clock.

Rain was just beginning to fall as I came in, and the wind was rising. It promised an ugly night. The alley looked dismal and dreary, and the hall of the house, as I passed through it, felt chilly as a tomb. It was the first stormy night I had experienced in my new quarters. The draughts were awful. They came criss-cross, met in the middle of the room, and formed eddies and whirlpools and cold silent currents that almost lifted the hair of my head. I stuffed up the sashes of the windows with neckties and odd socks, and sat over the smoky fire to keep warm. First, I tried to write, but found it too cold. My hand turned to ice on the paper.

What tricks the wind did play with the old place! It came rushing up the forsaken alley with a sound like the feet of a hurrying crowd of people who stopped suddenly at the door. I felt as if a lot of curious folk had arranged themselves just outside and were staring up at my windows. Then they took to their heels again and fled whispering and laughing down the lane, only, however, to return with the next gust of wind and repeat their impertinence.

On the other side of my room a single square window opens into a sort of shaft, or well, that measures about six feet across to the back wall of another house. Down this funnel the wind dropped, and puffed and shouted. Such noises I never heard before. Between these two entertainments I sat over the fire in a great-coat, listening to the deep booming in the chimney. It was like being in a ship at sea, and I almost looked for the floor to rise in undulations and rock to and fro.

Oct. 12.—I wish I were not quite so lonely—and so poor. And yet I love both my loneliness and my poverty. The former makes me appreciate the companionship of the wind and rain, while the latter preserves my liver and prevents me wasting time in dancing attendance upon women. Poor, ill-dressed men are not acceptable "attendants."

My parents are dead, and my only sister is—no, not dead exactly, but married to a very rich man. They travel most of the time, he to find his health, she to lose herself. Through sheer neglect on her part, she has long passed out of my life. The door closed when, after an absolute silence of five years, she sent me a cheque for £50 at Christmas. It was signed by her husband. I returned it to her in a thousand pieces and in an unstamped envelope. So at least I had the satisfaction of knowing that it cost her something! She wrote back with a broad quill pen that covered a whole page with three lines, "You are evidently as cracked as ever, and rude and ungrateful into the bargain."

It had always been my special terror lest the insanity in my father's family should leap across the generations and appear in me. This thought haunted me, and she knew it. So, after this little exchange of civilities the door slammed, never to open again. I heard the crash it made, and, with it, the falling from the walls of my heart of many little bits of china with their own peculiar value—rare china, some of it, that only needed dusting.

The same walls, too, carried mirrors in which I used sometimes to see reflected the misty lawns of childhood, the daisy chains, the wind-torn blossoms scattered through the orchard by warm rains, the robbers' cave in the long walk, and the hidden store of apples in the hay-loft. She was my inseparable companion then—but, when the door slammed, the mirrors cracked across their entire length, and the visions they held vanished for ever. Now I am quite alone. At forty-one cannot begin all over again to build up careful friendships, and all others are comparatively worthless.

Oct. 14.—My bedroom is 10 by 10. It is below the level of the front room, and a step leads down into it. Both rooms are very quiet on calm nights, for there is no traffic down this forsaken alley-way. In spite of the occasional larks of the wind, it is a most sheltered strip. At its upper end, below my windows, all the cats of the neighbourhood congregate as soon as darkness gathers. They lie undisturbed on the long ledge of a blind window of the opposite building, for after the postman has come and gone at 9.30, no footsteps ever dare to interrupt their sinister conclave, no step but my own, or sometimes the unsteady footfall of the son who "is somethink on a homnibus."

Oct. 15.—I dined at an "A.B.C." shop on poached eggs and coffee, and then went for a stroll round the outer edge of Regent's Park. It was tea o'clock when I got home. I counted no less than thirteen cats, all of a dark colour, crouching under the lee side of the alley walls. It was a cold night, and the stars shone like points of ice in a blue-black sky. The cats turned their heads and stared at me in silence as I passed. An odd sensation of shyness took possession of me under the glare of so many pairs of unblinking eyes. As I fumbled with the latch-key they jumped noiselessly down and pressed against my legs, as if anxious to be let in. But I slammed the door in their faces and ran quickly upstairs. The front room, as I entered to grope for the matches, felt as cold as a stone vault, and the air held an unusual dampness.

Oct. 17.—For several days I have been working on a ponderous article that allows no play for the fancy. My imagination requires a judicious rein; I am afraid to let it loose, for it carries me sometimes into appalling places beyond the stars and beneath the world. No one realises the danger more than I do. But what a foolish thing to write here—for there is no one to know, no one to realise! My mind of late has held unusual thoughts, thoughts I have never had before, about medicines and drugs and the treatment of strange illnesses. I cannot imagine their source. At no time in my life have I dwelt upon such ideas as now constantly throng my brain. I have had no exercise lately, for the weather has been shocking; and all my afternoons have been spent in the reading-room of the British Museum, where I have a reader's ticket

I have made an unpleasant discovery: there are rats in the house. At night from my bed I have heard them scampering across the hills and valleys of the front room, and my sleep has been a good deal disturbed in consequence.

Oct. 19.—The landlady, I find, has a little boy with her, probably her son's child. In fine weather he plays in the alley, and draws a wooden cart over the cobbles. One of the wheels is off, and it makes a most distracting noise. After putting up with it as long as possible, I found it was getting on my nerves, and I could not write. So, I rang the bell. Emily answered it.

"Emily, will you ask the little fellow to make less noise? It's impossible to work."

The girl went downstairs, and soon afterwards the child was called in by the kitchen door. I felt rather a brute for spoiling his play. In a few minutes, however, the noise began again, and I felt that he was the brute. He dragged the broken toy with a string over the stones till the rattling noise jarred every nerve in my body. It became unbearable, and I rang the bell a second time.

"That noise *must* be put a stop to!" I said to the girl, with decision.

"Yes, sir," she grinned, "I know; but one of the wheels is hoff. The men in the stable offered to mend it for 'im, but he wouldn't let them. He says he likes it that way."

"I can't help what he likes. The noise must stop. I can't write."

"Yes, sir; I'll tell Mrs. Monson."

The noise stopped for the day then;

Oct 23.—Every day for the past week that cart has rattled over the stones, till I have come to think of it as a huge carrier's van with four wheels and two horses; and every morning I have been obliged to ring the bell and have it stopped. The last time Mrs. Monson herself came up, and said she was sorry I had been annoyed; the sounds should not occur again. With rare discursiveness she went on to ask if I was comfortable, and how I liked the rooms. I replied cautiously. I mentioned the rats. She said they were mice. I spoke of the draughts. She said, "Yes, it were a draughty 'ouse." I referred to the cats, and she said they had been as long as she could remember.

By way of conclusion, she informed me that the house was over two hundred years old, and that the last gentleman who had occupied my rooms was a painter who "'ad real Jimmy Bueys and Raffles 'anging all hover the walls." It took me some moments to discern that Cimabue and Raphael were in the woman's mind.

Oct. 24.—Last night the son who is "somethink on a homnibus" came in. He had evidently been drinking, for I heard loud and angry voices below in the kitchen long after I had gone to bed. Once, too, I caught the singular words rising up to me through the floor, "Burning from top to bottom is the only thing that'll ever make this 'ouse right." I knocked on the floor, and the voices ceased suddenly, though later I again heard their clamour in my dreams.

These rooms are very quiet, almost too quiet sometimes. On windless nights they are silent as the grave, and the house might be miles in the country. The roar of London's traffic reaches me only in heavy, distant vibrations. It holds an ominous note sometimes, like that of an approaching army, or an immense tidal-wave very far away thundering in the night.

Oct 27.—Mrs. Monson, though admirably silent, is a foolish, fussy woman. She does such stupid things. In dusting the room, she puts all my things in the wrong places. The ashtrays, which should be on the writing-table, she sets in a silly row on the mantelpiece. The pen-tray, which should be beside the inkstand, she hides away cleverly among the books on my reading-desk. My gloves she arranges daily in idiotic array upon a half-filled book-shelf, and I always have to rearrange them on the low table by the door.

She places my armchair at impossible angles between the fire and the light, and the tablecloth—the one with Trinity Hall stains—she puts on the table in such a fashion that when I look at it I feel as if my tie and all my clothes were on crooked and awry. She exasperates me. Her very silence and meekness are irritating. Sometimes I feel inclined to throw the inkstand at her, just to bring an expression into her watery eyes and a squeak from those colourless lips. Dear me! What violent expressions I am making use of! How very foolish of me! And yet it almost seems as if the words were not my own, but had been spoken into my ear—I mean, I never make use of such terms naturally.

Oct. 30.—I have been here a month. The place does not agree with me, I think. My headaches are more frequent and violent, and my nerves are a perpetual source of discomfort and annoyance.

I have conceived a great dislike for Mrs. Monson, a feeling I am certain she reciprocates. Somehow, the impression comes frequently to me that there are goings on in this house of which I know nothing, and which she is careful to hide from me.

Last night her son slept in the house, and this morning as I was standing at the window, I saw him go out. He glanced up and caught my eye. It was a loutish figure and a singularly repulsive face that I saw, and he gave me the benefit of a very unpleasant leer. At least, so I imagined.

Evidently, I am getting absurdly sensitive to trifles, and I suppose it is my disordered nerves making themselves felt. In the British Museum this afternoon I noticed several people at the reader's table staring at me and watching every movement I made. Whenever I looked up from my books, I found their eyes upon me. It seemed to me unnecessary and unpleasant, and I left earlier than was my custom. When I reached the door, I threw back a last look into the room, and saw every head at the table turned in my direction. It annoyed me very much, and yet I know it is foolish to take note of such things. When I am well, they pass me by. I must get more regular exercise. Of late I have had next to none.

Nov. 2.—The utter stillness of this house is beginning to oppress me. I wish there were other fellows living upstairs. No footsteps ever sound overhead, and no tread ever passes my door to go up the next flight of stairs. I am beginning to feel some curiosity to go up myself and see what the upper rooms are like. I feel lonely here and isolated, swept into a deserted corner of the world and forgotten. . . . Once I actually caught myself gazing into the long, cracked mirrors, trying to see the sunlight dancing beneath the trees in the orchard. But only deep shadows seemed to congregate there now, and I soon desisted.

It has been very dark all day, and no wind stirring. The fogs have begun. I had to use a reading-lamp all this morning. There was no cart to be heard today. I actually missed it. This morning, in the gloom and silence, I think I could almost have welcomed it After all, the sound is a very human one, and this empty house at the end of the alley holds other noises that are not quite so satisfactory.

I have never once seen a policeman in the lane, and the postmen always hurry out with no evidence of a desire to loiter.

10 p.m.—As I write this, I hear no sound but the deep murmur of the distant traffic and the low sighing of the wind. The two sounds melt into one another. Now and again a cat raises its shrill, uncanny cry upon the darkness. The cats are always there under my windows when the darkness falls. The wind is dropping into the funnel with a noise like the sudden sweeping of immense distant wings. It is a dreary night. I feet lost and forgotten.

Nov. 3.—From my windows I can see arrivals. When anyone comes to the door, I can just see the hat and shoulders and the hand on the bell. Only two fellows have been to see me since I came here two months ago. Both of them I saw from the window before they came up, and heard their voices asking if I was in. Neither of them ever came back.

I have finished the ponderous article. On reading it through, however, I was dissatisfied with it, and drew my pencil through almost every page. There were strange expressions and ideas in it that I could not explain, and viewed with amazement, not to say alarm. They did not sound like my *very own*, and I could not remember having written them. Can it be that my memory is beginning to be affected?

My pens are never to be found. That stupid old woman puts them in a different place each day. I must give her due credit for finding so many new hiding places; such ingenuity is wonderful. I have told her repeatedly, but she always says, "I'll speak to Emily, sir." Emily always says, "I'll tell Mrs. Monson, sir." Their foolishness makes me irritable and scatters all my thoughts. I should like to stick the lost pens into them and turn them out, blind-eyed, to be scratched and mauled by those thousand hungry cats.

Whew! What a ghastly thought! Where in the world did it come from? Such an idea is no more my own than it is the policeman's. Yet I felt I *had* to write it. It was like a voice singing in my head, and my pen wouldn't stop till the last word was finished. What ridiculous nonsense! I must and will restrain myself. I must take more regular exercise; my nerves and liver plague me horribly.

Nov. 4.—I attended a curious lecture in the French quarter on "Death," but the room was so hot and I was so weary that I fell asleep. The only part I heard, however, touched my imagination vividly. Speaking of suicides, the lecturer said that self-murder was no escape from the miseries of the present, but only a preparation of greater sorrow for the future. Suicides, he declared, cannot shirk their responsibilities so easily. They must return to take up life exactly where they laid it so violently down, but with the added pain and punishment of their weakness.

Many of them wander the earth in unspeakable misery till they can *reclothe* themselves in the body of someone else—generally a lunatic, or weak-minded person, who cannot resist the hideous obsession. This is their only means of escape. Surely a weird and horrible idea! I wish I had slept all the time and not heard it at all. My mind is morbid enough without such ghastly fancies. Such mischievous propaganda should be stopped by the police. I'll write to the *Times* and suggest it. Good idea

I walked home through Greek Street, Soho, and imagined that a hundred years had slipped back into place and De Quincey was still there, haunting the night with invocations to his "just, subtle, and mighty" drug. His vast dreams seemed to hover not very far away. Once started in my brain, the pictures refused to go away; and I saw him sleeping in that cold, tenantless mansion with the strange little waif who was afraid of its ghosts, both together in the shadows under a single horseman's cloak; or wandering in the companionship of the spectral Anne; or, later still, on his way to the eternal rendezvous at the foot of Great Titchfield Street, the rendezvous she never was able to keep. What an unutterable gloom, what an untold horror of sorrow and suffering comes over me as I try to realise something of what that man—boy he then was—must have taken into his lonely heart.

As I came up the alley, I saw a light in the top window, and a head and shoulders thrown in an exaggerated shadow upon the blind. I wondered what the son could be doing up there at such an hour.

Nov. 5.—This morning, while writing, someone came up the creaking stairs and knocked cautiously at my door. Thinking it was the landlady, I said, "Come in!" The knock was repeated, and I cried louder, "Come in, come in!" But no one turned the handle, and I continued my writing with a vexed "Well, stay out, then!" under my breath. Went on writing? I tried to, but my thoughts had suddenly dried up at their source. I could not set down a single word. It was a dark, yellow-fog morning, and there was little enough inspiration in the air as it was, but that stupid woman standing just outside my door waiting to be told again to come in roused a spirit of vexation that filled my head to the exclusion of all else. At last, I jumped up and opened the door myself.

"What do you want, and why in the world don't you come in?" I cried out. But the words dropped into empty air. There was no one there. The fog poured up the dingy staircase in deep yellow coils, but there was no sign of a human being anywhere.

I slammed the door, with imprecations upon the house and its noises, and went back to my work. A few minutes later Emily came in with a letter.

"Were you or Mrs. Monson outside a few minutes ago knocking at my door?"

"No, sir."

"Are you sure?"

"Mrs. Monson's gone to market, and there's no one but me and the child in the 'ole 'ouse, and I've been washing the dishes for the last hour, sir."

I fancied the girl's face turned a shade paler. She fidgeted towards the door with a glance over her shoulder.

"Wait, Emily," I said, and then told her what I had heard. She stared stupidly at me, though her eyes shifted now and then over the articles in the room.

"Who was it?" I asked when I had come to the end.

"Mrs. Monson says it's honly mice," she said, as if repeating a learned lesson.

"Mice!" I exclaimed; "it's nothing of the sort. Someone was feeling about outside my door. Who was it? Is the son in the house?"

Her whole manner changed suddenly, and she became earnest instead of evasive. She seemed anxious to tell the truth.

"Oh no, sir; there's no one in the house at all but you and me and the child, and there couldn't 'ave been nobody at your door. As for them knocks—"

She stopped abruptly, as though she had said too much.

"Well, what about the knocks?" I said more gently.

"Of course," she stammered, "the knocks isn't mice, nor the footsteps neither, but then—"

Again, she came to a full halt.

"Anything wrong with the house?"

"Lor', no, sir; the drains is splendid!"

"I don't mean drains, girl. I mean, did anything—anything bad ever happen here?"

She flushed up to the roots of her hair, and then turned suddenly pale again. She was obviously in considerable distress, and there was something she was anxious, yet afraid to tell—some forbidden thing she was not allowed to mention.

"I don't mind what it was, only I should like to know," I said encouragingly.

Raising her frightened eyes to my face, she began to blurt out something about "that which 'appened once to a gentleman that lived hupstairs," when a shrill voice calling her name sounded below.

"Emily, Emily!" It was the returning landlady, and the girl tumbled downstairs as if pulled backward by a rope, leaving me full of conjectures as to what in the world could have happened to a gentleman *upstairs* that could in so curious a manner affect my ears *downstairs*.

Nov. 10.—I have done capital work; have finished the ponderous article and had it accepted for the —— *Review,* and another one ordered. I feel well and cheerful, and have had regular exercise and good sleep; no headaches, no nerves, no liver! Those pills the chemist recommended are wonderful. I can watch the child playing with bis cart and feel no annoyance; sometimes I almost feel inclined to join him. Even the grey-faced landlady rouses pity in me; I am sorry for her: so, worn, so weary, so oddly put together, just like the building. She looks as if she had once suffered some shock of terror, and was momentarily dreading another.

When I spoke to her today very gently about not putting the pens in the ashtray and the gloves on the bookshelf she raised her faint eyes to mine for the first time, and said with the ghost of a smile, "I'll try and remember, sir," I felt inclined to pat her on the back and say, "Come, cheer up and be jolly. Life's not so bad after all." Oh! I am much better. There's nothing like open air and success and good sleep. They build up as if by magic the portions of the heart eaten down by despair and unsatisfied yearnings. Even to the cats I feel friendly. When I came in at eleven o'clock tonight they followed me to the door in a stream, and I stooped down to stroke the one nearest to me.

Bah! The brute hissed and spat, and struck at me with her paws.

The claw caught my hand and drew blood in a thin line. The others danced sideways into the darkness, screeching, as though I had done them an injury. I believe these cats really hate me. Perhaps they are only waiting to be reinforced. Then they will attack me. Ha, ha! In spite of the momentary annoyance, this fancy sent me laughing upstairs to my room.

The fire was out, and the room seemed unusually cold. As I groped my way over to the mantelpiece to find the matches, I realised all at once that there was another person standing beside me in the darkness. I could, of course, see nothing, but my fingers, feeling along the ledge, came into forcible contact with something that was at once withdrawn. It was cold and moist. I could have sworn it was somebody's hand. My flesh began to creep instantly.

"Who's that?" I exclaimed in a loud voice.

My voice dropped into the silence like a pebble into a deep well. There was no answer, but at the same moment I heard someone moving away from me across the room in the direction of the door. It was a confused sort of footstep, and the sound of garments brushing the furniture on the way. The same second my hand stumbled upon the matchbox, and I struck a light. I expected to see Mrs. Monson, or Emily, or perhaps the son who is something on an omnibus. But the flare of the gas jet illumined an empty room; there was not a sign of a person anywhere.

I felt the hair stir upon my head, and instinctively I backed up against the wall, lest something should approach me from behind. I was distinctly alarmed. But the next minute I recovered myself. The door was open on to the landing, and I crossed the room, not without some inward trepidation, and went out. The light from the room fell upon the stairs, but there was no one to be seen anywhere, nor was there any sound on the creaking wooden staircase to indicate a departing creature.

I was in the act of turning to go in again when a sound overhead caught my ear. It was a very faint sound, not unlike the sigh of wind; yet it could not have been the wind, for the night was still as the grave. Though it was not repeated, I resolved to go upstairs and see for myself what it all meant. Two senses had been affected—touch and hearing—and I could not believe that I had been deceived. So, with a lighted candle, I went stealthily forth on my unpleasant journey into the upper regions of this queer little old house.

On the first landing there was only one door, and it was locked.

On the second there was also only one door, but when I turned the handle it opened. There came forth to meet me the chill musty air that is characteristic of a long unoccupied room. With it there came an indescribable odour. I use the adjective advisedly. Though very faint, diluted as it were, it was nevertheless an odour that made my gorge rise. I had never smelt anything like it before, and I cannot describe it.

The room was small and square, close under the roof, with a sloping ceiling and two tiny windows. It was cold as the grave, without a shred of carpet or a stick of furniture. The icy atmosphere and the nameless odour combined to make the room abominable to me, and, after lingering a moment to see that it contained no cupboards or corners into which a person might have crept for concealment, I made haste to shut the door, and went downstairs again to bed. Evidently, I had been deceived after all as to the noise.

In the night I had a foolish but very vivid dream. I dreamed that the landlady and another person, dark and not properly visible, entered my room on all fours, followed by a horde of immense cats. They attacked me as I lay in bed, and murdered me, and then dragged my body upstairs and deposited it on the floor of that cold little square room under the roof.

Nov. 11.—Since my talk with Emily—the unfinished talk—I have hardly once set eyes on her. Mrs. Monson now attends wholly to my wants. As usual, she does everything exactly as I don't like it done. It is all too utterly trivial to mention, but it is exceedingly irritating. Like small doses of morphine often repeated, she has finally a cumulative effect,

Nov. 12.—This morning I woke early, and came into the front room to get a book, meaning to read in bed till it was time to get up. Emily was laying the fire.

"Good morning!" I said cheerfully. "Mind you make a good fire. It's very cold."

The girl turned and showed me a startled face. It was not Emily at all!

"Where's Emily?" I exclaimed.

"You mean the girl as was 'ere before me?"

"Has Emily left?"

"I came on the 6th," she replied sullenly, "and she'd gone then." I got my book and went back to bed. Emily must have been sent away almost immediately after our conversation. This reflection kept coming between me and the printed page. I was glad when it was time to get up. Such prompt energy, such merciless decision, seemed to argue something of importance—to somebody.

Nov. 13.—The wound inflicted by the cat's claw has swollen, and causes me annoyance and some pain. It throbs and itches. I'm afraid my blood must be in poor condition, or it would have healed by now. I opened it with a penknife soaked in an antiseptic solution, and cleansed it thoroughly. I have heard unpleasant stories of the results of wounds inflicted by cats.

Nov. 14.—In spite of the curious effect this house certainly exercises upon my nerves, I like it. It is lonely and deserted in the very heart of London, but it is also for that reason quiet to work in. I wonder why it is so cheap. Some people might be suspicious, but I did not even ask the reason. No answer is better than a lie. If only I could remove the cats from the outside and the rats from the inside. I feel that I shall grow accustomed more and more to its peculiarities, and shall die here. Ah, that expression reads queerly and gives a wrong impression: I meant *live and die* here. I shall renew the lease from year to year till one of us crumbles to pieces. From present indications the building will be the first to go.

Nov. 16.—It is abominable the way my nerves go up and down with me—and rather discouraging. This morning I woke to find my clothes scattered about the room, and a cane chair overturned beside the bed. My coat and waistcoat looked just as if they had been *tried on* by someone in the night. I had horribly vivid dreams, too, in which someone covering his face with his hands kept coming close up to me, crying out as if in pain, "Where can I find covering? Oh, who will clothe me?" How silly, and yet it frightened me a little. It was so dreadfully real. It is now over a year since I last walked in my sleep and woke up with such a shock on the cold pavement of Earl's Court Road, where I then lived. I thought I was cured, but evidently not. This discovery has rather a disquieting effect upon me. Tonight, I shall resort to the old trick of tying my toe to the bedpost

Nov. 17.—Last night I was again troubled by most oppressive dreams. Someone seemed to be moving in the night up and down my room, sometimes passing into the front room, and then returning to stand beside the bed and stare intently down upon me. I was being watched by this person all night long. I never actually awoke, though

I was often very near it. I suppose it was a nightmare from indigestion, for this morning I have one of my old vile headaches. Yet all my clothes lay about the floor when I awoke, where they had evidently been flung (had I so tossed them?) during the dark hours, and my trousers trailed over the step into the front room.

Worse than this, though—I fancied I noticed about the room in the morning that strange, fetid odour. Though very faint, its mere suggestion is foul and nauseating. What in the world can it be, I wonder? .... In future I shall lock my door.

Nov. 26.—I have accomplished a lot of good work during this past week, and have also managed to get regular exercise. I have felt well and in an equable state of mind. Only two things have occurred to disturb my equanimity. The first is trivial in itself, and no doubt to be easily explained. The upper window where I saw the light on the night of November 4, with the shadow of a large head and shoulders upon the blind, is one of the windows in the square room under the roof. In reality it has *no blind at all!*

Here is the other thing. I was coming home last night in a fresh fall of snow about eleven o'clock, my umbrella low down over my head. Half-way up the alley, where the snow was wholly untrodden, I saw a man's legs in front of me. The umbrella hid the rest of his figure, but on raising it I saw that he was tall and broad and was walking, as I was, towards the door of my house. He could not have been four feet ahead of me. I had thought the alley was empty when I entered it, but might of course have been mistaken very easily.

A sudden gust of wind compelled me to lower the umbrella, and when I raised it again, not half a minute later, there was no longer any man to be seen. With a few more steps I reached the door. It was closed as usual. I then noticed with a sudden sensation of dismay that the surface of the freshly fallen snow was *unbroken.* My own footmarks were the only ones to be seen anywhere, and though I retraced my way to the point where I had first seen the man, I could find no slightest impression of any other boots. Feeling creepy and uncomfortable, I went upstairs, and was glad to get into bed.

Nov. 28.—With the fastening of my bedroom door the disturbances ceased. I am convinced that I walked in my sleep. Probably I untied my toe and then tied it up again. The fancied security of the locked door would alone have been enough to restore sleep to my troubled spirit and enable me to rest quietly.

Last night, however, the annoyance was suddenly renewed in another and more aggressive form. I woke in the darkness with the impression that someone was standing outside my bedroom door *listening*. As I became more awake the impression grew into positive knowledge. Though there was no appreciable sound of moving or breathing, I was so convinced of the propinquity of a listener that I crept out of bed and approached the door. As I did so there came faintly from the next room the unmistakable sound of someone retreating stealthily across the floor. Yet, as I heard it, it was neither the tread of a man nor a regular footstep, but rather, it seemed to me, a confused sort of crawling, almost as of someone on his hands and knees.

I unlocked the door in less than a second, and passed quickly into the front room, and I could feel, as by the subtlest imaginable vibrations upon my nerves, that the spot I was standing in had just that instant been vacated! The Listener had moved; he was now behind the other door, standing in the passage. Yet this door was also closed. I moved swiftly, and as silently as possible, across the floor, and turned the handle. A cold rush of air met me from the passage and sent shiver after shiver down my back. There was no one in the doorway; there was no one on the little landing; there was no one moving down the staircase.

Yet I had been so quick that this midnight Listener could not be very far away, and I felt that if I persevered, I should eventually come face to face with him. And the courage that came so opportunely to overcome my nervousness and horror seemed born of the unwelcome conviction that it was somehow necessary for my safety as well as my sanity that I should find this intruder and force his secret from him. For was it not the intent action of his mind upon my own, in concentrated listening, that had awakened me with such a vivid realisation of his presence?

Advancing across the narrow landing, I peered down into the well of the little house. There was nothing to be seen; no one was moving in the darkness. How cold the oilcloth was to my bare feet.

I cannot say what it was that suddenly drew my eyes upwards. I only know that, without apparent reason, I looked up and saw a person about half-way up the next turn of the stairs, leaning forward over the balustrade and staring straight into my face. It was a man. He appeared to be clinging to the rail rather than standing on the stairs. The gloom made it impossible to see much beyond the general outline, but the head and shoulders were seemingly enormous, and stood sharply silhouetted against the skylight in the roof immediately above.

The idea flashed into my brain in a moment that I was looking into the visage of something monstrous. The huge skull, the mane-like hair, the wide-humped shoulders, suggested, in a way I did not pause to analyse, that which was scarcely human; and for some seconds, fascinated by horror, I returned the gaze and stared into the dark, inscrutable countenance above me, without knowing exactly where I was or what I was doing.

Then I realised in quite a new way that I was face to face with the secret midnight Listener, and I steeled myself as best I could for what was about to come.

The source of the rash courage that came to me at this awful moment will ever be to me an inexplicable mystery. Though shivering with fear, and my forehead wet with an unholy dew, I resolved to advance. Twenty questions leaped to my lips: What are you? What do you want? Why do you listen and watch? Why do you come into my room? But none of them found articulate utterance.

I began forthwith to climb the stairs, and with the first signs of my advance he drew himself back into the shadows and began to move too. He retreated as swiftly as I advanced. I heard the sound of his crawling motion a few steps ahead of me, ever maintaining the same distance. When I reached the landing, he was half-way up the next flight, and when I was half-way up the next flight he had already arrived at the top landing. I then heard him open the door of the little square room under the roof and go in. Immediately, though the door did not close after him, the sound of his moving entirely ceased.

At this moment I longed for a light, or a stick, or any weapon whatsoever; but I had none of these things, and it was impossible to go back. So, I marched steadily up the rest of the stairs, and in less than a minute found myself standing in the gloom face to face with the door through which this creature had just entered.

For a moment I hesitated. The door was about half way open, and the Listener was standing evidently in his favourite attitude just behind it—listening. To search through that dark room for him seemed hopeless; to enter the same small space where he was seemed horrible. The very idea filled me with loathing, and I almost decided to turn back.

It is strange at such times how trivial things impinge on the consciousness with a shock as of something important and immense.

Something—it may have been a beetle or a mouse—scuttled over the bare boards behind me. The door moved a quarter of an inch, closing. My decision came back with a sudden rush, as it were, and thrusting out a foot, I kicked the door so that it swung sharply back to its full extent, and permitted me to walk forward slowly into the aperture of profound blackness beyond. What a queer soft sound my bare feet made on the boards! How the blood sang and buzzed in my head!

I was inside. The darkness closed over me, hiding even the windows. I began to grope my way round the walls in a thorough search; but in order to prevent all possibility of the other's escape, I first of all *closed the door.*

There we were, we two, shut in together between four walls, within a few feet of one another. But with what, with whom, was I thus momentarily imprisoned? A new light flashed suddenly over the affair with a swift, illuminating brilliance—and I knew I was a fool, an utter fool! I was wide awake at last, and the horror was evaporating. My cursed nerves again; a dream, a nightmare, and the old result—walking in my sleep. The figure was a dream-figure. Many a time before had the actors in my dreams stood before me for some moments after I was awake. . . . There was a chance match in my pyjamas' pocket, and I struck it on the wall.

The room was utterly empty. It held not even a shadow. I went quickly down to bed, cursing my wretched nerves and my foolish, vivid dreams. But as soon as ever I was asleep again, the same uncouth figure of a man crept back to my bedside, and bending over me with his immense head close to my ear, whispered repeatedly in my dreams, "I want your body; I want its covering. I'm waiting for it, and listening always." Words scarcely less foolish than the dream.

But I wonder what that queer odour was up in the square room. I noticed it again, and stronger than ever before, and it seemed to be also in my bedroom when I woke this morning.

Nov. 29.—Slowly, as moonbeams rise over a misty sea in June, the thought is entering my mind that my nerves and somnambulistic dreams do not adequately account for the influence this house exercises upon me. It holds me as with a fine, invisible net. I cannot escape if I would. It draws me, and it means to keep me.

Nov. 30.—The post this morning brought me a letter from Aden, forwarded from my old rooms in Earl's Court. It was from Chapter, my former Trinity chum, who is on his way home from the East, and asks for my address. I sent it to him at the hotel he mentioned, "to await arrival."

As I have already said, my windows command a view of the alley, and I can see an arrival without difficulty. This morning, while I was busy writing, the sound of footsteps coming up the alley filled me with a sense of vague alarm that I could in no way account for. I went over to the window, and saw a man standing below waiting for the door to be opened. His shoulders were broad, his top-hat glossy, and his overcoat fitted beautifully round the collar. All this I could see, but no more. Presently the door was opened, and the shock to my nerves was unmistakable when I heard a man's voice ask, "Is Mr. —— still here?" mentioning my name.

I could not catch the answer, but it could only have been in the affirmative, for the man entered the hall and the door shut to behind him. But I waited in vain for the sound of his steps on the stairs. There was no sound of any kind. It seemed to me so strange that I opened my door and looked out. No one was anywhere to be seen, I walked across the narrow landing, and looked through the window that commands the whole length of the alley There was no sign of a human being, coming or going. The lane was deserted. Then I deliberately walked downstairs into the kitchen, and asked the grey-faced landlady if a gentleman had just that minute called for me.

The answer, given with an odd, weary sort of smile, was *"No!"*

Dec. 1.—I feel genuinely alarmed and uneasy over the state of my nerves. Dreams are dreams, but never before have I had dreams in broad daylight.

I am looking forward very much to Chapter's arrival. He is a capital fellow, vigorous, healthy, with no nerves, and even less imagination; and he has £2,000 a year into the bargain. Periodically he makes me offers—the last was to travel round the world with him as secretary, which was a delicate way of paying my expenses and giving me some pocket-money—offers, however, which I invariably decline. I prefer to keep his friendship. Women could not come between us; money might—therefore I give it no opportunity. Chapter always laughed at what he called my "fancies," being himself possessed only of that thin-blooded quality of imagination which is ever associated with the prosaic-minded man.

Yet, if taunted with this obvious lack, his wrath is deeply stirred. His psychology is that of the cross materialist—always a rather funny article. It will afford me genuine relief, none the less, to hear the cold judgment his mind will have to pass upon the story of this house as I shall have it to tell.

Dec. 2.—The strangest part of it all I have not referred to in this brief diary. Truth to tell, I have been afraid to set it down in black and white. I have kept it in the background of my thoughts, preventing it as far as possible from taking shape. In spite of my efforts, however! it has continued to grow stronger.

Now that I come to face the issue squarely, it is harder to express than I imagined. Like a half-remembered melody that trips in the head but vanishes the moment you try to sing it, these thoughts form a group in the background of my mind, *behind* my mind, as it were, and refuse to come forward. They are crouching ready to spring, but the actual leap never takes place.

In these rooms, except when my mind is strongly concentrated on my own work, I find myself suddenly dealing in thoughts and ideas that are not my own! New, strange conceptions, wholly foreign to my temperament, are for ever cropping up in my head. What precisely they are is of no particular importance. The point is that they are entirely apart from the channel in which my thoughts have hitherto been accustomed to flow. Especially they come when my mind is at rest, unoccupied; when I'm dreaming over the fire, or sitting with a book which fails to hold my attention. Then these thoughts which are not mine spring into life and make me feel exceedingly uncomfortable. Sometimes they are so strong that I almost feel as if someone were in the room beside me, thinking aloud.

Evidently my nerves and liver are shockingly out of order. I must work harder and take more vigorous exercise. The horrid thoughts never come when my mind is much occupied. But they are always there—waiting and as it were alive.

What I have attempted to describe above came first upon me gradually after I had been some days in the house, and then grew steadily in strength. The other strange thing has come to me only twice in all these weeks. *It appals me.* It is the consciousness of the propinquity of some deadly and loathsome disease. It comes over me like a wave of fever heat, and then passes off, leaving me cold and trembling. The air seems for a few seconds to become tainted. So, penetrating and convincing is the thought of this sickness, that on both occasions my brain has turned momentarily dizzy, and through my mind, like flames of white heat, have flashed the ominous names of all the dangerous illnesses I know. I can no more explain these visitations than I can fly, yet I know there is no dreaming about the clammy skin and palpitating heart which they always leave as witnesses of their brief visit.

Most strongly of all was I aware of this nearness of a mortal sickness when, on the night of the 28th, I went upstairs in pursuit of the listening figure. When we were shut in together in that little square room under the roof, I felt that I was face to face with the actual essence of this invisible and malignant disease. Such a feeling never entered my heart before, and I pray to God it never may again.

There! Now I have confessed. I have given some expression at least to the feelings that so far, I have been afraid to see in my own writing. For—since I can no longer deceive myself—the experiences of that night (28th) were no more a dream than my daily breakfast is a dream; and the trivial entry in this diary by which I sought to explain away an occurrence that caused me unutterable horror was due solely to my desire not to acknowledge in words what I really felt and believed to be true. The increase that would have accrued to my horror by so doing might have been more than I could stand.

Dec. 3.—I wish Chapter would come. My facts are all ready marshalled, and I can see his cool, grey eyes fixed incredulously on my face as I relate them: the knocking at my door, the well-dressed caller, the light in the upper window and the shadow upon the blind, the man who preceded me in the snow, the scattering of my clothes at night, Emily's arrested confession, the landlady's suspicious reticence, the midnight listener on the stairs, and those awful subsequent words in my sleep; and above all, and hardest to tell, the presence of the abominable sickness, and the stream of thoughts and ideas that are not my own.

I can see Chapter's face, and I can almost hear his deliberate words, "You've been at the tea again, and underfeeding, I expect, as usual. Better see my nerve doctor, and then come with me to the south of France." For this fellow, who knows nothing of disordered liver or high-strung nerves, goes regularly to a great nerve specialist with the periodical belief that his nervous system is beginning to decay.

Dec. 5.—Ever since the incident of the Listener, I have kept a night-light burning in my bedroom, and my sleep has been undisturbed. Last night, however, I was subjected to a far worse annoyance. I woke suddenly, and saw a man in front of the dressing-table regarding himself in the mirror. The door was locked, as usual. I knew at once it was the Listener, and the blood turned to ice in my veins. Such a wave of horror and dread swept over me that it seemed to turn me rigid in the bed, and I could neither move nor speak. I noted, however, that the odour I so abhorred was strong in the room.

The man seemed to be tall and broad. He was stooping forward over the mirror. His back was turned to me, but in the glass, I saw the reflection of a huge head and face illumined fitfully by the flicker of the night-light. The spectral grey of very early morning stealing in round the edges of the curtains lent an additional horror to the picture, for it fell upon hair that was tawny and mane-like, hanging loosely about a face whose swollen, rugose features bore the once seen never forgotten leonine expression of—— I dare not write down that awful word.

But, by way of corroborative proof, I saw in the faint mingling of the two lights that there were several bronze-coloured blotches on the cheeks which the man was evidently examining with great care in the glass. The lips were pale and very thick and large. One hand I could not see, but the other rested on the ivory back of my hair-brush. Its muscles were strangely contracted, the fingers thin to emaciation, the back of the hand closely puckered up. It was like a big grey spider crouching to spring, or the claw of a great bird.

The full realisation that I was alone in the room with this name-less creature, almost within arm's reach of him; overcame me to such a degree that, when, he suddenly turned and regarded me with small beady eyes, wholly out of proportion to the grandeur of their massive setting, I sat bolt upright in bed, uttered a loud cry, and then fell back in a dead swoon of terror upon the bed.

Dec. 6.—. . . . When I came to this morning, the first thing I noticed was that my clothes were strewn all over the floor. . . . I find it difficult to put my thoughts together, and have sudden accesses of violent trembling. I determined that I would go at once to Chapter's hotel and find out when he is expected. I cannot refer to what happened in the night; it is too awful, and I have to keep my thoughts rigorously away from it. I feel lightheaded and queer, couldn't eat any breakfast, and have twice vomited with blood. While dressing to go out, a hansom rattled up noisily over the cobbles, and a minute later the door opened, and to my great joy in walked the very subject of my thoughts.

The sight of his strong face and quiet eyes had an immediate effect upon me, and I grew calmer again. His very handshake was a sort of tonic. But, as I listened eagerly to the deep tones of his reassuring voice, and the visions of the night time paled a little, I began to realise how very hard it was going to be to tell him my wild, intangible tale. Some men radiate an animal vigour that destroys the delicate woof of a vision and effectually prevents its reconstruction. Chapter was one of these men.

We talked of incidents that had filled the interval since we last met, and he told me something of his travels. He talked and I listened. But so full was I of the horrid thing I had to tell, that I made a poor listener. I was for ever watching my opportunity to leap in and explode it all under his nose.

Before very long, however, it was borne in upon me that he too was merely talking for time. He too held something of importance in the background of his mind, something too weighty to let fall till the right moment presented itself. So that during the whole of the first half-hour we were both waiting for the psychological moment in which properly to release our respective bombs; and the intensity of our minds' action set up opposing forces that merely sufficed to hold one another in check—and nothing more. As soon as I realised this, therefore, I resolved to yield. I renounced for the time my purpose of telling my story, and had the satisfaction of seeing that his mind, released from the restraint of my own, at once began to make preparations for the discharge of its momentous burden.

The talk grew less and less magnetic; the interest waned; the descriptions of his travels became less alive. There were pauses between his sentences. Presently he repeated himself. His words clothed no living thoughts. The pauses grew longer. Then the interest dwindled altogether and went out like a candle in the wind. His voice ceased, and he looked up squarely into my face with serious and anxious eyes.

The psychological moment had come at last!

"I say—" he began, and then stopped short.

I made an unconscious gesture of encouragement, but said no word. I dreaded the impending disclosure exceedingly. A dark shadow seemed to precede it.

"I say," he blurted out at last, "what in the world made you ever come to this place—to these rooms, I mean?"

"They're cheap, for one thing," I began, "and central and—."

"They're too cheap," he interrupted. "Didn't you ask what made 'em so cheap?"

"It never occurred to me at the time."

There was a pause in which he avoided my eyes.

"For God's sake, go on, man, and tell it!" I cried, for the suspense was getting more than I could stand in my nervous condition.

"This was where Blount lived so long," he said quietly, "and where he—died. You know, in the old days I often used to come here and see him, and do what I could to alleviate his—" He stuck fast again.

"Well!" I said with a great effort "*Please* go on—faster."

"But," Chapter went on, turning his face to the window with a perceptible shiver, "he finally got so terrible I simply couldn't stand it, though I always thought I could stand anything. It got on my nerves and made me dream, and haunted me day and night."

I stared at him, and said nothing. I had never heard of Blount in my life, and didn't know what he was talking about. But, all the same, I was trembling, and my mouth had become strangely dry.

"This is the first time I've been back here since," he said almost in a whisper, "and, 'pon my word, it gives me the creeps. I swear it isn't fit for a man to live in. I never saw you look so bad, old man."

"I've got it for a year," I jerked out, with a forced laugh; "signed the lease and all. I thought it was rather a bargain."

Chapter shuddered, and buttoned his overcoat up to his neck. Then he spoke in a low voice, looking occasionally behind him as though he thought someone was listening. I too could have sworn someone else was in the room with us.

"He did it himself, you know, and no one blamed him a bit; his sufferings were awful. For the last two years he used to wear a veil when he went out, and even then, it was always in a closed carriage. Even the attendant who had nursed him for so long was at length obliged to leave. The extremities of both the lower limbs were gone, dropped off, and he moved about the ground on all fours with a sort of crawling motion. The odour, too, was—"

I was obliged to interrupt him here. I could hear no more details of that sort. My skin was moist, I felt hot and cold by turns, for at last I was beginning to understand.

"Poor devil," Chapter went on; "I used to keep my eyes closed as much as possible. He always begged to be allowed to take his veil off, and asked if I minded very much. I used to stand by the open window. He never touched me, though. He rented the whole house. Nothing would induce him to leave it."

"Did he occupy—these very rooms?"

"No. He had the little room on the top floor, the square one just under the roof. He preferred it because it was dark. These rooms were too near the ground, and he was afraid people might see him through the windows. A crowd had been known to follow him up to the very door, and then stand below the windows in the hope of catching a glimpse of his face."

"But there were hospitals."

"He wouldn't go near one, and they didn't like to force him. You know, they say it's *not* contagious, so there was nothing to prevent his staying here if he wanted to. He spent all his time reading medical books, about drugs and so on. His head and face were something appalling, just like a lion's."

I held up my hand to arrest further description.

"He was a burden to the world, and he knew it. One night I suppose he realised it too keenly to wish to live. He had the free use of drugs—and in the morning he was found dead on the floor. Two years ago, that was, and they said then he had still several years to live."

"Then, in Heaven's name!" I cried, unable to bear the suspense any longer, "tell me what it was he had, and be quick about it."

"I thought you knew!" he exclaimed, with genuine surprise. "I thought you knew!"

He leaned forward and our eyes met. In a scarcely audible whisper, I caught the words his lips seemed almost afraid to utter:

"He was a leper!"

The Touch of Pan

1

An idiot, Heber understood, was a person in whom intelligence had been arrested—instinct acted, but not reason. A lunatic, on the other hand, was someone whose reason had gone awry—the mechanism of the brain was injured. The lunatic was out of relation with his environment; the idiot had merely been delayed *en route*.

Be that as it might, he knew at any rate that a lunatic was not to be listened to, whereas an idiot—well, the one he fell in love with certainly had the secret of some instinctual knowledge that was not only joy, but a kind of sheer natural joy. Probably it was that sheer natural joy of living that reason argues to be untaught, degraded. In any case—at thirty—he married her instead of the daughter of a duchess he was engaged to. They lead today that happy, natural, vagabond life called idiotic, unmindful of that world the majority of reasonable people live only to remember.

Though born into an artificial social clique that made it difficult, Heber had always loved the simple things. Nature, especially, meant much to him. He would rather see a woodland misty with bluebells than all the *châteaux* on the Loire; the thought of a mountain valley in the dawn made his feet lonely in the grandest houses. Yet in these very houses was his home established. Not that he underestimated worldly things—their value was too obvious—but that it was another thing he wanted. Only he did not know precisely *what* he wanted until this particular idiot made it plain.

Her case was a mild one, possibly; the title bestowed by implication rather than by specific mention. Her family did not say that she was imbecile or half-witted, but that she "was not all there" they probably did say. Perhaps she saw men as trees walking, perhaps she saw through a glass darkly. Heber, who had met her once or twice, though never yet to speak to, did not analyse her degree of sight, for in him, person-

233

ally, she woke a secret joy and wonder that almost involved a touch of awe. The part of her that was not "all there" dwelt in an "elsewhere" that he longed to know about. He wanted to share it with her. She seemed aware of certain happy and desirable things that reason and too much thinking hid.

He just felt this instinctively without analysis. The values they set upon the prizes of life were similar. Money to her was just stamped metal, fame a loud noise of sorts, position nothing. Of people she was aware as a dog or bird might be aware—they were kind or unkind. Her parents, having collected much metal and achieved position, proceeded to make a loud noise of sorts with some success; and since she did not contribute, either by her appearance or her tastes, to their ambitions, they neglected her and made excuses. They were ashamed of her existence. Her father in particular justified Nietzsche's shrewd remark that no one with a loud voice can listen to subtle thoughts.

She was, perhaps, sixteen—for, though she looked it, eighteen or nineteen was probably more in accord with her birth certificate. Her mother was content, however, that she should dress the lesser age, preferring to tell strangers that she was childish, rather than admit that she was backward.

"You'll never marry at all, child, much less marry as you might," she said, "if you go about with that rabbit expression on your face. That's not the way to catch a nice young man of the sort we get down to stay with us now. Many a chorus-girl with less than you've got has caught them easily enough. Your sister's done well. Why not do the same? There's nothing to be shy or frightened about."

"But I'm not shy or frightened, mother. I'm bored. I mean *they* bore me."

It made no difference to the girl; she was herself. The bored expression in the eyes—the rabbit, not-all-there, expression—gave place sometimes to another look. Yet not often, nor with anybody. It was this other look that stirred the strange joy in the man who fell in love with her. It is not to be easily described. It was very wonderful. Whether sixteen or nineteen, she then looked—a thousand.

★★★★★★★★★★★★

The house-party was of that up-to-date kind prevalent in Heber's world. Husbands and wives were not asked together. There was a cynical disregard of the decent (not the stupid) conventions that savoured of abandon, perhaps of decadence. He only went himself in the hope of seeing the backward daughter once again. Her millionaire parents afflicted him, the smart folk tired him. Their peculiar affectation of a special language, their strange belief that they were of importance, their treatment of the servants, their calculated self-indulgence, all jarred upon him more than usual. At bottom he heartily despised the whole vapid set. He felt uncomfortable and out of place. Though not a prig, he abhorred the way these folk believed themselves the climax of fine living.

Their open immorality disgusted him, their indiscriminate love-making was merely rather nasty; he watched the very girl he was at last to settle down with behaving as the tone of the clique expected over her final fling—and, bored by the strain of so much "modernity," he tried to get away. Tea was long over, the sunset interval invited, he felt hungry for trees and fields that were not self-conscious—and he escaped. The flaming June day was turning chill. Dusk hovered over the ancient house, veiling the pretentious new wing that had been added. And he came across the idiot girl at the bend of the drive, where the birch trees shivered in the evening wind. His heart gave a leap.

She was leaning against one of the dreadful statues—it was a satyr—that sprinkled the lawn. Her back was to him; she gazed at a group of broken pine trees in the park beyond. He paused an instant, then went on quickly, while his mind scurried to recall her name. They were within easy speaking range.

"Miss Elizabeth!" he cried, yet not too loudly lest she might vanish as suddenly as she had appeared. She turned at once. Her eyes and lips were smiling welcome at him without pretence. She showed no surprise.

"You're the first one of the lot who's said it properly," she exclaimed, as he came up. "Everybody calls me Elizabeth instead of Elspeth. It's idiotic. They don't even take the trouble to get a name right."

"It is," he agreed. "Quite idiotic." He did not correct her. Possibly he had said Elspeth after all—the names were similar. Her perfectly natural voice was grateful to his ear, and soothing. He looked at her all over with an open admiration that she noticed and, without concealment, liked. She was very untidy, the grey stockings on her vigorous legs were torn, her short skirt was spattered with mud. Her nut-brown hair, glossy and plentiful, flew loose about neck and shoulders. In place of the usual belt, she had tied a coloured handkerchief round her waist. She wore no hat. What she had been doing to get in such a state, while her parents entertained a "distinguished" party, he did not know, but it was not difficult to guess. Climbing trees or riding bareback and astride was probably the truth. Yet her dishevelled state became her well, and the welcome in her face delighted him. She remembered him, she was glad. He, too, was glad, and a sense both happy and reckless stirred in his heart.

"Like a wild animal," he said, "you come out in the dusk——"

"To play with my kind," she answered in a flash, throwing him a glance of invitation that made his blood go dancing.

He leaned against the statue a moment, asking himself why this young Cinderella of a parvenu family delighted him when all the London beauties left him cold. There was a lift through his whole being as he watched her, slim and supple, grace shining through the untidy modern garb—almost as though she wore no clothes. He thought of a panther standing upright. Her poise was so alert—one arm upon the marble ledge, one leg bent across the other, the hip-line showing like a bird's curved wing. Wild animal or bird, flashed across his mind: something untamed and natural. Another second, and she might leap away—or spring into his arms.

It was a deep, stirring sensation in him that produced the mental picture. "Pure and natural," a voice whispered with it in his heart, "as surely as *they* are just the other thing!" And the thrill struck with unerring aim at the very root of that unrest he had always known in the state of life to which he was called. She made it natural, clean, and pure. This girl and himself were somehow kin. The primitive thing broke loose in him.

In two seconds, while he stood with her beside the vulgar statue, these thoughts passed through his mind. But he did not at first give utterance to any of them. He spoke more formally, although laughter, due to his happiness, lay behind:

"They haven't asked you to the party, then? Or you don't care about it? Which is it?"

"Both," she said, looking fearlessly into his face. "But I've been here ten minutes already. Why were you so long?"

This outspoken honesty was hardly what he expected, yet in another sense he was not surprised. Her eyes were very penetrating, very innocent, very frank. He felt her as clean and sweet as some young fawn that asks plainly to be stroked and fondled. He told the truth: "I couldn't get away before. I had to play about and——" when she interrupted with impatience:

"*They* don't really want you," she exclaimed scornfully. "I do."

And, before he could choose one out of the several answers that

236

rushed into his mind, she nudged him with her foot, holding it out a little so that he saw the shoelace was unfastened. She nodded her head towards it, and pulled her skirt up half an inch as he at once stooped down.

"And, anyhow," she went on as he fumbled with the lace, touching her ankle with his hand, "you're going to marry one of them. I read it in the paper. It's idiotic. You'll be miserable."

The blood rushed to his head, but whether owing to his stooping or to something else, he could not say.

"I only came—I only accepted," he said quickly, "because I wanted to see *you* again."

"Of course. I made mother ask you."

He did an impulsive thing. Kneeling as he was, he bent his head a little lower and suddenly kissed the soft grey stocking—then stood up and looked her in the face. She was laughing happily, no sign of embarrassment in her anywhere, no trace of outraged modesty. She just looked very pleased.

"I've tied a knot that won't come undone in a hurry——" he began, then stopped dead. For as he said it, gazing into her smiling face, another expression looked forth at him from the two big eyes of hazel. Something rushed from his heart to meet it. It may have been that playful kiss, it may have been the way she took it; but, at any rate, there was a strength in the new emotion that made him unsure of who he was and of whom he looked at. He forgot the place, the time, his own identity and hers. The lawn swept from beneath his feet, the English sunset with it.

He forgot his host and hostess, his fellow guests, even his father's name and his own into the bargain. He was carried away upon a great tide, the girl always beside him. He left the shore-line in the distance, already half forgotten, the shore-line of his education, learning, manners, social point of view—everything to which his father had most carefully brought him up as the scion of an old-established English family. This girl had torn up the anchor. Only the anchor had previously been loosened a little by his own unconscious and restless efforts . . .

Where was she taking him to? Upon what island would they land?

"I'm younger than you—a good deal," she broke in upon his rushing mood. "But that doesn't matter a bit, does it? We're about the same age really."

With the happy sound of her voice the extraordinary sensation passed—or, rather, it became normal. But that it had lasted an appreciable time was proved by the fact that they had left the statue on the lawn, the house was no longer visible behind them, and they were walking side by side between the massive rhododendron clumps. They brought up against a five-barred gate into the park. They leaned upon the topmost bar, and he felt her shoulder touching his—edging into it—as they looked across to the grove of pines.

"I feel absurdly young," he said without a sign of affectation, "and yet I've been looking for you a thousand years and more."

The afterglow lit up her face; it fell on her loose hair and tumbled blouse, turning them amber red. She looked not only soft and comely, but extraordinarily beautiful. The strange expression haunted the deep eyes again, the lips were a little parted, the young breast heaving slightly, joy and excitement in her whole presentment. And as he watched her, he knew that all he had just felt was due to her close presence, to her atmosphere, her perfume, her physical warmth and vigour. It had emanated directly from her being.

"Of course," she said, and laughed so that he felt her breath upon his face. He bent lower to bring his own on a level, gazing straight into her eyes that were fixed upon the field beyond. They were clear and luminous as pools of water, and in their centre, sharp as a photograph, he saw the reflection of the pine grove, perhaps a hundred yards away. With detailed accuracy he saw it, empty and motionless in the glimmering June dusk.

Then something caught his eye. He examined the picture more closely. He drew slightly nearer. He almost touched her face with his own, forgetting for a moment whose were the eyes that served him for a mirror. For, looking intently thus, it seemed to him that there was a movement, a passing to and fro, a stirring as of figures among the trees . . . Then suddenly the entire picture was obliterated. She had dropped her lids. He heard her speaking—the warm breath was again upon his face:

"*In the heart of that wood dwell I.*"

His heart gave another leap—more violent than the first—for the wonder and beauty of the sentence caught him like a spell. There was a lilt and rhythm in the words that made it poetry. She laid emphasis upon the pronoun and the nouns. It seemed the last line of some delicious runic verse:

"In the *heart* of the *wood*—dwell *I* . . ."

And it flashed across him: That living, moving, inhabited pine wood was her thought. It was thus she saw it. Her nature flung back to a life she understood, a life that needed, claimed her. The ostentatious and artificial values that surrounded her, she denied, even as the distinguished house-party of her ambitious, masquerading family neglected her. Of course, she was unnoticed by them, just as a swallow or a wild-rose were unnoticed.

He knew her secret then, for she had told it to him. It was his own secret too. They were akin, as the birds and animals were akin. They belonged together in some free and open life, natural, wild, untamed. That unhampered life was flowing about them now, rising, beating with delicious tumult in her veins and his, yet innocent as the sunlight and the wind—because it was as freely recognised.

"Elspeth!" he cried, "come, take me with you! We'll go at once. Come—hurry—before we forget to be happy, or remember to be wise again——!"

His words stopped half-way towards completion, for a perfume floated past him, born of the summer dusk, perhaps, yet sweet with a penetrating magic that made his senses reel with some remembered joy. No flower, no scented garden bush delivered it. It was the perfume of young, spendthrift life, sweet with the purity that reason had not yet stained. The girl moved closer. Gathering her loose hair between her fingers, she brushed his cheeks and eyes with it, her slim, warm body pressing against him as she leaned over laughingly.

"*In the darkness*," she whispered in his ear; "*when the moon puts the house upon the statue!*"

And he understood. Her world lay behind the vulgar, staring day. He turned. He heard the flutter of skirts—just caught the grey stockings, swift and light, as they flew behind the rhododendron masses. And she was gone.

He stood a long time, leaning upon that five-barred gate . . . It was the dressing-gong that recalled him at length to what seemed the present. By the conservatory door, as he went slowly in, he met his distinguished cousin—who was helping the girl he himself was to marry to enjoy her "final fling." He looked at his cousin. He realised suddenly that he was merely vicious. There was no sun and wind, no flowers—there was depravity only, lust instead of laughter, excitement in place of happiness. It was calculated, not spontaneous. His mind was in it. Without joy it was. He was not natural.

"Not a girl in the whole lot fit to look at," he exclaimed with peevish boredom, excusing himself stupidly for his illicit conduct. "I'm off in the morning." He shrugged his blue-blooded shoulders. "These millionaires! Their shooting's all right, but their mixum-gatherum weekends—bah!" His gesture completed all he had to say about this one in particular. He glanced sharply, nastily, at his companion. "*You* look as if you'd found something!" he added, with a suggestive grin. "Or have you seen the ghost that was paid for with the house?" And he guffawed and let his eyeglass drop. "Lady Hermione will be asking for an explanation—eh?"

"Idiot!" replied Heber, and ran upstairs to dress for dinner.

But the word was wrong, he remembered, as he closed his door. It was lunatic he had meant to say, yet something more as well. He saw the smart, modern philanderer somehow as a beast.

2

It was nearly midnight when he went up to bed, after an evening of intolerable amusement. The abandoned moral attitude, the common rudeness, the contempt of all others but themselves, the ugly jests, the horseplay of tasteless minds that passed for gaiety, above all the shame-lessness of the women that behind the cover of fine breeding aped emancipation, afflicted him to a boredom that touched desperation.

He understood now with a clarity unknown before. As with his cousin, so with these. They took life, he saw, with a brazen effrontery they thought was freedom, while yet it was life that they denied. He felt vampired and degraded; spontaneity went out of him. The fact that the geography of bedrooms was studied openly seemed an affirmation of vice that sickened him. Their ways were nauseous merely. He escaped—unnoticed.

He locked his door, went to the open window, and looked out into the night—then started. For silver dressed the lawn and park, the shadow of the building lay dark across the elaborate garden, and the moon, he noticed, was just high enough to put the house upon the statue. The chimney-stacks edged the pedestal precisely.

"Odd!" he exclaimed. "Odd that I should come at the very moment——!" then smiled as he realised how his proposed adventure would be misinterpreted, its natural innocence and spirit ruined—if he were seen. "And someone would be sure to see me on a night like this. There are couples still hanging about in the garden." And he glanced at the shrubberies and secret paths that seemed to float upon the warm June air like islands.

He stood for a moment framed in the glare of the electric light, then turned back into the room; and at that instant a low sound like a bird-call rose from the lawn below. It was soft and flutey, as though someone played two notes upon a reed, a piping sound. He had been seen, and she was waiting for him. Before he knew it, he had made an answering call, of oddly similar kind, then switched the light out. Three minutes later, dressed in simpler clothes, with a cap pulled over his eyes, he reached the back lawn by means of the conservatory and the billiard-room. He paused a moment to look about him. There was no one, although the lights were still ablaze. "I am an idiot," he chuckled to himself. "I'm acting on instinct!" He ran.

The sweet night air bathed him from head to foot; there was strength and cleansing in it. The lawn shone wet with dew. He could almost smell the perfume of the stars. The fumes of wine, cigars and artificial scent were left behind, the atmosphere exhaled by civilisation, by heavy thoughts, by bodies overdressed, unwisely stimulated— all, all forgotten. He passed into a world of magical enchantment. The hush of the open sky came down. In black and white the garden lay, brimmed full with beauty, shot by the ancient silver of the moon, spangled with the stars' old-gold. And the night wind rustled in the rhododendron masses as he flew between them.

In a moment he was beside the statue, engulfed now by the shadow of the building, and the girl detached herself silently from the blur of darkness. Two arms were flung about his neck, a shower of soft hair fell on his cheek with a heady scent of earth and leaves and grass, and the same instant they were away together at full speed—towards the pine wood. Their feet were soundless on the soaking grass. They went so swiftly that they made a whir of following wind that blew her hair across his eyes.

And the sudden contrast caused a shock that put a blank, perhaps, upon his mind, so that he lost the standard of remembered things. For it was no longer merely a particular adventure; it seemed a habit and a natural joy resumed. It was not new. He knew the momentum of an accustomed happiness, mislaid, it may be, but certainly familiar. They sped across the gravel paths that intersected the well-groomed lawn, they leaped the flower-beds, so laboriously shaped in mockery, they clambered over the ornamental iron railings, scorning the easier five-barred gate into the park. The longer grass then shook the dew in soaking showers against his knees.

He stooped, as though in some foolish effort to turn up something, then realised that his legs, of course, were bare. *Her* garment

241

was already high and free, for she, too, was barelegged like himself. He saw her little ankles, wet and shining in the moonlight, and flinging himself down, he kissed them happily, plunging his face into the dripping, perfumed grass. Her ringing laughter mingled with his own, as she stooped beside him the same instant; her hair hung in a silver cloud; her eyes gleamed through its curtain into his; then, suddenly, she soaked her hands in the heavy dew and passed them over his face with a softness that was like the touch of some scented southern wind.

"Now you are anointed with the Night," she cried. "No one will know you. You are forgotten of the world. Kiss me!"

"We'll play for ever and ever," he cried, "the eternal game that was old when the world was yet young," and lifting her in his arms he kissed her eyes and lips. There was some natural bliss of song and dance and laughter in his heart, an elemental bliss that caught them together as wind and sunlight catch the branches of a tree. She leaped from the ground to meet his swinging arms. He ran with her, then tossed her off and caught her neatly as she fell. Evading a second capture, she danced ahead, holding out one shining arm that he might follow. Hand in hand they raced on together through the clean summer moonlight. Yet there remained a smooth softness as of fur against his neck and shoulders, and he saw then that she wore skins of tawny colour that clung to her body closely, that he wore them too, and that her skin, like his own, was of a sweet dusky brown.

Then, pulling her towards him, he stared into her face. She suffered the close gaze a second, but no longer, for with a burst of sparkling laughter again she leaped into his arms, and before he shook her free, she had pulled and tweaked the two small horns that hid in the thick curly hair behind, and just above, the ears.

And that wilful tweaking turned him wild and reckless. That touch ran down him deep into the mothering earth. He leaped and ran and sang with a great laughing sound. The wine of eternal youth flushed all his veins with joy, and the old, old world was young again with every impulse of natural happiness intensified with the Earth's own foaming tide of life.

From head to foot, he tingled with the delight of Spring, prodigal with creative power. Of course, he could fly the bushes and fling wild across the open! Of course, the wind and moonlight fitted close and soft about him like a skin! Of course, he had youth and beauty for playmates, with dancing, laughter, singing, and a thousand kisses! For he and she were natural once again. They were free together of those long-forgotten days when "Pan leaped through the roses in the month of June . . .!"

With the girl swaying this way and that upon his shoulders, tweaking his horns with mischief and desire, hanging her flying hair before his eyes, then bending swiftly over again to lift it, he danced to join the rest of their companions in the little moonlit grove of pines beyond . . .

3

They rose somewhat pointed, perhaps, against the moonlight, those English pines—more with the shape of cypresses, some might have thought. A stream gushed down between their roots, there were mossy ferns, and rough grey boulders with lichen on them. But there was no dimness, for the silver of the moon sprinkled freely through the branches like the faint sunlight that it really was, and the air ran out to meet them with a heady fragrance that was wiser far than wine.

The girl, in an instant, was whirled from her perch on his shoulders and caught by a dozen arms that bore her into the heart of the jolly, careless throng. Whisht! Whew! Whir! She was gone, but another, fairer still, was in her place, with skins as soft and knees that clung as tightly. Her eyes were liquid amber, grapes hung between her little breasts, her arms entwined about him, smoother than marble, and as cool. She had a crystal laugh.

But he flung her off, so that she fell plump among a group of bigger figures lolling against a twisted root and roaring with a jollity that boomed like wind through the chorus of a song. They seized her, kissed her, then sent her flying. They were happier with their glad singing. They held stone goblets, red and foaming, in their broad-palmed hands.

"The mountains lie behind us!" cried a figure dancing past. "We are come at last into our valley of delight. Grapes, breasts, and rich red lips! Ho! Ho! It is time to press them that the juice of life may run!" He waved a cluster of ferns across the air and vanished amid a cloud of song and laughter.

"It is ours. Use it!" answered a deep, ringing voice. "The valleys are our own. No climbing now!" And a wind of echoing cries gave answer from all sides. "Life! Life! Life! Abundant, flowing over—use it, use it!"

A troop of nymphs rushed forth, escaped from clustering arms and lips they yet openly desired. He chased them in and out among the waving branches, while she who had brought him ever followed, and sped past him and away again. He caught three gleaming soft brown bodies, then fell beneath them, smothered, bubbling with joyous laughter—next freed himself and, while they sought to drag him captive again, escaped and raced with a leap upon a slimmer, sweeter outline that swung up—only just in time—upon a lower bough, whence she leaned down above him with hanging net of hair and merry eyes. A few feet beyond his reach, she laughed and teased him—the one who had brought him in, the one he ever sought, and who for ever sought him too....

It became a riotous glory of wild children who romped and played with an impassioned glee beneath the moon. For the world was young and they, her happy offspring, glowed with the life she poured so freely into them. All intermingled, the laughing voices rose into a foam of song that broke against the stars. The difficult mountains had been climbed and were forgotten. Good! Then, enjoy the luxuriant, fruitful valley and be glad! And glad they were, brimful with spontaneous energy, natural as birds and animals that obeyed the big, deep rhythm of a simpler age—natural as wind and innocent as sunshine.

Yet, for all the untamed riot, there was a lift of beauty pulsing underneath. Even when the wildest abandon approached the heat of orgy, when the recklessness appeared excess—there hid that marvellous touch of loveliness which makes the natural sacred. There was coherence, purpose, the fulfilling of an exquisite law: there was worship. The form it took, haply, was strange as well as riotous, yet in its strangeness dreamed innocence and purity, and in its very riot flamed that spirit which is divine.

For he found himself at length beside her once again; breathless and panting, her sweet brown limbs aglow from the excitement of escape denied; eyes shining like a blaze of stars, and pulses beating with tumultuous life—helpless and yielding against the strength that pinned her down between the roots. His eyes put mastery on her own. She looked up into his face, obedient, happy, soft with love, surrendered with the same delicious abandon that had swept her for a moment into other arms. "You caught me in the end," she sighed. "I only played awhile."

"I hold you for ever," he replied, half wondering at the rough power in his voice.

It was here the hush of worship stole upon her little face, into her obedient eyes, about her parted lips. She ceased her wilful struggling.

"Listen!" she whispered. "I hear a step upon the glades beyond.

244

The iris and the lily open; the earth is ready, waiting; we must be ready too! *He* is coming!"

He released her and sprang up; the entire company rose too. All stood, all bowed the head. There was an instant's subtle panic, but it was the panic of reverent awe that preludes a descent of deity. For a wind passed through the branches with a sound that is the oldest in the world and so the youngest. Above it there rose the shrill, faint piping of a little reed. Only the first, true sounds were audible—wind and water—the tinkling of the dewdrops as they fell, the murmur of the trees against the air. This was the piping that they heard. And in the hush the stars bent down to hear, the riot paused, the orgy passed and died. The figures waited, kneeling then with one accord. They listened with—the Earth.

"He comes . . . He comes . . ." the valley breathed about them.

There was a footfall from far away, treading across a world unruined and unstained. It fell with the wind and water, sweetening the valley into life as it approached. Across the rivers and forests, it came gently, tenderly, but swiftly and with a power that knew majesty.

"He comes . . . He comes . . .!" rose with the murmur of the wind and water from the host of lowered heads.

The footfall came nearer, treading a world grown soft with worship. It reached the grove. It entered. There was a sense of intolerable loveliness, of brimming life, of rapture. The thousand faces lifted like a cloud. They heard the piping close. And so, He came.

But He came with blessing. With the stupendous Presence there was joy, the joy of abundant, natural life, pure as the sunlight and the wind. He passed among them. There was great movement—as of a forest shaking, as of deep water falling, as of a cornfield swaying to the wind, yet gentle as of a harebell shedding its burden of dew that it has held too long because of love. He passed among them, touching every head. The great hand swept with tenderness each face, lingered a moment on each beating heart.

There was sweetness, peace, and loveliness; but above all, there was—life. He sanctioned every natural joy in them and blessed each passion with his power of creation . . . Yet each one saw him differently: some as a wife or maiden desired with fire, some as a youth or stalwart husband, others as a figure veiled with stars or cloaked in luminous mist, hardly attainable; others, again—the fewest these, not more than two or three—as that mysterious wonder which tempts the heart away from known familiar sweetness into a wilderness of undecipherable magic without flesh and blood . . .

To two, in particular, He came so near that they could feel his breath of hills and fields upon their eyes. He touched them with both mighty hands. He stroked the marble breasts, He felt the little hidden horns ... and, as they bent lower so that their lips met together for an instant, He took her arms and twined them about the curved, brown neck that she might hold him closer still . . .

Again, a footfall sounded far away upon an unruined world ... and He was gone—back into the wind and water whence He came. The thousand faces lifted; all stood up; the hush of worship still among them. There was a quiet as of the dawn. The piping floated over woods and fields, fading into silence. All looked at one another.... And then once more the laughter and the play broke loose.

4

"We'll go," she cried, "and peep upon that other world where life hangs like a prison on their eyes!" And, in a moment, they were across the soaking grass, the lawn and flower-beds, and close to the walls of the heavy mansion. He peered in through a window, lifting her up to peer in with him. He recognised the world to which outwardly he belonged; he understood; a little gasp escaped him; and a slight shiver ran down the girl's body into his own. She turned her eyes away. "See," she murmured in his ear, "it's ugly, it's not natural. They feel guilty and ashamed. There is no innocence!" She saw the men; it was the women that he saw chiefly.

Lolling ungracefully, with a kind of boldness that asserted independence, the women smoked their cigarettes with an air of invitation they sought to conceal and yet showed plainly. He saw his familiar world in nakedness. Their backs were bare, for all the elaborate clothes they wore; they hung their breasts uncleanly; in their eyes shone light that had never known the open sun. Hoping they were alluring and desirable, they feigned a guilty ignorance of that hope. They all pretended.

Instead of wind and dew upon their hair, he saw flowers grown artificially to ape wild beauty, tresses without lustre borrowed from the slums of city factories. He watched them manoeuvring with the men; heard dark sentences; caught gestures half delivered whose meaning should just convey that glimpse of guilt they deemed to increase pleasure. The women were calculating, but nowhere glad; the men experienced, but nowhere joyous. Pretended innocence lay cloaked with a veil of something that whispered secretly, clandestine, ashamed, yet with a brazen air that laid mockery instead of sunshine in their smiles. Vice masqueraded in the ugly shape of pleasure; beauty was degraded into calculated tricks. They were not natural. They knew not joy.

"The forward ones, the civilised!" she laughed in his ear, tweaking his horns with energy. "*We* are the backward!"

"Unclean," he muttered, recalling a catchword of the world he gazed upon.

They were the civilised! They were refined and educated—advanced. Generations of careful breeding, mate cautiously selecting mate, laid the polish of caste upon their hands and faces where gleamed ridiculous, untaught jewels—rings, bracelets, necklaces hanging absurdly from every possible angle.

"But—they are dressed up—for fun," he exclaimed, more to himself than to the girl in skins who clung to his shoulders with her naked arms.

"*Un*dressed!" she answered, putting her brown hand in play across his eyes. "Only they have forgotten even that!" And another shiver passed through her into him. He turned and hid his face against the soft skins that touched his cheek. He kissed her body. Seizing his horns, she pressed him to her, laughing happily.

"Look!" she whispered, raising her head again; "they're coming out." And he saw that two of them, a man and a girl, with an interchange of secret glances, had stolen from the room and were already by the door of the conservatory that led into the garden. It was his wife to be—and his distinguished cousin.

"Oh, Pan!" she cried in mischief. The girl sprang from his arms and pointed. "We will follow them. We will put natural life into their little veins!"

"Or panic terror," he answered, catching the yellow panther skin and following her swiftly round the building. He kept in the shadow, though she ran full into the blaze of moonlight. "But they can't see us," she called, looking over her shoulder a moment. "They can only feel our presence, perhaps." And, as she danced across the lawn, it seemed a moonbeam slipped from a sapling birch tree that the wind curved earthwards, then tossed back against the sky.

Keeping just ahead, they led the pair, by methods known instinctively to elemental blood yet not translatable—led them towards the little grove of waiting pines. The night wind murmured in the branches; a bird woke into a sudden burst of song. These sounds were plainly audible. But four little pointed ears caught other, wilder notes behind the wind and music of the bird—the cries and ringing laughter, the leaping footsteps and the happy singing of their merry kin within the wood.

And the throng paused then amid the revels to watch the "civilised" draw near. They presently reached the trees, halted, looked about them, hesitated a moment—then, with a hurried movement as of shame and fear lest they be caught, entered the zone of shadow.

"Let's go in here," said the man, without music in his voice. "It's dry on the pine needles, and we can't be seen." He led the way; she picked up her skirts and followed over the strip of long wet grass. "Here's a log all ready for us," he added, sat down, and drew her into his arms with a sigh of satisfaction. "Sit on my knee; it's warmer for your pretty figure." He chuckled; evidently, they were on familiar terms, for though she hesitated, pretending to be coy, there was no real resistance in her, and she allowed the ungraceful roughness. "But are we *quite* safe? Are you sure?" she asked between his kisses.

"What does it matter, even if we're not?" he replied, establishing her more securely on his knees. "But, as a matter of fact, we're safer here than in my own house." He kissed her hungrily. "By Jove, Hermione, but you're divine," he cried passionately, "divinely beautiful. I love you with every atom of my being—with my soul."

"Yes, dear, I know—I mean, I know you do, but——"

"But what?" he asked impatiently.

"Those detectives——"

He laughed. Yet it seemed to annoy him. "My wife is a beast, isn't she?—to have me watched like that," he said quickly.

"They're everywhere," she replied, a sudden hush in her tone. She looked at the encircling trees a moment, then added bitterly: "I hate her, simply *hate* her."

"I love you," he cried, crushing her to him, "that's all that matters now. Don't let's waste time talking about the rest." She contrived to shudder, and hid her face against his coat, while he showered kisses on her neck and hair.

And the solemn pine trees watched them, the silvery moonlight fell on their faces, the scent of new-mown hay went floating past.

"I love you with my very soul," he repeated with intense conviction. "I'd do anything, give up anything, bear anything—just to give you a moment's happiness. I swear it—before God!"

There was a faint sound among the trees behind them, and the girl sat up, alert. She would have scrambled to her feet, but that he held her tight.

"What the devil's the matter with you tonight?" he asked in a different tone, his vexation plainly audible. "You're as nervy as if *you* were being watched, instead of me."

She paused before she answered, her finger on her lip. Then she said slowly, hushing her voice a little:

"Watched! That's exactly what I did feel. I've felt it ever since we came into the wood."

"Nonsense, Hermione. It's too many cigarettes." He drew her back into his arms, forcing her head up so that he could kiss her better.

"I suppose it is nonsense," she said, smiling. "It's gone now, anyhow."

He began admiring her hair, her dress, her shoes, her pretty ankles, while she resisted in a way that proved her practice. "It's not *me* you love," she pouted, yet drinking in his praise. She listened to his repeated assurances that he loved her with his "soul" and was prepared for any sacrifice.

"I feel so safe with you," she murmured, knowing the moves in the game as well as he did. She looked up guiltily into his face, and he looked down with a passion that he thought perhaps was joy.

"You'll be married before the summer's out," he said, "and all the thrill and excitement will be over. Poor Hermione!" She lay back in his arms, drawing his face down with both hands, and kissing him on the lips. "You'll have more of him than you can do with—eh? As much as you care about, anyhow."

"I shall be much more free," she whispered. "Things will be easier. And I've got to marry someone——"

She broke off with another start. There was a sound again behind them. The man heard nothing. The blood in his temples pulsed too loudly, doubtless.

"Well, what is it this time?" he asked sharply.

She was peering into the wood, where the patches of dark shadow and moonlit spaces made odd, irregular patterns in the air. A low branch waved slightly in the wind.

"Did you hear that?" she asked nervously.

"Wind," he replied, annoyed that her change of mood disturbed his pleasure.

"But something moved——"

"Only a branch. We're quite alone, quite safe, I tell you," and there was a rasping sound in his voice as he said it. "Don't be so imaginative. I can take care of you."

She sprang up. The moonlight caught her figure, revealing its exquisite young curves beneath the smother of the costly clothing. Her hair had dropped a little in the struggle. The man eyed her eagerly, making a quick, impatient gesture towards her, then stopped abruptly. He saw the terror in her eyes.

"Oh, hark! What's that?" she whispered in a startled voice. She put her finger up. "Oh, let's go back. I don't like this wood. I'm frightened."

"Rubbish," he said, and tried to catch her by the waist.

"It's safer in the house—my room—or yours——" She broke off again. "There it is—don't you hear? It's a footstep!" Her face was whiter than the moon.

"I tell you it's the wind in the branches," he repeated gruffly. "Oh, come on, *do*. We were just getting jolly together. There's nothing to be afraid of. Can't you believe me?" He tried to pull her down upon his knee again with force. His face wore an unpleasant expression that was half leer, half grin.

But the girl stood away from him. She continued to peer nervously about her. She listened.

"You give me the creeps," he exclaimed crossly, clawing at her waist again with passionate eagerness that now betrayed exasperation. His disappointment turned him coarse.

The girl made a quick movement of escape, turning so as to look in every direction. She gave a little scream.

"That *was* a step. Oh, oh, it's close beside us. I heard it. We're being watched!" she cried in terror. She darted towards him, then shrank back. He did not try to touch her this time.

"Moonshine!" he growled. "You've spoilt my—spoilt our chance with your silly nerves."

But she did not hear him apparently. She stood there shivering as with sudden cold.

"There! I saw it again. I'm sure of it. Something went past me through the air."

And the man, still thinking only of his own pleasure frustrated, got up heavily, something like anger in his eyes. "All right," he said testily; "if you're going to make a fuss, we'd better go. The house *is* safer, possibly, as you say. You know my room. Come along!" Even that risk he would not take. He loved her with his "soul."

They crept stealthily out of the wood, the girl slightly in front of him, casting frightened backward glances. Afraid, guilty, ashamed, with an air as though they had been detected, they stole back towards the garden and the house, and disappeared from view.

And a wind rose suddenly with a rushing sound, poured through the wood as though to cleanse it, swept out the artificial scent and trace of shame, and brought back again the song, the laughter, and the happy revels. It roared across the park, it shook the windows of the house, then sank away as quickly as it came. The trees stood motionless again, guarding their secret in the clean, sweet moonlight that held the world in dream until the dawn stole up and sunshine took the earth with joy.

The House of the Past

One night a Dream came to me and brought with her an old and rusty key. She led me across fields and sweet-smelling lanes, where the hedges were already whispering to one another in the dark of the spring, till we came to a huge, gaunt house with staring windows and lofty roof half hidden in the shadows of very early morning. I noticed that the blinds were of heavy black, and that the house seemed wrapped in absolute stillness.

"This," she whispered in my ear, "is the House of the Past. Come with me and we will go through some of its rooms and passages; but quickly, for I have not the key for long, and the night is very nearly over. Yet, perchance, you shall remember!"

The key made a dreadful noise as she turned it in the lock, and when the great door swung open into an empty hall and we went in, I heard sounds of whispering and weeping, and the rustling of clothes, as of people moving in their sleep and about to wake. Then, instantly, a spirit of intense sadness came over me, drenching me to the soul; my eyes began to burn and smart, and in my heart, I became aware of a strange sensation as of the uncoiling of something that had been asleep for ages. My whole being, unable to resist, at once surrendered itself to the spirit of deepest melancholy, and the pain of my heart, as the Things moved and woke, became in a moment of time too strong for words. . . .

As we advanced, the faint voices and sobbings fled away before us into the interior of the House, and I became conscious that the air was full of hands held aloft, of swaying garments, of drooping tresses, and of eyes so sad and wistful that the tears, which were already brimming in my own, held back for wonder at the sight of such intolerable yearning.

"Do not allow all this sadness to overwhelm you," whispered the Dream at my side. "It is not often They wake. They sleep for years and

253

years and years. The chambers are all full, and unless visitors such as we come to disturb them, they will never wake of their own accord. But, when one stirs, the sleep of the others is troubled, and they too awake, till the motion is communicated from one room to another and thus finally throughout the whole House. . . . Then, sometimes, the sadness is too great to be borne, and the mind weakens. For this reason, Memory gives to them the sweetest and deepest sleep she has, and she keeps this old key rusty from little use. But, listen now," she added, holding up her hand: "do you not hear all through the House that trembling of the air like the distant murmur of falling water? And do you not now. . . perhaps . . . *remember?*"

Even before she spoke, I had already caught faintly the beginning of a new sound; and, now, deep in the cellars beneath our feet, and from the upper regions of the great House, as well, I heard the whispering, and the rustling and the inward stirring of the sleeping Shadows. It rose like a chord swept softly from huge unseen strings stretched somewhere among the foundations of the House, and its tremblings ran gently through its walls and ceilings. And I knew that I heard the slow awakening of the Ghosts of the Past.

Ah, me, with what terrible inrushing of sadness I stood with brimming eyes and listened to the faint dead voices of the long ago. . . . For, indeed, the whole House was awakening; and there presently rose to my nostrils the subtle, penetrating perfume of age: of letters, long preserved, with ink faded and ribbons pale; of scented tresses, golden and brown, laid away, ah, how tenderly! among pressed flowers that still held the inmost delicacy of their forgotten fragrance; the scented presence of lost memories—the intoxicating incense of the past.

My eyes o'erflowed, my heart tightened and expanded, as I yielded myself up without reserve to these old, old influences of sound and smell. These Ghosts of the Past—forgotten in the tumult of more recent memories—thronged round me, took my hands in theirs, and, ever whispering of what I had so long forgot, ever sighing, shaking from their hair and garments the ineffable odours of the dead ages, led me through the vast House, from room to room, from floor to floor.

And the Ghosts—were not all equally clear to me. Some had indeed but the faintest life, and stirred me so little that they left only an indistinct, blurred impression in the air; while others gazed half reproachfully at me out of faded, colourless eyes, as if longing to recall themselves to my recollection; and then, seeing they were not recognised, floated back gently into the shadows of their room, to sleep again undisturbed till the Final Day, when I should not fail to know them.

"Many of them have slept so long," said the Dream beside me, "that they wake only with the greatest difficulty. Once awake, however, they know and remember *you* even though you fail to remember them. For it is the rule in this House of the Past that, unless you recall them distinctly, remembering precisely when you knew them and with what particular causes in your past evolution they were associated, they cannot stay awake. Unless you remember them when your eyes meet, unless their look of recognition is returned by you, they are obliged to go back to their sleep, silent and sorrowful, their hands unpressed, their voices unheard, to sleep and dream, deathless and patient, till. . . ."

At this moment, her words died away suddenly into the distance, and I became conscious of an overpowering sensation of delight and happiness. Something had touched me on the lips, and a strong, sweet fire flashed down into my heart and sent the blood rushing tumultuously through my veins. My pulses beat wildly, my skin glowed, my eyes grew tender, and the terrible sadness of the place was instantly dispelled' as if by magic. Turning with a cry of joy, that was at once swallowed up in the chorus of weeping and sighing round me, I looked . . . and instinctively stretched forth my arms in a rapture of happiness towards . . . towards a vision of a Face . . . hair, lips, eyes; a cloth of gold lay about the fair neck, and the old, old perfume of the East—ye stars, how long ago—was in her breath.

Her lips were again on mine; her hair over my eyes; her arms about my neck, and the love of her ancient soul pouring into mine out of eyes still starry and undimmed. Oh, the fierce tumult, the untold wonder, if I could only remember! . . . . That subtle, mist-dispelling odour of many ages ago, once so familiar . . . before the Hills of Atlantis were above the blue sea, or the sands had begun to form the bed of the Sphinx. Yet wait; it comes back; I begin to remember. Curtain upon curtain rises in my soul, and I can almost see beyond. But that hideous stretch of the years, awful and sinister, thousands upon thousands. . . . . My heart shakes, and I am afraid. Another curtain rises and a new vista, farther than the others, comes into view, interminable, running to a point among thick mists. Lo, they too are moving, rising, lightening.

At last, I shall see . . . already I begin to recall . . . the dusky skin . . . the Eastern grace, the wondrous eyes that held the knowledge of Buddha and the wisdom of Christ before these had even dreamed of

255

attainment. As a dream within a dream, it steals over me again, taking compelling possession of my whole being . . . the slender form . . . the stars in that magical Eastern sky . . . the whispering winds among the palm trees . . . the murmur of the river's waves and the music of the reeds where they bend and sigh in the shallows on the golden sand. Thousands of years ago in some aeonian distance. It fades a little and begins to pass; then seems again to rise. Ah me, that smile of the shining teeth . . . those lace-veined lids.

Oh, who will help me to recall, for it is too far away, too dim, and I cannot wholly remember; though my lips are still tingling, and my arms still outstretched, it again begins to fade. Already there is a look of sadness too deep for words, as she realises that she is unrecognised . . . she, whose mere presence could once extinguish for me the entire universe . . . and she goes back slowly, mournfully, silently to her dim, tremendous sleep, to dream and dream of the day when I *must* remember her and she must come where she belongs. . . .

She peers at me from the end of the room where the Shadows already cover her and win her back with outstretched arms to her age-long sleep in the House of the Past.

Trembling all over, with the strange odour still in my nostrils and the fire in my heart, I turned away and followed my Dream up a broad staircase into another part of the House.

As we entered the upper corridors, I heard the wind pass singing over the roof. Its music took possession of me until I felt as though my whole body were a single heart, aching, straining, throbbing as if it would break; and all because I heard the wind singing round this House of the Past.

"But, remember," whispered the Dream, answering my unspoken wonder, "that you are listening to the song it; has sung for untold ages into untold myriad ears. It carries back so appallingly far; and in that simple dirge, profound in its terrible monotony, are the associations and recollections of the joys, griefs, and struggles of all your previous existence. The wind, like the sea, speaks to the inmost memory," she added, "and that is why its voice is one of such deep spiritual sadness. It is the song of things for ever incomplete, unfinished, unsatisfying."

As we passed through the vaulted rooms, I noticed that no one stirred. There was no actual sound, only a general impression of deep, collective breathing, like the heave of a muffled ocean. But the rooms, I knew at once, were full to the walls, crowded, rows upon rows. . . . And, from the floors below, rose ever the murmur of the weeping

Shadows as they returned to their sleep, and settled down again in the silence, the darkness, and the dust.

The dust. . . . Ah, the dust that floated in this House of the Past, so thick, so penetrating; so fine, it filled the throat and eyes without pain; so fragrant, it soothed the senses and stilled the aching of the heart; so soft, it parched the tongue, without offence; yet so silently falling, gathering, settling over everything, that the air held it like a fine mist and the sleeping Shadows wore it for their shrouds.

"And these are the oldest," said my Dream, "the longest asleep," pointing to the crowded rows of silent sleepers. "None here have wakened for ages too many to count; and even if they woke you would not know them. They are, like the others, all your own, but they are the memories of your earliest stages along the great Path of Evolution. Someday, though, they will awake, and you must know them, and answer their questions, for they cannot die till they have exhausted themselves again through you who gave them birth."

"Ah me," I thought, only half listening to or understanding these last words, "what mothers, fathers, brothers may then be asleep in this room; what faithful lovers, what true friends, what ancient enemies! And to think that someday they will step forth and confront me, and I shall meet their eyes again, claim them, know them, forgive, and be forgiven . . . the memories of all my Past. . .

I turned to speak to the Dream at my side, but she was already fading into dimness, and, as I looked again, the whole House melted away into the flush of the eastern sky, and I heard the birds singing and saw the clouds overhead veiling the stars in the light of coming day.

LEONAUR

ALSO FROM LEONAUR
AVAILABLE IN SOFTCOVER OR HARDCOVER WITH DUST JACKET

MR MUKERJI'S GHOSTS *by S. Mukerji*—Supernatural tales from the British Raj period by India's Ghost story collector.

KIPLINGS GHOSTS *by Rudyard Kipling*—Twelve stories of Ghosts, Hauntings, Curses, Werewolves & Magic.

THE COLLECTED SUPERNATURAL AND WEIRD FICTION OF WASHINGTON IRVING: VOLUME 1 *by Washington Irving*—Including one novel 'A History of New York', and nine short stories of the Strange and Unusual.

THE COLLECTED SUPERNATURAL AND WEIRD FICTION OF WASHINGTON IRVING: VOLUME 2 *by Washington Irving*—Including three novelettes 'The Legend of the Sleepy Hollow', 'Dolph Heyliger', 'The Adventure of the Black Fisherman' and thirty-two short stories of the Strange and Unusual.

THE COLLECTED SUPERNATURAL AND WEIRD FICTION OF JOHN KENDRICK BANGS: VOLUME 1 *by John Kendrick Bangs*—Including one novel 'Toppleton's Client or A Spirit in Exile', and ten short stories of the Strange and Unusual.

THE COLLECTED SUPERNATURAL AND WEIRD FICTION OF JOHN KENDRICK BANGS: VOLUME 2 *by John Kendrick Bangs*—Including four novellas 'A House-Boat on the Styx', 'The Pursuit of the House-Boat', 'The Enchanted Typewriter' and 'Mr. Munchausen' of the Strange and Unusual.

THE COLLECTED SUPERNATURAL AND WEIRD FICTION OF JOHN KENDRICK BANGS: VOLUME 3 *by John Kendrick Bangs*—Including twor novellas 'Olympian Nights', 'Roger Camerden: A Strange Story', and ten short stories of the Strange and Unusual.

THE COLLECTED SUPERNATURAL AND WEIRD FICTION OF MARY SHELLEY: VOLUME 1 *by Mary Shelley*—Including one novel 'Frankenstein or the Modern Prometheus', and fourteen short stories of the Strange and Unusual.

THE COLLECTED SUPERNATURAL AND WEIRD FICTION OF MARY SHELLEY: VOLUME 2 *by Mary Shelley*—Including one novel 'The Last Man', and three short stories of the Strange and Unusual.

THE COLLECTED SUPERNATURAL AND WEIRD FICTION OF AMELIA B. EDWARDS *by Amelia B. Edwards*—Contains two novelettes 'Monsieur Maurice', and 'The Discovery of the Treasure Isles', one ballad 'A Legend of Boisguilbert'and seventeen short stories to cill the blood.